KT-440-923

# ROSIE THOMAS

# SUNRISE

ARROW

Published by Arrow Books in 2001

1 3 5 7 9 10 8 6 4 2

Copyright © Rosie Thomas 1984

Rosie Thomas has asserted her right under the Copyright, Designs and Patents Act,
1988 to be identified as the author of this work

This novel is a work of fiction. Names and characters are the product
of the author's imagination and any resemblance to actual persons,
living or dead, is entirely coincidental

This book is sold subject to the condition that it shall not,
by way of trade or otherwise, be lent, resold, hired out, or
otherwise circulated without the publisher's prior consent in
any form of binding or cover other than that in which it is
published and without a similar condition including this
condition being imposed on the subsequent purchaser

First published in the United Kingdom in 1984
by Fontana Paperbacks

Arrow Books Limited
20 Vauxhall Bridge Road, London, SW1V 2SA

Random House Australia (Pty) Limited
20 Alfred Street, Milsons Point, Sydney,
New South Wales 2061, Australia

Random House New Zealand Limited
18 Poland Road, Glenfield
Auckland 10, New Zealand

Random House (Pty) Limited
Endulini, 5a Jubilee Road, Parktown 2193, South Africa

Random House Group Limited Reg. No. 954009

www.randomhouse.co.uk

A CIP catalogue record for this book
is available from the British Library

Papers used by Random House
are natural, recyclable products made from wood grown in
sustainable forests. The manufacturing processes conform to
the environmental regulations of the country of origin

ISBN 0 09 940644 6

Printed and bound in Germany by
Elsnerdruck, Berlin

# CHAPTER ONE

'Good girl. Nearly there now.'

The midwife's mouth was pursed professionally as she watched the little green bleeps of the monitor. The room went quiet for an instant, waiting. The exhausted medical student glanced up too. Blearily he saw the strong green pulse of the foetal heartbeat tracing across the screen. Routine. Another routine birth. The ninth he'd seen in three days.

Baptism by fire, he thought, this part of the course. Or no, not so much fire as water, blood, and animal screams and yelps. Not for him, obstetrics. Much rather something serene, academic. Haematology, perhaps.

'*Ohhh.*' It was the girl's first moan, and it came from low down in her throat.

'Are you assisting at this birth, Mr Porter?' The midwife's voice was acid.

The student leapt forward, his face scarlet.

'One more push now, if you can,' he said, trying to sound both soothing and imperative. The lavender-pink perineal skin glistened as it stretched tight over the wet, black, impatient head of the baby. There was the flash of a hypodermic needle and then a sound like ripping canvas as the midwife made her slice into the muscle.

The moan came again, the uncontrolled jungle noise of an intent animal. The student shuddered in spite of himself. Thank God he was a man.

The girl was struggling upright, fighting against the junior nurses who held her. Her face, damp with sweat, looked even younger than theirs.

'Brave girl,' the midwife told her. 'One last push and you'll have your baby.' There was no need for her instructions. The girl was utterly in control, riding the waves from her own womb.

'Oh.' Her voice was different this time, rising in triumph.

The baby's head was born, and the student saw that it was the same, sudden, crimson knot of features that it always was. It punctuated his off-duty dreams. The other staff were still for a moment. It was just another labour and another baby, but the instant of birth never lost its impact. The delivery room door was still closed. No-one had come in, but they were one more.

The baby's body followed almost at once, streaked with blood and grey-white vernix. The eyes opened, very black and deep. Then the tiny chest fluttered, the mouth opened and there was a long, ragged howl of protest.

The midwife chuckled, deft and cheerful again. 'A boy. and quite a little tiger. Well done, mum.'

The girl brushed aside her practised patter. 'Give him to me,' she said quietly. 'Now.'

They glanced curiously at her as her arms reached out for her son. She drew him to her, slipping one shoulder out of the green hospital gown and offering him the small, puckered nipple. The baby's head turned, searching for it.

'There,' she murmured. 'There.'

The medical student saw that the look of extreme youth had left her. Her face was lit with a satisfaction as old as motherhood itself. He sighed, feeling the weight of his own cynicism. This birth was different from the others he had witnessed because there was no tense, queasy father hovering at the bedhead. There was no beaming face to peer down proudly now when the midwife made her ritual insistence on the new-born's likeness to his brand-new father.

This girl had nobody.

'Come on now, dear,' they were saying to her. 'You can have him back in five minutes. We've got to attend to you, and clean him up for you as well.' They took the infant out of her arms. The messy, painful business of mopping and stitching went on, but the girl seemed to be oblivious. Her eyes never left her baby.

At last they were finished with her. The machines and monitors were wheeled away and the baby in its white blanket was handed back. She gave a small, contented sigh as the bundle fitted against her. The baby was already asleep, one clenched fist against his cheek.

The student had dutifully performed the stitching under his tutor's eye. His job was finished now. Normally he would have bolted in search of a few hours' sleep before his name climbed inexorably to the top of the rota list and the whole thing started all over again. Yet this time something held him back, loitering in the way of the efficient nurses.

The girl smiled shyly at him.

'Thank you,' she whispered.

'Thank you. You were terrific, you know. Made it easy for us.'

She had combed her fine, fair hair back behind her ears, leaving just a straight fringe like an earnest schoolgirl's. But now, when she shook her head and grinned at him, it swung free again in a loose bell. She was pretty, he realized. He caught himself wondering how the pig of a father could have left her alone like this.

'I didn't expect it to be like this,' she murmured to him. 'I didn't think that it would be so much.'

He saw the tenacious arms around the baby, and the light in her face, and knew what she meant. He nodded, silenced.

The girl lifted her face and kissed his cheek, as naturally as if he was her brother.

'Thank you,' she said again.

Lightly, he touched her shoulder. 'Good luck.' As he left the room he saw that her gaze was back on the puckered, sleeping face at her breast.

The delivery room was empty now except for one brisk woman in a sister's blue uniform. She was sitting on the girl's bed, counting her pulse against the little watch hanging at her apron front. As she finished, the baby stirred and the girl touched the tiny head with her fingertips.

'Such a lot of black hair,' she said to herself. 'Like his father.' She seemed barely aware that she was speaking aloud.

The sister looked shrewdly at her.

'You're on your own, aren't you?' Hardly more than a

child yourself, she was thinking.

'Yes.'

'Are you going to keep the baby?'

The girl's glance was shrivelling. 'Of course. I want him more than anything in the world.' Then, as if afraid that she might have hurt the sister's feelings, she added 'I had no mother of my own. She died when I was born. I know how much mothers matter.'

'Babies need fathers too. And you're very young,' the sister said gently. The fierceness came back at once. 'Mine doesn't. I'm eighteen years old. I can manage.'

It was not a topic to be pursued.

'Do you want to telephone anyone?' The blue uniform rustled as she stood up. 'I can wheel in the trolley for you. It's more private for you here than up on the ward.'

The girl shook her head. 'No. No, thank you, sister.'

All right. I'll go and find a porter to help us upstairs with you.' At the door, she asked 'What's the baby's name?'

'William. William Owain.'

'That's nice.'

'It's a family name, you see. My father's. If I'd been a boy, I would have been William too. Instead of just a girl,' she added to herself.

'That's nice,' the sister said again, automatically. 'Now, where are those porters?'

Left alone, the girl looked down again at the unbelievable, delicate lids over her baby's dark eyes.

'Just us,' she whispered to him. 'But it won't matter to us. I promise you. I'll make it right for you. I will.'

As the tears pricked in her own eyes, she hugged the baby to her as if her love would break them both in half.

Yet when the porter came clattering through the door with his wheelchair and his tired, labour-ward joke, she found a smile for him. Pretending was beginning to come naturally. Perhaps soon she wouldn't notice it at all.

A day later she looked on from her quiet corner of the post-natal ward. She was breaking the rules in keeping the sleeping baby drawn against her, protected by the white wall of bedcovers. Twice the ward sister had told her that he should be left in the clinical glass crib at the bedside. The girl had said nothing, but the baby stayed in her arms. With resigned tact the nursing staff had begun to leave her alone and now, at visiting time, she lay in a pool of deepening isolation. The ward was noisy with clattering arrivals, exclamations and the pop and whirr of cameras, but she turned calmly away from it. She only looked up when the tap of leather soles on polished linoleum stopped at her bed.

'Hullo, Anne.'

Her visitor was a broad, pink-faced man in a well-cut suit worn with an air of constriction. He was carrying a pyramid of red roses and a Harrods carrier bag. The girl he had called Anne looked up with the same smile that had sent yesterday's medical student whistling out into the sunshine.

'Jamie?'

He dropped the roses on the end of the bed and held out the Harrods bag. 'Why didn't you tell me? I called at your room to see if you were okay, and couldn't find you. So I telephoned here and they told me. Let's have a look at the little beggar.'

She turned down the covers for him to see the tiny red face.

'God, why are they always so hideous?'

Anne laughed, quite certain that he was wrong. 'William isn't. To me he's just like . . . well, just like I knew he would be.'

Jamie proffered the carrier bag again and she rummaged in the tissue paper like a child with a birthday. The present was a classic, fat, golden-yellow teddy bear with a pale blue ribbon round his neck.

'Thank you,' she said simply. 'And for the flowers. They'll all stop looking sympathetically at me now I've got some too.'

Jamie glanced up the ward at the scenes of family celebration beside every bed, and the pinkness of his face deepened. He put one finger up to ease his starched collar.

The silence between them became embarrassed, the sign of people who don't know each other very well caught in a moment of unwonted intimacy.

9

Jamie broke it at last, apparently steeling himself to say something that might seem not quite polite.

'What are you going to do now? Now you've got the baby, I mean?'

Anne's face contracted with anxiety.

'I was afraid that's what you'd come to ask. I want to go on working for you, if you'll let me. Please, won't you? William can come with me for a bit. He can sleep in his Moses basket. He won't be in the way, I promise. I need the job, Jamie.'

He nodded slowly.

'You cook like an angel. You know that. You can go on working in the restaurant as long as you like. But it's hardly a life for you, is it? Long hours, and nothing at the end of it but a bedsitter and a baby who won't be the joy of your life for every single minute. You aren't trained. You can probably earn just enough to feed yourself and him and keep a roof over your heads. But what kind of future does that give you, or him?'

Anne bent her head. Her hair swung forward to leave the nape of her neck bare and Jamie thought with resigned irritation how vulnerable she was. The offer he was about to make was crazy, but he knew that he was going to have to make it just the same.

'I know all this,' Anne whispered. 'But I'll make it work, somehow.' She was echoing her promise to the baby. 'Just help me by letting me keep the job, will you?'

'Hear me out, please,' Jamie said. Resolution made his voice sound brusque. 'I'll make you a business proposal. You're an instinctive cook, good enough to be exceptional if you're trained properly. You won't get that training where you are now in Pierre's kitchen because he hasn't the time to devote to it. Listen, will you?' He was impatient with her for trying to insist that yes, she could pick things up as she went along.

'You could use part of what I pay you now – more than you're worth as it stands, incidentally – to pay your way through cookery school. Wait. That is if, if, you're not paying huge sums in rent for some poky room.

10

'Now, I live in a mansion block off Sloane Square. At the end of the corridor I have an empty room with another, smaller room opening off it. The maid used to live there, so don't think it's grander than it is. Both rooms are full of old tennis racquets and mackintoshes now, but I can clear them out for you. You and the baby can move in and live there rent free during the time that you are training – provided that you also continue to work at Duff's part-time as you do now, and for some specified period that we can agree between us when your training is complete. I'll be happy with that as a bargain if it suits you too.'

He was on his home ground now, fluent and lawyer-like, negotiating an out-of-court settlement. He stopped expectantly, and then something else occurred to him. 'No strings, of course. It's just a business arrangement.'

'You didn't have to say that,' she told him quickly. 'Of course I didn't think you wanted . . .'

'Well?' he interrupted, heading off their embarrassment.

'Do you really want to clutter up your domestic sanctum with a part-time chef and a baby?'

'Not at all. But I'm away a good deal, and it's a large flat. The offer stands, anyway. But first, will you promise me something?'

'Anything. No, anything reasonable.' He hadn't seen her perky humour before, and he was surprised how different her face looked without the preoccupied anxiety that had marked it during the last weeks.

'Will you think seriously about going home? Back to your people? I know you're not a real waif, even though you turned up at my restaurant like one. Are you sure, Anne, that you and the baby wouldn't be happier back where you belong?'

She looked past him and the shiny, pale green hospital walls vanished. Instead she saw the haphazard cluster of low grey stone and slate houses against the curve of hillside. The sun of her imagination went in as a door opened and a man, older than his years, came out into the familiar street. She heard the exact sound of the door latch, and smelt coal smoke thick on the mild air. The house behind him was

11

empty, and the street was empty, and the fields beyond it across the few miles to the other house were empty too. They would stay empty for her, however full they were of other lives.

'No,' she said, 'I wouldn't be happier. We don't belong, either of us. See, I'm even getting used to being called Anne.'

'I can't pronounce the other,' he complained, not for the first time.

'Angharad,' she said. The soft *r* curled and brought out the Welsh lilt that she usually struggled to suppress.

'Angharad,' he repeated, and laughed. 'When I say it it sounds like a patent rotary clothesline.'

'Doesn't matter.' Her smile came back. 'Anne is a fine London name. But I'll keep the Owain, because that's his name by rights too.' She stroked the downy head and at once everything else was forgotten.

Her visitor stood up.

'Okay then. Make sure you give me a ring when they say you can come home, and I'll see someone from Duff's picks you up. Better put your roses in some water before they die of thirst.' He nodded at her casually and went away up the ward.

Thank you, she whispered under her breath. Thank you, funny English inhibited Jamie Duff. You see? Her finger touched the baby's cheek. It will all be all right. Trust me, won't you?

The girl in the next bed looked across at her, relieved to see some signs of normality about her odd neighbour.

'Was that . . . was that him?' she asked inquisitively.

Anne stared back astonished.

'My baby's father? Oh no.' She began to laugh at the idea. 'Oh no. His father is nothing like that at all.'

And she turned away again to look through the green hospital walls into a landscape that lived on inside her head.

# CHAPTER TWO

Nothing had changed.

The way home was almost unbearably familiar. Over the last two miles, after they left the main road and began to climb the lane to the village, Angharad knew the outline of every patch of moss on the stone walls, and the branched pattern of every tree showing through the last ragged leaves.

She peered sideways at her father. He looked the same too, but she was aware that there was a difference between them. They had driven the long way from school in almost total silence. That was nothing new in itself, because her father always drove with a concentration that reflected his mistrust of machinery. But in the old days Angharad would have filled the silence with chatter that didn't call for an answer. Now an uneasy shyness kept her quiet. She wasn't sure how much she had changed in the long weeks she had been away, and she was afraid that her unhappiness would show and disappoint him.

She caught herself wondering how she should present herself, as a happy schoolgirl coming back for her first visit home, or as forgivably homesick, and the very thought silenced her. Only weeks ago she had just been Angharad Owain, and there had been none of these uncomfortable avenues of possibility ahead of her. Now she felt severed from her father and from her old self. She had counted the hours to this half term, yet here she was coming home almost as a stranger.

Angharad looked fiercely up at the oak tree that hung over the road as it curved into the village. She had perched in the branches as a little girl, ·playing the forbidden game of aiming pebbles at the tops of rare passing cars.

It looks the same, she thought bitterly, but it isn't. Nothing is, any more. They turned the corner and came into the long, straggling street. It was as familiar to Angharad as her own face.

Most of the houses were grey stone, roofed in Welsh slate that was spotted with whorls of yellow lichen. Others, dropped haphazardly in between, were newer, shiny red Ruabon brick with yellow facings around the windows. The doors almost all opened straight on to the pavement, and Angharad knew the families behind each one and all their histories. Against the grey-white sky hung low billows of smoke from each house. It was mid-afternoon and fires were being lit before children came back on the school bus. There was no school in the village now, because there were too few village children to attend it. Angharad's Aunt Gwyn lived in the Victorian schoolhouse and grew geraniums in tubs in the girls' yard.

The car stopped in front of the last house in the street.

'Home,' Angharad said, savouring the word.

Angharad had always been pleased that she lived in one of the grey stone houses, with a door in the middle and two windows on either side like a house in a child's drawing. It had once been the vicarage, and it was a shade larger than the other houses. Angharad had always considered this appropriate too, because, after all, her father was different from the other men in the village. Beyond the house was the low wall of the churchyard, a fat yew tree, and the grey church tower rising among the gravestones. The Methodist chapel, hideous in red brick, sat trenchantly at the opposite end of the village.

Beyond the houses and the church were open fields, dipping and rising to the skirts of The Mountain. It was only one of the range that ran from the sea down into the heart of mid-Wales, but it was The Mountain in the village, to Angharad and everyone else, and its homely outline dominated the horizon. The summit of it was brown now with dead bracken, and the lower slopes were dark squares of symmetrical Forestry Commission conifers.

'Home,' her father repeated. 'Are you pleased to be back?'

'Yes.' Angharad forgot the constraints of the drive. 'Oh yes.'

The car door slammed open and she scrambled out,

transformed back into the child who had been driven so reluctantly away in her scratchy school uniform. The air surprised her with its milky sweetness, overlaid with the distinctive drift of coal smoke. For a second it was so quiet that Angharad could hear the stream trickling in the hollow beyond the churchyard. She ran the few steps to the front door, clicked the old-fashioned latch and it swung open. It was never locked.

'It may be 1965, but you'd never know it in Cefn, thank God,' her father was fond of saying. 'When it's time to lock the doors against your neighbours, it's time to move somewhere else.'

The door opened straight into the square room that was the centre of the house. Her father's study was off to the right, but this room was where they lived. It looked smaller to Angharad after the echoing linoleum spaces of school, but otherwise just the same. The rugs and the few pieces of battered but solid furniture stood in the same places on the flagged floor. The alcoves were lined with books and a grandfather clock with the sun and moon painted on its face ticked solidly. The scrolled top touched the black beams of the ceiling. A new fire smelling of freshly chopped sticks crackled in the stone hearth.

Angharad listened to the sounds of the old house for a moment and then shouted, 'Aunty Gwyn, are you here? I'm home!'

Gwyn Owain came out from the kitchen at the back of the house. Angharad beamed at the sight of her in her perennial tubular tweed skirt, snagged pullover and laced-up brown shoes worn with man's grey socks. Her intelligent face was lined and puckered, and her faded hair was cut short with a firm consideration of convenience and none of style.

Angharad had never known her own mother, and her father's spinster sister had mothered her uncomplainingly from birth. Gwyn Owain was too independent to live as part of her brother's household, even for the sake of his orphaned daughter, but she lived close enough for Angharad to love her and depend on her as if she were her real mother. She had taken her aunt's forthrightness, and her occasional

15

eccentricity, for granted for the whole of her life. Gwyn wiped her hand absently on the best white tablecloth she was holding and then wrapped her arms around her niece.

'Welcome home, pet lamb.' Then she blinked, and looked at her again. 'What's happened to your lovely hair?'

Angharad's hands flew up to her bare ears, and back came the memory of the bleak school bathroom and the knot of giggling, jeering girls around her.

It had been her dormitory initiation.

'Plaits?' they had said incredulously. 'No one wears plaits any more.' There had been a metallic click as the scissors were lifted, and two jagged bites that wrenched her head back as the twists of hair were cut off. In the sudden, slightly awed silence that followed she heard the tiny crinkling noise as the hair unwound from the stumps of her plaits and frizzed into abandon.

'I cut them off,' she said quickly. 'None of the girls had plaits, Aunty Gwyn.'

After they had gone away and left her alone, another girl, a tall girl with very clear eyes, had come in and found Angharad staring at herself in the mirror as if at a stranger.

'What did they do?'

'They said it was my initiation.'

The image in the glass in front of her, her own round face with the ridiculous sawn-off hair and the dark, oval one above it, had blurred with tears. The dark girl had made an impatient noise and gone to fetch her own scissors. She had made Angharad sit on a bathroom stool, and with her black eyebrows drawn together in a frown, she had evened up the ragged ends. She snipped and trimmed decisively until she had turned Angharad's ravaged hair into a smooth bell.

When Angharad dared to look at herself again she stared in disbelief and then in dawning gratitude.

'How wonderful. You've made me look just like everyone else.'

The dark girl had said, drily, 'Well now, aren't you lucky.'

To their surprise they found themselves laughing.

The dark girl's name was Laura Cotton, and Angharad had loved her from that moment. Somehow, the awkward

16

scholarship girl and the elegant, aloof Laura, seemingly older by years than her contemporaries, had become friends. Laura had made the lonely privation of school endurable for Angharad.

Gwyn was clicking her tongue in disapproval.

'I'm surprised at you. Why do you have to look like everyone else? What do you think about it, Will?'

William Owain looked vaguely surprised. 'I hadn't noticed. She always looks nice to me. Surely she's old enough now to decide about her hair for herself?'

Angharad went to him and kissed him. As her lips touched his face, she felt how the skin of his cheeks was loosening into folds. Her father was getting old, here on his own without her.

A sudden touch of grown-up fear came to her. Everything was changing, and she couldn't stop it. Angharad hugged her father with a fierce, possessive love. Their separation made her see him more clearly. Externally he was a mild, preoccupied man, uninterested in conventional achievements and happy in his beloved Welsh countryside. But Angharad knew that her father's mildness was deceptive. There was a passionate streak in him that could make him flare into anger, sometimes irrational, and it made her afraid of him as well as loving. Angharad understood too, without ever having explored the idea, that her father had never overcome his bitterness and grief over his young wife's loss. His daughter had always known that his feelings for her were shadowed by that memory, and that her physical likeness to her mother was a pain as well as a pleasure to William. Her cautiousness towards him had taken her running instead to Aunty Gwyn with all the problems and pleasures of her childhood.

Yet it was William she had missed, painfully, in the weeks away from Cefn village.

Her father stroked her smooth hair now and said, 'Go and help your aunt with the tea. I've got some work to finish. You can tell us everything about school while we're eating.'

The last sun of the afternoon was striking through the kitchen windows at the back of the house. Angharad saw that

17

her busy lizzies on the windowsill had been faithfully watered, and were a mass of bright scarlet flowers. There was a fire here too, in the old tiled range, dulled to a sullen red glow by the bright sunlight. A fat white cat was asleep in the rocking chair.

'Eirlys.' Angharad pressed her face into the soft fur and the cat stretched lazily in its sleep. 'I have missed you all.'

Gwyn had taken a pot out of the oven and was prodding at the contents.

'Lamb hot-pot,' she said unenthusiastically. 'Nothing like as good as yours.'

Neither her aunt nor her father was interested in cooking, but Angharad had been fascinated for as long as she could remember. She took the dish from her aunt, with a sudden memory of herself as a solemn eight-year-old, sitting at this same square scrubbed table. She had had a recipe book propped up in front of her while she wrestled with a mass of dough for puff pastry.

'It's fine,' she said now, tasting the hot-pot. 'Needs more salt, that's all.'

'I'll do it, if you lay the table.'

Angharad went automatically to the drawer in the dresser and took out the cutlery. She set three places, touching the thin silver gently as she laid it down. She was dimly aware that these delicate spoons and bone-handled knives, and the forks engraved with the entwined 'WO', were somehow part of her father's past, and didn't properly belong here in the little stone house any more than her father did himself.

Her new, uncomfortable perspectives made her suddenly aware of how little she knew, and how little she understood.

'Is Dad all right?' she asked abruptly.

'What, lamb? Your Dad? Oh yes, I think so. He'll be finished with his book soon, and he's been lucky with other work lately.'

William was an historian, once a teacher, but he had retreated years ago to his study to write scholarly books on remote Welsh history. The negligible income from that was supplemented with book reviewing, and occasional pieces on Welsh culture or characters for magazines. There had never been any money, and Angharad had never thought about it until confronted with her shaming lack of it by her new contemporaries. They had laughed, not quite behind her back, at her clothes and her unsophisticated tastes. Except for Laura, who had told her that clothes were peripheral – although her own were beautiful – and that she should be proud of having won her free scholarship.

'I didn't mean that,' Angharad said now, frowning. Nothing was simple, any more. 'I meant . . . what will happen to him while I'm away? When I grow up, and he gets old?'

'He's younger than me,' Gwyn said cheerfully. 'I notice you're not worried about your poor old aunt. Quite right too, and you shouldn't worry about your father either, because he can look after himself. You enjoy yourself while you can. Now, go and call him in for his tea.'

So I'm still not old enough for a serious answer, Angharad thought, as she walked through to the study. Old enough to go away on my own, old enough to cut my own hair, but not old enough to know anything about anything.

None of the questions that were beginning to ferment inside her would be answered yet.

'Not tea-time already is it?' her father said, as he always did. It was getting dark outside, and Gwyn drew the check curtains at the window. They sat down in their accustomed places at the best white tablecloth.

'Well then.' Her father peered over his spectacles and his eyebrows drew up into peaks. 'Let's hear all about it. You didn't say much in your letters.'

Angharad looked from one face to the other.

They were proud, and expectant, and anxious for her happiness. The words of complaint dried up on her tongue, and she swallowed the truth back hurriedly. 'It was strange to begin with. It's so big, and noisy, and there are so many people.' She was careful to keep her voice light, as if none of these things mattered to her now. 'And my uniform, and books, aren't quite the same as . . . everyone else's. Not that it matters, of course.' Her free-scholar's books and uniform were second-hand, and bore the marks of it. In spite of

19

Laura's dismissiveness she still minded. Angharad rushed on before she gave herself away. 'The lessons are okay, quite easy really, and I've started to do Latin . . .'

'Good. You'll need that to get a University place.' Her father nodded approvingly.

'. . . And French, and European History. The only thing they don't have is proper cookery classes, only stupid lessons where you learn about flower arranging and table setting and how to make tea. Home management, it's called.'

'You can't earn your living at cooking,' her father said briskly. 'You concentrate on your Latin instead.'

Aunty Gwyn winked at her.

Angharad cast around for something else to say that wouldn't betray her loneliness, and her bewilderment, and her hatred of the whole ugly, strange-smelling turmoil of school. Except for Laura. Of course, she could tell them about Laura.

'There's a girl I've made friends with. Different from all the other stupid ones.'

Laura led, and Angharad followed without question. Laura had an uncompromising intelligence that Angharad admired, and if she was sometimes sharp-tongued, Angharad understood it was because her cleverness made her impatient. Angharad was clever in her own, much gentler way, and that was a bond between them. But their closest link was forged when Angharad discovered that Laura was from Wales too, and that under her cool exterior she was as homesick as herself.

'I wish I was proper Welsh, like you,' Laura had said once. 'Not just born there, but from Welsh people for generations. My father came from Lancashire. Do you think I count?'

'Of course you do,' Angharad said, in all the security of her own firm roots. 'If you believe that you're Welsh, then you are.'

'Talk some more Welsh to me,' Laura commanded, and Angharad did as she was asked, teaching her simple words and laughing as Laura tried to get her stiff tongue around the soft, liquid sounds.

*Gwallt*, Laura repeated doggedly, *llygad*, *trwyn*. Angharad

20

taught her to pronounce her own name with the soft, throaty 'r' that spoke so clearly of home.

In her turn, Laura talked of her own home. She came from a place called Llyn Fair, describing it as 'an old, old stone house, beside a secret lake in a hidden valley.'

Angharad had never heard of it, although it was not many miles from Cefn.

'It's beautiful,' Laura told her. 'The most beautiful place in the world.' And after a little pause, when Angharad judged that she was being evaluated all over again, Laura said, 'You must come and see it. You'll meet my brother. He's . . . my best friend. The only friend I wanted, until you. You'll like him, Angharad. It would be odd, and nice, to be three instead of only two at Llyn Fair.'

Laura's eyes shone, and her face glowed, and she looked beyond the clamorous school dining-room to somewhere Angharad couldn't follow. Jealousy bit at her.

'What's his name?' she asked, not wanting to know. She didn't want to share Laura with anyone.

'His name is Harry.' Angharad had seen the pleasure that it gave Laura just to say his name aloud, and she had turned away, biting her lip.

She became aware now that William and Gwyn were waiting, watching her with curious expectancy.

She smiled at them happily.

'Her name's Laura. She's older than me, and much cleverer. She's going to go to Oxford after she's left school, and then to London to be a television producer. The best thing is that she's Welsh too. Only honorary Welsh, she calls it. She lives quite near here, at somewhere called Llyn Fair.'

There was a sudden, icy silence.

The chill of it spread from the circle of light bathing the table out into the shadowy corners of the room. Startled, Angharad looked from one face to the other. Gwyn, after her first shocked gasp, was looking away from her, down at the edge of the tablecloth. She lifted the corner of it and began to pull so fiercely at the hem that Angharad was sure she would tear it. When she turned to William, she saw that his face had darkened with anger, and there were sharp lines beside his mouth. It was an expression she knew, and feared.

'What did you say her name is?'

'Laura.'

'*Laura who?*'

'Dad? Laura Cotton . . .'

Her father's cup smashed down into his saucer. The force of it made the spoons and plates rattle. Angharad stared at him, bewildered.

'How many girls are there at your school?'

'Why? What . . . ?'

'How many, Angharad?'

'Six hundred and twenty.'

'And out of six hundred and twenty girls, you have to choose to make friends with a Cotton child?'

The sarcasm in his voice bit into Angharad and she shrank into her chair.

'William, she couldn't know . . .'

'Be quiet, Gwyn. Listen to me, Angharad. When you go back to your school, you will make friends with someone else. Anyone else you please. I don't want to hear you mention anyone called Cotton from Llyn Fair again. Understood?'

'But . . .'

'You heard what I said, Angharad.'

Her father jerked to his feet and swung away from the table. They heard the door to his study close behind him and silence fell again. There was a brown stain on the best tablecloth where William's tea had slopped over. Angharad stared dully at it for a moment and then raised her eyes to her aunt's.

'What have I done wrong?'

'Come here, my lamb.' Her voice sounded heavy. Angharad stumbled to her and buried her face against the knobbly grey shoulder. Tears of shock came welling into her eyes and she shook with fright.

'It isn't your fault,' Gwyn soothed her. 'Your father isn't angry with you. He's angry about something that happened long ago, before you were born, and your friend's name and . . . and the place where she lived reminded him of it.' Gwyn's hands tightened on Angharad's arms, and her voice grew firm, and stern in a way that Angharad had never heard before. 'But he's right. You should find yourself another friend. There must be dozens of nice girls to choose from.'

'There aren't,' Angharad sobbed. 'They are all horrible except Laura. They only talk about clothes and boys and kissing.'

She would have gone on, if she hadn't felt that her aunt's thoughts were elsewhere. She was thinking about something so cold and unwelcome that it took all the kindliness out of her face.

'Clothes and boys?' Gwyn repeated at last, with a visible effort. 'Darling, that's normal and natural. Girls of your age are starting to be interested in things like that, and so should you be. It's part of growing up. You've been too much on your own here with only your father and me for company. Being with all the other girls will be good for you. You'll see, you'll soon start to like them.'

Angharad knew, with unshakeable conviction, that she never would.

'But I've got friends here,' she said desperately. The thought of going back to school, with even the solace of Laura's friendship mysteriously denied her, was unbearable. 'Friends I've had all my life.' She counted the names off on her fingers, children from the village who had sat next to her at primary school and who lived behind the doors down the street. She knew everything about them, as they did about her. Weren't they good enough any more? Why was the world suddenly so complicated?

'I know, I know.' Gwyn was smiling. 'And they'll stay your friends, I'm sure. But truly, you've always preferred your own company, or ours, haven't you? You see, your father doesn't want you to stay here all your life. He's proud of you, and he wants you to make something of yourself. You'll learn things at your school, in classes and out of them, that you'll never learn here.'

That's true, Angharad thought bitterly. About French kissing, and pop records.

Laura was the only person who had shown her anything

23

she really wanted to know. She thought back over them, all kinds of things.

'Haven't you read *Jane Eyre*?' Laura had said. 'You should.'

Angharad had dutifully picked it up, and it had swept her into another world for three whole days.

'Yes, the Beatles are good,' Laura had agreed. 'But listen to *this*.' It was the *Pastoral Symphony*, and Angharad was entranced. There was music at home, but listening to it with Laura made it quite different.

Laura had even shown her how to tame the elastic tentacles of her suspender belt so that Angharad's blue woollen stockings were as smooth as her own. She had wound the ends of her hair on to big spongy rollers for her, so that they curved elegantly inwards to frame her round face.

And now their friendship was forbidden.

Why? It made no sense. And Angharad liked to have answers to things. Her deep-seated instinct was to obey her father, but the rest of her cried out against it.

'Aunty Gwyn,' she said carefully, 'why can't I be Laura's friend? You'd like her, and Dad would too. I know you would.'

Gwyn sighed and stared over Angharad's head. At last she said, 'I'm going to tell you this because suddenly it seems to affect you. There would have been no need otherwise. Old bitterness is best forgotten. It happened a long time ago, just after your mother and father were married. A man called Joe Cotton, your friend's father, cheated our family out of something that was important to us. And as a result of that, something else happened that hurt your father and me deeply. That's all you need to know. Your father has never forgiven him, and it hurts him still to this day. Hearing those names again, and from you, was a shock to him. Do you see?'

Angharad said nothing. She was struggling to take in Gwyn's words. Laura's father? Laura was real to her, vivid and important, but her father was less than a shadow. Angharad couldn't recall Laura even having mentioned him. She frowned, trying to remember. Laura talked about her mother, in passing, and about her brother in moments

24

which flattered Angharad with their intimacy, even though jealousy still pricked her. But never her father. What could he have done, so long ago but so damagingly, to cause so much turmoil now?

'Cheated us out of what?' she asked.

Gwyn shook her head. Her lips were pressed together.

'That doesn't matter now. It's all past. Just do as your father says, and make friends with someone else. For his sake, Angharad.' Clearly the conversation was at an end. Angharad pulled away from her aunt and mechanically set about clearing the tea-table. The left-overs were put away in the cold stone pantry, the dirty dishes stacked beside the deep, old-fashioned sink, just as always. She knew that Gwyn was watching her but she kept her face averted. She felt heavy, and cold, and cut off. It was strange to feel lonely in this warm, homely place.

'What is it, lamb?' Gwyn asked at last. 'Is this girl so important to you? Aren't you happy at your school?'

Something in Angharad, a little secret reserve of pride, as well as anger that her aunt wouldn't trust her with her father's story, kept the truth locked inside her.

'Of course I am,' she said stiffly. 'I love it. It took a little bit of getting used to, that's all.'

They finished the washing-up in silence. Angharad, staring into the greasy water, felt the first ache of her dilemma. Part of her wanted, and needed, to obey her father. But another, the new Angharad who was emerging out of the shell of being a little girl, dictated differently.

Laura was her own friend. Neither of them owed anything to the distant past. *It doesn't matter*, she thought fiercely.

But Dad . . . She remembered how she had felt the loose skin masking his face like an old man's. And he had never asked her for anything before. Nothing that would cost her anything to give. The realization settled around her like a heavy weight. Of course she would have to do as he asked. Somehow, when they sent her back to the brass bells, and the dust and chalk smells, and the relentless unprivate monotony of school, she would have to turn her back on Laura too.

25

*Unfair*.

Hot tears stung her eyes again and Angharad had to duck her head to hide them from her aunt.

Gwyn opened the back door and the sweet, damp night air spilled into the kitchen.

'I think I'll go back home,' she said. 'Unless you'd like me to stay and keep you company?'

Angharad knew that she could still have called her back, and let herself be comforted, but she didn't.

'No,' she said. 'I'm just going to read for a while.'

The house was very silent after Gwyn had gone. Eirlys, the white cat, was still asleep in the rocker. Angharad walked through and looked at the closed door of her father's study. She thought of running in and climbing up on to his knee, as she might have done years ago, and telling him that it was all, all right. She would do whatever he wanted, however mysterious or hurtful it seemed, because she loved him.

But the study door stayed shut, and after a moment Angharad turned away. Up in her bedroom, with the little square sash window looking out over the street, Angharad stared at the shelf of battered children's classics over her bed. *Alice in Wonderland. The Wind in the Willows. What Katy Did.* There was nothing to solace her there now.

Angharad ran back downstairs to the alcove shelves. Towards the top, on the left-hand side, under her father's meticulous classification, she found something that drew her hand. Next to *Jane Eyre* there was a fat book with a worn, brown spine. She peered at the dim gilt title. *Wuthering Heights*. Angharad took the book upstairs with her, undressed, and drew the blankets over her head to make a protective cave. The book fell open at the first page and she began to read.

In the morning, when he came down, William said nothing about the night before. Angharad didn't expect that he would. The storm had subsided, for this time, and provided that he was obeyed her father was his normal, calm, kindly self again.

Angharad laid the breakfast table and they sat down together.

'It's a beautiful day,' William said. 'What are you going to do with it?'

'I don't know.'

Angharad had got up early, her eyes still gritty with reading late. She had stood barefoot on the stone doorstep, looking away down the street. The day was clear and sharp, smelling of leaf-mould and damp earth. The sky over the shiny, wet slate roofs was duck-egg blue, unsmudged with smoke before the day's fires were lit. Elfed the Milk rattled round the corner under the oak tree in his pick-up loaded with crates, and he had waved to her as he began clinking the bottles in pairs on to the doorsteps. As she had watched him, she had asked herself the same question, what she should do and had been disconcerted by it. She had never needed to think about filling her days at Cefn before.

'I'm going to St Winefride's Well,' William said. 'Would you like to come with me?'

William was not the man to put his arms around his daughter in an open attempt at reconciliation. This invitation was his own way of putting things to rights. It took Angharad back at once to their times together before she had been banished to school. They had often gone off on expeditions to historical sites, and she had stood at his side half-understanding his explanations and wholly enthralled by his company. Those were the best times with her father.

She weighed it up now, balancing her pride against her unhappiness at being at odds with him.

'Yes,' she said awkwardly. 'I've never seen it. I'd like to come.'

The well was half a dozen miles away, and they drove through the narrow lanes at first in silence and then, slowly, picking up the threads of inconsequential talk.

Angharad wondered if this was what being grown-up was like, talking about things that didn't matter while all you could think about were the things that did.

But when they reached their destination on the outskirts of the little local town, the awkwardness between them fell instantly away. William left his old car just where it stopped,

27

at an angle to the kerb, and strode across the narrow street into the shadow under the wall of the old monastery. Angharad scrambled after him, at once a child again, ready to enter into the world that he was always able to recreate for her.

'Look,' William said, pointing up to the façade that Angharad had passed dozens of times yet somehow had never seen before. She saw the simple Norman arches and the solid pillars within, and the hollows in the stone steps worn so deeply that the centre of the step was almost gone.

'Can you imagine the pilgrims, columns of them, with their cloaks and bundles and their dusty feet, shuffling patiently up these steps? There has been a holy place here since the twelfth century.'

Angharad followed him in under the round arch, and into the cold dimness of the shrine. They came down some more hollow steps and ahead of them was a column of light. The shrine opened to the sky and Angharad saw green water enclosed by mossed grey stone, and on the slabs at the bottom of the pool the glitter of coins. William looked down at them.

'This is where the pilgrims came. Look, there are votive offerings to the saint, even today. Pennies thrown in with a wish, just the same as lighting a candle with a prayer.'

They sat down on the steps and Angharad felt the chill of centuries-old shadow, and the invisible press of pilgrims all around her. It was her father's special talent to bring such places alive for her.

'Do you know the story?' William asked.

'Tell me.'

'Winefride lived in the seventh century. She was the daughter of well-to-do parents, and the niece of Saint Bueno. Winefride was a devout girl, promised to a nunnery when she came of age.

'One day a local princeling came to her home, hot and thirsty from a day's hunting. It would have been Winefride's special responsibility, as the daughter of the house, to offer the welcome of their home to any traveller who needed it. That was the Welsh tradition. She would have brought the prince the best food they had, and offered to wash his feet or play the harp for him. Can you see her, bringing the dishes in, in her white veil over her dark cloak, with plaid wraps over her shoulders?

'She would have kept her eyes on the floor, never looking once directly at her guest. But the prince saw at once how beautiful she was, and he wanted her. Perhaps there was a struggle. Maybe the veil was torn off, ripped between them and trampled in the mud from the hunting field. Somehow Winefride broke free and ran to sanctuary in the church. But the prince caught up with her on the threshold, drew his hunting sword in his rage, and hacked the girl's head from her body.

'Saint Bueno came out of the church and saw his beautiful, mutilated niece at his feet. He cursed the murderer, and the ground opened at once at their feet and the prince was swallowed alive. The saint knelt and prayed for the girl's life to be restored, and it was. She came back to life, and the only sign was a thin white line around her neck. On the spot where her head had fallen, a fountain sprang up. Just here, Angharad.'

Angharad looked down into the water and saw the tiny crystal bubbles rising. Winefride was as real as herself.

'What happened to her?'

'Winefride lived for fifteen years. She became a nun, as she had promised. Her shrine here slowly gathered a great reputation as a holy place. The sick came on pilgrimages, and so did hundreds of thousands of ordinary people. Great men came too, even Kings. Henry V was one, and Edward IV. James II was the last King to come here. And Henry Tudor chose Winefride as one of the stone saints who guard his tomb in his chapel at Westminster.'

They sat in the little square of light within the thick walls. The bubbles rose endlessly from somewhere deep in the rock, up through the still water, and escaped at last.

Twelve hundred years, Angharad thought.

The unimaginable time had the effect of sharpening her own small fear and loneliness instead of dimninishing it.

She turned and rested her head against the comforting

solidity of her father's knee.

'I miss you,' she said. 'Can't I come home again?'

Her father stopped looking at the old stonework and the crude decorative carvings over the arches and smiled down at the top of her head.

'Do you think that I don't miss you?'

'No,' Angharad said, and then corrected her sulky tone at once. 'Yes, I know you do. That's why it doesn't make sense. Let me come home again.'

'It will take you a little while to get used to being away,' William said, in the unarguable voice that Angharad dreaded. 'But it is the best possible thing for you. You need the company and influence of other women because you'll be a woman yourself soon. We can't go on here on our own together.'

'Why not?' she asked, mulishly.

'Because it isn't suitable, that's why.' Angharad could see that her father was smiling, but it was a thin smile, devoid of happiness. 'Don't argue with me, Angharad. And do one more thing to please me. Find yourself another friend. That shouldn't be too difficult, should it?'

Yes, she wanted to say. Impossible, because I know that there isn't anyone like Laura.

'Mayn't I know why?' she asked, with a meekness that she didn't feel.

There was a long pause, and Angharad counted the bubbles as they soared upwards. William's thin smile cut bitter creases into his face, and he made a defensive gesture over her head as if to fend something off.

'It's past. There's isn't any need,' William reiterated.

Angharad didn't answer, and she felt the divide between them as thick as the old walls themselves.

At last William said heavily, 'I'll just go and collect the documents I need.' They left the green light behind, and the brief moment of closeness that Winefride had brought them, and went out into the traffic once again.

Back home once more, Angharad wandered through the little house. She had the chilly feeling of not belonging anywhere, any more. As soon as the thought came to her, she frowned and shook herself. She would go out somewhere, just as she would always have done.

Angharad found her wellingtons, still caked with the mud of the last rainy days of the summer holidays, and her old coat with the darned woollen gloves in the pocket. She scrambled over the low point in the churchyard wall and swished through the long grass between the headstones. The short-cut led to the back lane that wound in turn towards The Mountain. As she came down the lane she could see that there were children moving round a huge clump of red-brown brushwood in the centre of the field. They were her friends from the village street, building the annual Guy Fawkes bonfire. Angharad could see the tangle of orange-red curls belonging to Jessie Rhys, and the Williams twins beside her, Dicky and Gareth, and the others she had played with across these fields for as long as she could remember. She hesitated, and then stopped. Once she would have run to join them, but now she felt that she didn't belong here any more than she fitted in at school. Angharad stuck her hands in her pockets and turned away, staring up instead at the long summit of The Mountain. Beyond it, somewhere, was the mysterious place Llyn Fair. She wondered what Laura was doing, and thought that Laura wouldn't care about being left out of the building of a stupid bonfire.

I wish I was like Laura, Angharad whispered.

A heavy, cold weight pressed on her, as it had done ever since last night. It was much worse than not being part of the Guy Fawkes preparations, and worse than not knowing what to do with herself now. Almost as bad as being at odds with her father. On Sunday night she was going to have to find some way of telling Laura that they weren't friends any more. She pictured Laura's cool, inquiring stare, then miserably shut her eyes on it.

There was nothing to be done.

Angharad went for a long walk. She followed the deserted lane and pushed herself harder as it petered out into the track past Pendre Farm and began to rise with The Mountain. There were deep tractor ruts in the dried mud, and a ridge of coarse grass between them. The slope grew steeper and

Angharad found herself panting for breath. She strode on, frowning unseeingly at the path in front of her, deliberately thinking of nothing but the effort of climbing on upwards.

It grew very still and silent as the avenues of dark conifers closed around her, then suddenly they dropped behind and she was out on close springy turf with the wind clawing her hair back from her face. This was open grazing land, and a flock of wiry, grey sheep scudded away in front of her. Angharad kept her eyes on the skyline until she reached a little hollow just below the high point of The Mountain. She sank into its shelter out of the wind, and turned to look at the view.

In the far distance on one hand was the flat grey line of the sea, and on the other the undulating ridges of other low summits like this one. In front of her was the uneven green and ochre patchwork of farmland, laced with hedges and little belts of trees. Tiny grey or white oblongs of farmhouses stood between the bigger red-brown barns, and when Angharad screwed her eyes up she could pick out tractors inching through the winter ploughing.

Beyond that the land flattened, perceptibly richer, and rolled towards England. The village was a haphazard tumble of little grey blocks directly ahead of her, with the blue smoke hanging above it. As she stared she saw the sun glint sharply off a car turning down towards the main road. Her own home was hidden, but she could see Aunty Gwyn's old schoolhouse a little to one side, and almost pick out the white-painted fretted board that ran under the gables.

Her eyes began to water with the effort of staring, but still the absence that she had noticed with the very first glimpse nagged at her. It was very beautiful, but it might have been any picture-postcard view, anywhere.

Chillingly, the hills and hollows no longer reassuringly read *home* to her.

With a small, angry noise Angharad scrambled out of her sheltered spot and ran the last few yards to the summit. The wind up here took her breath away. It was rising in the west and sweeping with it top-heavy clouds that meant heavy rain. Angharad let herself hang against it, poised as if she wanted to swoop down away from the village and into the wilder landscape on the other side. Here the peaks were jagged and the valleys between them darker and narrower. The mountains rose sharply, grey under the grey sky, into splintered ridges that were blanketed in cloud.

Angharad quartered the wild scenery with her eyes, wondering if one of the houses isolated by folds of rock and .urf might be Llyn Fair. A heavy raindrop drove against her cheek and a glance at the sky told her that an autumn storm was breaking over the mountains. It was time to turn back.

She scrambled and ran down the same steep tracks, pursued all the way by the rain. Cae Mawr was deserted and the bonfire already darkened by the deluge as she passed by. By the time she reached the old schoolhouse, she was soaked.

Gwyn's door stood wide open and the rain was making dark pockmarks on the stone passage floor. Angharad slammed it behind her and made her way through to Gwyn's studio in what had once been the infant classroom. Her aunt was humming in her blue overall, oblivious as she pinched and moulded clay.

'Aunty Gwyn, the door was open. And the floor was getting all wet.'

'Mmm? Wet? Why, is it raining?' She peered out of the window in surprise and then back at Angharad. '*Cariad*, you're all wet yourself.'

'I've been up The Mountain. Got caught in the rain.'

Gwyn's air of preoccupation vanished. She bustled Angharad into one of her own shapeless jerseys, then sat her down in the warmest corner with a mug of hot tea. The room was still heated by the old pot-bellied classroom stove inside its tall barred fireguard. All winter Gwyn fed it with coke, and sometimes it got so hot that the old cast iron glowed red.

'What are you making?' Angharad asked. Gwyn was a potter, and the studio was furnished with a small kiln and a kick-wheel. Her interest lay in creating strange, fragile, sculpted shapes in translucent porcelain, looking oddly unlike herself, but she made her living by selling souvenir pottery to the tourist shops on the coast and in the more picturesque local towns.

33

'I had a lovely big order from Y Gegin Fach for these.' Gwyn pointed to a tray of brown jugs and bowls, slip-glazed in white stripes and the wobbly words '*siwgr*' and '*llaeth*'. 'Aren't they hideous?'

'They are, rather.' Angharad laughed with her. The comfortable companionship took her back to the times when she had played all day in here, picking up discarded lumps of clay from under the table and rolling them into animal shapes before trying to bake them hard on the stove top. She remembered how she had chattered endlessly while Gwyn had worked and listened. Or probably not listened, Angharad thought now. But the undemanding warmth made her want to talk again.

'I saw Jessie and the others at Cae Mawr finishing the bonfire. Only I won't be here for the Fifth and I couldn't see the point of helping.' She picked up a piece of clay and began to twist it aimlessly in her fingers. Gwyn glanced at her from under her thick eyebrows, but said nothing. 'So I went up The Mountain for a walk. Looking out over this side I thought . . . I thought just for a minute that it was nothing to do with me, as if I'd never seen it before. Then I went up and looked the other way. There was wind and the clouds racing along, and all that space. I felt like jumping off and sailing down into it. As if it was there I belonged. Not here, any more.'

She looked up at her aunt for her reaction, and saw that she was frowning.

'That's just fanciful, Angharad.' The word surprised her. She had never heard her aunt use it in a derogatory way before. 'Here's where you live. This is your home and where you belong, with your Dad and me. Don't talk any more nonsense. Of course you have to go away, to school and then to your own life with some future in it afterwards. You don't want to stay here and end up a solitary old duck like me, do you? But you can always come back home. Never forget that. No one can take your home away from you.'

Angharad saw Gwyn turn sharply away and look out of the windows again.

'Not now,' she added.

In the silence the coke hissed in the stove, and the rain drummed bleakly against the glass. Angharad had a sudden insight, and was shocked by her past blindness.

'You're lonely too, Aunty Gwyn, aren't you?'

'Everyone is sometimes. You'll have to learn that, pet. I have been, although not so much now. I've had you, and your father, after his own fashion, after all. But I'm ordinary enough to have wished for a husband and a family of my own. There was nobody for me here, and I never managed to get away anywhere else. Perhaps I should have made the best of it and married Twm Ty Coch after all.' It was a family joke that the local coal haulier had been in love with Gwyn since their schooldays. 'You take your chances, Angharad. You've everything in front of you.'

Everything? Angharad thought savagely that if everything meant the regimented school life that she hated, then the world could keep it. She would rather stay here and turn into an old duck, whatever that was.

If Laura hadn't been forbidden her, it would be different.

'I don't like school,' she said in a small voice.

'I know,' Gwyn said gently, smiling at her. 'But won't you try to, just for a little while longer?'

After a moment Angharad nodded submissively. But her docility hid a little ripple of resentment. She would do as they wanted her to, but only because there was no alternative.

'Look,' she said at last in a different, brittle voice. 'I've made a sheep.' She held up the lump of clay to show Gwyn.

'A better one than I could manage,' Gwyn encouraged her. 'Leave it and I'll fire it for you in he next batch.'

The offer would once have delighted Angharad. Now she shrugged and said 'Not worth it.' The little sheep was crushed back into a shapeless mass and tossed with the other pieces under the table again. Angharad stood up and took her steaming coat off the stove guard.

'I'd better go.'

Gwyn watched her. It was several minutes before she turned with a sigh back to her work.

For the rest of the longed-for weekend, the passions of Cathy and Heathcliff were more real for Angharad than her own dull discomforts. She wrapped herself in *Wuthering Heights* and insulated herself within its drama.

The grey house was very quiet. The ticking of the grandfather clock was the single sonorous counterpoint to the crackle and hiss of the fire. Angharad and her father were gently courteous to each other when they met, steering their talk through neutral channels that increased Angharad's first understanding of adult ways of saying things and meaning something quite different.

When the time came for them to make the long drive back to school, Angharad was relieved as much as reluctant. As the old car trundled down the street, she looked back once at the double row of houses, the windows decently veiled with lace curtains, and at Gwyn with her hand still raised in a wave. Then Angharad jerked her head round again and set her face firmly forward.

The grey school quadrangle was oppressive.

In the moment or two of silence after they parked at the end of the row of parents' cars, Angharad waited for her father to qualify his prohibition. Without being quite aware of it, she longed for him to reward her for this painful emergence from childhood with his trust, and his secret, whatever it was.

But the silence lengthened and her father's hands remained tensely on the wheel. At last she whispered, 'It's time for me to go in.'

Her father took her suitcase off the back seat and handed it to her.

'Remember what I said.' His voice was stern, unwavering.

Angharad kissed his cheek and turned sadly away. The impression that he was beginning to stoop like an old man clung with her.

She went heavily up the steps and the echoes of the high, bare corridors closed around her.

Laura was sitting on the floor of the bathroom at the end of their dormitory, where the other girls had cut off Angharad's plaits. She was leaning against a tall, ridged radiator with her legs stretched out in front of her and her hands loosely folded in her tunic lap. She had been looking ahead of her, her expression remote, but when Angharad came in, her head turned so quickly that her dark hair swung around her face.

'I'm so glad you're back,' she said. 'I can't bear it here.'

Angharad dropped to her knees beside her so that their faces were level. It was important to say what she had to say now, at once.

'Laura. My father wants me to find someone else – anyone else – to make friends with,' she blurted out. 'He said . . . he said it doesn't matter who, so long as it isn't a Cotton from Llyn Fair.'

Laura and Angharad heard only the silence that followed, not the endless hiss of steam in the old pipes overhead.

Angharad saw that Laura flinched a little, only a little, and then the welcoming glow faded from her face, leaving it set and pale. *Don't*, she wanted to say, I'm still your friend. I don't care what happened years ago.

At last Laura asked, 'Am I allowed to know why?'

'He wouldn't tell me. He was very angry, I don't understand why. It's something that happened before I was born, even. I asked Aunty Gwyn, and all she would say is that . . . your father cheated our family out of something that belonged to us, and my father has never forgotten or forgiven him.'

The dark curves of Laura's hair swung to hide her face as she bent her head. 'That doesn't surprise me.'

Angharad stared in astonishment. In her rehearsals of the scene she had imagined Laura leaping angrily to her father's defence. She had assumed that they would quarrel and so the breach would be made. But Laura's quiet acceptance nonplussed her.

'My father does do things like that. I've know it since I was quite small. But I can't hope to change him, can I?'

'I suppose not,' Angharad said faintly.

'Do you think your father's right to dictate whether we should like each other or not?'

As she thought, Angharad did hear the clank of the pipes and the insistent dripping that reminded her of the night of her initiation. Laura had rescued her.

She felt the stoop of her father's shoulders that suddenly brought him almost down to her own height, and the corded skin of his face as it touched her own. Not infallible, she thought. Surely he is wrong, this time? Laura had recognized her own father's fallibility when she was a little girl. Was that part of being grown-up, then, too, seeing the tall fixtures of childhood foreshortened by wider perspectives across which the cold winds blew?

'No,' she whispered. 'I think he's wrong.'

'And do you like me?' Laura had lifted her head and her dark stare drew Angharad's eyes. They looked at each other and Angharad had the fleeting impression that she could see past the flesh and bone of her friend's face and into her head.

'Yes,' she answered. 'No one can stop us from being friends.'

The power of her own decision jumped intoxicatingly inside her, setting her free at a stroke from the weight of the weekend.

She was her own person. She could decide for herself.

'I'm glad.'

Laura reached out and her hand closed over Angharad's. The physical touch unbalanced her again.

'Did you enjoy your half-term?' she asked, clumsily, to hide it.

'No.' Laura's voice was chill, but then passion broke through it. 'Harry wasn't there. I knew he wasn't going to be. His half isn't until next weekend. But being at home without him is like having a very lavish Christmas, with all the best and loveliest trappings, completely alone, with no one to share them with. And that makes it much worse, much, than ordinary, dull days alone. Can you understand that?'

Angharad's hand was released and she knew that she was forgotten. Jealousy of the intrusive Harry reared again inside her. But she put her arm around Laura's shoulders and comforted her, as Laura had once consoled her.

'Look, it's only, how many – seven? weeks until Christmas really comes. He'll be home then, won't he?'

Laura nodded. 'Only seven weeeks. If you know it's going to end sometime, I suppose you can stand anything.'

Suddenly she turned to face Angharad so that their faces were almost touching. 'You'll know him too. You will come to Lyn Fair with me one day, won't you?'

Angharad didn't want to share Laura with her brother, and she couldn't see how her father would ever allow her to go. But she understood that Laura was offering her something rare and valuable.

'I'd like that,' she said simply.

Slowly Laura moved her face so that her lips brushed the angle of Angharad's cheek. Her skin felt very cool as Angharad's instantly flamed scarlet.

'So would I,' Laura said.

Angharad knew that a pact was sealed between them. It would see her through her days in this place, but it went beyond that and it would last much longer. She had disobeyed her father, and she didn't care, because she had this. In the bleak bathroom, deaf to the insistent clanging of the school bells, Laura and Angharad smiled at each other.

# CHAPTER THREE

It was more than two years before Angharad saw Llyn Fair. She arrived alone that first time, on a hot summer morning, torn between excitement and guilt that she had lied to get herself here.

'This is your stop now,' the bus conductor shouted to her down the length of the empty bus. The driver leant on his wheel and winked at her as she passed, and Angharad climbed down the steps. The fresh air welcomed her after the stuffy, jolting journey. The way to Llyn Fair had been made longer by having to change buses with a long wait in between. She had told her father that she was going to stay with a friend in Chester, and he had driven her to the stop for the express bus and waved unsuspectingly as it pulled away.

But Angharad had got off again a mile down the road and waited in the heat for the slow country bus going the other way. Now she watched its reassuring green rear as it ground away along the valley road, and then looked around her.

She was at a crossroads marked by a small white cottage and a wooden signpost, just as Laura had described. Otherwise there was nothing but the narrow roads, only just wide enough for the bus to pass with the long grass brushing both sides, and the country rolling away beyond. At the roadside, shadowed by knotty trees, the grass was moist and verdant, but in the sunlight where it began to rise sharply it was bleached to strawy dryness and splashed with gorse and heather. Higher up still Angharad could see outcrops of bare rock and the skyline jagged and almost black against the blue sky. Nothing moved except the sheep against the hill. When the rumble of the bus had died away, the only sound was the song of a skylark spiralling over its territory in the rough grass.

Angharad squinted against the sun down each of the four roads in turn. She had no idea which direction to set off in, and Laura had said that they would come to meet her. A glance at her watch told her that the bus had been exactly on time. Angharad thought for a moment, then hoisted her overnight bag into the shade of a tree and sat down in the grass to wait.

The sound of the car began as a low hum, then swelled rapidly into a powerful roar. Angharad knew that it was travelling very fast even before it shot round a corner ahead of her. She had a glimpse of a low, dark green chassis before the car braked at the crossroads in a plume of dust. For a moment she thought that it was Laura's dark head behind the windscreen, and began to scramble to her feet. But when the driver turned and looked straight at her, she saw the resemblance, and the difference. It was Harry.

He vaulted out of the open car and came towards her. His long hair, almost as long as Laura's, was slicked back by the wind of the drive and it showed that his face was darker and more taut than his sister's. He was wearing jeans, and a white shirt with rolled-up sleeves that made his forearms look very tanned. Shyly Angharad looked away from him to the car. It was a Morgan two-seater with a rakish brown leather strap across the bonnet and a silver radiator grille that dazzled in the sun. Laura had told her that it had been Harry's seventeenth birthday present a month ago. Angharad felt that she was almost grown-up now, and not easily impressed, but in that summer of 1968, Harry's car seemed the ultimate in sophistication.

'Angharad.'

She jumped, nervously. Harry had come close to her while she was staring at the car and now his shadow fell across her face.

'Angharad?'

He said her name right, just as Laura did.

'Yes.'

Harry smiled, a sudden gipsyish flash that was like the sun coming out. 'I'm sorry you had to wait. I had to spend at least four minutes convincing Laura that there wasn't room

41

for her to come. A two-seater means two people, don't you agree? Here, give me that.' Gently he took her bag, and Angharad realized that she had been clinging to it like a lifebuoy. Harry opened the passenger door with a flourish and Angharad ducked into her seat. She was surprised by the opulent embrace of the leather seat and the low, beckoning perspective of the road over the length of the shiny bonnet.

'Hold on to your hat.' Harry glanced at her and in the second as the engine roared into life she felt his eyes on her hair and the planes of her face. Then his hands were braced on the wheel and he was watching the road again. The car shot forward, squeezing a gasp of breath out of her. Angharad felt a flicker of fear as the road hurtled towards her and was swallowed by the car's green jaws, but at the same time the warm wind raked her face and she felt the exhilaration of speed mounting within her.

Harry swung the car into a sharp turn and they were speeding up an even narrower lane into a deep cutting between two steep hillsides. The sound of the car's racing engines drummed back at her from the high banks and she found that her head was thrown back and she was laughing out loud. The road wound on, taking them with it as if they were part of it. Angharad saw how the hills curved round in front of them to meet, making a blind end to the little valley. Then they were slowing down, and slower, until they passed a white barred gate with the words 'Llyn Fair. Private Road' lettered in black on it.

An avenue of trees closed overhead, amplifying the drumming of the car, then opened to the sky again and they swept into a wide sunlit space enclosed by the hills on three sides. Harry turned the car in a scatter of gravel and the engine purred into silence.

Angharad looked around her. Her first impression was of the marriage of sunlight and dense shadow, the shimmering opacity of open water and the solid weight of dark pine trees against it. She heard the musical splash of water ahead of her and then louder, confused splashing as ducks rose from the surface of the water and soared overhead. The lake was a sheet of silver underlaid with jade green, protected from the

42

hillside on two sides by the dense, mysterious trees.

Llyn Fair House stood against the third slope. It was grey stone and blue-purple slate, but it was heightened and given elegance by the rows of tall Georgian sash windows, white-painted, and the intricate wood and wrought-iron verandah that ran along the lake frontage. The carving was smothered with creamy honeysuckle and with the opulent purple flowers of a clematis. On the tongue of gravel between the house and the arc of roses above the drop to the lake a tame goose waddled, honking derisively. Laura had been sitting in a white basket chair in the shade of the verandah with a black and white cocker spaniel asleep at her feet. She jumped up as the car stopped and sauntered towards them, hands in the pockets of her white tennis skirt.

Harry's hands dropped from the wheel and his eyes met Angharad's.

'Welcome to Llyn Fair.'

'Thank you. And thank you for the ride. I enjoyed it.'

Harry laughed, gipsyish again. Before her eyes turned to Laura, Angharad had the sense that she had met a challenge. The notion both pleased and irritated her.

Laura bent over the low door to kiss her.

'What kept you?' she asked in her cool voice.

'Kept us? We didn't drop below seventy all the way. By rights, your friend should have been scared senseless. But she wasn't.' Harry leaned across to release her from the front seat. Angharad was intensely aware of the two dark heads close to hers.

Then Harry was out of the car and strolling away towards the house. Laura linked her arm through Angharad's and drew her to the lip of ground above the lake. Ten feet below a rowing boat was moored to a primitive wooden jetty. There was sunshine on crumbly grey stone, and a white-painted seat at the water's edge with a straw hat hanging on one corner.

'I'm glad you're here,' Laura said. 'At last. You're the only person I've ever wanted to bring home, to this.' The jerk of her chin took in the trees and the water, the grey house and the low green car in its own slewed tyre marks on the gravel.

'It's beautiful,' Angharad said softly. The sheltered hollow cupped the light and warmth of the day, and the stillness radiating from the calm water seemed almost enchanted.

'There's just the three of us. You, and Harry, and me.' There was an almost gloating light in Laura's face. Angharad glanced involuntarily, but Harry had disappeared under the verandah, whistling. 'Pa and Ma will be out until late tonight. It's why I especially wanted you to come today, so that there would be just the three of us. Did you manage to escape all right?'

'Yes.' Angharad was abrupt. 'I don't much like lying to Dad, but it's done now.'

'Yes,' Laura responded in her cool voice. 'It's been done for almost three years, hasn't it?'

Angharad understood that the enforced secrecy of their friendship rankled with Laura as much as it troubled herself. Her father had never spoken of it again, and she knew that he assumed her complete obedience. She had held back from this visit because of the extra deception it seemed to involve, and because of her unwillingness to meet Laura's father. The quarrels of years ago were nothing to do with Laura or herself, but she had no wish to encounter her own father's enemy.

Yet in the end, her longing to see Laura's home and her curious desire to meet her brother had overcome her.

Laura laughed to dispel the shadow that threatened to fall between them and, taking her hand, led Angharad towards the house.

'We can eat lunch out here in the shade, and then do whatever you like. Tennis?'

There was a grass court beyond the house, spruce with fresh white lines.

Angharad groaned. 'What for, when you always beat me?'

'Then we can take on Harry together. It'll do him good to be trounced for once.'

They passed in through the heavy front door and into the cool of the hall. Angharad had a brief impression of old stone floors and oak doors obscured by effects that were just a little

44

too grand for the reserved simplicity of the old house. There was a heavy Persian runner on the floor, and an ornate polished buffet that drew the focus away from the tall window at the opposite end. Everything was surgically clean, and smelt of beeswax polish. Angharad could hear Harry still whistling somewhere and Laura followed the sound, her head cocked to it.

'In the kitchen,' she said. 'Foraging for food.'

The kitchen was terracotta-tiled, with a big square table and windsor chairs, and an Aga set under an arch hung with copper pans and a plait of garlic. Harry was standing at the open door of the largest refrigerator Angharad had ever seen.

'No immediate inspiration,' he said cheerfully. 'Yoghurt with leftover green beans? Tomatoes in some of Mrs Parry's ginger pudding?'

'Mrs Parry usually cooks,' Laura explained. 'It's her day off.'

Angharad looked around Harry's shoulder. 'I'll make something, if you like,' she offered shyly. There were eggs in a basket, and from the kitchen window she could see across a little yard herringbone-paved in brick to a kitchen bed lush with herbs. 'Omelettes fines herbes and a salad?'

Laura was already waltzing to load a tray with cutlery and glasses. 'Angharad,' she said, 'is the best cook in the world. She cooks like a composer . . . no, a painter, with a taste for *chiaroscuro*.'

Harry bowed her to the big, round black plates of the Aga under their hooded lids. 'If the best cook will tell me what she wants from the garden, I'll be honoured to lay it before her.'

He had blue eyes, very dark but perfectly clear. His face was quite serious but somewhere, belying the straight lines, he was laughing too. Angharad felt red-cheeked and gauche, and aware that much more than the two years in their ages separated them. She felt a sudden fierce desire for Laura's brother to like her, as much as she knew Laura did. It was as if a piece of her knowledge of Laura, which she had denied until this moment, had slipped smoothly into place. The brother and sister were part of each other, opposite sides of the same coin, uniquely minted up here in this remote, sun-filled cup of valley.

The kitchen was quiet except for the faintest ring of the glasses where Laura had set them on the tray.

'Yours to command,' Harry murmured.

'Chervil,' Angharad mumbled. 'Basil, if you have it. and some parsley, and lettuce and a few radishes . . .'

When he was gone, Angharad bent hurriedly to crack eggs into a copper bowl. Laura stood with her fingertips resting on the oak tabletop.

'You like him, don't you?'

There was a note in her voice Angharad didn't understand. It might have been command, or warning.

'Of course,' she answered simply. 'He's your brother.'

She had the impression that, behind her, Laura's rigid shoulders relaxed a little.

'It's just that it feels strange, sharing. I've always had Harry to myself. And you to myself. I wanted us all three to be together. Yet now . . .' She stopped, and then said much more softly, 'I must be a very possessive person.'

Angharad recognized the truth, and it failed to disturb her. She was sure of her loyalty to Laura, more confident of that than anything else. And it was a relief, no more, to discover that she was prepared to like Harry too, was even anxious for it, without the jealousy or resentment she had feared.

There was nothing to be afraid of. Nothing to do at all, except to enjoy the perfection of today.

Harry's shadow fell across the floor, and then he was tossing the contents of his garden basket on to the table.

'Is this enough of this feathery stuff?'

They looked, and burst out laughing. 'Enough for us and about forty others,' Angharad told him.

'Harry, you're absurdly greedy.' Laura's voice was warm again.

They ate lunch in the shade of the verandah, with the shadow tendrils of honeysuckle and clematis weaving patterns on the white table.

46

Harry brought out a bottle of white wine, saying, 'I plundered this from Joe's cellar. To do justice to Angharad's lunch.'

'Plundered is right,' Laura responded. 'I bet he knows exactly how many bottles of that he's got left.'

'Too bad. I shall justify myself when the explosion comes by saying it was perfect for this food, and this sunshine, and the three of us. And that we enjoyed every mouthful of it. Which is no less than the truth.' He filled their glasses with the pale gold wine and they raised them to one another and then drank.

Angharad was unused to alcohol of any sort and she felt it beguilingly loosen her tongue. She leant comfortably back in her chair, smiling between the faces that were so similar yet teased her with their difference.

'Tell us about Cefn,' Harry said gently. 'Tell us what you left behind this morning.'

Laura knew everything already, but Angharad sensed that she wanted it repeated, shared with Harry.

'It's no more than a long, uneven street with a church, and a shop, and a pub. I know every crack in the paving, and the sound of everyone's voice, and what they'll say when you see them. I've lived there all my life and I belong to it in one way. But in another I don't belong at all, any more. My Dad and Aunty Gwyn aren't quite like everyone else. They haven't always lived there, although I don't know any more than that. And since I've been away to school I feel even less part of it. I go away, and come back, and everything goes on without me. And since I've known Laura . . . .'

Angharad flashed a glance from Laura to Harry. 'You know about your Dad, and mine, and what he said?'

'Just that,' Harry said. 'I can't guess at why any more than Laura, or you. But it doesn't surprise me.'

The same words that Laura had used when she had first told her, Angharad remembered. But there was more bitterness, more resentment in Harry's voice. Angharad guessed that Laura, cool and self-contained, simply turned away from her father, cutting him out of her life. But there was more heat in Harry, and less control. Angharad knew

47

that instinctively. There would be open and probably dangerous conflict between Joe Cotton and his son. The thought of meeting the father cast a dark little finger of shade over the brightness of Angharad's afternoon.

'Cefn is my home, but yet it isn't,' she went on softly. Her eyes travelled over the expanse of lake, from the black water under the pine trees to the curve where it licked and splintered into a million points of light under the sun. Light and shade, brightness and secrecy. 'I feel more at home here,' she said, and the truth surprised her. 'It must be because I'm with you.'

She had meant to look at Laura, but it was Harry's glance which held hers.

'I hope so,' he said. A second or two of silence ticked away. Then Laura stood up, scraping her chair as she moved. 'But Llyn Fair's very special. Isn't it, Lolly?'

'You haven't called me that for years.' Laura leaned forward now and put her arms around Harry's shoulders. Her hair fell forward and as it mingled with Harry's, Angharad saw that it was exactly the same shade. The blackness was almost blue, and where the sun caught it there were silvery lights. Laura kissed her brother's forehead, and as if to answer her his hands closed over hers for a second.

How close they are, Angharad thought.

'It's too hot now for tennis.' Harry's voice was light. 'Shall we row on the lake instead?'

They went down the stone steps to the little sloping jetty and clambered one by one into the rocking boat. There was a seat with a padded cushion in the prow, and Laura steered Angharad into it. Then she produced another cushion and settled herself amidships with her dark head resting in Angharad's lap. Angharad stroked the fanned-out threads of hair back into a smooth cap and Laura sighed contentedly, letting her eyes close.

Harry took up the oars and they slid away from the jetty. From under her eyelashes Angharad saw the spray from the blades refracting into tiny rainbows. In the dead centre of the lake, close to the wavering line between light and shade, he rested on his oars and they drifted, close to the margin and then away again. Once they slipped into the shade so that a dark line fell across Harry's face. He smiled absently and paddled gently with one oar to take them into the sun again. Then he shipped the oars and lay back in the stern with his straw hat tipped over his eyes. Angharad listened to the splash of water over the dam at the end of the lake, and the faint breath of wind in the pines. Laura's head was warm and heavy in her lap, and she saw that Harry's tanned arm had dropped so that his fingers brushed against Laura's bare ankle. She felt that the touch connected them all in their isolation on the lapping water.

Dimly, she thought, I wish I could hold on to this moment. Keep it. But her own eyelids were heavy with sunshine and wine, and at last she let them close on the shimmering afternoon.

When she woke up again it was with a start and the impression that everything had suddenly gone dark. But the sun was simply moving to the west and the shadowed arc of lake was beginning, slowly, to eat up the sunlit portion. Harry woke up at the same instant. He blinked, and then shot her his dazzling smile. Gesturing her to silence he picked up the oars and then whispered, 'Ready . . . *paddle.*'

The boat leapt forward across the water in a shower of spray. Laura screamed as the cold drops splashed over her skin, and flung herself upright.

'You savage!'

Angharad felt the cold, empty place where her head had rested. Laura lurched forward to grab Harry's wrists. The boat rocked violently as they stood, wrestled briefly, and then, with a mocking shout from Harry and an anxious cry from Angharad, the brother and sister locked together for an instant before tipping in a flailing arc into the water.

Angharad clung desperately to her seat as the boat bobbed like a cork, her heart in her mouth. But then she saw the sleek heads surfacing together in a plume of white water. They were choking with laughter and still struggling together, rolling over in the water like seals. Then Harry was gone, surging towards the jetty with a powerful crawl that left Laura trailing behind him.

Angharad retrieved the splayed oars and clambered gingerly into Harry's seat. Then, with the boat ploughing like a tub, she began to row ashore after them. They were dancing up and down on dry land, waiting for her, when the boat bumped the jetty. They were still laughing, but contrite too.

'It was mean of us to leave you out there.'

'But she does row like a pro.'

'I'd rather row ashore than swim, thank you.'

'Quite right. God, that water's cold. I must have been in there a million times and I still forget.'

The lake water, bubbling from an underground spring deep in the rock, was icy. Angharad had trailed her fingers languidly in it and had drawn them out numb. Something made her shiver, now.

'Dry clothes then, and I'll beat you both at tennis.'

'You don't stand a chance.'

In fact they were only nearly a match for Harry. He was quicker, and much more powerful, and he made no allowances. Angharad's game was by far the weakest and she hovered at the net, jabbing an occasional volley between the powerful shots that whizzed past her. Harry's concentrated frown under his sweatband as he prowled on the back line waiting for her loopy service made her giggle, and Laura's stern instructions made it worse.

They took the game so seriously that it made Angharad see another side of them. They were competitive, but only with each other. The rest of the world was a sideshow. Angharad understood how the Laura she had first known had been so self-contained. She had needed no one to match herself against except Harry.

In the end, after three close sets, Harry was the victor. He threw his racket in the air and crowed while Laura scowled and told Angharad, 'I was sure with you I'd beat him. But you were no help.'

'I know,' she laughed. 'I just don't care enough about winning. How can I change myself?'

Harry came up behind them and his arms dropped around their shoulders. The heat of his skin through his thin shirt struck through to Angharad's. He kissed them both, laughing and still panting a little, and she recognized the same clean scent as Laura's. Lemons and grass.

'Good game. For girls, that is.'

Laura's swung racket narrowly missed him and he sprang away, taunting them as he went with, 'Dinner at eight, I hope?'

Amused by Laura's irritation Angharad slid her arm through her friend's. They walked slowly away past the draped nets of the court and through the lengthening shadows. The lake surface was dimpled with the rise and fall of tiny insects. Under the verandah the scent of honeysuckle hung powerfully on the still air.

In Laura's pretty bedroom there were twin beds, with Angharad's bag standing at the foot of one. There was a bathroom adjoining the room and Angharad followed Laura into it.

'Is this your own bathroom?'

'Sure. Do you want to shower first, or shall I?'

'You.'

'Stay and talk, then.'

Angharad sat down on a low stool. Through the glass shower partition she watched the shape of Laura blurring under the stream of water. Laura was almost as tanned as Harry, except for the narrow white strips of her bikini. She lifted her hands to her hair and Angharad saw the rivulets of foam chasing over her skin.

Then the water was turned crisply off and Laura was stepping out, sleek, brown and black and creamy white.

'I wish I was as pretty as you,' Angharad said.

Laura looked at her. She put out her hand for her white bathrobe and only when she had enveloped herself in it did she answer.

'You are. You're like . . . a piece of china. A very rare piece, painted by hand somewhere a long time ago. Angharad?'

'Mmm?' The sudden urgency in Laura's voice surprised her.

'Don't change, will you?'

51

'Don't get more motivated at tennis after all, d'you mean?'

She knew that that wasn't what Laura meant at all, but a kind of shyness, and reserve, stopped her from acknowledging it.

'No. Or yes, if you like.'

The moment was past. 'Come on, have your shower. We'd better go and rustle up something for supper.'

They ate grilled trout from the lake in the polished, formal expanse of the Cottons' dining-room.

Laura had put on a dress and found one for Angharad too. Harry had whistled through his teeth when he saw them and gone away to change out of his jeans. When he came back he was wearing a white jacket, a pleated white shirt and a black bow tie. There was a red rosebud in his buttonhole. With his hair slicked back behind his ears he looked older, from another generation. He leant in the doorway, one eyebrow raised, waiting for their reaction.

'Very nice,' Laura said coolly. 'Are you going to sing, "Give Me the Moonlight"?'

But she was smiling, and her eyes were bright. Angharad suddenly felt too shy of him again to say anything, but she acknowledged to herself that he looked very beautiful.

The room grew dim as they ate and Laura leaned gracefully over to light the candles in the branched candelabrum in the centre of the table. Pools of golden light reflected back from the polished wood. Outside the last of the daylight lingered on the slopes of the hills and the lake water lay as black and as still as a mirror.

Angharad put down her knife and fork with a sigh of happiness.

'It's so beautiful here. You're so lucky. What does your father do, to have a house in a place like this?' It was the first time, since the beginning, that she had mentioned him to Laura.

There was a tiny silence.

Then Laura said 'Property.' It was Laura's way to give the necessary information and then, if it didn't interest or displeased her, to turn herself away from it as if it didn't exist.

But Harry was different. He picked up his glass and tilted it sideways in the candlelight.

'Yes, property. You've read about the sort of glamorous thing he does, I'm sure. He buys houses and parcels of land from people, old ladies mostly, for a few hundred pounds. Then he sells them again, for lots of thousands. And if the old ladies don't want to sell, he manages to buy anyway. Somehow or other.'

'Harry . . .'

He turned sharply to Laura. His face had turned dark.

'You deal with it by refusing to think about it. But that doesn't make it any less true. He's a profiteer. Yes, all this is beautiful.' He waved at the room, and the still water beyond. 'But it's tainted.'

Angharad listened, wishing that she didn't have to. She was frightened by the sudden rawness in Harry's voice, and unwilling to believe that he could think so badly of his father. Love for her own father touched her, and the thought that just by sitting here she was deceiving him. Harry's father, Laura's father, had cheated him. And very soon, in a few hours, she would have to meet the same Joe Cotton as a guest in his house.

For the first time, she wished that she had never come to Llyn Fair.

'You profit from the profiteering,' Laura was saying, wearily, as if they had thrashed over this ground together a thousand times before. 'You live here, don't you? You didn't refuse to accept that car a month ago. You don't look as if you think it's tainted when you polish it and fondle it. It's the same for all of us. We take from Joe, so we're as guilty of whatever it is as he is himself.'

No, that isn't true, Angharad thought.

Harry leapt to his feet with a violent gesture that sent his wineglass skidding across the polished table.

'I won't be for any longer than I have to. A few more months. Once I'm at college I'll be through with it.'

Angharad suddenly saw that the veneer of his sophistication had melted away. Harry was an angry boy, confused by his own anger.

As soon as she knew it, she loved him.

There was none of Harry's confusion in Laura.

'Taking your Morgan with you?' she asked him, softly now.

Harry stood still for a second, staring at her. Then he jammed his hands into the pockets of his beautiful white jacket and walked away.

Laura sighed and began calmly to gather up the plates and glasses.

'It's painful, being an idealist rather than a realist. Do you think Harry and I quarrel all the time? We don't, as it happens. We reinforce each other. What he hasn't got, I can give him. And what I lack, I find in Harry.'

There was a quiet, satisfied glow in her face, and when she saw it Angharad felt the first, disturbing clawings of anxiety.

Perhaps Laura's fierce devotion to Harry wasn't ordinary, or healthy. What would happen to them both when they were grown up, when someone tried to come between them?

A shiver, gone as soon as she had felt it, brushed cold wings over her. But who could help admiring Harry, she asked herself. Laura, myself, everyone he meets, probably.

'Hadn't you better go after him?' Angharad asked aloud.

'I know what he's doing. He'll be across in his room. We can go when we've finished here.'

Half an hour later they were crossing the little brick-paved kitchen yard. Over the stable block at right-angles to the house was a row of lighted windows, with a flight of wooden steps leading up to a door. Laura ran up the steps and the door swung open on the latch.

Harry's room was long and narrow, bisected by low beams. The walls were painted red and the floor was strewn with books, record sleeves, discarded clothes and tennis rackets. In the midst of the confusion Harry was lying back in a deep sofa with his eyes closed, strands of his dark hair spread across the cushions behind him. A long cigarette dangled in his fingers. As they came in his eyes snapped open.

'Bitch,' he said to Laura.

'Dopehead,' she countered, equally. Harry smiled crookedly and stretched out one hand. Laura took it, and

54

folded herself into the corner of the sofa beside him. Harry patted the cushions on his other side.

'Come on,' he ordered.

Angharad felt for an instant that she couldn't move, and couldn't be so close to him. But he raised one eyebrow, cynical, at her hesitation and she fell awkwardly into the place beside him. With his arm around her shoulders she didn't dare to move, although her legs were crushed uncomfortably beneath her.

Laura took the long, fat cigarette from Harry's fingers and drew deeply on it, then exhaled on a long, slow breath. Angharad stared in amazement, and her eyes opened still wider when Laura held the cigarette out to her. She shook her head, suddenly understanding. *Dopehead*, Laura had said.

'Go on. It's nice.'

'Don't push it at her, if she doesn't want it.' Harry's voice startled them with its sharpness, and Laura shrugged.

To Angharad a gulf had suddenly opened between her and them, mocking their physical closeness. The two of them took drugs together, did dangerous things., They were older, and knowing. All their shared years excluded her. Angharad felt isolated, and excluded from their partnership.

As if he sensed it, Harry's arm tightened around her shoulders.

'Will you choose a record for us?'

Gratefully she-slid away from him and began to flip through the albums littering the floor. The hectic graphics puzzled her and most of the names meant nothing. Who or what were The Doors? Pretending that she couldn't find what she wanted, Angharad went on searching.

'What about something classical?' she ventured at last. Harry pointed to a loaded shelf and at last she chose some Beethoven late quartets. She knew that Laura liked those. The sonorous music soared up to the beams.

'Clever of you,' Harry said, and she felt a little glow of pleasure. She ventured back to the sofa and his arm circled her shoulders again. She tried to memorize exactly how it felt, so that she could remember it again whenever she wanted.

A quick glance told her that Laura and Harry both looked peaceful and content, busy with their own thoughts and the private pictures behind their eyelids. She let her head fall back against Harry's shoulder. Suddenly she felt as she had done in the boat on the lake. At home, and happy. Harry.

His name reverberated in her head, and all through her. He was so like Laura, and all the things that Angharad admired and loved in her friend. The thought of them together as they had been today made her mouth curve into a smile. Being with her brother softened Laura's sharpness, as if she wanted to be at her best for him.

And who wouldn't want that? Angharad asked herself. I do. I want him to like me.

For there was something about Harry, in the way he looked a challenge at her, that was nothing like Laura at all. It made her want to meet the challenge and it set off a hundred different, dizzy sensations inside her. It made her want to jump up and down to attract his attention, and at the same time to hide, and cover her confusion.

Angharad turned her head, so gently that she was sure he wouldn't feel it, but far enough for her cheek to rest against the white stuff of his sleeve, and far enough for her to be able to look from under her eyelashes at his black hair, the corner of his mouth, recalling the supple way he moved and the easy, arrogant manner.

Yet across the dinner table she had seen him angry, a confused and vulnerable boy. Not cool, like Laura, but passionate. Unknown, and with a fascination that confused her with its power.

Of course he was different. Harry was a man, and the first she had known. The significance of what she suddenly felt struck home to Angharad. What would Laura, jealous Laura, say if she discovered that Angharad might fall in love with Harry?

As if to answer her, and reassure her, Harry turned his head and smiled straight into her eyes.

Laura heard the car first, but she didn't move an inch. Harry stopped smiling and his eyes slid away from Angharad's. She felt his muscles tense under her cheek, and then he cocked his head to the sound.

'Smashed again,' he said bitterly. 'Listen to him taking that bend. He must be doing eighty.'

'You can talk.' Laura was mild, relaxed against her brother's quivering tautness.

Angharad knew that the dreaded moment had come. Joe Cotton was back. The car stopped with a squeal of brakes somewhere beyond the house. A door slammed and everything went quiet, but the silence was oppressive where it had once been tranquil.

Without looking at each other, Laura and Harry moved deftly around the room. The ashtray was emptied and carefully polished, and the cigarettes and a little twist of paper were locked away in a drawer. Then Laura turned the record over and they sat down again, still in silence, clearly waiting for something.

The moments ticked by. Angharad could just hear the water running over the dam. Laura hadn't lifted the pick-up arm and the only sound in the room was the faint swish of the record revolving on the turntable.

Then the door slammed in the kitchen yard and a man's voice shouted, 'Harry? Laura? You up there?'

Angharad sat nervously upright but the others didn't move. Footsteps came across the brick paving and up the steep flight of wooden steps. When the door to Harry's loft was flung open, Angharad saw a tall, bulky man with the flattened features of a boxer. As he looked from one to another of them, she saw that his eyes were not quite focussed.

'So here you are,' he said. 'You might have come down to see your mother, at least.' When his children didn't answer, he stepped forward, stumbled against a low table, and his face contracted with sudden anger. The red flush over his cheeks and forehead deepened. 'It stinks in here,' he said. 'What the hell have you been doing?'

Harry stared at his father as if he had momentarily forgotten who he could be. 'I'm sorry about that,' he said very clearly. 'But I don't remember asking you to join us. If you don't like it in here, why not just go away again?'

'Harry.' Laura spoke under her breath, imploringly. Angharad sat frozen, wishing herself a thousand miles away.

Like an enraged bear, Joe Cotton swung around to his son. The jacket of his blue suit rode up his broad back in wrinkles as he reached out for Harry. He seized him by the lapels and hauled him to his feet, shaking him like a puppy.

Harry's mouth curled in contempt.

Then Joe drew back one heavy fist and struck him in the face. Every tiny muscle in Angharad's body tensed ready to run to him, but shock and fear held her motionless.

'Joe? Joe!'

Someone was running up the steps. A woman in a red dress stopped in the doorway and her hands flew to her mouth. Harry had fallen back into his seat, but his eyes were open and fixed on his father. Blood was running from his nose and on to the front of his white jacket. Laura slid to her knees and held her handkerchief up to his face. He took it without looking at her and then dabbed at the blood.

Joe ran his hands wearily over his forehead. The red flush had subsided, leaving him unhealthily grey.

'Little bastard,' he mumbled. 'I'm your father, remember that. Everything you've got, you owe to me. Look at it all.' He swung his arm clumsily.

Angharad, with her eyes on Harry, understood the tense lines in his face. Why do the ways that people love each other hurt so much, she wondered? Sadness enveloped her like a shroud.

'Hush, Joe,' his wife said. 'Not now. That's enough for tonight.' She took his arm and guided him towards the door.

'I'm coming, Monica,' he said. But he looked straight at Angharad. 'Who are you?'

Laura lifted her head from Harry. 'This is Angharad Owain, my friend from school. I told you she was coming to stay the night.'

'Owain? Any relation to William Owain?'

'Yes. I'm his daughter.' Her voice sounded reedy, as if she hadn't used it for days.

Joe Cotton turned heavily away again. 'I thought so. You've the look of your mother.' He went away without a backward glance at any of them.

Monica hovered behind for a moment. 'Are you all right, darling?'

Harry nodded, smiling lopsidedly. 'Me, yes. My jacket, probably not.'

'Don't make him angry when he's had a few drinks,' she whispered. Then, with an attempt at brightness, 'Have you all had a nice day together? Good. See you in the morning then, darlings. And Angharad. How nice to have you here.'

Monica's children had inherited her neat features, but their colouring and the set of their eyes was all Joe's. His own black hair was bristled with silver and his brown skin was blotched and reddened, but he had set his looks on both of them like a stamp.

As soon as they were alone again, Harry hauled himself upright and came over to Angharad.

'That wasn't a very pretty display,' he said, looking candidly at her. Angharad felt a pulse beating in her throat, and her limbs began to shake with the after-effects of shock. 'Don't look like that. I'm sorry. Will you forgive us?'

She nodded blindly, thinking that she would forgive Harry anything.

'Every time,' Laura said bitterly behind them. 'You just can't let it go, can you? You have to bait him like a boy with a bear. Why?'

'Because I can't ignore him, like you can.'

They looked at each other for a moment and Angharad studied their profiles. The same, but different, she thought again. Then Harry put out his arms and Laura hung back for only a second before letting him pull her close. Her head bent and her hair swung forward, showing the white nape of her neck.

'I love you,' she whispered fiercely. 'I could kill him for hurting you.' And she brushed the angry red mark on his face with her mouth. All her coolness was gone, and she was shaking with passion, anger and resentment.

Angharad bit her lip and looked away. No wonder their

closeness excluded her, commanding intensity like that from Laura.

'I know,' she heard Harry say, low-voiced. 'I know that. At least he doesn't touch you. If he laid a finger on you, I would kill him.'

Their vehemence frightened Angharad. It was Joe who had drawn it out of them, and Joe was frightening. She remembered the heaviness of his movements, the big hands, and the stare that didn't quite see. *You've the look of your mother*, he had told her. Angharad shivered. When she looked at Harry and Laura again they were standing a little apart, remembering her presence. Harry dabbed the handkerchief to his nose, looked at the blood, and attempted a casual shrug.

'Look,' he said, to the air between them, 'it's late. I'm going to bed with an ice-bag on my nose. Tomorrow, you'll see, we'll be the pattern of a perfect family. Angharad?'

She understood that he was making the effort to put the ugly little scene behind them, and she wondered how many times a similar something had happened before.

'Yes,' she said, as normally as she could, 'Yes, of course.'

'You can't escape now, can you?' Laura said. 'You're really part of the family. You belong to us.'

Escape, she had said. It was an odd word to choose. She wanted to belong to Laura and Harry, but the thought gave her none of the uncomplicated happiness that it would have done that afternoon.

They said their subdued goodnights to Harry and walked down to the dark house together in silence.

In her bed in Laura's room, Angharad stared up into the blackness, thinking about Joe Cotton. How well must he have known her mother, to see her features in a strange girl fifteen years later? *Cheat*, her father had said. And what was Harry's word? *Profiteer*. What had he done, so long ago?

Angharad shivered in spite of the warmth of the night. The primitive bluntness of Joe Cotton's features still frightened her, and gave rise to speculations that she had no wish to entertain in the darkness. But there was a kind of weariness and bafflement too, when he looked at his son, that triggered different feelings altogether.

Angharad turned her head on the pillow, heavy with anxiety and puzzlement. However tightly she screwed up her eyes she couldn't rid herself of the sight of Harry, white-faced and with blood dripping, and Joe rocking over him with his fists still clenched.

Then a small sound in the blackness made her eyes snap wide open again. It was a single sob, muffled at once. Laura was crying.

'Laura?'

No answer.

Angharad slid out of bed and crossed to Laura's side.

'Don't cry.' She put out her hand to touch her friend's shoulder and felt that it was rigid, rejecting her.

'Oh, don't.' Unthinkingly Angharad lay down beside her and put her face close to the dark blur of Laura's head on the pillow. She stroked her arms and shoulders and felt Laura shiver under the thin sheet. Angharad was murmuring meaningless, disjointed words of comfort, not knowing what else to say or do. It was utterly unlike Laura to break down, and yet so like her to go on trying to keep it to herself.

'Tell me. I'm part of the family. We belong together,' Angharad reminded her gently.

Suddenly Laura turned to face her and Angharad felt the warmth of her breath on her cheek.

'Harry,' she said, as if that explained everything.

Angharad tried to read her expression, but it was too dark.

'I know,' she whispered back. 'I understand.' I do, she thought sadly. There could be nothing more natural in the world than loving Harry. And nothing more complicated.

At once she had the illusion that it was Harry and not Laura lying beside her. Dark blue eyes wide open and watching, and the pulse beating in his throat as she had seen it across the dinner table. Harry and Laura. So alike and so different. Two halves of one whole.

Angharad lay very still, afraid of something that was hidden close at hand, afraid that even the slightest movement might reveal it. Beside her Laura's breathing

61

slowed, barely perceptibly, and at last it sank into the even rhythm of sleep. Angharad went on staring at the two faces beyond the blackness until they blurred, and dissolved into one.

She hadn't expected to sleep, but the warmth of Laura beside her was soothing, and she felt her eyes and limbs grow heavy. The fear of moving a single muscle drifted away and she rolled over to her side. Her cheek fell against the softness of Laura's hair and she dropped into sleep.

When Angharad opened her eyes once more it was with a jolt of disorientation. It was broad daylight, and she could see the sky through the open curtains. It was pale unbroken grey, and the air was cool.

The confusion of her dream world left her.

The warm weight beside her had gone, and Laura was singing and splashing in the shower. Angharad groped her way out of bed and wrapped herself hastily in her dressing-gown. When Laura came back she was sitting on the window seat staring out at the lake. Ducks were trailing long, rippling Vs in the water. Laura touched her shoulder.

'Breakfast time. Come down soon.' She was smiling quite naturally, last night's tears apparently forgotten.

Angharad said, 'Your father, and Harry . . .' The smoothness with which his name came out surprised her. 'What will happen after last night?' If there was going to be any hint of any more violence, Angharad thought, she couldn't bear to see it. She would start out for her bus now, at once, regardless of what they might think of her.

Laura shrugged airily. 'Nothing. Until the next time. Just like always.'

She waited while Angharad dressed, and they went down the wide stairs together. Angharad's fingers lingered on the polished wood of the old banisters as if she wished it could hold her back. The colour was high in her cheeks at the thought of seeing Harry in this new, garish light. And she had no wish to encounter Joe at all.

The dining-room was airy and fragrant with the honeysuckle wreathing the windows. In the daylight it looked quite different from the dim grandeur of the night before, with Harry lounging in his white jacket across the candlelit table.

Monica Cotton was reading a magazine at one end of the table, absently stirring her coffee in slow circles. She was chic in a neat silky suit, and perfectly groomed, but there was an extinguished air about her, as if she had long ago given up an unequal struggle. She greeted the girls faintly and went back to her fashion pages.

Out of the corner of her eye Angharad saw the dark height of Harry, turning at the sideboard. Her neck felt stiff, unable to carry her head, and a humming in her ears almost deafened her. She groped to her seat and when the mist cleared she saw him, in a frayed grey sweater and an open shirt that showed the hollow at the base of his throat, more clearly than she had ever seen anyone else. Every line of his face, from the straight black eyebrows meeting over his unusually clear eyes, to the full top lip and square, set chin seemed precious to her. She wanted to reach out and touch the blotched bruise spreading across from the wing of one nostril to the corner of his mouth.

She had never felt so physically, electrically aware of anyone.

Harry was saying something to her, and she nodded, not trusting herself to speak. In response he handed her a plate of food, but all she could see was the bone at his wrist and the sinews running along the back of his hand.

Last night he and Laura had blurred together. Now she knew that there was no chance of ever mistaking him again. Beside him Laura seemed pale, and abstract.

Harry was warm, solid and vibrating with life, and she wanted him to wrap his arms around her, she wanted to feel his mouth against hers, and she wanted him to look at her the way he had looked at his clever, possessive sister.

*I love you, Harry.*

Angharad tried out the words in her head, and felt the colour hot in her cheeks. She sat down quickly opposite Monica.

Harry and Laura were talking in light voices when the

door opened. In a grey, wide chalk-striped suit, Joe's bulk seemed even more formidable. His silvery hair was brushed flat and sleek, and his colour was normal again. He was every inch the prosperous businessman as his glance flicked over them. He sat down carefully, as if the chair was too small for him. 'Good morning,' he said deliberately, so that the Midlands twang in his voice sounded clearer. His children murmured, and Angharad stared miserably. Harry's face was neutral, but with her tense sensitivity to him Angharad could feel the anger and confusion within him as clearly as if they were her own.

Joe unfolded his napkin and touched the *Financial Times* beside his plate. But clearly he was making a fumbling attempt at reconciliation.

'Well then. What have you all got planned for today?'

'Hairdresser. And some shoppng,' Monica said. Joe's glance swung to the three of them.

'Angharad has to go home this morning. We'll take her to the bus.' Now Joe's flat, expressionless eyes were fixed on Angharad.

'Does your father know where you are?'

'No,' she whispered through dry lips.

'I thought not. Well, that's something. It's not just my own kids who don't know how to behave.'

Harry made a tiny start, but under the table Laura's cool hand restrained him.

They finished their breakfast in uneasy quiet, painfully aware of Joe's blunt head behind the newspaper. At last he drained his cup and stood up.

'Car going OK, son?'

Angharad understood that he was asking, not about the car, but Harry himself. She wondered if Harry knew that too.

'Yes. Thanks.'

'Take mine this morning if the three of you want to go somewhere. I've only got the office and a round of golf later. I'll go in the station wagon.'

The peace-offering hung between the two men, and Angharad saw Harry struggling with it. He's cleverer and prouder than his father, she thought, and just as difficult. I wish . . . But she shut off her wish, and swallowed back the love for him that rose chokingly inside her.

'Thanks.'

'Don't forget we've got dinner tonight with Lloyd-Jones the Bank,' Monica said.

'Aw, Christ.'

As soon as Joe was gone, the wheels of the station wagon crunching roundly on the gravel, the atmosphere lifted like a blanket.

Harry tipped back in his seat and ran his fingers through his crest of black hair.

'Joy-riding in the Jag for us this morning, then. Angharad, darling, we'll take you all the way home.'

*Darling*. He was jokey, unaffected, yesterday's frivolous boy again. He wouldn't think about it, she was sure, so he would never guess how potently he had struck through to her.

'Just to the stop for the other bus,' she murmured. 'My Dad'll be waiting to meet me off it.'

An hour later they waved to Monica who was ensconced in her chair on the verandah. The big white car rolled forward, and Angharad turned for a last look at the lake, lying like a sheet of mirror glass under the dull sky. It needed the sun to bring back the dazzle and the seductive shade of yesterday.

The arch of trees closed over the car and then opened out again. They were at the white gate, and nosing down the valley road. Harry gave a whoop of pleasure, the engine snarled, and they shot away from the secret hollow of Llyn Fair.

In her place beside them, with their bare brown arms brushing hers, Angharad felt happiness flowing back. Warm smells of hay and tar swept in through the open windows, and with Laura's fingers on the dial the car filled with bouncy, cheerful music.

'I'm glad, she thought. I'm glad all of it happened. I wouldn't want anything to take it away. She swayed against Laura, and then as the car cornered again, she felt the opposite prickle of Harry's touch, and saw his sidelong grin at her. Nothing can happen if I just think about him, she told herself. Nothing can take the memory away.

She smiled at the hurtling road in front of her, and heard the words of the radio song bubbling out of her mouth.

At the bus stop Harry lifted her bag out of the car and he and Laura stood shoulder to shoulder, smiling at her.

''Bye, kid,' he said, and she accepted it meekly, concentrating on the graze of his mouth against the corner of hers. He was so vividly, physically real to her that at that moment she felt no anxiety at leaving him.

It was Laura who wrapped her arms around her, and kissed her properly. She whispered under the bell of Angharad's hair, 'Until next term. I've never looked forward to school before, but I will now.'

Her words touched Angharad with a tiny shadow. It came to her that she was a little afraid of Laura, and all her cool possessiveness. Did she belong to Laura now, just as Harry did?

The bus came. and they stood to wave to her. Laura had moved in front of Harry, half shielding him. She didn't move until the bus had trundled away again, and they had waved Angharad out of sight.

# CHAPTER FOUR

Angharad put her book down for the dozenth time.

She looked around the room, seeing how small it was, and how shabby it had grown. Beside her chair the grandfather clock measured the slow minutes with its infuriatingly steady *tock, tock*. Angharad jumped up and and went to the window, but the street outside looked narrow and dull, without even a prowling cat for her eyes to follow.

'What's the matter with me?' she asked herself, also for the dozenth time. School was behind her now. She was grown up, she told herself, and the longed-for time had come at last. She had come home, but instead of feeling free and triumphant, she was chafed with boredom and irritation. The summer stretched ahead of her, three long months of it before she could escape to university. and even that escape would be to a safe, redbrick foundation which had seemed a sensible choice when she applied to it, but which now threatened to be no more than lacklustre.

Angharad moved away from the window, turning her back on the lifeless street. It was uncomfortable to be bored with Cefn, and bored with the prospect of her neat future running on well-oiled, unassuming tracks into the dim distance.

'*What's the matter with me?*' she repeated, and the lack of an answer drove her upstairs, for the fourth time in an hour. Impatiently she saw that her bedroom still looked like a child's, with its pink bedcover and row of children's classics ranged on the shelf over it. There was another book on the table, the general history book that had topped the reading list sent by her college. Angharad picked the book up quickly, opened it and looked down at the fading photograph tucked inside.

The snapshot crackled faintly in her fingers. They were sitting on the wooden steps of the school games pavilion.

Angharad was in front on the lower step, with Laura behind her, higher up, her forearms resting on Angharad's shoulders and her hands stretched out as if to ward off the photographer's unwelcome intrusion. Angharad was laughing, but Laura's face was serious, her dark eyebrows drawn together.

The picture had been taken at the beginning of Laura's last school term. Angharad had pinned it up in the senior room they had shared, and she remembered exactly how Laura had leaned over to watch her.

'It makes me look like Harry.'

Yes. Their two faces stared out challengingly over her own happy one. She kept it because it was secretly a picture of both of them.

Laura and Angharad had drawn closer together after Llyn Fair. Laura had let her friend feel that she was an initiate, and Angharad had seized upon the deeper intimacy gladly, for Laura's own sake and for Harry. The two girls hadn't wanted or needed anyone else in their senior years. Their friendship had flowered in their shared room, and the irksome boundaries of school had mattered less. It had been easy to create their own world, reading and talking through the nights, making grandiose plans for the future which suddenly seemed close enough to reach out and touch, or weaving hilarious fantasies about the mistresses and other girls. They had worked too, long hours at the desks placed side by side under the window.

Although, separately, they thought of Harry constantly, they spoke of him very little.

'I've had a letter,' Laura would say brightly, and then she would fold it away in her pocket. Angharad knew that he had gone to college, leaving Llyn Fair and his Morgan behind him.

'And Joe,' Laura told her. 'Joe wanted him to join the business, but Harry would never, ever do that. Joe tried to force him to, but Harry wouldn't.'

Angharad wondered what kind of force Joe would have applied, and shivered for Harry.

After the next letter Angharad learned that he had given

up college and was setting off to hitchhike across America, aiming for Los Angeles.

'Films. He's dreaming about films,' Laura said.

It seemed so far away from the set school routines that he might have been embarking for another planet. Angharad had not seen him again, but the memory of him stayed with her as vividly as if he was her constant companion, rather than Laura.

Nor had they tried to repeat the stolen day at Llyn Fair.

Laura had left school two terms earlier than Angharad, after her successful Cambridge scholarship papers. Joe Cotton had sent her to be finished at an exclusive establishment in Switzerland. Her letters, crackling with satirical descriptions of her new companions and their expertise at spending money, had been Angharad's main lifeline in the dull intervening months. Angharad had longed to get home to Cefn, believing that Laura would be home from Switzerland at the same time, that somehow they would meet, and the world would come alive again. Perhaps, even, Harry might come home again too.

Angharad looked down at the photograph again, at the two faces in one, and felt the disappointment afresh. The news had come almost as an afterthought in Laura's last letter.

'Remember me telling you about Gaby d'Erlanget? Whose papa is head of the Académie Française? Or editor of *Le Monde*, or President of France, I forget which. Well, Gaby and I are to spend a sybaritic few weeks at her family holiday home on Cap Ferrat. I gather that it is only a little smarter than the heyday of Villa Mauresque. I must go, of course. It means that I can't see Llyn Fair, or Cefn, or my lovely Angharad before September. Will you wait for me? Adore you. L.

'PS. Harry has disappeared. He did have a job as assistant to somebody's assistant at a studio in Hollywood, but he got into a fight and was drummed out. *Méchant fils.*'

The brittle tone was new. Angharad wondered if it was an essential requirement for someone who had been 'finished'.

Frowning, she put the photograph carefully back between

69

the pages of her history book.

No Laura, and no Harry, and no prospect of seeing them.

Laura was probably drinking champagne amongst the bougainvillaea, sparring wittily with rich, clever people against the background of a postcard-blue sea. While Angharad was alone in Cefn, with only her books for company. Angharad had never been abroad, and it was impossible not to feel jealous and abandoned.

And Harry . . . it was impossible even to imagine what Harry was doing. Wandering in America. Images from *On the Road* filled Angharad's head, and she wondered if freedom from Llyn Fair and Joe had quenched his anger. Or, a darker thought, if separation from Laura had eased his confusion. His face was as vivid to Angharad at that moment as it had been when he stood a little behind Laura, both of them waving her out of sight on the Cefn bus.

Angharad went downstairs again and into the kitchen. She made a pot of coffee, very slowly and carefully, measuring out the beans exactly and grinding them to just the right consistency. Then she laid a tray with her father's favourite china cup, and one for herself. She cocked her head, listening for a break in the pecking of the typewriter from William's study, and then carried the tray through.

William looked up at her, impatience flickering in his face before it was replaced with polite tolerance.

'Oh. Thank you, Angharad. I wasn't expecting coffee.' She poured it out for him and sat down with her own cup.

'How's it going?' she asked cheerfully, wanting and needing to talk to someone. William was immersed in the research for a huge, abstruse history of the last princes of Wales. Angharad was already enough of a historian to know that he was unlikely to finish the task, and even if he did that the work was unlikely to find a publisher. She suspected that William knew it too, and it made his uneven temper even less predictable.

'Fine,' he said shortly, impatience gaining the upper hand again. 'I'm surprised you don't have work of your own to do, Angharad. I must get on with mine.' Dismissively he turned back to the typewriter. Angharad picked up her cup and left

70

the room, and the peck-peck started up even before she closed the door. Loneliness gathered around her again. The peace and satisfaction she had once felt in the evenness of life in Cefn with her father had deserted her as completely as if they had never existed.

'I'll go and see Gwyn,' she said, to the unhearing rattle of the typewriter.

Angharad had spent hours of those first few days of unwelcome freedom sitting in Gwyn's studio. Listlessly she helped her aunt to load her kiln, or packed pots in boxes ready for delivery. In the intervals when she could no longer stand her aunt's concerned stare or leading questions, she went for long, pointless walks. Often, from the summit of The Mountain, she looked westwards towards Llyn Fair. She had worked out long ago which pleats of rocky hillside hid its sunny hollow, but there was no point even in looking towards it if Harry and Laura were not there.

Today in the studio, as Angharad carelessly pushed aside a teetering pile of pots, Gwyn said with unusual sharpness, 'Be careful. That represents two days' labour for me. You may have nothing to do but mope about, but the rest of us have to work.'

'I'm sorry,' Angharad mumbled, contrite at once. 'I just feel . . . impatient, and lethargic, all at once. It's horrible.'

'I know, *cariad*. What happened about your school friend, the one in Chester, who you were going to see such a lot of this summer?'

Before Laura's last letter, Angharad had prepared the ground carefully. Her fictional friend was to be her alibi again.

'Um. She went to France, unexpectedly.'

The single postcard from Laura, unwittingly handed over by William across the breakfast table, was supposed to have come from the same friend. It showed a view of the Promenade des Anglais at Nice. On the reverse Laura had written 'It's Nice here'.

I bet it is, Angharad had thought bitterly.

'What about getting a job?' Gwyn asked now. 'I could ask at Y Gegin Fach, if you like. They've got a regular cook, but

71

they might need some extra help now it's the busy season.'

'Good idea. Please do,' Angharad said, without enthusiasm. Y Gegin Fach sold pottery, knick-knacks made out of Welsh slate, dolls in national costume and 'hand-carved' love spoons in one room, and had a popular, folksy restaurant in another. Angharad thought that the stock was twee and the food a perfect match for it.

Two days later Gwyn told her the answer. 'They do need someone to cook a couple of shifts a week, and to do the fetching and carrying for the rest. They'll have to give you a trial, but I've told them what a good cook you are, better than a professional any day.'

'Oh, Aunty Gwyn.' Angharad was exasperated at the thought of having to prove her skills in the gingham-festooned cosiness of Y Gegin Fach. But lack of anything better to do took her down to the restaurant.

The proprietor was a canny businesswoman who had, Angharad grudgingly admitted to herself, judged her market to perfection. The customers, mostly elderly, straggled out of the shop laden with their souvenirs of Wales and into the restaurant. They weren't demanding diners. They wanted something plain, wholesome, and notionally Welsh.

'Welsh lamb cutlets with parsley butter, mostly, dear,' said the owner. 'Can you cope?'

'I think so,' Angharad said, smiling in spite of herself.

The little kitchen behind the restaurant was hot, busy and cheerful. The regular cook was a plump, beaming woman whom Angharad had often seen on the local bus. She was making pastry at a marble slab and Angharad admired the light touch of her podgy fingers in the dough. Mrs Price was a natural cook. She winked at Angharad as if to acknowledge that she understood the restrictions of the place too. Angharad felt her spirits rise as she smiled back.

'Fruit pies are very popular too,' the owner said. 'How's your pastry?'

'Not as good as Mrs Price's, I shouldn't think, but I'll do my best.'

'Have a try now, dear, for us, will you?'

Obligingly Angharad demonstrated that she could grill

cutlets and make pastry, half-listening as she worked to the two young waitresses clumping in and out and giggling together, and the ancient washer-up sniffing lugubriously in her wellington boots at the stone sink.

There were people here, she thought, doing things. It helped.

'Can you start on Wednesday?' the owner said, and Angharad nodded and thanked her with genuine enthusiasm that would have amazed herself an hour before.

And on Wednesday she went to work, leaving the silent house behind her with relief. For two or three days she watched Mrs Price, trying to copy her deftness, laughing with the waitresses, and preparing endless baskets of local fruit and vegetables. The produce was excellent, she saw. There was scope, definite scope, and it excited her. On the fourth day Angharad made William's favourite Welsh broth, using a stock base that was one of her own inventions, and the owner and Mrs Price nodded their approval of its savoury richness.

The fifth day was Mrs Price's day off, and Angharad worked a long, hard shift. The girls had accepted her, and she enjoyed the simple sense of belonging that seemed to have been missing from her life for months. When at last she came home and dropped into bed, she realized that she had hardly had time to think of Laura and Harry, or her own unfair isolation.

As Angharad settled into the routine of Y Gegin Fach, the challenges of professional cooking began to interest her more deeply, and she met them with increasing energy. As the days passed she began to score little victories, persuading her co-workers to leave the beetroot out of the salads, and to reduce the cooking times of the vegetables. They were small triumphs, but she was proud of them and of her employer's approval. As the time went by she was entrusted with small amounts of marketing, haggling cheerfully with the local butcher, and getting up at dawn to greet the early stallholders in the weekly vegetable market in the nearby town.

Gradually the more interesting buying and planning

became Angharad's job and she spent more time at that, and less churning out pies in the kitchen.

And so it was that she was standing in the old market square at six o'clock on a perfect midsummer morning, watching shrewdly as the produce was unloaded from the vans. She balanced her big, flat-bottomed wicker basket on her hip and waited. One old farmer in ancient ·corduroys, from whom she always bought carrots and onions in the brisk auction that was the market's centrepiece, raised his greasy cap to her as he passed. The cobbled inner square began to fill with striped awnings sheltering glistening mountains of strawberries and leafy punnets of early raspberries. Cabbage leaves and wisps of straw spread over the worn stones.

There had been a market in this square for hundreds of years, originally for cattle and the little, spare sheep of the surrounding hills. The rough crates of scraggy hens were the only living relic of that, but the square was always still known as the Beast Market.

Angharad shifted her basket on her hip. The auction wouldn't start for another half an hour, but now was her chance to earmark what she would bid for. She was planning to slip ratatouille on to the menu for the week and her glance shifted to the tattooed Liverpudlian in the corner who traded in the most exotic vegetables.

The light on the grey walls enclosing the square began to change from the thin brightness of dawn to the rounder dapple of full daylight. The pub on the corner, open for eighteen hours on market day, was already busy. Angharad caught the snatches of talk around her.

'S'mae, Dic?'

'Iawn, diolch. Syda'chi?'

Then, standing no more than three yards away, she saw a tall, spare figure. His face was obscured by the viewfinder of a cumbersome, hand-held film camera. Slowly, as she watched, the black barrel tracked towards her and held her exposed in its sights. The clamour of the square stopped as if turned off by a huge switch. Angharad stood rooted to the cobblestones. The Beast Market vanished, and a hundred splintered images danced in its place. Sun and deep shade on still water, blood on a white jacket. Hands and mouths, barely distinguishable, and a pulse beating at Harry's throat.

As soon as she had seen him, no more than a glimpse from the corner of her eye, she knew that it was Harry.

Slowly he lowered his camera and looked full at her. The black brows were heavier, and the hollowness of his cheeks made him look older. But then he smiled, and at once she saw the handsome boy at the wheel of his gleaming new car.

'I wonder,' he said, 'if you have any idea how perfect you look, standing there in that blue shirt with your basket, and all that behind you?' A tiny movement of the camera took in the crowded square.

*He doesn't recognize me*, she thought, panic stifling her. I'm just a girl, a frame in his film, whatever it is. Why should he remember a single day, two years ago?

But then in two steps Harry was right in front of her, so close that they almost touched each other. He put his camera down on the cobbles beside them. His hands came out, as she went on staring dumbly at him, and cupped her face.

'Angharad, I know it's you. You look just the same, except not a little girl any more. Don't you remember me?'

His fingers combed through her hair, and he smiled down at her.

Angharad moistened her lips, feeling that they were dry enough to crack, and whispered, 'Harry.'

'That's better. I didn't believe you could have forgotten.'

She wanted to look away, to say something light, and casual. But her eyes clung to him, seeing that a cleft had developed between his eyebrows, that the long, hippie-ish hair had been cut short, a little raggedly. His eyes were exactly the same clear, dark blue that she remembered. How old was he? She calculated, irrelevantly, nineteen to her seventeen.

'What are you doing?' she asked at last. 'I . . . heard you were in America.'

'That's one more thing than I've heard about you.' His fingers touched the bones of her cheeks as if measuring them, and then let her go. He stepped back a pace and looked at her, his head on one side. She saw that he was wearing light trousers tucked into calf-length boots, and a baggy sweater made of some fine, grey stuff. He was unshaven, and the dark shadow accentuated the sharp, almost feminine points of his top lip. Without looking at it, evidently as familiar with it as if it was part of him, he stooped to pick up the heavy camera and hoisted it under his arm. Then he held out his other hand.

'Come and have breakfast.'

Angharad forgot the list of things she had wanted to bid for at the auction. She forgot the restaurant, and Cefn, and everything else. She put her hand into Harry's and followed him out of the Beast Market.

There was a little grey van parked in a side-street. Harry dismantled his camera and nested it in a complicated case, then put her basket in the back beside it. Neither of them spoke, but as they left the little town behind them Harry looked at her, just once. He was rewarded with Angharad's rarest smile that tilted and then dissolved all the composed angles of her face. Their eyes met, and held each other for so long that the little van wandered and bumped dangerously against the grass verge.

Harry laughed as he pulled the wheel back, and Angharad, with her eyes firmly on the way ahead again, said, 'Be careful.' The empty road was white in front of them, and the banks were starred with tiny flowers. It was the most beautiful morning Angharad had ever seen.

A few moments later they turned off the road and followed a track up to the edge of a wood that hung over a low hill. In the shelter of the trees was a derelict stone cottage, hardly more than a shed, with a corrugated-iron roof and a rainwater barrel beside the peeling brown-painted door. At the doorway Harry stood aside to let her pass, sweeping a low bow.

'Welcome to the Heulfryn Hilton.'

She blinked in the dimness and then saw the single room, bare-floored, with a table and two chairs, a gas-ring, and a narrow bed covered with a scarlet blanket. On a rickety table beside the bed was a tottering pile of books, the only personal touch that she could see. Angharad remembered the cushioned comfort of Llyn Fair, the gleaming Morgan and Harry's other room strewn with expensive possessions.

'Why?' she asked him, and then checked herself. 'At least, I know why, but . . .' Over his shoulder she had caught the view through the open door. The green and sepia fold of the vale lay in front of her, running down in a fertile spread to the invisible sea. In the far distance she could just see the squat grey church tower of Cefn. This was the calm, open side of The Mountain. On the other side lay the jagged rocks and changeable skies over Llyn Fair.

'The view is one reason,' Harry said quietly. 'The other reasons are all negative ones. Won't you let me give you something to eat, first, before we talk?'

Angharad sat in one of the chairs that he held out for her, and rested her chin in her cupped hands to watch him. He made coffee in a blue jug, and then cracked eggs into a bowl. She thought about the arrogant boy who had assumed that food would just appear at Llyn Fair, and compared him with this different man moving economically around his barren room. She wondered what else had changed in him. He was noticeably thinner, but his shoulders had broadened. The new, short hair accentuated the firmness of his jaw. The fey, whimsical air of two years ago had vanished. Harry looked certain of himself now and, Angharad thought, there was a glitter of danger in him.

'Why did you cut your hair?' she asked, and blushed. She wanted to ask him a thousand questions, and had to begin with the silliest. Harry put a mug of coffee into her hand, folding her fingers firmly around it.

'It was cut off for me, down in Texas. I was bumming around, dreaming about movies and wishing I was Dennis Hopper. I got into an argument and then a fight, ended up in jail, and I was discharged with a free haircut. When I got round to looking at myself, I thought I liked it better this way anyway.'

'Laura mentioned another fight, too.'

'Yep. Must be something of Joe coming out in me. I'm trying to give it up.'

77

Their eyes met again at the mention of Joe, remembering the night at Llyn Fair.

Harry put a plate down in front of her and sat down in the opposite chair. The scrambled eggs and bacon were perfect and they began to eat, ravenously, smiling across the table.

'You know, you're the only person I've ever brought up here? I've been living on my own for weeks.'

'What were you doing with a camera, at six o'clock in the morning in the Beast Market?'

Angharad's hand was resting loosely on the table. Harry took it and spread the fingers out flat, studying each one intently. Angharad felt the small vibrations from his touch spread through her wrist and up her arm. Harry began to talk, still looking down at her fingers, their fingertips touching.

'Filming. I want to make films. No, I've got to make films. I started at film school in London, you know, but it was all pissing little pointless exercises. I stopped that. Bought a one-way ticket to New York and hitched across the States. Got very hungry for a while in LA, then lied my way into a studio job. Hocked everything I owned to get a camera, worked at the studio job during the day and my own stuff at night, popping lots of pills to keep going. It made me very irritable, can you believe that?' His eyes widened in mock surprise as he looked up at her.'

'You amaze me.'

'I thought it would. But, unlikely though it sounds, it wasn't too long before I fell out with some fat little shit who thought he was Orson Welles. Whereas, of course, if anyone around there ranked with Welles it was me. So, after a brief, colourful interval I found myself at the bus station, my camera bag in my hand. I went south, right down to New Mexico and back. Looking for something, "ideas", I suppose, God help me. Then I ended up in jail on a vagrancy charge.

'I thought one morning that if I was going to make a career out of vagrancy I might as well do it back home in Wales. All the time I was away, pretending to think about art, I only had one real idea.

78

'There's an old farmer who lives on the hill across there. Been there all his life, and his father and grandfather, and back before that. Scratching a living out of a few sheep and some vegetables. I kept thinking about him, all that time. The old man's past seventy now, crippled with rheumatism. He's got two sons. One works at Massey-Ferguson, and the other down in the steelworks at Shotton. Good money for both of them, nice houses on an estate somewhere. They both drive shiny Fords. So, after the old man goes, the farm goes with him. The end of – what? – a hundred years taken to build up something that never stood a chance of being anything anyway. I've no doubt that Joe will come along after he's gone, pay the old girl a couple of thousand, and do the place up as a holiday home for city folk. I thought I'd come home before it was too late, and make a film about that. The end of a way of life. Flickering out.

'I'm shooting what I can, very slowly, in black and white because I can't afford colour stock. So, to answer your question, that's what I was doing this morning in the Beast Market. D'you think I'm being completely absurd?'

Angharad shook her head. Her eyes were very bright. 'No. I think it's just what you should be doing.'

Harry didn't answer, but she didn't miss the flash of gratitude in his face.

After a moment Angharad said, 'Joe and Monica don't know you're here?'

'No. I don't want to be part of that, any more.'

'Does Laura?'

'Nope. Not even Laura. She's joined the fat-cats, hasn't she? Swanning around Cap Ferrat with decaying European royalty?'

'She has, rather.' Laughter bubbled between them again. Harry took her hand and held it between his own.

'So,' he said very softly, 'that just leaves you and me.'

Angharad thought that perhaps she should look away, defuse the moment in some modest way, but she didn't want to. She went on meeting Harry's stare, suddenly electrically conscious of the sun edging into the room with the beginning of warmth, the smell of coffee, the red blur of the blanket

79

seen out of the corner of her eye.

Harry was still talking. '. . . In the Beast Market, of all places. All those dun-coloured men, piles of carrots. Then, suddenly, in a shaft of light, there you were. In a blue shirt with a ridiculous basket, like a woman in a primitive painting. I fell in love with you there and then, did you know?'

He was only joking. His eyebrows were raised, the cleft between them smoothed away by a smile. But Angharad didn't care. She wondered what he would say if she told him, *I've loved you for two years. I've loved you, through your sister, all that time.* The memory of Laura came like a shadow, but she pushed it aside. Laura was a thousand miles away.

Instead she asked, 'And will I be in the film?'

Harry laughed. 'Oh, yes. I shall have to find some way to work you into the story. I couldn't waste a shot like that. Or perhaps I won't need to. I think you're already part of it.'

Again the soft silence in the room, and the sunlight on the homely breakfast things on the table between them. Harry touched her wrist lightly with his finger.

'It's still very early. Shall we go for a walk? I've been walking a lot, mostly when it's just light, when the world's empty. It would be a treat to do it with you. Will you come?'

'I've been walking too,' Angharad told him. 'Up and down the side of The Mountain, looking down to the sea, and over the top towards Llyn Fair. Thinking that you and Laura were so far away that it was stupid to be looking at it.'

Harry drew her chair back for her. 'I wonder why we never met each other? We'll go together now.'

As they walked down the lane Harry drew her arm through his. The sun sloped through the leaves overhead, and threw sharp early shadows in front of them. It felt quite natural to be walking side by side, shoulders and hands touching, unthinkingly in step. Angharad felt less shy of Harry than she had ever been with anyone, even Laura. Laura could sometimes silence her with a cutting word, but she knew that Harry would not. He listened intently, as if anything she could tell him was important. Secure in his attention, the floodgates lifted. Angharad talked and talked,

80

as if she had been in solitary confinement for months. She described the last bleak times at school for him, the mechanical submission to exams and dim plans for the future. He nodded when she told him of her isolation at Cefn, and the unshakeable depression that had threatened to swamp her.

'That's over now, isn't it?' he asked, and she said, simply, 'Yes.'

At the top of the bare hill, the wind drove in from the sea and Angharad shivered. Harry wrapped his arms around her shoulders at once and turned her to face inland, sheltering her. She felt the weight of his chin resting on her head, and his warmth at her back. The short turf was springy under her feet, and she thought that she could easily jump, and fly. Nothing was heavy, or solid, any more.

'What shall we do now?' His breath was warm against her hair.

'Nothing,' she said lazily. 'Anything you like.' But then with a jolt she remembered her basket, and the busy Beast Market. As soon as she thought about it, it seemed incredible that she could have forgotten. 'Harry. The auction. I was supposed to buy aubergines, and tomatoes, and strawberries for flans . . . and get them to the restaurant in time for lunch . . .'

Already he was pulling her by the wrist. 'Quick then. Run. We'll go and blitz the market. I'll find you the best aubergines in Wales.'

*Yours to command*, he had said once, in the kitchen at Llyn Fair. Angharad's heart lifted almost into her throat, and blindly she followed Harry in their headlong rush down the hill and back to Heulfryn cottage. She was only just getting her breath back by the time they whirled into the market square again.

The auction was long over, but Harry was undeterred. He led her from stall to stall, bargaining fiercely, determined to secure prices as good as those at the auction. Her basket was full and she begged him to stop.

'No more. I'll never be able to come and face them again, on my own.'

'Don't come on your own,' he said seriously. 'Don't do anything without me.' He drove her to the road that led down to Y Gegin Fach, and before the last bend she put out her hand to stop him.

'Drop me here,' she said.

He looked at her, the cleft between his eyebrows deepening again.

'What are you ashamed of?'

She bit her lip, anxious at once. 'I'm not ashamed. It's because of my father. And yours.'

'Angharad, I don't live at Llyn Fair any more. I haven't seen Joe for months. Can't I meet your father? Stop being treated like a pariah because of Joe?'

Angharad knew William well enough to understand that it wasn't possible.

'Please, Harry.'

He softened àt once. 'If it matters so much.'

He helped her out, and delivered the loaded basket into her charge. 'What will you do now, for the rest of the day?'

Laughing at his interest in her trivial doings, she told him.

'And after you've done all that?'

Angharad looked straight up into his eyes and said, 'I'll wait to see you again.'

'You mean that there's no muscular swain waiting to sweep you off to live the high life in Rhyl or somewhere?'

'Nobody at all.'

'In that case, count on me. Eight o'clock.' He leant over her briefly and she thought that his kiss just brushed the top of her head.

'By the old fountain,' she called after him. 'At the bottom of Cefn hill.'

She turned and walked down to the restaurant only after the little grey van had wound out of sight. She hummed as she unloaded the vegetables, handling them as if they were precious because Harry had touched them. Through new eyes, she saw that the looped gingham curtains with their red ribbon bows looked pretty rather than affected. She smoothed the tablecloths as she laid them, and brought posies of sweet-peas in from the back fence for the tables. She beamed over the interminable pies as they shuttled in and out of the ovens.

'Won the Pools, have you?' asked Old Lil the washer-up, already at the sink in her wellingtons.

'Something like that, Lil.' How many hours until eight o'clock? What was he doing now, this minute? The day's change had been so dizzying that it was too early to question it. It's not a dream, she reassured herself, over and over. Harry was here, a mile or two away. He wanted her too. She had nothing to do but count through the hours until the evening brought him back again.

'I'm going out tonight,' she told William when she got in from work. 'Just with ... some friends.'

William barely looked up from his book, and she realized with a wave of relief that so long as she seemed respectably occupied, she could do as she liked. Gwyn called in just as she was leaving the house, and took in Angharad's glowing face with a single keen glance. 'Have a good time,' she said. 'Anyone we know, by the way?'

'No. Look, I don't want to be late. See you both tomorrow.'

Gwyn watched her go, but William only had eyes for his work.

Angharad slipped out into the deserted street. There was no one to be seen, but she knew that half a dozen pairs of eyes would be watching her from behind the lace curtains. Smiling to herself, she supplied the commentary. *Angharad Owain, going off walking again. Strange girl, that one.* There was no harm in going for a walk, she thought. But it would be wise not to be seen with the striking figure of Harry anywhere near Cefn. Within hours, everyone would know about it.

The sky was the fragile pinky-grey of summer dusk, but beyond the village where the road sloped under a tunnel of old trees, it was already twilight. It was only twenty to eight. Angharad walked slowly, intensely aware of the small, sharp stones under the thin soles of her shoes, the rustle of a small prowling animal in the dry leaves on the other side of the wall, the muted night scents already rising from the earth. She had never felt so vividly alive, or so aware of everything around her, as if each of her senses had been separately sharpened. The beating of her own heart sounded unnaturally loud, and it was impossible not to measure her steps in time to it.

It was exactly eight o'clock when Angharad came out of the trees and saw the triangular stone of the old drinking fountain. A little to one side of it was Harry's grey van, almost invisible in the shadow.

She ran, everything else forgotten. Harry came to meet her and they stopped in the middle of the wide road. His arms came round her and she buried her face against him, laughing and talking incoherently, all at once.

'Hey,' he said, lifting her chin with one finger. He kissed her, as lightly as a butterfly grazing the corner of her mouth, and then they looked into each other's eyes. Then Harry's smile teased the question away. 'Shall we stand here in the middle of the road until the next motorist mows us down? Or shall we move on?'

'I don't think I care,' Angharad said, But she followed him, and they rattled away in the old van. 'Where are we going?'

'To eat the most exotic celebratory dinner that the west can command. In other words, not exotic at all. We shall have to use our imaginations to supply whatever's lacking.'

'What are we celebrating?'

Harry's gaze didn't waver from the road ahead. 'Finding each other,' he said. 'Didn't you know?'

'Yes,' Angharad answered. 'But I wanted to hear you say it.'

In the dim light she saw the white flash of Harry's teeth as he laughed. 'Don't ever change, Angharad, will you? You're unbelievably honest, and you are so clear that every ripple of feeling shows up in your face.'

That wasn't true, she thought. She had been dissembling successfully to her father for years, ever since she had known Laura. Another recollection came to her at the same moment. Laura had said exactly the same thing. *Don't ever change.*

*I won't*, Angharad promised herself. If I don't change, perhaps nothing else will either. And nothing could ever be more perfect than now, this minute. As she looked sideways at the straight lines of Harry's profile, she felt happiness and excitement so strong inside her that she could taste them on her tongue.

Later, when she tried to recall their first evening together, she could see it only in a series of static images, like stills from Harry's film. In one of them they were leaning towards each other across a white tablecloth, foreheads almost touching. In another, Harry was pouring a silver froth of champagne into her glass, with the glow of candlelight deepening the hollows of his eyes and cheeks so that he looked broodingly serious. In yet another they were outside under a high, white moon that made a perfect reflection of itself in the black water of a millpond. Behind them were the tangled lights of a carpark, but they were alone in their own world.

By contrast, the memory of their talk ran through her head like an uninterrupted sound-track. She had never talked so much to anyone, or believed that anyone could listen so minutely. She wanted Harry to know everything, and she craved just as much to know the smallest detail of his life. He made her laugh until she almost choked with bizarre stories of his American journey, and she reciprocated with stories of the people of Cefn.

Delightedly, she found that he was just as diversely well-read as Laura, but where Laura would deliver her razor-sharp judgement of anything and leave no room for disagreement, Harry would listen gravely and then say with his eyebrows raised an inch, 'Well, that's an interesting perspective. Completely unhinged, of course, but interesting . . .' which would send her off into peals of laughter again. Another of her still-memories of the evening was of surprised and faintly envious faces turned towards their table as they dissolved into their private merriment again.

It was only at the end of the evening that the still-pictures jerked and began slowly to move again. They turned reluctantly away from the luminous reflection in the millpond and Harry said, 'It's midnight, Cinderella. What

85

time does your father expect you back? Or no, not Cinderella. Juliet, perhaps?'

It was an oddly sombre note, but Angharad brushed it lightly aside. 'Oh, no, not Juliet. What about Cinders in reverse?' She patted the grey roof of the van. 'At the twelfth stroke this will turn into a white Rolls Corniche, and this,' she pointed to her plain cotton dress, 'into a glittering creation starred with a million sequins.'

'I'll take the Rolls. The sequins are your department. And what about me? Transformed into a handsome prince, as wealthy as he's wise and witty?'

As Angharad shook her head, Harry saw the roundness of her cheek, and the curve of her eyelashes over it. He tightened his grip on her wrist so that she looked up into his face to answer him.

'No, thank you,' she whispered. 'I'd rather have you just as you are.'

'Do you mean that?' He was turning her to face him, drawing her closer so their hips met, and their feet fitted between each other like the smooth pieces of an ancient puzzle.

'Yes.'

Harry's dark head blotted out the moon. His mouth jarred against hers and his tongue between her teeth was an instant's violence before she met it with her own. She had a confused impression of the hardness of his jaw, and all the complex bones knitted under the taut skin. He felt rough, and foreign, and so exciting that she was giddy with the strangeness of it.

She had never kissed anyone except Laura.

Under his insistent weight and her own dizziness, Angharad swayed backwards. She felt the ridges of the van's side at her back, digging into her flesh as he pinioned her against it. Her eyes opened and she saw the moon, sliding away now, and the thick powdering of stars. Harry's tongue teased insistently at her own, drawing it from her mouth so that it probed between his teeth, answering him. She felt that she wanted to drink him in, draining every last drop.

Then, through the thin fold of her dress as he rolled

against her, she felt his erection. Angharad knew her biology. She could have recited the Latin names, and described the processes with clinical exactness. But the size, and the insistent hardness of this, was utterly surprising. In response she felt a startling mixture of pride and elation. Her mouth curved in a smile and Harry's face rubbed hers as he made a small groan deep in his throat. Angharad's hands fluttered, helplessly at first, and then moved to touch him. Harry's eyes were shut and she felt how his face contracted fiercely as her fingers brushed him. His mouth moved from hers to the arch of her throat, and he drew the skin between his lips as if he was tasting it. His hands slid from her shoulders and over her small, hard breasts, then spanned her ribs. She felt him draw in his breath, sharply, against her bare neck and then his hands dropped heavily to his sides. His head lifted and he was blinking, not seeing her any more.

Angharad drew back her hand as if it was burnt.

'What is it? Shouldn't I do that?'

Harry seemed to be groping for his bearings. 'I'm sorry. Something reminded me . . .' But the words were bitten off before they came out. In a second more he had collected himself. When he smiled again it was crooked, and not quite convincing. 'Brrr. Must have been someone walking over my grave. Anyway we shouldn't be doing this in the carpark like a couple of kids. I'd better take you home before it's too late.'

Angharad bundled herself into her seat, humiliation silencing her. She was afraid that she must have done something shockingly inappropriate, and she stared in bewilderment at the darkness as the headlamps sliced into it. They had gone several miles before Harry put his hand out and touched her.

'Are you all right?'

'Yes. Did I do something wrong?'

'Wrong? Of course you didn't.' He pulled into the side of the road again and hugged her, kissing her eyelids and the tip of her nose. 'I told you. Someone walked over my gave. Doesn't it ever happen to you?'

'Yes,' she lied, wanting very much to believe him.

'Well, then,' he coaxed her. 'Can we forget it? In fact it was rather neat timing on the part of whatever passer-by in the cemetery. Without him, I would have ravished you, there and then, in the carpark of the Mill Restaurant. And that would have been uncomfortable, and not very romantic. I don't want it to be like that, do you?'

He disarmed her utterly with his mixture of arrogance and humility. Angharad smiled at him, and the cold moment was forgotten. They drove on with his arm around her, and her head against his shoulder.

At the old fountain she said, 'I'll walk from here.'

'No, you won't.' His voice was firm. 'Not on your own, in the middle of the night.'

'I'll be quite safe. I've wandered these lanes at all hours. And I'd like a walk now.'

Harry turned her chin and kissed her again, then reluctantly let her go. 'I don't want anything to happen to you.'

Angharad said lightly, 'You've happened to me. That's enough for one day.'

Their fingers were still locked together and she was afraid that she couldn't let go, even for a few hours. But at last her hand dropped.

'Tomorrow,' Harry said as she turned away into the blackness under the tunnel of trees. She knew that he was watching her and before the road took her out of his sight, she turned to wave, hoping that he could see the white glimmer of her hand in the dark.

The night air was very sweet and still. Angharad could see nothing but she knew the road so well that she trod unthinkingly, aware of nothing but the happiness inside her. Harry's strange withdrawal was forgotten, and she had accepted his explanation as part of this perfect, transforming day. There were no lights showing as she came along the village street, and the low line of the rooftops showed only as deeper blackness against the sky. Even in midsummer there was the faintest drift of coal smoke. Angharad felt that she had never loved the place so much. As her hand closed on the front door latch she heard quite clearly, although it was more than a mile away, the low throb of Harry's van as he drove off. He had waited until she must be safely home. Angharad smiled as she let herself into the quiet house. The grandfather clock ticked steadily, its face a white circle that reminded her of the moon in the millpond.

She had imagined that she would never sleep, but as soon as she lay down and closed her eyes it claimed her, and she slept dreamlessly until morning.

For two more evenings she met Harry beside the fountain. On the first she cooked for him on the gas ring in his cottage, and they sat opposite each other at the table to talk, greedy for the details of the hours that they had spent apart. Harry had been filming the old man out on the hillside with his dogs, rounding up the sheep for the dip.

'Intricate patterns,' he said, 'spreading in skeins across the hill. The man and the dogs, working perfectly together. Christ, I hope I caught it. I'm no good if I didn't.' She saw how fierce he was about his film, and understood how much of himself he was investing in it. She felt proud and anxious, equally.

'All I did was make pies,' she said ruefully.

'Exquisite pies, I bet.'

The next evening they went to a tiny pub halfway up a mountain, and sat in the bar under the fairylights, hand in hand.

In all their hours of talk there was only one topic that jarred between them. Angharad found that Laura's name came easily, too easily. For six years Laura had been her mentor and guide, as well as her best friend. Everything she had read or seen she had talked about with Laura, and every opinion she held had been formed alongside Laura's. More than that, with Harry's face in front of her, it was impossible not to see Laura too. She might almost have been there with them. Sometimes Angharad believed that she really was.

But Harry didn't want to hear Angharad talking about his sister. Whenever her name came out, he would lightly change the subject, looking away so that Angharad couldn't see into his eyes.

Alone in bed at night, or as she sliced vegtables in the kitchen at Y Gegin Fach, Angharad tried to puzzle out why.

The prudence that had made her hide her feelings from Laura was consumed by the flame of her new happiness. As she looked back, she was amazed that she had never given away how much the thought of Harry meant to her. And now, with calm optimism, she looked forward to sharing her happiness with Laura. All three of them were grown up now. The very fact that Laura was away, living her own life, proved that. *It's Nice here.* When she came home, after her first surprise, she would surely accept that Harry would not be exclusively hers for ever. The three of them would just draw closer together, Angharad thought, staring wide-eyed into the future. Her love for Laura wouldn't change. It had been like a gentle initiation for this new, fierce, and compelling feeling.

I'm grown up now, she told herself. Ready to be really in love.

But for all the luminous clarity with which she saw the future herself, she couldn't convey it to Harry. He wouldn't talk about Laura, and she didn't attempt to press him. She excused him by calling it loyalty, to Laura and to her friendship which he was taking over for himself while she was away. If Laura was here, Angharad thought, forgetting the possessive light in her friend's eyes, it would all be quite simple. But even so her shadow began to lengthen between them, out of place in the brilliance that bathed everything else.

On their third evening together, Angharad told him, 'I have to work tomorrow, and on Sunday evening. It's our busy time, and they need extra hands in the kitchen.'

Harry frowned. 'Two days without you? And after that what happens?'

'Two days completely free.'

At once he presssed her hands between his. 'Wonderful. Do you think you could get away from home for just one night?'

Angharad's heart leapt into her throat. The time was coming, and she knew that they were both ready. Each evening it was harder to part, and each evening it seemed less reasonable to try. Now she looked at Harry and saw his slow, interrogative smile.

'Yes.'

Her friend could come back from France just as unexpectedly as she had gone away.

'That's good. You can come with me to the August Meeting.'

Angharad stared at him, astonished. She knew about the August Meeting, but she had never been. At dawn on the first of August, people came from miles around to a tiny tin chapel at an isolated crossroads. Crammed into the chapel and overflowing into the rough paddock around it, they listened raptly to singing and verse-reading and passages from the Bible. There was no programme. Those who felt like contributing simply stood up and did it. Angharad's father said that the festival had ancient, pagan origins and had only borne its mild religious significance for the last two hundred years.

She bit the corners of her mouth to hide her smile. It could hardly have been more different from what she had imagined Harry was going to say.

'That would be nice,' she said innocently. 'But I don't need to spend the night away from home just for the August Meeting. I can be up out of my own bed, if I must, in plenty of time for the dawn.'

Harry grinned.

'So you could. But you'd miss the fun beforehand, wouldn't you?'

The parties held locally before the Meeting were equally legendary. The most dedicated revellers didn't bother to go to bed, and their head-on meetings with the sober early risers at the chapel contributed to the electric atmosphere.

Angharad was beginning to see. Reluctantly she said, 'I've just thought of something. There'll be all kinds of people I know there. I can't go with you.'

She wished that she could have put it differently, and Harry brushed aside her objection irritably. He had little patience with Angharad's insistence on secrecy. 'If we take care and time it right, no one will know or care who the hell you're with the night before. And at the chapel the preacher

91

says I can film, so I'll be prowling around the edges. You can sit by yourself and pretend to be alone, if you like.'

And so it was agreed.

On the last night of July, Angharad went to bed as usual. She lay wide awake in the darkness and listened to her father moving heavily around downstairs. At last the wooden boards of the landing creaked and the door opposite hers opened and closed. As she waited, counting the minutes until he must be asleep, she promised herself that soon, somehow, she would tell him about Harry and Laura. They had come like a wedge between William and herself, and every lie that she told now drove the wedge deeper. And again, for the thousandth time, she came up short against the blank wall of her ignorance. There was no way to prise the old secrets out of the past, and with every day they went on breeding new ones.

At last a faint snore told her that William was asleep. Silently she slid into her clothes and, treading softly to avoid the familiar creaking board, she padded downstairs and let herself out into the midnight air. Harry was waiting for her and she saw the white glimmer of his smile. He enveloped her in a hug and she felt a prickle of excitement nudge away the guilt.

'Thank you for coming. I love you.' His breath was warm against her ear. She didn't answer, but she took the words and hoarded them.

As they drove away from Cefn they might have been the only people awake in the world. Even in the village nearest to the chapel, there were only two or three lighted windows, and the front door of the old square pub was shut and barred. But the carpark was full, and the curtains glowed red at the windows.

'In full swing,' Harry murmured, 'And still three hours until dawn.' With his camera case in one hand he guided Angharad round to the back door. He tapped casually, and waited.

'Yes?'

'Harry Cotton. That you, Daffydd?'

The door opened at once. Warm light and the clamour of

92

talk and singing swept at them like a tidal wave. The bar was packed. Harry's friend was huge. He winked at them, redfaced and with wet black curls clinging to his forehead.

'*Iechyd da*. Pint in the pump for you, Harry boy.' To Angharad he said, 'Hello, love. Mind yourself with this one, won't you? Come straight to Daffydd if he's any trouble.'

The party swallowed them up at once. Harry seemed to know everyone, and he was greeted like an old friend by a dozen people.

'How?' Angharad asked breathlessly in a moment's lull. As far as she could see, she recognized no one. 'I thought I belonged here. And you said you lived like a hermit at Heulfryn. Or is that only one half of a double life?' Harry rocked back against the bar and lifted his drink. He looked as at home here as she had ever seen him, with his lean dark features softened by good humour. Only the camera case, carefully guarded at his feet, distinguished him.

'They're good people. I like to be alone when I'm working. Except for you.' Angharad only just caught the last words before he swept on. 'But I can't work all the time. Can't film in here without lights. And you'd never see my man in here. Early to bed and straight to the chapel, for him.' He broke off to wave across the room to Daffydd, who was staggering up on to a low dais with a microphone stand. 'I used to come to places like this a lot, when I couldn't stand Llyn Fair any more. And just lately, when I got so lonely without . . .' He said something else, but this time the words were completely lost. Angharad could have cursed the cheerful babble around them. Had he said *without Laura*? It would be the first time he had spoken her name without prompting. But then his eyes turned down to her, and she was certain that he couldn't have done. His look, that look, could be for no one but herself and it isolated them in all the clamour. 'And now I don't need to,' Harry said softly, 'Because I've got you. But shall we enjoy ourselves just the same?'

Angharad did enjoy herself. It wasn't the several drinks, although they blurred the edges of the room forgivingly and took away her shyness. It wasn't even being with Harry, although the warmth of that underlaid all the other sensations of the night. It was just that the simple determination of everyone in the room to have a good time swept her along.

She jigged to jukebox music with beaming men she had never seen before, then found herself beached beside friendly women who gave her slices of pickled egg and peanuts before the dancing grabbed her back again. When Daffydd mounted the dais to sing against a storm of clapping, she joined in the choruses of the old songs, and when they came to '*Ystlys wen a chynffon, wen, wen, wen!*' she banged her glass on the table for emphasis like everyone else.

Much later, when the heat and noise were at their height, an anonymous-looking young man in a collar and tie, with two layers of knitted waistcoat showing under his suit jacket, leapt up on to the dais. At once the clapping and stamping settled into an encouraging rhythm. The man unknotted his tie and waved it over his head. His collar stud pinged into the crowd and then his jacket sailed with spread arms over their heads. The knitted waistcoats followed. The barmaid caught one and waved it like a trophy. When the shirt was unbuttoned the cheering became a roar. From behind Angharad two old ladies, with identical iron perms and white cardigans, came elbowing their way forward. One of them grinned toothlessly at Angharad. 'Might as well see what there is to see, eh?'

'She doesn't need to. Stands more chance of a close-up at her age.'

A wave of laughter rose inside Angharad and threatened to choke her. Across the throbbing room she saw that Harry was watching her. *I love you too*, she shouted inside herself, and she knew that he heard. His laughter met and matched hers.

'Off! Off!' The impromptu stripper unzipped his trousers and they fell around his ankles, hobbling him. He lurched, grabbing at the toe of one black sock in an attempt to wrench it off. Daffydd was at the piano now, crashing thunderous climactic chords. The young man's trousers were off and were hauled from the stage by the turnups. In one sock and his underpants he struck a pose before the lights flashed off, on again, and the underpants were stripped away as he capered naked, and hopelessly innocent, away into the arms of his cronies.

'Is that all?' howled one of the old ladies. '*Duw*, then things have changed since my day.'

The pub was rocking with laughter. Then there was another chord at the piano and at once, with no hint of incongruity, the singing soared up again. Out came the old, loved hymns and Angharad knew without looking at her watch that it was the still, waiting time just before dawn.

Without warning, tears pricked behind her eyelids.

Out of the crowd Harry's hand reached for hers, and gently he drew her away. The back door clicked shut behind them and the singing was swallowed up at once.

'I'm glad you enjoyed it,' Harry said softly.

She saw behind him that the sky was streaked with lemon and gold.

On the road to the old tin chapel, the people were straggling along in twos and threes. They filed in through the rusty gate and were swallowed up by the dark porch. Angharad left Harry to his camera, and joined the line of people. The inside of the chapel was gloomy and bare, undecorated except for a varnished board at one end with a forbidding text. The light coming through the plain glass windows in the whitewashed walls was only dully grey. She took her place in a high wooden pew and waited. Within minutes the chapel was full, and still people pressed inside. There were coughs and shuffles, and discreet waves. Facing the main body of the chapel were the black suits and stern expressions of a full male voice choir. To her surprise, Angharad picked out amongst them the red faces of some of her friends from the party. After a moment she saw Harry deep in the shadow of an aisle, whispering to the silver-haired preacher. The old hill farmer had come in and found a place, sitting with his knobbed stick between his knees.

As the light strengthened, the murmuring died away. There was a moment of total silence. Then, through the line of east windows, came the first rays of the sun.

Out of the corner of her eye Angharad saw Harry lift his

camera. Like a a long black ripple the choir stood up. The leader gave a single, pure note and the tenor voices rose like a perfect instrument over the bass humming.

It was '*Ar Hyd Y Nos*', and sung more perfectly than Angharad had ever heard it. There was no accompaniment, and the acoustics were wretched. But it was singing for the joy of it and it held her, the fine hairs raised at the back of her neck, until the last low note fell into silence. At last she turned her hed and saw that the old farmer had a starched white handkerchief at his eyes. And she knew, without looking further, that Harry held him in his camera's black eye.

After the choir the preacher stood up in the plain wooden box under the text at the end and read from the Bible. An anguished teenage boy forgot the words of a complicated Welsh poem. He stumbled back to his seat, to be followed by an angelic-faced band of tiny children with recorders and tambourines. Everyone joined in the singing.

Angharad was enchanted. It was neither a service nor a concert, but an unselfconscious celebration for all of them. Heads bobbed happily up one after another to perform in their own ways. She lost track of the individual items and drifted away on the tide of her own thoughts, watching the specks of dust as they whirled in the wedges of light from the window shafts. The sun was fully up now, and it struck across the chapel to the old man, sitting with his head bent and his hands clasped over his stick.

A boy of eight or nine stood up, snub-nosed and stiff in his Sunday-best suit. The crowd rustled expectantly, and Angharad's attention focussed again.

The child lifted his head and began to sing.

*Early one morning.*
*Just as the sun was rising,*

The piercing, exquisite soprano cut through the stillness.

*I heard a maiden singing*
*In the valley below.*

The clear light was gilding the bare corners of the chapel. Angharad saw beyond the whitewashed walls to the valley under The Mountain, and over the other side across the rocks to Llyn Fair.

> *Oh, don't deceive me,*
> *Oh, never leave me,*
> *How could you use a poor maiden so?*

At the last, quivering note Angharad shivered. Harry had been standing close to the child. Now he stepped backwards and slowly padded down the side aisle, tracking away until the frame held all of the congregation. With one movement they were on their feet. The Meeting was over, and the Welsh anthem was hammering at the dusty beams of the old roof.

Afterwards she waited in her place on the uncomfortable wooden bench through the clapping and cheering that followed, and the babble of talk and greetings as the people pushed out into the sunshine. At last she was the only person left, and the chapel felt hollow and cold. Angharad shook herself, frowning. The child's solo had left her with a chill feeling that she couldn't explain.

Then someone gently touched her shoulder.

'Come on,' Harry said. 'Let's go home to bed.'

Angharad smiled at him, and the moment was forgotten. 'I couldn't sleep now.'

Harry's fingers knotted fiercely in hers. 'Who said anything about sleep?'

Heulfryn Cottage looked as it always did, as if it might finally decay at any moment and melt back into the landscape. Angharad had half expected that this morning it would look different. More significant, because of what was going to happen there.

Inside it was just the same too. Her eyes flickered over the books, yesterday's unfolded newspaper, an empty coffee mug and the red blanket on the narrow bed.

Harry poured something into a glass and handed it to her. She sipped, and the brandy warmed her.

'You look frightened,' he said. He turned her to him so that she looked up into his face. 'Angharad. I love you and I want to make love to you. But only if you want it too.'

With odd detachment she looked at his mouth, thinking that the slightly crooked smile was Laura's, too. But where

97

Laura would have gone straight on, Harry was waiting. Looking up into his eyes Angharad saw the clear blue irises, rimmed with a darker circle. She felt a band tighten around her chest. Slowly she moved her cheek against his and felt the rough prickle of beard. It was easy now to put the memory of Laura out of her head. She closed her eyes and answered.

'I do want to.'

The kiss he gave her was almost brotherly. 'I want to look at you,' he whispered.

She felt absurdly like a little girl as her fingers fumbled obediently at her buttons. She wore no bra under her shirt. Her breasts seemed to vanish under Harry's big hands, and when he kissed them, she stared down into the dark points of his hair. Gently he peeled off the rest of her clothes. Angharad stood unmoving, so electrically conscious of her skin that she felt the sun shining right through it to show the nerves and bones underneath.

Harry's mouth brushed across her belly, touched the hollows beside her hips where the blue veins showed, and the tuft of pale blonde hair.

'You're so fair,' he said.

He lifted her up and laid her on the bed. The red blanket brushed all along the length of her spine. Not afraid any more, and with a languid confidence that surprised her, through half-closed eyes she watched him undress. Dark hair curled across his chest, and a narrow line ran over his stomach to the inverted V beneath it. From it his – and she stumbled over the word in her head – his thing lifted. The impatient profile startled her, as if it was something not part of Harry at all.

'I'm not as pretty as you,' he said, seeing her face. Unwelcome into her mind's eye came Laura's sleek body, like a photographic negative of her own.

'I think you are,' she told him, and held out her arms.

He lay down beside her. The brush of curling hair and the hardness of muscle beneath was different, and much more urgent. Angharad felt the first slow shudder of impatience begin to gather under her skin.

Harry propped his head on one hand to look down at her. The fingers of his other hand traced over her until they came down between her legs.

'Is it the first time?' he asked gently. She was half lost in the sensations stirred by his hand.

'Yes. The first time,' she whispered. 'And you?'

From the smile in Harry's eyes, she read the idiocy of her question. Two years since they had first met. Two years in which he had lived in London and ranged all over the States.

'No. Do you mind very much?'

'I'm glad. One of us should know what we are doing.' She smiled lazily, and her fingers knotted in the hair on his chest.

Suddenly Harry reached over her. His tongue searched for hers and as she answered it, her hips lifted from the mattress to meet his. The expected weight nudged against her belly.

'Touch me,' he ordered her, 'like this.' His hand guided hers until her fingers closed around him. The heat and the hardness was both fascinating and frightening.

There isn't room inside me, she thought, panic fluttering over the impatient circles summoned by his hand. Harry's fist over hers showed her how to stroke, long smooth movements. When he took his hand away she went on, not thinking about herself any longer, but overflowing with love for him as she watched the fierce lines deepen in his face. His head fell back and she kissed his throat, where she had seen the pulse beating. Once she looked down and saw a single bead of moisture on the purple tip between her fingers.

Harry rolled so that he hung over her. He lifted his hand and she wanted to say, *No, I like it like that*.

Instead his knees forced hers apart until he knelt between them. His hands came underneath her and lifted her to meet him. She felt the intrusive pressure hard enough to bruise the fragile skin.

'Don't be afraid,' he whispered. There was an instant of sharp pain so that she almost cried out, but then it was gone. When she looked down she saw that her own blonde hair was tangled with his blackness, and the length of Harry was buried inside her

Crazily she wanted to laugh, and say, *So that's what happens*.

But Harry was moving again, no more than an inch at first, but then deeper so that the long, slow strokes built up again. Angharad looked over his shoulder at a damp blotch on the old wall, to match her rhythm to his. But the sensations inside her were confused now, warring with each other. She felt that Harry was rushing away from her, and she was falling behind him. She saw that his black eyelashes were glued into sweaty spikes, and she twisted her head to kiss them.

But then she felt the muscles bunch all along his back, and he moaned something that she couldn't hear. It wasn't her own name. They rolled together, and she hugged him, surprised at how vulnerable he felt in her arms.

Angharad found herself laughing in spite of her own disappointment.

After a long moment Harry opened his eyes. 'I'm sorry,' he whispered, contrite. 'That wasn't very clever of me. Next time . . .' But she put her fingers over his mouth. She watched the angles of his face, and thought how simple and how inevitable it was to be in love with him.

Almost at once he was the leader again.

'I'll show you something else,' he said, and there was a teasing note now. She looked down, and saw that a thin thread of pale blood hung between them. That's all it was, she thought distantly, but then she felt Harry's black hair brush over her skin. Gently his tongue moved. Angharad gasped. The confusion disappeared, swallowed by certainty. She heard someone cry out, not in her own voice at all.

At last, when the world reassembled itself into its component parts of warm skin, prickly wool and sunlight, she opened her eyes. Harry was watching her, his head propped on one elbow again.

He smiled, and she felt that they knew each other perfectly. There was no need for any more questions, because they could see clearly into one another. Harry kissed the corner of her mouth, greeting her.

'I'm glad you're here,' he said, and she knew that she had arrived somewhere important, somewhere that she couldn't imagine ever wanting to leave. With the knowledge came the realization that she was exhausted. The sunlight on the stone floor blurred, and the red blanket made a rainbow fuzz in front of her eyes. She let her eyelids fall, just for a second, and at once fell asleep.

She dreamed of Laura. They were playing tennis on a grass court shaded by the long arms of copper beech trees, and Laura was winning effortlessly. Every so often she would wave her racket and call out 'Come on. You aren't trying.' And Angharad would try harder, biting her lips and pushing the sweat-damp hair out of her eyes, but always with the knowledge that she couldn't match Laura's score.

When she woke up again and saw black hair on the pillow beside her and olive-brown skin, it was with the thought that it was Laura. She lay very still because she didn't want her to wake up. Then, with clearer consciousness, she remembered that it was Harry.

The rush of relief and happiness was so strong that she tightened her arms around him, nuzzling up against him like a child, willing him to wake up and share her pleasure with her.

'Harry.'

He yawned and smiled at her, catching her happiness.

'Mmmm. Mmmm. Well, what do you think?'

She opened her mouth to tell him, but he kissed her mouth to stop her and said, 'Don't tell me until next time. I really meant, do you think I should get up now to make us some coffee, or later?'

Angharad wound her arms around his neck. 'Later.'

'How wanton.' Then, simply, 'You are lovely, you know.'

Everything was much slower now. It was as if they had time to stop and look at each other, memorizing every detail as they went, and to listen, as well as just to touch and taste.

Afterwards she asked him humbly, 'That was nearly right, wasn't it?'

'Yes.' His face was so close to hers that she could see herself reflected in his eyes. 'I think, if we practise enough, we shall do quite nicely.' They fell back against the pillows, laughing together.

Later, when they got up, they sat across the little table

watching each other and drinking coffee, in quietness that was as companionable and untroubled as if they had been together for a hundred years.

# CHAPTER FIVE

William was waiting for her.

Angharad clicked the front door latch and walked into the dimness of the house. Her father was sitting in the chair under the grandfather clock, waiting, not even with a book in his hands.

Angharad stopped short, disorientated by the sameness of everything here when all the world outside had changed so radically.

'Where have you been?' William's voice was dangerously quiet. Her answer came quickly, and she forced nonchalance into it so that it wouldn't sound as if she had been rehearsing it all the way home.

'I got up in the middle of the night to go to the August Meeting. I thought I ought to do it, just once.'

Could he see that her mouth looked bruised? Surely she must look as different as she felt, as if there was light and not blood in all her veins?

'Ah.' William took off his spectacles and rubbed his hands over his face. 'That was one thing I hadn't thought of. I was worried about you.'

Remorse hit her. Forgetting herself, she knelt down beside him and rubbed his hands, seeing that his spectacles had left deep crimson marks beside the bridge of his nose.

'I'm sorry. It was thoughtless of me. But what could happen to me here? And it was fun . . .' She rushed on, self-dislike nudging at her. 'Someone I know, the brother of a friend of mine from school, is making a film about Mr Ellis the Bwlch. He was filming him being at the Meeting.'

William laughed suddenly. 'A film about old Ellis? Good God, they'll be wanting to make one about me, next.'

'I went to have lunch with him afterwards as it's my day off. The film man, I mean, not Mr Ellis. I didn't think you'd mind,' she added humbly. 'You've been so busy, lately.'

William's smile faded as he stroked her hair. 'I know. Not much of a father to you, am I?'

*A better father than I'm a daughter.* She almost said it aloud, but instead she rested her head against him and said, 'You are. You work too hard, that's all.'

I'll tell you everything, she promised inside her head, just as soon as I can. Old, forgotten things won't matter any more. You'll like Harry too. *I want you to.*

'Don't be out half the night again without letting me know, will you?' William ordered, and she nodded. Be careful, she warned herself, but at once her thoughts went back to Harry and she felt that even her bones were melting.

'Make me a cup of tea, love?' William asked, and she rushed to do it, glad to hide her face and glad to do something for him, however tiny.

I'll make it up to you, she promised her father's bent head as she handed him his cup. William's attention was already wandering back to his work. And it can't be so wrong, can it? To love someone like this? Because if it is, the whole world's wrong. And I don't care.

The grass under the willows was lush green. Dragonflies zipped over the stream in sudden darts of colour and the trickle of water over the stones was an endless, low accompaniment to Harry's voice. He was reading aloud to her and she shut her eyes, only half listening, letting the words of the poem weave patterns in her head.

'That is no country for old men. The young
in one another's arms, birds in the trees . . .'

Harry read on and Angharad thought *that's us*, lying here listening to the birds. The image of old men and time passing made her shiver. It seemed ever more important to seize all these minutes, somehow to stop them escaping from her forever. Their first days together had seemed eternal, resonant with every touch and every word they exchanged. Now they had a bloom like a ripe apricot, and were just as short-lived.

'Sad?'

Angharad opened her eyes. 'A little. Only because it's a sad poem.'

'It's not meant to be. It's about finding compensations in growing old.' Harry smiled as he looked down at Angharad in the grass. Her thin dress was caught up and the stalks made waving shadows over the skin of her thigh. 'Although I must agree that, looking at it from this angle, it isn't all that convincing.'

Angharad laughed and put her arms around his neck. With Harry, it was impossible to be sad for long.

'I love you,' he said.

'Don't go,' she responded, suddenly greedy for him. Over the last days Harry had unlocked something inside her that surprised them both. Now as she fastened her hands behind him, she felt her eyes losing their focus and the warm summer afternoon its physical reality.

'Never,' he whispered, with his mouth against her neck. The word reassured her. He was stroking the smooth skin of her inner thigh and she felt hot and constrained.

He was still smiling at her, challenging her a little, as he lifted her dress over her head. The sun warmed her shoulders and the grass was deliciously cool and sappy underneath her.

'I think,' she teased him, 'you think I'm going to be embarrassed about doing this out of doors.'

'I wouldn't think anything of the kind. You're far too original.'

'Anyway, I'm not embarrassed. I want you too much. Besides, there's no one for miles.'

Laughter swept over them.

'You've worked it all out already?'

'Of course I have.'

Harry took off his clothes and knelt beside her in the grass. The long stalks tickled and the sharp scent of grass sap rose around them. The air felt cool and silky over their skin. Angharad reached out for him. She was learning how the hard muscles moved under her fingers, and to recognize the changing lights in Harry's eyes as he guided her. The strangeness had gone, replaced by intrigued pleasure that deepened every day.

Harry drew her down into the green hollow in the grass. Dreamily she watched a tortoiseshell butterfly folding its wings for a second on a curving stem.

Harry. Harry.

His hand was searching for her, and then the dreaminess was driven away by a harder edge. Angharad rolled fiercely so that she was above him, with her hair hanging over his face, and then with her tongue traced the shape of his mouth. She was ready not to be led any more

One of her hands reached for his wrists and held them until he fell back into the green shadow, mock-yielding. Gently Angharad slid over him until she found him and then, reversing what he had wordlessly taught her, began to lift herself and sink back over him. It was exciting suddenly to taste her own power and to play with the currents that she generated between them. She could take him deeper into her so that the sensation jarred between pleasure and pain, and then draw away again until he frowned and reached back blindly for her. There was no sense of being outrun, any more. They were equal and opposite, and they belonged together.

She bent again to kiss him so that her hair brushed over him, then leant away with her back arched to see the complete bowl of the sky. Confidence suffused her, and with it came a deeper throb of pleasure than she had ever known before.

'Now,' she whispered to him, and in answer Harry caught her hips and plunged, once, so that the shock spilled through them both like the flame of the same fire.

Gasping, they rolled together through the plumes of grass, and they lay still while the minute world of petals and fronds and gaudy insects composed itself again in front of their eyes. Angharad found that she was laughing softly, and she felt the warm breath of Harry's response against her neck.

'Unmanned,' he teased her.

'Be quiet, or I'll attack you all over again.'

'Please.'

Angharad felt a slight breeze stirring the fine hairs at the bare nape of her neck. On a sudden impulse she scrambled up and ran to the bank of the stream. The water was no more than a silver trickle over the fronds of weeds but she splashed into it so that rainbows of spray sparkled behind her. A hump of weed was like a soft pillow as she half-fell against it and the water ran with icy fingers over her hair and face.

'Ouch.' Angharad jumped up again, the shock of the cold water taking her breath away. She looked to the bank, just as the first of a procession of tall clouds sailed over the sun. A wall of shadow swept over her, and over Harry who was sitting in the grass, arms wrapped around his knees, watching her. Angharad shook herself, her hair darkened with water and clinging to her skin. The sudden shade had drained the colour out of everything.

'Come on, love-in-idleness,' she called to Harry. 'Into the water.'

He stared at her, seeing her slick and dark with the water, and then turned sharply away.

'Don't call me that.' The jagged edge to his voice shocked her. With the surprise a little window of memory opened up. Laura had used the same words once to her, love-in-idleness, as she lay drowsing in the narrow bed in their school room. It sounded just like her, pretty and veiled in mockery. Shivering, Angharad ran the few steps and dropped beside Harry in the grass.

'I'm sorry,' she whispered. Somehow it had been tacitly understood between them that Laura was a chord not to be touched on.

The taboo disturbed Angharad, who believed that Laura would share and deepen, rather than disturb their happiness. But two or three times now she thought that the shadow of her friend had come between them, although Harry had never given that much away. He simply withdrew from her, and she was touched by the icy fear of being without him.

But now the tower of cloud slipped momentarily away again, and brilliant sunshine brought colour flooding back. Harry turned to her with his gipsy smile and wound a coil of damp fair hair around his finger. 'I'm sorry too. Don't

107

change,' he begged her again. 'Anything.'

Perhaps, Angharad thought to reassure herself, he feels just like I do, wanting to keep and freeze all these moments we've had together, but feeling them slipping away and vanishing.

'Nothing,' she promised him, and he leant forward to kiss the end of her nose. He rubbed her dry with his sweater until her skin tingled, and they then sat and watched the changing sky until the first fat drops of summer rain exploded on their upturned faces. Hand-in-hand they ran, shouting to each other, to the shelter of Harry's little grey van and Heulfryn Cottage.

'Who is he?' Gwyn asked one afternoon.

Angharad's face immediately burned scarlet. Gwyn's stare was shrewd and penetrating, and there was nothing in the cluttered studio to deflect it. Angharad shrank under it.

'Is it so obvious?' she asked at last, seeing that it was hopeless to pretend. Every day she had promised herself that after just one or two more secret days she would tell her family about Harry Cotton. But the days had rippled by and she had said nothing.

'Transparently, to me,' Gwyn said crisply. 'I'm not sure about your father. If he knows, he's chosen not to mention it to me. Who is he?'

Angharad groped for the right words. At length she said, 'Nobody you know. But yes, I have met someone who has changed everything. I love him, Aunty Gwyn.'

Gwyn smiled, but Angharad thought it was a sad smile. Lines of anxiety showed in her face and there was a shade of disappointment in her eyes.

'Couldn't you have brought him home?'

'I will, soon,' Angharad promised desperately. 'It's just that . . .' and her voice trailed away. Gwyn was still looking at her and she thought, *She's guessed. Somehow, she knows.*

After a long, long silence Gwyn said, 'I hope you're being careful, Angharad, and I don't just mean in the obvious way. I wouldn't like to see you hurt yourself. Or anyone else.' *Dad. She means Dad, of course.*

'I know.'

Both women knew that there was nothing else to say, and the quiet closed uncomfortably around them.

Careful? The word dinned in Angharad's head, amplified by a new anxiety that had only just started to flicker within her.

Harry hadn't been careful with her, she knew that. He was nineteen years old, and he was handsome, and clever, and arrogant, and fatally used to getting his own way. She recognized all that, and forgave him, and loved him for his passion and vitality. Harry drew more out of her than she had ever dreamed existed. He made her laugh like a child, and then silenced her with the incredible adult reality of loving her in return. He made her feel open, and relaxed, and confident that whatever she said or did he would understand. Not even her closest friend, not even Laura, had ever made her feel like that.

But Angharad had been innocent, and Harry, impetuous and not innocent at all, had made love to her without thinking about it. It was only three days later that he said to her, 'You aren't on the Pill or anything like that, are you?'

She had answered him as lightly as he had asked. 'No. I suppose I should be.'

'There are clinics you can go to. Would you like me to come with you?'

Angharad had declined his help, fortified by an independent pride that half surprised her. The clinic, when she tracked it down, turned out to be a shabby outpost of the local hospital. Her 'case' was handled by a voluntary worker who reminded her uncomfortably of Aunty Gwyn.

'And what's your fiancé's name, dear? You are engaged, aren't you?' Blushing, Angharad sat on her suddenly shamefully naked fingers and gave Harry's name. Thereafter they had called her 'Mrs Cotton' until she was ready to scream. But she had come back with a bald, domed rubber cap which, when it wasn't in use, lived in a discreet pink plastic case like a bulbous powder compact.

So that was being carefully, wasn't it? If . . . But Angharad shut her mind to the black shaft opened by that *if*.

109

But in the other, unobvious ways that Gwyn had meant too, she knew that she was being fatefully reckless.

The longer she delayed it, the harder it would be to tell William what was happening to her. And the angrier he would have every right to be for the deception. She began to wish that she had had the courage, right at the very beginning, to tell her father and to meet the consequence then.

Now, with every day that passed, Harry grew more a part of her. He lived under the electrically sensitive surface of her skin, and walked behind her eyes. The hours apart from him stretched, and their times together burned up so fiercely that it frightened her. She had explored and learned every inch of him with her eyes and hands, and had given herself as openly in return. Nor was it just their bodies, but heads and minds and hearts. Angharad saw that behind Harry's old mask of casual smiles and flippancy, a different, passionate Harry stalked. He loved her just as much as she loved him, except when Laura's long arm reached out for him, and took him away from her with an abruptness that Angharad didn't understand.

August was nearly over, and she began to feel almost feverish. There was a lurid, overblown tinge to their happiness that told her it couldn't last. *I love you*, they told each other, over and over, in the dimness of the cottage and out on the open side of The Mountain. They clung to each other avidly, and fell asleep in exhaustion only to wake and start all over again.

Something will happen soon, Angharad comforted herself. With Harry, I can face anything.

At the end of the month, she began counting the days.

A day late. That's nothing. It's happened before.

Two days late. It'll start today. Or tomorrow, at the latest.

Three days. It isn't that. It's just because of what's been happening. Intense physical and emotional excitement are bound to have an effect. Probably hormonal changes too. There's no need to worry yet. We've been careful. Except at the very beginning.

The fourth day she spent with Harry at Heulfryn. The

long, intensely hot summer had come to an abrupt end. Needles of grey rain pinged at the windows today, and the damp rising from the bare floor told Angharad what she already knew, that Harry couldn't live here very much longer. His film was almost completed. She often caught him looking at the pile of black cans which held the exposed film, stacked safely in the coolest corner of the cottage.

'What happens next?' she had asked him, and he had answered vaguely.

'A lot of work. Cutting and editing. Sound mixing.'

Today she kept her eyes averted from the cans of film. She had cooked lunch for them as she had done so often before, and when they had eaten, Harry stood up and came round to the back of her chair. His hand slid over her shoulders and she felt his cheek against her hair.

'Angharad,' he murmured. 'Come and lie down with me?'

Under the red blanket, needing it for warmth now, they lay and looked at each other. Harry's face was very soft and serious in the grey light, with all the teasing smiles and taut, confident lines rubbed away. The tiny light squares of the window were reflected in the clear blue of his eyes, and as she looked past the reflections she saw how much he loved her too. The happiness of the knowledge was tempered with anxiety.

'I think I'm frightened,' she told him.

Not just the specific fear now, but of the sudden importance, and fragility, of everything.

'I know.' Harry was watching the shadows cupped in her collarbone and at the sides of her throat. 'It started so simply, didn't it? And now it isn't simple at all. It's real. I don't want anything to change, and I don't want to leave here, and I don't want to lose you.'

Angharad heard the unspoken words ballooning threateningly between them.

But things must change, however often we promise each other that we won't let them.

I have to leave, because I can't go on living here.

And I don't want to lose you, but . . .

'You won't lose me,' she said firmly. Harry cupped her face in his hands and kissed her.

'I hope not.'

Watching him, she recalled the other moods she had seen him in, intent on his work or indolent in the sunshine, frivolous and slightly drunk or angry with some trivial detail, companionable or passionately demanding, and thought that now he was none of those things. Seeing him like this, quiet and serious and touched with sadness, she thought that this must be the plain, unvarnished Harry that Laura loved.

It was as if she had spoken the name aloud.

Harry answered her by saying, very quietly, 'I had a letter from Laura. She'll be home on Friday.'

Wednesday today.

Angharad's heart thumped painfully in her chest. She heard her own voice, coming from a long way off.

'I'm glad. She's been away too long. There's such a lot to talk to her about.' Harry said nothing at all. She waited for him to, but he didn't. Instead he hugged her, and kissed her so that her hair spread over their faces, and then she let herself cling to him too. For a few minutes she forgot her specific fears and the other, vaguer ones that were in a way more threatening.

They were very tender with each other now. In the last days their love-making had grown almost violent, but the time for exploration and feverish dsicoveries was past. Harry stroked her shoulders and touched her breasts as if for the first time, and Angharad's fingers counted the rounded knobs of his spine like beads in a familiar necklace. When he came inside her, they moved together slowly, as if they were afraid of hurting each other. Their eyes stayed open, not wanting to lose sight of one another, and they watched how their own reflections moved like films over the nakedness beneath. The gentleness and slowness made Angharad think that this must be how people who had known each other for a long, long time made love. Married people. Grown-up people.

Even as she gasped, and shivered under the waves of intense pleasure, a tiny voice asked her *Grown-up*? But we are

112

grown-up. We have to be, now. And people who have babies are married, aren't they?

Afterwards she shut her eyes, longing to keep everything at bay for just a few seconds more.

'I love you.'

'I love you.'

Neither of them had anything else to say. Angharad sighed and heavily began to dress herself and get ready to go back to Cefn. A resolution was forming inside her head. She would begin, at least, to fight her way out of the net that was closing around her by telling her father that she had fallen in love with Joe Cotton's son. The decision made her feel a little better. When that hurdle was crossed, she would see. After all, she wasn't sure about anything else, yet.

The unprotected Harry had slid away again behind a brisk, positive veneer. 'I'm going home to Llyn Fair,' he told her, making a wry face. 'Better present myself to Joe and Monica before Laura gets back. And,' with a quick, sardonic smile, 'I want to make some calls to LA. Easier to do it from there than the kiosk outside the shop.'

'Of course.' She didn't ask him what the calls were about. The thought of him moving on, pursuing his films, was frightening enough.

By the old fountain he hugged her and kissed the top of her head. 'Okay? I'll see you at the weekend sometime. Laura and I could make you a special supper at Heulfryn.'

He was suddenly cheerful and Angharad went cold. She knew what he meant. That she needn't cook for once, that it would be a party for her. But she didn't want that. It wasn't *Laura and I* anything, any more.

Was it?

Seeing Harry's surprised stare, she said, 'Yes, I'm okay. Tell Laura how much I'm looking forward to seeing her.'

Abruptly she turned away and began to walk up the shiny, wet road towards the village.

The house was claustrophobic. Angharad wandered from room to room, picking things up and putting them down again. From the study came the irritable peck, peck of her father's typewriter. Angharad prepared a meal, watching the clock and knowing that there wasn't time, now, to talk to William before going out to do her evening's work. She served their early supper and ate it in listless silence. William looked at her over the top of his glasses and said, 'Do you feel ill?'

She answered, 'No, of course not.'

Another day. Five days late, now. On Thursday, Angharad worked the day shift, and she came home at six in the evening utterly exhausted. The empty evening opened ahead of her, offering no refuge of an excuse.

Tonight she would have to face her father.

She thought briefly about Harry, wondering what he was doing. Perhaps packing up his few possessions ready to leave the old cottage. But he seemed remote, oddly not a part of the anxieties that possessed her now.

After supper, William picked up the newspaper and made as if to go back into his study.

Angharad said quickly, 'Shall I make us some coffee? I'd like to . . . I'd like to talk to you.'

He beamed at her, full of affection, and she quailed. 'Ah, that would be nice. I don't feel that I've seen you properly for days. About College, is it? How much work have you been able to fit in, with playing about down at that pie-shop?'

'No, not exactly about that.' Angharad laid a tray for coffee and ground the beans, wondering if William could tell from the rattle of the china how much her hands were shaking. They went into the living-room and sat down under the moon-face of the grandfather clock.

'Well now, what's all this about?'

The clock ticked, unbelievably firm and measured when everything else in the world was racing and swaying.

'I . . . Dad, remember I told you I met a friend at the August Meeting?'

William snorted, still cheerful. 'Making a film. What nonsense.'

'Please, Dad. I want to tell you this as directly as I can. I've seen a lot of him, lately, and I've grown very fond of him. He's unusual, and special. And important to me. I've fallen in love with him.' Angharad spread her hands out wide,

114

thinking how feeble and jejeune she sounded.

Amusement and suspicion dawned together in William's face. 'In love?' There was a pause before he nodded, as if considering, and went on, 'I suppose it's natural, and charming in a way, that you should feel that at seventeen. And I'm flattered that you should take me into your confidence, Angharad. I've thought, lately, that we had somehow gone past that. If you want my reaction, it's that I can't see any reason why you shouldn't be in love at your age, provided that you don't do anything stupid and it doesn't interfere with your work.'

*Interfere?* A wave of panic brought the sweat out on her palms and at the nape of her neck under her hair.

'What's the boy's name?'

Tick, tock. The clock's ornate hands stood at ten minutes past nine, and she wished that she could freeze them there for ever.

'That's what I have to tell you. Harry Cotton. Joe Cotton's son.'

It was worse, much worse than her worst imaginings. William's head snapped round like a puppet's under the hand of a manic puppetmaster.

'*Who?*'

Angharad moistened her lips, trying to say the name again, but there was no need. William had heard clearly enough. He had gone white with anger, and there was a fleck of froth at the corner of his mouth.

'You dare to sit there and tell me that you are in love with the son of that scum? What do you know about love? Not the first thing. Not even love for me or any of your family, obviously. What did I say to you, six years ago? Or have you conveniently forgotten? I told you that you were to have nothing to do with the Cotton family. And that I never wanted to hear the name mentioned in this house. And now you creep up to me and say that you love them.'

Her childhood terror of his rages came back to Angharad and she shrank under his words as if they were blows. But at the same time her spirit sprang up inside her. She wanted to run and hide, yet she heard herself flinging back at him,

'I didn't say them. I don't care for his parents. I don't know what they've done to you because you've never chosen to tell me. But Laura Cotton is my friend and I love Harry. Yes. However much you shout or mock at me, you can't change that.'

William was carried away, so consumed by his anger that his face terrified her. 'Your friend? I told you six years ago that you could choose another friend, any one of the bloody little girls in the world except that one. But you couldn't, could you? And you've been deceiving me, like a meek little mouse, for all that time?'

Angharad's chin went up and her eyes blazed back at him. She was furious, and terrified, and torn so hard by loyalty that she wished she could break in half.

'Yes.'

William's hand flashed out and caught her cheek. It was no more than a brief, stinging slap but it whirled them apart so that they stood, separated by the domestic space of the hearthrug, staring at each other. Angharad's fingers went to the blazing red mark on her cheek. The hands of the clock had moved on only a couple of minutes, but it might have been a lifetime.

'Don't,' he breathed, 'ever . . . let me . . . hear you say those names again. I've failed with you, Angharad, and I'm bitterly ashamed. You're too old now for me to forbid you. Or to try to give you a sense of what is morally correct. You must do what your distorted reasoning dictates. But don't ask me. Do you understand? I don't want to know about you,' William heard the harshness of his own words, then, and tried to temper them, 'unless you promise me, here and now, that you will see no more of any member of that family. That might convince me that you are my daughter after all.'

It was Angharad's turn for blind anger now. Unreasonable. Vicious. Rigid and bigoted and destructive. Her father was all those things, and if he didn't want her, then – she didn't want him, either.

'Never. I won't ever. And you're a fool to force a choice on me, because I won't choose you and then we'll be lost to each other for ever.'

116

Hurt sprang into her father's face, the flood of it pushing aside the bitterness, and she wished that she could snatch the words back. But it was too late.

Painfully, as if his joints hurt, William drew himself up straight. 'I see. Well then, we understand each other. Good night, Angharad.'

Knowing that she couldn't bear to see him turn away from her and walk away, Angharad whirled around herself. The narrow stairs curved away in front of her and she ran up them, squeezing the hot tears back behind her eyelids so that he wouldn't catch a glimpse of them. Once the door of her room was shut and bolted behind her, she threw herself down on her bed and cried as if she would never be able to stop.

For a long moment William stood staring at the foot of the stairs. Then, still moving as if he was in pain, he walked through into his cluttered study. The top right-hand drawer of his desk was locked, but his fingers groped for the key on top of a cupboard and found it at once. Inside the drawer was an old black and white snapshot. It showed a woman, smiling and holding her hair back from her eyes, with a wide, rippling stretch of water behind her. The shape of her face, and the lines of her eyes and mouth, were exactly Angharad's.

William looked down into the woman's face, and then, with a little sound deep in his throat that might have been pain, he thrust the picture back into the drawer and locked it up again. Then he sat down in his creaking chair and buried his face in his hands.

In the next room the grandfather clock struck the half-hour and then ticked imperturbably on into the night.

When she woke up Angharad winced and closed her eyes against the intrusive light. Her face was tight, and her eyelids were so swollen that they felt like tiny lead weights. The memory came back at once, dully familiar, as if it had been with her all night. She half-turned restlessly under the blankets and laced her fingers across her stomach.

Every word, every gesture from last night's horrible scene

117

burned in her head. Much worse than all the anger was the hurt that she had seen in her father's eyes.

And that just because she had confessed to loving Harry Cotton.

What would her father say when she told him that she was going to have Harry Cotton's child?

Angharad rolled over and bit against the corner of the pillow to stop herself choking. Never. She could never tell him. Once more she counted the days off in her head, hopelessly praying that she might somehow have made a mistake. Six days now. And her periods had always been as regular as the ticking of the clock downstairs.

Angharad was sure, now, that she was pregnant. There was a faint, metallic taste in her mouth that she couldn't get rid of, however hard she tried, and it made the food taste dusty and nauseating in her mouth. She felt exhausted, and at the same time misaligned with everything, as if her physical responses had subtly changed. There was no point, any longer, in trying to see it as anything else.

She was pregnant.

Staring up at the tracery of cracks in the ceiling, as she had done as a child ill in bed, Angharad tried to work out what she should do.

Tell Harry, first. Except that today Laura would be home. She imagined them, too vividly, beside the lake, exchanging the stories of their summer apart. What would Harry say? She realized that she had no idea. All her confidence in their closeness began to crumble away. Love. Her father had mocked the idea, and she had a sickly fear that he might be right. What if nothing had any reality, except what was growing inside her?

Tormented, Angharad pushed back the bedcovers and flung herself out of bed. At once she felt sick, but she fought it back and went downstairs. William was sitting at the breakfast table. He didn't look up at her, and his expression still held yesterday's mixture of anger, hurt and bitterness. It was the first time she could remember that rest and reflection had failed to lighten his mood.

'I'm sorry, Dad.' Her voice sounded weary in her ears.

118

'Yes. And does being sorry extend to a promise to leave the Cotton family alone?'

Angharad thought about Harry, trying to measure what he meant to her, and then abandoned the attempt. It was too complicated. Harry filled too many corners of her that had been empty before. She loved him, and it was impossible to imagine not doing so. She was right, and her father was wrong.

'No,' she whispered. 'I can't promise that. I told you, last night.' She was looking at the familiar bright colours of the cereal packet now, dully resenting the good-morning brightness, and she didn't see her father's face.

'In that case, as I told you last night, you are on your own.' His voice was clipped and cold. Angharad knew that he meant it, and she listened to him going away without lifting her head. Funny, she thought, how just a few weeks have changed everything so that there's no chance of going back, ever.

In the oppressive silence in the house the hours dragged by. William and Angharad didn't speak to each other, and she wondered how they would ever cross the breach again.

She sat by the clock and tried to read, but her eyes were on the black telephone on the little table beside it. She had made no arrangement with Harry, and there was no telephone at the cottage. She could do nothing except wait for him to call her. Laura would be home by now. What were they doing? At last, on Sunday morning when she thought she would go mad with the strain, the phone rang. She was sitting beside it, and picked it up half way through the first ring.

'Cefn 339.'

'Why do you sound so frightened?' By contrast Harry's voice was warm and lazy. He was certain of her, of course. Angharad sank bank in her chair, closing her eyes in relief.

'Harry. I . . . it seems such a long time.'

'I know. I couldn't call before. We're at Heulfryn now. Can you come?'

'I'll be there as soon as I can. I want to see you so much. Is Laura with you?'

'Yep. Rather full of her fashionable summer. And looking

119

forward to seeing you. Don't be too long.'

He was gone before Angharad realized they had both forgotten that there was no bus on Sundays. Well, that didn't matter. She would hitch a ride somehow. All she could think of was getting to Harry, and leaving the silent house behind her.

She snatched up a sweater and almost ran to the door. Outside William's study she hesitated for an instant, wondering whether to call out to him. But to tell him what? Chillingly, she remembered *You are on your own*. No, there was no point in telling William where she was going. Angharad closed the door softly behind her and set off down the street.

The morning was bright, but with the thin brightness of autumn, and there was a hint of mist still trapped in the corners where the sun hadn't penetrated. The church bell was ringing, three unvarying insistent peals, 'Come *to* church, come *to* church,' that punctuated every Sunday. She passed several people on their way up to the church, or in the opposite direction to chapel, black hymn books under their arms. Everyone smiled and greeted her, and every greeting turned a knife in her.

'How's your Dad? Must be nice for him to have you home for good.'

'Not going to church, are you, Angharad? Ah, I thought not. Haven't you got the dinner in the oven, then?'

'Lovely morning. Makes you feel glad to be alive, doesn't it?'

Angharad imagined herself walking along here in six or seven months' time, with her winter coat not meeting any more across her stomach. She had seen it happen to one or two other girls, and had ached with pity for them. The sharp eyes had followed them, calculating and speculating, and the gossip had been just as sharp. It would be even worse for her. It hadn't been her own choice, but she had been set a notch above everyone else, with her smart school and now her college place. They would all be shocked when they knew, but there would be relish in it too. Village opinion was like that. Angharad felt sick again, and with it an overwhelming longing to be anonymous. Just so that she could live through

120

whatever was coming to her away from prying eyes.

I can't do it here, she thought, standing still so that the nausea would leave her alone. I can't have a baby here. I'm not brave enough. I'll have to do something. What do people do? Harry would know. The thing to do was to get to Harry, and to let him help her.

At the bottom of the village she saw Elfed the Milk in his pick-up truck, finishing the late Sunday milk-round. He would be driving back home along the Heulfryn road. Angharad ran, waving to him.

'Can I have a lift?' she begged. He looked at her, inquisitive bright blue eyes sunk in red cheeks, and opened the truck door. They settled into the ancient vehicle and drove away with the milk crates rattling behind them.

'I hear you're off to Uni-versity,' Elfed said.

'That's right.' Was she imagining it, or was there sly speculation in his sidelong stare.

'Ah, well. A clever girl like you, you'll be going off and leaving us all behind you.'

'I don't think so,' she said weakly.

*Heard about Angharad Owain? Got herself in trouble. Seventeen years old and supposed to be so clever. Says she's in love with the father. Even my Bronwen's got more sense than that.*

That's what they would be saying. Elfed was definitely staring at her now. She wondered if she was going to make it to the Heulfryn turning before throwing up. 'I haven't decided exactly what I'm going to do, yet,' she told him with a bright, tight smile, and turned her face to look out at trees that were showing the first brown wrinkles of autumn.

Angharad clambered thankfully out of the truck at the bottom of the lane, and with her head down and her hands in her pockets began the steep walk up the hill. She knew that if she looked up she could just see the grey corner of the cottage in its shroud of trees. The brisk scramble in the open air cleared her head, and she felt better as she came up to the peeling old door. Harry's grey van was parked in its usual place, and her heart started thumping with the thought of his closeness.

Angharad pushed the door open and walked in. Her eyes

121

searched for and found Harry's supple height. His face was in shadow, but she thought she should have seen the white flash of his smile. Her gaze flicked to Laura, and was held there.

Laura was sitting at the table, in Angharad's usual chair, tilting it back at a dangerous angle. Her hair was longer, and it waved voluptuously around her face. Angharad thought she looked different. Older, and somehow riper, as if her mouth had widened and her eyes brightened with seeing new things. She was smoking, and her head was encircled with a blue haze.

'Darling Angharad,' she said. Her red mouth was smiling, but her dark eyes were not. They stared at Angharad, perfectly level. Angharad saw that Laura was wearing a creamy blouse with full sleeves caught tight at the wrists. The pale colour made her throat and hands, with silver rings on all the fingers, look even more glowingly tanned. She was wearing a long, full skirt that made Angharad want to tug at her own skimpy hemline.

'Welcome home,' she managed to say.

Laura's eyebrows arched. 'Home?' She looked round the cottage and laughed, a new, throaty laugh. 'I don't think so. It's different, but I think that's all there is to be said for it. Harry, you've got so eccentric.'

'And you've spent too long with the idle rich.' Harry came out of the shadow and Laura's brown fingers caught his arm as he passed her.

'Much too long,' she agreed and Angharad saw their eyes lock for a second. Then Harry turned abruptly away, to Angharad.

'I forgot about the bus. Are you all right? You look very white.' He kissed her cheek, but awkwardly, so that their foreheads bumped.

'I felt sick, but I'm okay now. Can I make myself a cup of tea?' She began to move around the room, finding the tea-caddy and a mug, filling the kettle at the single cold tap and settling it on the gas ring. All the time she felt Laura's level eyes on her back.

'Tell me about France,' she said out of her dry throat. 'You

122

look as though you've had a very glamorous time.'

'Very. And what about you? You seem quite at home here.'

The gas hissed softly, echoed by the wind in the chimney. Angharad understood. Harry hadn't told his sister about their weeks together. Angharad had been invited here this morning on the old basis, as privileged spectator at the ringside of Harry and Laura's perfect match.

Anger with Harry mounted inside her, but when she looked at him, it melted away again. She saw the black hair falling in points over his forehead, and the impatient dark-blue stare. He looked strained, with a trace of uncharacteristic anxiety. Harry would hate this, she thought. His instinct would be to set himself free. She loved him more than ever, and even now she ached for the feel of him.

Laura saw, of course. Sharp-eyed, clever Laura knew at once. She looked coolly from Angharad to the red cover on the narrow bed, and the curve of her mouth tightened.

'Quite at home,' she repeated softly.

Harry's black eyebrows drew together and he stuck his hands in the pockets of his jeans, looking away from both of them.

How could I, Angharad thought, have been so naive? And so dim-wittedly optimistic as to imagine that Laura would let me have him? She'll never let anyone have him. Least of all me. With the realization came the chilling thought that she had lost a friend. And Laura would make a dangerous enemy.

Harry had simply stepped aside. She might have blamed him for that, but she didn't. He had promised her nothing. All through the summer Laura had been the dark shadow between them, and now that she was here, Angharad felt her sight clearing as if it had been fogged until now with happiness.

Harry loved her, she was certain of that. But not to the exclusion of Laura. Laura had shared all his life, up in the mysterious isolation of Llyn Fair, and for some reason that she only partly understood, he couldn't desert her. It would be desertion, of course. It was all or nothing, with Laura. And with Harry she had always had all.

The direction in which Angharad's thoughts were leading her made the hairs prickle warningly at the nape of her neck. She stopped thinking, at once. The two women sat looking at one another. Laura's head was still ringed with lazy blue smoke, and her lovely face was calm. Angharad thought that she had never see her look so beautiful, or so cold.

Well then. If Harry chose to stay aloof, then the battle lines would have to be drawn with Laura. Angharad wanted to fight, she was sure of that.

'Yes,' she answered her. 'Heulfryn does feel like home. It's been a wonderful summer.'

Laura's glance flicked to the window, and the grey rain outside.

'What a pity it's over.'

They might almost have been talking about the weather.

'You've been away such a long time. I want to hear about all the things you've been doing and seeing while Harry and I haven't been further than the other side of The Mountain.'

Laura shrugged gracefully. 'Oh, I enjoyed it. Gaby's parents are absurdly rich, and know everyone. There were lots of parties. On yachts. Around white marble swimming pools. At the Casino. I met all kinds of people. I sat next to George Harrison at dinner. Danced with David Niven. A French racing driver – Jean-Louis Grégoire, you know? – sent me flowers every day for two weeks.' Laura's head turned on her slim neck. 'I even fell in love. With an American movie actor called Richard Latimer.'

At the sink Harry threw the potato peeler with a clatter on to the metal draining board. The corners of Laura's mouth lifted a little, but the look in her eyes didn't change.

'He the handsomest man I've ever seen.'

'He's a prick.'

Angharad saw it. Jealousy in Harry's face, unmistakeable.

'You dont' know him, Harry.'

'I know enough about him.'

'It was Angharad who asked. I was telling her. Go away, if you don't want to hear, and we can have a girls' talk.'

It isn't just me, Angharad thought. She wants to punish Harry too. She must feel that we've both betrayed her. Poor Laura, if everyone she cares for must belong exclusively to her. And I've got something of Harry's now that she can never have. Poor Laura. Poor all of us. It's a mess. A horrible, sickening mess that I can't see how to disentangle. Harry.

'Well then, why don't you two regale me with stories of Heulfryn and Cefn, instead?'

'I don't think we could compete,' Harry said shortly.

It was a miserable meal. Harry ate as if he wanted to attack the food. Angharad consumed what she could, feeling sick and heavy, and pushed the rest endlessly around her plate. Laura didn't touch hers, but she smoked incessantly and went on talking in her bright, brittle voice. There were flashes of the old witty Laura as she described the rigorous French formality of days at the d'Erlangets' villa, and the stark contrast of night-life with Gaby when the pair of them slid into wilder and wilder parties.

'At one of them I saw a model, whose face, incidentally, was on the cover of last month's *Vogue*, walk down the length of the dinner table wearing nothing but bracelets of feathers around her wrists and ankles. At each place she pushed the crystal glass off the table with the tip of her toe. When she reached the end, a man walked barefoot over the broken glass and carried her away. At another party I was handed a Fabergé egg with sugar cubes in it. Very strange things happened after that.'

Harry said, 'How tiresome.'

Laura smiled at him, suddenly a real smile. 'Not exactly tiresome. Repetitive, rather, after a while. I'd rather have been here with you. I don't know why I wasn't.'

Angharad guessed that Laura was very unhappy. It was so like her to veil it with cynical brightness. But if Laura had spent the summer away in a deliberate search for diversions, or new perspectives, then she had failed to find them. She had come home with a luscious, provocative world-weariness, but it was in conflict with a restlessness that Angharad had never seen in her before. Laura had always seemed calm and tranquil. But there was a feverish glitter about her now, and Angharad was frightened of it.

When Angharad put down her knife and fork at last, Laura ground out yet another cigarette.

'And what shall we three do now?' she asked, flicking her little gold lighter again.

'Go back to Llyn Fair,' Harry said. To Angharad he explained, 'My mother and father are leaving tomorrow for a month's holiday. Laura will have gone up to Cambridge by the time they get back, and I . . . have to leave soon, too.' He gestured at the pile of film cans in the corner. It was no more than Angharad had expected in her heart, but she went cold. What would he say, when she told him? What could they do?

Harry made a quick, wry face. 'We're expected. Why don't you come back too, and help us out?'

'Yes,' Angharad said firmly. 'I'll come.'

Laura gave no reaction. She was rolling her lighter idly across the table.

They drove to Llyn Fair pressed together in the front of the grey van. Laura smelt of some exotic, musky scent, and the bare skin of her arm against Angharad's felt hot and dry. Angharad's thoughts went back to the morning two years ago, when they had sat like this in Joe's Jaguar, laughing and singing to radio music. Had they all been happy, then? It was hard to believe that it was Laura who had been her friend. Had she really known this hard, bright stranger as well as she knew herself? Or as well as she knew Harry, now?

They came to the crossroads where she had first seen him, long-haired at the wheel of his gleaming car, and had mistaken him for Laura. As they began the climb up to Llyn Fair where he had shown off his driving and she had refused to be frightened, she saw his head turn a fraction and knew that he was thinking of it too. They passed the white barred gate, under the dripping tunnel of trees, and came out into the grey light at the end of the valley. The lake was flat and hostile, pockmarked with falling rain. The rain had darkened the slate and stone of the old house too, so that it looked grim against the black hillside. Harry stopped the van and in the silence that followed the rain drummed against the roof.

Laura looked sadly out at the grey veils. The brittle armour dissolved for an instant.

Almost in a whisper she said, 'Why does everything always have to change for the worse? Even us?'

Harry looked past Angharad to Laura's shadowed eyes and the melancholy twist at the corner of her mouth. Gently he said, 'Laura. Of course there has to be change. How could we stay here in this valley for ever?'

There was no answer, and the three of them sat imprisoned by the insistent rain.

'How could we? You'll go to Cambridge, and Angharad will go off too, and there'll be a thousand new faces and new things for both of you. All of us.' His voice was hollow, empty of its usual firm conviction.' And you know that I have to leave. If I stay Joe will try to suck me into his disgusting business. Just by being here I'm condoning it . . .'

Laura interrupted him savagely, and Angharad knew that for the moment she was forgotten. 'Don't try to pretend that's why.'

'Everything changes,' Harry repeated. 'It has to.'

Laura's hands fell to her sides and her shoulders sagged. Her voice was so low that Angharad barely caught the words. 'If only it didn't.'

She climbed out of the cramped space and walked away with the wind tugging at her pale, elegant clothes. Harry's fingers tightened on the wheel. He was looking after Laura and Angharad couldn't read his face, but she caught the impression of intense frustration and despair. Tentatively she put out her hand and touched his arm and at once he turned to her, his face softening.

'I'm sorry,' he said, attempting a laugh, but Angharad knew that whatever the truth was it couldn't be laughed away.

The implications frightened her, but she simply said, 'Harry, why didn't you tell her?'

'I think you know why.' His voice was low. Then, with a

sudden challenge that made him like Laura, 'Tell her exactly what, anyway?'

Only that we love each other. Only that I'm as important to you a she is. I must be. Especially now. Angharad could have cried out, but instead she kept her voice even and answered, 'About me. It wasn't fair to let her guess for herself. It hurt her.'

Harry tore the keys out of the ignition and flung the door open so that a damp gust of wind blew in at them.

'Nothing's fair. Do you still expect it to be? And I don't think, now, that there's any way to avoid hurting. Perhaps we should have thought of that earlier. Perhaps I should.' Then he was walking away from her, his shoulders hunched.

'Harry, she's only your *sister*!' Angharad shouted after him, but he gave no sign that he had heard her.

Joe Cotton came out of the house and stood on the verandah under the yellowing leaves of honeysuckle. Harry was standing beside him when Angharad reached them, inches taller than his father. Joe seemed to have shrunk, and spread sideways, and the grey of his flannel suit reflected up into his face. A little of his prosperous vitality had ebbed away, but Angharad thought it made him seem more rather than less threatening. Her fear and dislike of him was as intense as ever.

Joe took his cigar out of his mouth and stared at her. 'Mary Owain's daughter. Tell me, does your father know you're here this time?'

Coolly she told him, 'He does, as a matter of fact.' Harry turned sharply to stare at her but she passed them both as if they were standing aside to let her into the house. In the hallway was a huge, overblown arrangement of flowers, chrysanthemums and teasels and sprays of copper beech leaves. Monica Cotton was tweaking the last leaves into place, her head on one side. She greeted Angharad with ordinary civility, and it seemed out of place in this distorted day. Behind her mother, Laura was pacing up and down as if in a cage.

'I think, as it's so vile everywhere,' she said suddenly, 'we should play bridge. Don't you?'

'If you like, darling,' Monica said.

Harry was sharp. 'No, we won't.'

'I'm sure Angharad will make up a four?' Laura's voice was sweet. Angharad hated the game and played it badly, but her protestations were ignored. She was propelled to the table, and to her horror found herself partnering Joe. As she sat and watched Laura dealing the cards with deft, snapping movements, she was swept by bewilderment and panic. Suddenly she had lost all clue as to what she was doing here, so clearly unwanted and out of place. The nausea of the morning came back, and her chest and throat tightened so that she could hardly breathe. These people were strangers.

'Angharad?' The three faces were looking inquiringly at her. She stared down weakly at her cards.

'No bid.'

'Really?' Laura was silky. 'No bid at all?'

The game moved jerkily. Angharad became conscious of Harry to one side of them, standing with his arms outspread along the marble mantelpiece. She looked pleadingly towards him, but couldn't see his face through the nauseated blur around her. All she could sense was his eyes on her and then the movement as they turned to Laura. He was watching them both, held here in this civilized tableau. She wondered wildly how they looked to him, whether he was making comparisons. Her hair against Laura's. Her skin against Laura's. What she meant to him, against what his sister meant. She felt suffocatingly, sickeningly jealous, and convinced that Harry never would be hers. Never had been.

The conviction settled like a black knot in the pit of her stomach. *You're on your own, now.*

She had been wrong to come here. Mistaken determination to hang on, to go on being with Harry. Trying to prove something. She longed to escape, not to run home because there was nothing there, but to get outside, into the fresh air and emptiness.

The rubber came to an end and they started on another. The afternoon would never, ever be over. She would have to go on sitting here, like a butterfly pinned to a cushion, for the rest of her life.

But then Joe was totting the scores up on his pad. He was an excellent player, but Angharad's partnership had defeated him. Laura and Monica won easily. Laura leant back in her seat and said, 'That was fun.' In her relief that it was over, the sarcasm washed over Angharad.

The relief was short-lived. The day went dragging on, and she had no idea how to get away. At tea-time Joe began drinking whisky and Harry measured glass for glass with him. Laura made complicated cocktails for herself and her mother, clinking the glass and the silver shaker with little, icy noises. Angharad refused everything. Once she excused herself and went into the little cloakroom off the hallway to press a cold towel against her forehead. Her face stared back at her from the mirror, dead white and filmed faintly with sweat. Her eyes looked twice their normal size.

Dinner came next, around the table where she had sat and looked through the candlelight at Harry in his white jacket. She had thought that she understood his anger, and his confusion, and had fallen in love with him. What did that mean, now?

Watching the four of them, Angharad saw with unwilling fascination how the balance between them had changed. Harry and Laura held all the strength now. They sat opposite each other, as alike as reflections in a glass.

Angharad put down her knife, and her hand was shaking. Somehow, she would come between them. She must do. Not for herself, or even for what was happening inside her. But for Harry's sake. Even if he couldn't see that for himself.

'Are you all right, Angharad?' He was asking her again, and his eyes were concerned.

With an effort she said, 'I'm very tired. Perhaps after dinner you could take me home?'

'Of course.'

Down the table she saw Laura smile, a little, tight smile.

At last the meal was over. Joe had drunk a bottle of wine with his food and his eyes were half shut now, embedded in puffy flesh. He wouldn't look at Angharad as she said goodbye, but repeated, 'So like your mother. Aren't you?' She jerked her head away, not wanting to hear any more.

Monica said something absently, her eyes on her husband.

Laura came out with them on to the verandah. The rain had stopped and the air was cool and damp. The two women stood and faced each other.

'Good night, Angharad. We must have a long, long talk before I go to Cambridge. And you to – where is it?'

Angharad reminded her of her unfashionable redbrick university.

'Oh, yes. Before that.'

What a snob she is, Angharad thought. And how unhappy they all are, with their affluent life in their lovely house. No wonder Harry needed to escape so badly. How can he let himself be caught up in it again now? Of course he must go away again. Except that now there was the baby. Their baby. Harry's baby.

They were walking towards the van. Laura called after them, 'I'll still be up when you get back, Harry.' Then Angharad heard the crunch of her heels turning on the gravel. She sank into her seat, shivering.

The van was noisy and Harry was driving it too fast. There was no point in trying to shout over the engine roar. Angharad sat huddled in her place, trying to rehearse in her head how she would tell him.

Harry, I . . .

At the old fountain Harry stopped and they faced each other in the spreading pool of silence. He rubbed his hands over his face and the tight lines showed clearly.

'You told your father?' he asked gently.

'Yes.'

'And?'

'He was very angry. He wanted me to promise that I wouldn't ever see you again. I told him that I couldn't, and if he made me choose between you I wouldn't choose him. And so he told me I'm on my own, now.'

Harry was looking away, out into the dark. 'Families.' He almost spat the word. 'For perfect isolation. Poor Angharad. At least I had Laura to be lonely with.'

'We haven't been lonely this summer. We've had each other . . .'

But Harry didn't hear her. He was staring into the blackness beyond the windows with a driven look that she had never seen before. He drew a deep, ragged breath, and then, surprisingly, began to talk, the words tumbling out as if he had kept them dammed up all through their weeks together.

'Angharad, listen to me. You've given me the happiest summer of my life. It's been a kind of happiness that I don't deserve. I've taken it because it was so perfect I couldn't stop myself. And because I saw that it was making you happy too, and I kept putting off this moment. I love you, Angharad. That's not very much, but I do. I'd do anything not to hurt you.'

Angharad tried to break in, to tell him that she loved him too and that together they could face anything the future held, but he pressed his fingers against her lips.

'Please listen. I have to go away now. Right away, for quite a long time, I think. If I stay here any longer, I'll never be able to leave, and that terrifies me more than anything. I'd lose you, anyway.'

He turned to her and took her face in his hands, and kissed her so hard that her lips were bruised against her teeth. 'Love. My love, Angharad. It's for your sake too, don't you understand?

'I've got to ask you for two things I don't deserve, but I believe you'll still do them for me because you're the truest and most generous person I've ever known. I can't bear to leave you because I know it will hurt you. But I must, or it will hurt you more.'

Angharad saw the glitter in his eyes, and knew that Harry was on the edge of tears. There was a pain inside him that she had only half guessed at, and the mystery of it rose up around her more terrifyingly than all the other fears besetting her. With the fear came the certainty that she loved him deeply, and that she would never love anyone else in the same way.

'Two things.' Harry's voice had thickened with emotion, and his hands gripping hers were shaking. 'First, trust me. I haven't done anything to make you believe you should, I

132

know that, so I can only ask. I promise I will come back. When everything is clear and honest again, I'll come back to you. It may be that you will have somebody else, and you'll be so happy that I'll be completely forgotten. That will be my loss, my darling. But I will come back to you, and then you can decide whether you still want me.'

Again, he moved to silence Angharad before she could interrupt him. 'The second thing. To forgive me, if you can.' Harry was staring into her eyes, and holding on to her as if he would never let go. 'Do you understand why?'

Numbly Angharad looked back at him, trying to find the words to tell him that she didn't. All she knew was that she was going to have his baby, and needed him with her.

The sweeping headlights of a passing car caught something that still glittered at the corner of Harry's eye. He turned away from her to hide it, and then buried his head in his arms cradled against the steering wheel.

'Oh God, I don't think you do. I can't tell you why. *I can't tell you, Angharad.* Just believe that I wouldn't leave you if I didn't have to.'

His insistence was terrifying, and inexplicable. Angharad heard herself say 'Don't go. I need you. I want to tell you . . .'

'*Please.*'

Harry's passionate desperation overtook her own. Heavily, Angharad's hands dropped from his arms. They folded together in her lap, over her stomach. Harry wouldn't look at her now, and as she watched the loved angles of his profile and head, Angharad felt the walls of isolation sliding around her like thick sheets of glass. Harry wasn't part of herself, after all. He was just somebody else, another person. She really was alone.

Angharad couldn't have told him about the baby now, even if she had been able to find the words.

'All right. Whatever you want. Go, then.' She said it mechanically, her attention devoted to the movements that would take her out of the van, away from here, and up the hill to Cefn and the watching eyes. She groped, and found her way. Harry lunged after her, and his mouth burned against the back of her neck. She thought she heard him call her name as she ran, across the road and into the shelter of the trees. But it didn't come again, and as she half ran, half stumbled up the steep hill, she heard him drive away.

It was the worst week of her life. Sometimes Angharad thought that she was going mad as her mind circled round and round the same treadmill. Harry had withdrawn from her. Not forever, perhaps, but until he and Laura had learned to live without the unhealthy dependence that they all recognized. Angharad saw the sense of it, and would have loved him for his strength of mind. If only they hadn't begun by being so careless together. And now she was pregnant. Her thoughts rolled on around the mill to dwell on the comma of tissue growing irrevocably inside her. What was it like now? When would it have fingers, and toes? Eyelids, and eyelashes? Brutally, she made herself think about abortion and the lurid imaginings made her physically sick. How could she do that? Even if she knew where to go. Didn't it take money, lots of money, and she had none? Perhaps Harry could help her with that, at least. And so on, round and round interminably. A week went by, and then one morning she woke up with the conviction that she must go and see Harry, to try once more to talk to him before he went away and it was too late. She had no way of knowing for sure, but somehow she thought that he hadn't left yet. Perhaps it would be a way of precipitating something. Anything. Better than going on like this, with only her own thoughts and her father's angry averted face for company. They had hardly spoken to each other. Even Gwyn looked at her with a puzzled, anxious expression and said nothing. Aunty Gwyn was on her father's side, of course. Why should she not be?

Angharad pulled her clothes on and looked out of the window. It seemed as if it had been raining all week, and it was raining again now. It hardly mattered.

Once she had decided that she would see him, she could focus on nothing else. Briefly she wondered how to get to Heulfryn, and then thought of Gwyn's bicycle. Immediately she went up to the old schoolhouse and tapped on the studio door. There was no answer. Gwyn must have gone shopping on the early bus, but her old black bicycle stood propped up against the school wall. With only the thought of seeing Harry in her head, Angharad snatched it up and rode away The fine rain misted in her hair and over her clothes but she ignored it. She swooped down the village street and the long hill beyond with a sudden sense of freedom. The road wound away and she leaned forward, feeling the wind keen in her face. Someone hooted and waved at her, but she swerved away and pedalled on blindly. Almost at once, it seemed, the wide sweep of land where Mr Ellis and his dogs herded the sheep rose in front of her. Beautiful patterns, Harry had said.

There was the cottage. She dropped her bicycle into the hedge and ran towards the door. An empty space where the van usually stood. The brown door was shut, and a chained padlock held the hasp to the staple in the frame. Almost sobbing with frustration, Angharad pressed her face to the smeared windows and looked inside. The flagged floor was swept bare, the room completely empty. Harry had gone.

Angharad sank down against the wet bank and pressed the heels of her hands against her eyes. Llyn Fair. He must be there, alone with Laura. Of course. Joe and Monica had gone away. She didn't stop to think. She picked up the bicycle again and wheeled away.

The road stretched on interminably. She would never have believed that Llyn Fair was so far away, and she was moving at a snail's pace. Her clothes were wet and cold, but she was sweating and the palms of her hands slid on the handlebars. All thoughts of what she would do when she got there drained away, and she focussed grimly on the simple struggle to keep moving. Lack of food and sleepless nights had taken their toll, and she felt as weak as a child now.

It seemed to take a lifetime, but at last she was at the crossroads. The hill was steep here and her breath came in painful gasps. She lifted her hand to push the hair back from her face and found that it was streaming with wet.

She had driven along here with Harry, laughing, dazzled by him. How long ago?

Now, here. Llyn Fair in black letters on the white gate, and the avenue of trees before the open sky, the splash of falling water and ducks skimming over the still silver reaches.

Angharad looked and saw with a throb of relief that Harry's grey van was neatly parked beside a new red mini. That would be Laura's, of course. The tame goose came waddling over the pebbles towards her, honking, but the house looked silent and closed. Angharad let the bicycle fall with a crash to the gravel. Her legs and head felt as if they would float apart, and an agonizing stitch stabbed at her side. With her hand pressed to it, she stumbled to the front door under the dripping white metalwork of the verandah. Locked.

Angharad stood for a moment in the shelter, biting her lip and thinking. Then she remembered Harry's old room over the stable block. That's where he would be, not in the confines of Joe's house. She walked round the end gable of the old house and across the little brick-paved yard. Over there in the kitchen garden, Harry had picked herbs for her on that very first day.

At the flight of wooden steps leading up to the loft door, Angharad reached out to the handrail to steady herself. She was shaking as if in the grip of a high fever, and she had the sensation of being outside herself, watching detachedly as she padded up the steps to the door. It was on the latch, and swung open to her touch. In the middle of the floor were boxes, labelled and packed. Bare patches on the walls showed where pictures had hung. Angharad turned her head to the arch that led through to the bedroom. Silently she walked across to it.

Harry and Laura were in bed together.

At first she thought it was Harry alone, horribly distorted, but then she saw.

They were making love. Their skin was exactly the same colour, and the black hair tangled together. Harry's eyes were shut and his face was twisted, baring his teeth, as if he was in terrible pain. Sometimes when he had made love to Angharad he had been violent, but he had always turned to gentleness again. With Laura there was no tenderness. He was driving himself savagely into her like a weapon, as if he longed to hurt her. Angharad saw the sweat gather on his shoulders and then run down his back. He was groaning, and the groans sounded as if they were being dragged from him under torture. Laura's hands were at his hips, drawing him deeper into her. His back was scored with the long tracks of her nails. Her head was flung back and her arched throat was exposed to Harry's mouth. The crimson marks of his kisses stood out on it like livid scars.

Angharad's hand flew up to her mouth to stifle a scream, but they were oblivious of her. Harry was covered in sweat now. He moved faster and more desperately and Laura's mouth opened in a soundless cry. And then he moaned and buried his dark face against his sister's breasts. His body bucked over hers, and then drove down a last time with such force that it must have torn her. Laura's scream of release answered him, curdling in her throat, and her eyelids fluttered before her eyes snapped open.

For long seconds they shivered in each other's arms. The stillness in the room seemed to spill outwards to envelop the whole world. Then, with an abrupt movement, Harry rolled away. He wouldn't look at Laura but Angharad heard him whisper,

'I love you. Oh God, I hate you.'

Laura was looking past him. As soon as her eyes opened, she saw Angharad and the sight seemed to double the intensity of pleasure that swept through her. When it was done and Harry slid away from her, she smiled, and the smile was pure exultant triumph.

You see? it said. You see? Did you ever think that you could compete with me? With this? Did he ever do it to you like this?

Now Harry's eyes were open. He stared in disbelief and then Angharad saw the film of anger clouding them. He pulled himself upright and faced her with such venom that she believed he hated her as well.

'How dare you? I told you not to come prying here into what doesn't concern you. Well, and are you happy now that you really know? Oh Christ, you must be so stupid.' Angharad backed away, her fingers still pressed into her mouth. Harry called after her. 'Don't get yourself wound up in this, do you hear me? Stay away from it, keep yourself clean.'

His hand came up to his face, white-knuckled, and in an instant Angharad understood the rage and revulsion tearing at him. She almost ran to him, crying that she didn't care, that she knew Laura's power in just the same way, and that together they would win out over her.

But then, fatally, her eyes left Harry's haunted face and she saw Laura still smiling her triumphant smile. Her thin brown fingers curled on her brother's bare shoulder and her tumbled black hair fell against him. She hadn't spoken a word.

Angharad swung around, and once her back was turned to them, she couldn't bring herself to look back again. A wall of hateful silence rose behind her as she ran away, thudding down the wooden steps and over the warm red bricks. Gwyn's bicycle lay where she had left it, one wheel still quivering. Angharad lifted up the heavy frame with a wrench that jarred her bones and rode out of the valley as if it were the jaws of hell. Behind her the grey water lapped on expressionlessly at the jetty and the house stood, blind-eyed, against the high dark hill.

# CHAPTER SIX

The rain slashed cruelly into her face. Angharad felt the sopping weight of her clothes pulling at her as she struggled against the wind. Yet in a way it helped, and mutely she thanked the driving rain and the gale that fought to throw her sideways. By giving everything she had to the effort of moving doggedly onwards she could close the eyes inside her head against what she had just seen.

Keeping going was enough, so long as it was away from Llyn Fair, enough to block the knowledge that she had no idea where she was going, or why. She didn't think about it, but simple habit took her back towards Cefn, and at last she saw the stone fountain at the bottom of the long hill. The last stretch of road defeated her and she got off the old bicycle to push. Her legs were as heavy as lead, and she was shaking with long uncontrollable shivers. The soaking strands of hair clung to her cheeks and her fingers were too numb to push them back.

At last, as she came up the village street, she heard people calling cheerfully to her.

'Not much of a day for a bike-ride,' and 'You'd be better off in a rowing boat.'

Angharad was too exhausted and too stunned with shock even to look up. All she saw was the familiar contours of the street and the glittering, rotating spokes, sending out little cascades of spray as they turned round and round. Outside the old schoolhouse she was propping the bike up against the wall once more, still without a conscious motivating thought, when the studio door opened. Gwyn stared out at her.

'Dear God, Angharad. Get inside here at once.'

Angharad stumbled in after her and the cosy warmth struck her like a blow. Robbed of the drive to keep moving, to go on making her escape, painful awareness washed over her.

139

Harry and Laura. The arch, neatly framing the low bed against the warm red walls. Rain drumming against the windows, making a safe, secret world inside. Harry and Laura, locked together like two halves of a puzzle, and herself with her hand jammed against her mouth to stifle a scream that never came.

Years – how many years? – of deluding herself. She hadn't known, yet she had always known. She had herself so nearly fitted with them both. And what else, in truth, could their perfect closeness ever have meant? Angharad closed her eyes and felt herself swaying. All summer, then, Harry had been cheating her. Playing with her, to pass the time until Laura came back and he could turn in again to their shared secret landscape. A landscape that was blacker and more violent, but yet more fascinating, than anything she could have shared with him herself. The terrible, potent excitement of taboos, Angharad thought. She had tasted just a little of that herself, with Laura. But while their relationship had indeed been innocent because it had hurt or threatened nobody, this one was different. She had been the victim of it herself.

No.

Even in the saddle of her shock and despair, another part of Angharad sprang to Harry's defence. He hadn't deceived her. She hadn't asked him for the truth, even though she had felt Laura's shadow falling coldly between them. Harry had never lied to her. He had never promised anything, and he had taken nothing except what had been freely given because they loved each other.

And now, because of that . . . Unthinkably, assaulted by so much else, Angharad had almost forgotten about the baby.

Gwyn caught her before she fell. 'What have you been doing to yourself?' Her aunt's voice was harsh with anxiety. Angharad shook her head wearily, but she clung to Gwyn as her aunt's arms came around her. Gwyn had comforted her just like this after all the tiny bumps and shocks of childhood. At least, she thought, she still had one friend left. Until Gwyn found out, of course, as she would have to.

Angharad let herself be led into the bathroom. Gwyn

made her strip off the wet clothes and sit in a steaming hot bath. Her hair was briskly towelled dry, and she dressed herself again in the dry clothes that Gwyn handed to her. When she was sitting in the chair by the old coke stove, which was burning unseasonably early, Gwyn brought her a mug of hot milk. Angharad tasted it and found that it was liberally laced with whisky. The warmth spread hypnotically through her, and with an edge of hysteria, Angharad almost laughed. The old nursery standby topped up with invisible reserves of potent spirit. It was a perfect symbol for Gwyn herself. Of course she could talk to Gwyn. She had been a fool not to do it before now. Gwyn swung the heavy coke hod into the red mouth of the stove and fed it with a dusty rattle of fuel. Then she replaced the hod and brushed the dust sharply from her hands.

'Harry Cotton?' she asked.

'Dad told you?'

'Not at all. But I'm glad you had the courage to tell him yourself before he found it out. It must have been hard for you. I know what he's like now, but it'll make the difference in the end.'

I wouldn't have done, Angharad thought bitterly, if the other thing hadn't prompted me.

'Poor duck, did you think you could keep it a secret up here? Cath Jones saw you at the Mill, and told me. And you were with him in the Pandy Inn on the night of the August Meeting, weren't you?'

Of course the eyes had seen her. She had been too busy being happy to notice them.

Escape. She couldn't stay here, to be watched and judged. Where to? And to do what in the world, without Harry?

Angharad looked up at her aunt, and Gwyn winced to see the strange mixture of bare hurt and steely determination in eyes that only a few weeks ago had been clear and untroubled.

'I'm pregnant,' Angharad said. 'And I can't see him again. Ever. Don't ask me why.'

Never, she would never tell anybody why. The thought came to her that the hateful secret was an unbreakable yoke

141

that held her to the Cottons for ever, even if she never set eyes on them again. They did belong together, the three of them, in their misfortune.

Gwyn flexed her old hands on the high guard around the stove and stared down at the knobby red joints.

'Poor thing,' she said. 'My poor Angharad. I wish . . .' But Gwyn had learned to be too practical to indulge herself with wishing. Instead she said, as matter-of-fact as if it was something that she discussed every day; 'It needn't be the end of the world for you, you know. We'll see if we can work something out together. No good thinking about Dr Hughes, of course. Now, where should we go?'

Angharad saw that Gwyn had seized gratefully on the most obvious answer. She tried it out for herself. Abortion. Quick, sterile, and utterly final. The little mistake gone, and soon forgotten about. For all the world to see she would be clever Angharad Owain again, back on the well-oiled tracks, parcelling up her books and papers before setting off for college as they had all expected that she would. The whispers about Harry Cotton would soon die away again.

But to herself, inside, it wouldn't be like that at all. Hideous images rose up in front of her again, of blood and silent screams that never would be heard. Little fingers that would never uncurl, because of her cowardice. She couldn't let them rip Harry's baby out of her. It was all she had left of him now, the only thing that she could allow herself out of her love for Harry that was still the most potent and most beautiful thing in the distorted world.

She wanted the baby. As she sat huddled in the big chair beside Gwyn's purring stove, she felt the first primeval stirring of love for her son.

'I won't have an abortion. I want to keep the baby.' The tone of her voice left no leeway for persuasion.

'I think I can understand that.' Tolerant, liberal, but deeply moral Aunty Gwyn. 'You'll give the baby up for adoption, you mean?'

She didn't mean that at all, but she would cross that hurdle when she came to it.

'I can't stay here. I couldn't bear it, for Dad's sake or my own, with everyone looking and talking. I'll have to go away. Stay away.' The hugeness of the decisions she was making towered ahead of her. She knew that she was cutting herself off, severing herself from everything in life that had promised happiness and normality.

'And so what will you do?' Gwyn was very gentle with her.

'Go to London,' Angharad improvised desperately. The farthest, biggest, most anonymous place possible. She could lose herself there. 'Find somewhere to live, a bedsitter. Get a job of some kind. I can cook for someone. Be a housekeeper, perhaps.'

'Can you, with a baby coming?' She was still so gentle that Angharad wanted to cry. It felt like the first gentleness anyone had shown her for so long, and she knew it would be almost the last.

'I can work until I have to stop. After that there are places you can go to, aren't there? Anything will be better than staying here.'

'I can help you a little. I wish it was more. I can give you two hundred pounds now, and I'll send whatever else I can. There just isn't a great fortune in *siwgr* and *llaeth* pots.'

The two women stared at each other, and Angharad saw the unfamiliar sparkle of tears in Gwyn's eyes. Her aunt's tears swept away the last of her own defences and she cried too, with her face pressed against the knobby wool of Gwyn's old cardigan and with Gwyn's hand stroking her wet hair.

'You have chosen the hardest way,' Gwyn said, but Angharad shook her head.

'No. It isn't a choice. It's the only thing I can do. What . . . what shall I tell Dad?'

Gwyn sighed. 'You're asking me for advice that I shouldn't try to give. But, if you want it, I think you should just go quietly away. Leave your father to me, and when the time is right, I'll tell him what has happened. You know, he's always been a victim of his own sense of failure, rightly or wrongly. You must see that he will think of your choice as an extension of that, if you confront him with it now. It will only make him say, and do, things that he will regret.'

Angharad nodded dumbly, thinking of William on the

evening when she had confessed to loving Harry.

'But he loves you very much, and he will miss you equally. Once the shock and anger are over, he'll want you back as much as I do. And the child, too. When you are ready to come. I hope that's what will happen, Angharad.'

Angharad was looking out of the tall schoolroom windows into the rain. She had the chill sense that all her boats were burned. Gwyn's advice did no more than confirm her own feelings but, in her secret heart, she might have been hoping for something else. An escape loophole that would mean not having to confront the loneliness yawning in front of her. But there was nothing, and she would have to face what was coming.

'Well,' she said dully, 'it won't take me long to get ready. The sooner the better, I suppose.' It will be easier not to be here, where everything shouts Harry at me, she added silently.

Gwyn stroked her hair and said again, 'Poor love. Are you quite, quite certain that you want to carry this baby?'

Angharad's chin lifted, firmly pointed. 'I want him.'

She was leaving Cefn, the grey and blue huddle of houses against the long brown back of The Mountain, with its sharp mixture of loved familiarity and dull constriction. She was leaving Harry and Laura, and the thought of that wrung her heart more than the memory of what they had done to her. But she was carrying Harry's baby with her. She wouldn't, after all, be quite alone. Angharad was no fool. She knew that it would be a hard struggle. Yet, somehow, she would make it work for both of them.


Angharad had been to London only two or three times before in her life. This time she arrived with a single heavy suitcase and outside Euston Station she looked at the traffic and the pervading pall of soot with new eyes. This is where I live, she told herself, sniffing the acrid air. People bumped against her as they passed, but none of them glanced at her. She was as inconspicuous as one of the gnarled, scabby pigeons on the exhausted grass of the square. If she had been cherishing the faint hope that Harry might come after her, the hope died

144

as she watched the flow of commuters to the station. Harry would never find her in so many millions. Nobody would.

Angharad went to Earl's Court, for the simple reason that she had heard of it. Here she found a tall, dingy hotel with a red neon sign in one of the front windows saying 'Vacancies'. She took a 'family room' because that was all they said they had, and paid for it in advance with the first slice of the money that Gwyn had given her. There were two vast double beds and a third, child-size one, crammed almost under the washbasin. On her first evening in London, Angharad sat on the little bed, eating a sandwich supper and keeping her fear at bay with a list of priorities.

One, to find somewhere cheap to live. Gwyn's money wouldn't last long at this rate.

Two, to find a job. For the same reason.

Tomorrow she would buy newspapers and read the classifieds. She could look at the cards in newsagents' windows, too, if such homely things existed here. Angharad stretched out on the bed, hearing the roar of traffic out in the Earl's Court Road through the wedged-shut window as if it was in the room with her. The noise pursued her into her dreams when at last she fell asleep.

Angharad worked hard at her objectives. She ran through the advertisements for rooms in the early edition of the *Evening Standard*, and stood in a grimy booth at the tube station with a pile of change ready to make her calls. Quickly she discovered that most of the ads were placed by accommodation agencies, and began a wearying round of registering with them. The tube journeys and the walks to and fro were endless and yielded nothing. The few cards in newsagents' windows offered nothing but French lessons.

The search for a home took five days, interrupted by a wet Sunday when she sat for hours in her family room and fought to keep the despair at bay. Images of Harry kept coming cruelly back to her, lying with his face close to hers or laughing across the table at Heulfryn. The pain they brought was physical, doubling her up like savage cramps.

Angharad felt continually sick and her instinct was to stop eating to save money. But for the baby's sake she forced herself to drink pints of milk, and carefully reckoned up the valuable calories in bread, cheese and apples. She knew that she was physically strong, but she would risk nothing.

Then, on the sixth day, she found something. The room was on the first floor front of a tall, peeling stucco house not far from her hotel. It had been carved with hardwood partitions from a once-grand drawing-room. Half of an intricate and beautiful plaster cornice decorated the distant ceiling. The little room was higher than it was long, and was just wide enough to take a narrow bed beside the door. But the walls were freshly white-painted, and the tall, graceful window at the end made it airy and light. There was a spartan bathroom across the linoleum landing, and a kitchen cubby-hole, both to be shared with the other occupants of the floor.

'Four pounds ten a week,' the landlady said, looking not unkindly at her. 'Young ladies only. I live in the basement, and I stand no nonsense. But if you need anything, I'll help if I can.'

Angharad believed her. 'I'll take it,' she said, and paid her deposit and two weeks' rent in advance. Her reserves of cash were dwindling with frightening speed.

Finding a job was even more difficult. There were advertisements for catering jobs, but nearly all for kitchen porters or washers-up. It might yet come to that, Angharad thought grimly, remembering Old Lil at the sink in her wellingtons, but not just yet. She bought the trade papers and ringed the possible vacancies. Yet again and again her lack of experience and qualifications eliminated her before even the first round.

She went for one interview, for a job in the kitchens of a big restaurant chain near Leicester Square, but it was first thing in the morning and the sight of the huge, cylindrical metal bins overflowing with potato peelings and scraps of congealed food made her feel so ill that she had almost to run away.

Two weeks passed, and Angharad felt the tide of panic rising. She had almost resolved to give up the stupid pursuit of a cook's job. It was absurd and illogical to want one so

146

much when even the sight of food made her feel sick. Surely she could be something else? A filing clerk, or a telephonist? Yet she promised herself over and over again 'just one more day', and went on scanning the catering columns with stubborn hope.

One morning she found herself in the Fulham Road. It was a bright day at the very beginning of October, and the plane trees were showing a mixture of yellow and ochre with the dusty green. Angharad's attention had been caught by a restaurant frontage, and she had stopped to look at it because it was so pretty.

It was painted white, and the pavement was shaded with a scalloped green awning. Two round-clipped bay trees stood in terracotta pots on either side of a white front door with winking brass plates. 'Duff's' was painted in big white letters on the wide window, and the window boxes underneath it were full of late scarlet geraniums. A very young waiter in a white jacket was sweeping the step. He looked carefully to see that not a speck of dust remained, and saw Angharad. He smiled at her, and she noticed that he was very dark, probably Italian, with even white teeth.

Without giving herself time to think, she stepped up to him. 'I suppose,' she said diffidently, 'they don't need an extra kitchen hand in there?'

The waiter looked at her again. It was so long since she had thought about herself in relation to new people that she was astonished to see admiration kindle in his black eyes.

'Who knows?' He shrugged easily and jerked his thumb over his shoulder. 'You could try asking chef. Through the restaurant and past the double doors at the back.' He watched her go, twirling his broom and with his lips pursed in a whistle.

Angharad went inside. The room was lofty and cool. The floor was white terrazzo tiles, and there were baskets of lush ferns in the corners and hanging from the ceiling. Another waiter was laying up the wide-spaced tables for lunch, white starched cloths over green ones.

Angharad nodded at him and marched determinedly past. The swing doors into the kitchen were sparkling white too.

She pushed them open and found herself in a wide tiled space hung with scoured pans. A man in a spotless starched toque, white apron and chef's trousers was standing at a scrubbed table, slicing raw steak into melting pink curls.

'*Oui?*'

Angharad licked her lips. Her heart was thumping because this was, suddenly, so very important.

'I'm looking for a job. *Commis* chef, actually. I'm quite experienced. I've worked in a restaurant in Wales, completely responsible . . .' She exaggerated, but carefully. The chief listened with Gallic scepticism.

'Mmm. And where did you train?'

'Well, actually I haven't . . .' No good after all. But the swing doors behind them opened and someone came in. The chef put down his long, sharp knife and straightened his apron. Angharad looked, and saw a very tall young man in a dark suit. He had a pink, healthy face, short-cropped curling fair hair and a deeply-cleft chin.

'What's this, Pierre?'

'A young lady looking for a job. This,' he said to Angharad, 'is Mister Duff.'

The proprietor prowled round the table looking at her. He had very keen pale blue eyes. 'Well now. What can you do?'

Angharad started off again, but he cut her short. 'Tell me this. We've got a box of fine apples here, and we need a pudding for today, let's say. You know our menu, presumably, or you wouldn't waltz in here out of the blue to ask for a job. So, what will you make for us?'

Angharad's heart sank. Too clearly, there would be no hoodwinking Mr Duff. Frantically she pieced together a picture of a restaurant. Slick, but not pretentious. Young, prosperous clientele, like the owner himself. Healthy, with no taste for over-ornate food.

'Tarte aux pommes,' she said firmly. 'Simple pâté sucrée, apples sliced and poached in butter and sugar with a hint of vanilla. No glaze, just the pan juices swirled with a little calvados. Served hot. Cream, if they insist.'

Mr Duff laughed merrily. 'You pinched all that from Mrs David. But it's not a bad answer. Go on, then.'

Angharad stared but he nodded amiably at the marble pastry slab. 'Pierre will give you what you need. Or, wait. tell me first how many tarts you'd make. Forty-five covers for lunch.'

She was home at last. A summer of buying for Y Gegin Fach had made her confident of that. She reckoned quickly, and told him.

'Good. But one will do for now.'

Angharad set to work, and Mr Duff sat on a tall kitchen stool munching cheerfully at one of the apples. Pierre went quietly on with his work, but she knew that he was watching her too as she dripped in the iced water, moulded the pastry with quick, light fingertips, remembering Mrs Price at Y Gegin Fach. That seemed half a lifetime ago now. She left the pastry to rest while she prepared the apples. Soon the delicious buttery smell filled the kitchen. Angharad dared not let herself hope, but she wanted to work at Duff's.

While the pie was in the oven, Mr Duff said lightly, 'Are you honest?'

Angharad looked straight into the sharp blue eyes and said, 'Yes, of course.'

'Our last *commis* wasn't. You look the very opposite of him. What's your name?'

She told them, and added, 'It's Welsh. I've just come to London, from Wales.' At once she saw the shrewd, appraising flicker in Mr Duff's face, and shrank from it. She didn't want him to know anything about her beyond the fact that she could cook.

All he said was, 'Good Lord. I can't cope with that, and I'm certain Pierre can't either. May we call you Anne?' He held out his large hand. 'I'm Jamie Duff. I'm a lawyer, but my heart is in my stomach. Hence Duff's.' He waved, with distinct pride, around the orderly kitchen.

When the pie was ready, the restaurateur and his chef broke off a chunk of the crust apiece. Mr Duff held open the door into the restaurant courteously and said, 'Shan't keep you long.'

Angharad waited in the cool green and white space with her heart thumping painfully. If she couldn't work here, she didn't want to work anywhere else. *Please*, she whispered silently.

When Mr Duff pushed the door open again, he was smiling.

'Pierre says that it is most irregular, and I have to agree with him. But I've got one of my hunches, and he knows what that means. When can you start?'

'At once.'

'Fine. Twelve pounds a week, and a month's trial. More money after that, if you prove to be worth it. You work to Pierre, and do just as he tells you.' Then, with another smile and a nod, Jamie Duff was on his way.

Angharad felt herself shaking with relief. Pierre was looking warily at her and she took a deep breath. It would be best, now that the job was hers, to be as honest as she could.

'I'm not trained. But I can . . .'

Pierre interrupted her, but not unkindly. 'I can see zat. You are a cook, not a chef. But, you have a certain touch. You can be sure that I will not give you anything to do until I am convinced you are capable of it. Make yourself ready, therefore, for a good deal of vegetable preparation. Starting at ten a.m. sharp tomorrow, if you please.'

Angharad nodded meekly.

'At least,' the chef went on drily, 'I don't think you will be slipping the steak fillet into your handbag.'

They looked at each other, and exchanged the first ghost of a smile. Pierre would be a hard taskmaster. She would have to work, and watch, and learn everything she could to satisfy him. And she could do that, she thought, with a flutter of nearly forgotten hope. *I'm sure I can*.

Almost light-heartedly, Angharad went back to her bare room. She sat down at the table under the pretty window and wrote to Gwyn.

'Don't worry,' she wrote. 'I have found a room, tiny but light and clean, for only four pounds ten a week. And even better, I have a job, a real job, in a smart little restaurant under a French chef. I will be learning all the time, just think, and getting paid as well. Twelve pounds a week, to start with. I can live on that, I should think. As soon as I have my first pay-packet, I will send you back all your money that I have left. It will take me a little while to repay the rest, but I will do it.'

That much was easy. Angharad bit her pen and stared out at the teeming houses opposite. The rest was much harder. At last she scribbled the words in a rush. 'Is Dad all right? What did he say? I wish I had said goodbye instead of just running away like a coward. I wish I could tell him how much I love him, and how sorry I am for all of it, everything, including whatever happened years ago to hurt him so much. Please tell him I miss him. And that if he wants me, I'll come back somehow. Don't worry about me, Aunty Gwyn. I can do whatever I have to, for the baby's sake. You know I love you too, and how grateful I am.'

Angharad printed her address carefully and walked to the end of the road to post her letter. She let go of the white corner of it reluctantly, thinking that in just a few hours it would reach Cefn.

There was not a word of Harry in it, although she had felt the wild questions dinning in her head as she wrote. Please, have you seen him? Is there a letter for me, anything?

The thought of him, or rather the continuous ache of his absence, was with her every waking moment and his face was the recurring image of her dreams. He was still so close and vividly real to her, so much more true and real than anything else, that she couldn't believe he wouldn't appear, at her door, on the next street corner, or staring at her from the crowded opposite platform of the station.

Then she would remember her last glimpse of him. Black with anger, hounded by guilt and dread. He wouldn't ever come back. How could he, after that? Angharad would often see Laura's face too, and reflect sadly that she couldn't even assuage herself with hating her. Laura had been too long and too closely her friend. She found herself missing her, and sadness at the lost friendship added to her isolation.

At ten sharp the next morning Angharad presented herself at Duff's. Pierre greeted her formally, and introduced her to the other kitchen staff. Later the manager came in in his black jacket and shook her hand. Mario, the young waiter she had met on the front step, winked at her from behind the *sommelier*'s rigid back, and she half-smiled in spite of herself. Duff's was impeccably run, but there was a courteous, considerate feel about it that warmed her too.

As she began her first task, cleaning the day's vegetables brought back by Pierre from the Covent Garden market, Gwyn was holding her letter up to the light of the schoolroom window.

She read it through twice and then folded it back into its creases with a sigh. She had no good news to relay to Angharad. William had surprised and shocked her with his bitter rigidity. Gwyn had told him gently that Angharad had gone to London for a while, to find a job, and he had whirled round at her with his face white and deep, frightening lines etched from his nostrils to the corners of his mouth.

'Waste,' he had hissed at her. 'A waste of everything she has done and learned. She's no good, Gwyn. I don't want to hear any more.'

And he turned away again, with bowed shoulders. Gwyn had been unable to find the courage to tell him about Angharad's child. Harry Cotton's child.

Gwyn turned the folded piece of paper around in her fingers. No mention of the boy in it. What had Angharad said?

*I can't see him again. Ever.*

If only, Gwyn thought, it was possible to know whether she meant what she said. That would provide the answer to the impossible dilemma Gwyn found herself in.

Harry had come two days after Angharad's departure. Gwyn had opened the schoolhouse door to the insistent knocking and Harry confronted her, one hand still raised. Gwyn saw the light in his eyes and stepped back from him.

'Where is she?' Harry had asked.

Gwyn would have closed the door if she could, but Harry was already past her and pacing her little parlour like a caged animal.

'Gone,' she told him coldly. 'I don't know where to.'

It was almost the truth. She had no address yet, and

no idea where to reach Angharad.

'How was she?'

Gwyn forced herself to look at him, pushing back the weight of dislike and the memories that flooded back to her.

This, then, was Joe Cotton's son. Their physical likeness seemed so startling that Gwyn had to remind herself that this was only the son, not the father she had hated since the day of Angharad's birth.

'Please, how was she?' Harry repeated. Gwyn blinked, and suddenly it was an anxious boy standing in front of her, not Joe Cotton at all. There was none of Joe's coarseness and brutality here. Harry was strikingly handsome, with the ascetic features of a saint in a stained glass window. Except, of course, that Harry Cotton had proved himself to be no ascetic. The Cottons, father and son. Wrecking and maiming all over again. Hatred, hot and powerful, surged through Gwyn.

'How was she?' she repeated. 'More or less as you would expect. Or rather braver, perhaps.' Gwyn saw the pain in Harry's eyes. Yes, she thought. Not just for what you've done to my Angharad, but for all that your family has done to mine.

'I want to find her, Miss Owain. Will you help me?'

To hurt her again? Gwyn thought. Why should you be any different from your father?

'No,' she said, with brutal finality. 'I don't think she wants to be found. She told me, "I can't see him again. Ever".'

Harry's hands clenched, and then opened to hang loosely at his side. For a moment he looked as if Gwyn had struck him, but he quickly recovered his defiance.

'Well, I shall try to find her anyway. Does her father know where she has gone?'

'He doesn't. And I wouldn't advise you to try asking.'

'I'm not afraid to.'

The blue eyes holding hers were very clear and unwavering. Of course you're not afraid, Gwyn thought. Whatever your faults are, I'm sure fear isn't among them.

Harry turned to go, but at the door he faced her again. 'If

. . . if there's any message for me from her, will you see that it gets to me?'

Gwyn thought for a long moment, struggling against her instincts. She longed for Harry simply to go, to disappear out of Angharad's life and leave her niece in safety. But if Angharad wanted or needed Harry Cotton, however much Gwyn mistrusted him, then that was different. She made her decision.

'If Angharad asks me for news of you, or ever seems to need you, for her sake I'll let you know. But only if, do you understand? And for myself, I wish that you and your family had never existed.'

Harry barely flinched now. 'Thank you.' He was gravely polite. 'A message will reach me for the time being from Llyn Fair, over at . . .'

Gwyn cut him short, with a harsh note in her voice that startled him. 'Yes. I know where you live.'

Harry nodded once sharply and then walked away. Gwyn's eyes were on his back. She was thinking of Angharad alone in London, and the horror in her eyes when she had said that she could never see Harry again.

If only she was doing the right thing for Angharad. That was what mattered.


With her days divided between Duff's and the silent haven of her room, Angharad's life fell quickly into a routine. She was numbingly lonely, but that was partly her own choice. It would have been easy enough to make new friends through Duff's. Mario the waiter asked her out persistently; there was a pretty, bubbly girl not much older than Angharad who worked as the restaurant's PR, and even Pierre had invited her to his home on a Sunday to meet his wife and eat a 'proper French déjeuner'. Angharad refused all their overtures, as gently and tactfully as she could. It was as if a part of herself, the old friendly, outgoing Angharad, had withered away. All her energy was concentrated on starker imperatives now, on keeping going at her job, on the baby, and on bearing the loss of Harry and Laura, her family and her home.

There was no room for anything else.

Angharad found herself a doctor, and matter-of-factly explained her position. The doctor examined her and announced that she was in perfect health. She must expect to be tired sometimes; plenty of rest and the right food were essential.

Angharad rigorously followed his advice. When she was at Duff's, she worked with silent concentration, learning so quickly and avidly that she earned approving nods from Pierre. Sometimes she caught him looking at her with puzzled concern, and she smiled as happily as she could. Duff's provided its staff with excellent meals, and Angharad ate all the protein and fresh produce she could manage. Offduty, she lay on her bed in her room, thinking and waiting. She lived for her regular letters from Gwyn, seizing each new arrival with the feverish hope that it would bring her good news – of Harry, or her father.

They never did.

Gwyn tried to blur the harshness as best she could, writing that time would change everything but Angharad, reading between the lines, knew that William was unbending.

There was never a word of Harry. Angharad thought about him constantly. Sometimes she had the eerie sense that he was very close at hand, perhaps walking the same streets that she passed along every morning on her way to Duff's. It wasn't impossible. He could be here, editing his film, not knowing that she was so close. Perhaps their paths were endlessly passing and repassing, never meeting. At these times Harry became mysteriously identified with the baby growing inside her and she pressed her hands over her stomach, feeling his closeness deep within her as well as all around. She knew that she hadn't stopped loving him, and that she wouldn't ever stop.

At other times he seemed remote, a thousand miles or half a world away, busy and careless and forgetful of her. To Angharad, lying motionless on her narrow bed, these were the longest, loneliest hours.

She was simply waiting, making no plans. There was no point in planning, because she couldn't guess what they might say at Duff's when they found out she was pregnant.

All she could do was work, and make herself as close to irreplaceable as she could. She knew that she was successful at that, at least. After her month's trial Jamie Duff had confirmed her job, and paid her another two pounds a week. She had more than enough for her needs now. Pierre gave her more responsibility and she shouldered it willingly. Timidly she began to make suggestions of her own, and was flattered and pleased when her own dishes appeared on the menu.

Sometimes she felt so bone-tired that she was afraid that she couldn't go on standing at the pastry slab a moment longer. But somehow she found the energy to go on, knowing how important it was. It won't be long before they know, she thought, touching the smooth convexity of the skin between her hip bones. How long can I hide it?

The pre-Christmas rush came, when Duff's was packed every day and late into the night. Angharad was not the only one who was exhausted. Pierre had dark patches under his eyes and Jamie himself came to help out in the kitchen. He rolled up his striped shirtsleeves and worked as a relief porter or washer-up. Angharad even found herself directing him in the preparation of vegetables or salads. He was immensely cheerful and good-humoured, teasing her and joking just as if she was like everyone else. She found herself liking him in return, almost as her old self might have done.

'Don't you have to be in court?' she asked him half-seriously on one of these days. 'Unmasking diamond thieves or forgers under cross-examination?'

Jamie roared with laughter. 'My dear girl, I don't have anything to do with burglars. I'm a company lawyer, specializing in tax. Oh dear, has that destroyed a glamorous image? It's a good deal more lucrative than criminal law, believe me. I couldn't afford a little hobby like Duff's otherwise.'

'Isn't Duff's a success by itself?'

'Yes, it is, just at the moment, as it happens. We might even open another restaurant if I can find the right premises.'

Angharad thought that Jamie Duff was looking

thoughtfully at her, and she bent over her work so that her face was hidden.

The restaurant closed for two days over Christmas. Angharad got through the time by sleeping as much as she could, and dreaming of the next Christmas when she would have her baby for company. She would buy him presents, and take him out to see the tree lights winking in the windows.

Just after Christmas, she was found out.

She came into the restaurant early one morning and hung her coat up in its usual place. She was smoothing her white apron over her loose skirt when she heard Pierre say '*Merde*', very softly. She looked round in surprise. Pierre never swore. Angharad realized that she was standing in profile to him with one hand resting protectively on the round swelling. It was too late to try to hide it. Pierre's eye was far too shrewd. Angharad began to shake all over. She groped for the tall kitchen stool behind her and sank down on it, her wide eyes never leaving Pierre's face.

'It's none of my business,' Pierre said at last. 'Does Mr Duff know?'

Heavily Angharad shook her head. Pierre broke the long silence that followed by saying brusquely, 'Well then. If there is to be lunch today you had better look at the *cassoulet*.'

Angharad understood that he would not press her for confidences that she was unwilling to give, but she knew too that he would put the kitchen first. He would see it as his duty to tell Jamie.

Sure enough, two or three days later Jamie lounged into the kitchen, hands in the pockets of his charcoal grey suit. Angharad sensed that he was trying to look more at ease than he felt.

'Anne, which is your morning off this week?'

She glanced at the rota and managed to say, 'Thursday.'

'Fine. Perhaps you will have lunch with me? We could cast an eye over the competition.' He mentioned a popular nearby restaurant and said, very firmly, 'One o'clock.' There was no possibility of demur.

When Jamie had gone, Pierre shrugged his shoulders at

157

her, with such a perfectly Gallic mixture of apology and resignation that she found herself laughing out loud. 'I do understand,' she told him. 'He had to know sooner or later.' They went back to work, side by side in companionable silence.

'I've been so lucky up to now, Angharad thought. Might the luck hold for a little longer? If only they will let me stay.'

Thursday came, and at one o'clock a waiter ushered her to the table where Jamie was waiting for her. It was in a secluded corner, part-screened by a low partition. Jamie jumped up and pulled out her chair, and then pressed her to have a drink and look at the menu.

Angharad's breath, which had been coming in uncomfortable jagged gasps, drew in more easily. Surely, if he was going to sack her on that spot, Jamie Duff wouldn't do it like his?

'We must look at the menu very carefully,' he said, 'and reassure ourselves that it isn't a patch on ours.'

Meekly, Angharad turned her eyes to it. Jamie was adamant that they order three different courses each. They ate their way steadily through them, sampling each other's food and criticizing it liberally. Jamie was good company. He was fasincated by cooking and by the food business, and Angharad found herself talking easily and fluently to him, as to an equal. It was only when she heard herself insisting a little too vehemently that they should introduce some innovatory *nouvelle cuisine* dishes that she caught herself up short, blushing.

'No, please go on,' Jamie smiled at her. 'I'm interested. But that isn't Pierre's style, you know. He's a cream-and-wine sauce man, at heart. We'd have to do it somewhere other than Duff's.' The speculative light was back in his eyes, but the waiter was standing beside them with his coffee pot poised.

'Liqueur?' Jamie suggested. 'Brandy? Ah, no. Better not.'

For a little while they had forgotten the real motive for their meeting. But now it loomed inescapably. When the waiter had gone, Jamie leaned across the table. Angharad was staring down into her cup but she felt his closeness.

'Anne?' His voice was gentle, tentative. 'Pierre tells me that you are pregnant.' She nodded blindly. 'Don't you think that it would have been fairer to have told us that at the beginning?'

Angharad's head jerked up and hot colour filled her face. 'How could I? I wanted the job. You'd never have given it to me if you'd known. I've proved I can do it. I'm useful to you, I know that. Isn't it enough, for now? Won't you give me a little longer? Please, Mr Duff.'

'Jamie,' he corrected her. His clear English face was grave, the skin a little reddened over the cheekbones. 'You may look fragile, Anne, but – my God – you're tough where it counts.'

'I've got to learn to be tough,' she countered. 'I'm not ashamed or sorry for that. It won't be easy for us. Me and him.' Her fingers fluttered over the starched pink linen napkin on her lap. 'But we'll survive. You could help us by letting me stay at Duff's.'

There was admiration in Jamie's sharp eyes. Angharad saw it and felt a thrill of triumph. It meant that she was winning. Instead of recoiling from his blue stare, invasive of her precious privacy, she met it and held it. Involuntarily Jamie's hand reached out. It hung for an instant over hers, so close that the skin on her fingers prickled. Then, a split second later, she drew her hand gently but firmly away. Jamie Duff's fingers drummed instead on the bare pink cloth.

'Right,' he said, camouflaging with briskness something that his voice might otherwise have betrayed. 'You've persuaded me. You can stay at Duff's on the present basis until . . . damn it, I don't know anything about pregnant women. As long as you need. Tell me, have you seen a doctor and so forth?'

'Yes. I'm perfectly okay.'

'All right for money?'

'Yes.'

'Anne . . .' there was a pause, 'are you on your own?'

'Yes. But I don't need anything, Mr . . . um, Jamie, except to be allowed to go on as I am now.'

Jamie nodded. He wouldn't press her any more, and

she felt a wave of gratitude.

The bill had arrived in its white saucer. Angharad stood up a little unsteadily. Suddenly she wanted to get away, to break the thread of familiarity that was beginning to pull this man towards her. She was weak with relief and the release of tension, and she needed to be alone to restore herself.

But Jamie held her back. 'One more thing. I want you to make me a promise.'

'Of course.'

'That you will not give birth on, or anywhere near my premises. That kind of spectacle over lunch won't encourage the relaxed, expense-account trade we're working so hard to woo. Understood?'

'I'll do my very best.'

A ripple of laughter lapped between them. Jamie Duff looked up at Angharad, seeing her pink-cheeked and bright-eyed, in her best dress instead of a white apron, and thought, *Jesus, she's pretty.*

'Jamie?'

'Mm?'

'Thank you.' Angharad lifted her hand shyly and smiled her contradictory, half-ironic smile at him. Then she was gone, threading her way carefully between the tables. Jamie's eyes followed her until she was out of sight.

As soon as her secret was out, Angharad felt that she and Duff's were committed to each other. It was easier, suddenly, to accept the casual overtures of friendship. She went to the pictures with Mario, and was amused to notice that he treated her with Italian almost-reverence as a mother-to-be. One weekend she went to an art exhibition with the PR girl. Pierre nodded approvingly. As the weeks went by, they began to fuss around her. A high stool would materialize behind her as she stood at the table, Pierre or one of the waiters would give her a lift home instead of letting her wait for the bus. Angharad was still living alone in her own world, but the edges of it rubbed less painfully against the rest of reality.

As the baby grew, her awareness of it began slowly to push

other things out of her head. The first time she felt it moving, she was sitting on the top deck of a bus watching the heads bobbing at a busy intersection. She was combing the crowds with he eyes, as she had done every day since leaving Cefn, wondering if Harry was among them. Then she felt the tiny, butterfly stroke inside her. Once, and then again, unmistakeably. Amazement took her breath away. It was her own flesh, and Harry's, but yet another individual, a bud of life moving of its own accord. At her stop she jumped off the bus and almost ran home, seeing in her mind's eye the tiny, knobbly limbs stirring in their mysterious inner sea. For the first time, she was oblivious to the faces passing by. At that moment Harry might have walked in front of her and she wouldn't have seen him.

After that the movements grew more insistent every day. She could feel the press of a heel or the prod of fingers against the constricting muscle. 'You're doing fine,' they told her at the hospital, but there was no need. She knew that they were both perfect. Anghared felt that she was running a long race, and the white tape was inching closer. In the last month she felt breathless and exhausted, but triumphant.

Jamie came into the kitchen and said, 'I'm putting you on part time for this last month.' She tried to protest but he silenced her. 'You've put in six valuable months here. We owe you some kind of maternity concession. Same pay, less hours. No argument.'

Jamie smiled at her, hiding his concern for the misshapen clumsiness of the pregnant shape superimposed on her fragile figure. Her eyes looked unnaturally wide and the skin of her face seemed too taut over her cheekbones. He wanted to put his arm protectively around her, but he kept his fists clenched in his pockets.

Anghared accepted the new arrangement, and spent the extra hours of freedom sitting in the sun at her window. She was surprised at how natural it felt just to sit, resting her swollen ankles with her hands folded over the bulge, waiting.

She bought a wicker basket for the baby, blankets and a few tiny babyclothes. She stared at the minute socks, wondering how a foot could ever be so small. In spite of the simplicity of her preparations there was no room in the little bedsitter and she knew that she would have to move on. The brusque landlady had already indicated as much. Drowsily Angharad set the thought side. Once she had the baby, held him in her arms, she would know what to do.

The baby was due in the last week of April. The week came and went, and Angharad waited tranquilly. He was moving much less now, and she slept deeply and dreamlessly.

On the first day of May, she woke up in the early morning light to feel a slow, tightening wave pass over the weight of her stomach. As she lay still, smiling, it rolled away again. Then, with a sudden almost audible *pop*, there was a rush of water. Angharad got up, cleared up her wet things, and then went downstairs to telephone the hospital that she was on her way.

It was a week later when she came back into the room. She was panting after the climb up the stairs and the effort of lifting the wicker cradle around corners without bumping it. Angharad laid the basket gently on the bed and lifted the folded blanket. William was asleep with his clenched fist against his cheek and his hair very black against the pristine white covers. For a moment she looked at him, half smiling, then lifted her head to stare round the room. It was familiar, yet obliquely different, as everything had been since the moment of William's birth.

Jamie had sent a message this morning to say that he had to be in court. He had arranged for a cab to collect her from the hospital and bring her back here. She was to collect her things together and then call the cab once more to drive her to Jamie's flat in Godolphin Mansions. Angharad fingered the unfamiliar shape of the keys he had sent for her.

She had so few possessions that it didn't take her long to pack them, even though she moved slowly and fumblingly. When she was ready, she stood unwillingly in the doorway, wishing that she could stay. The bare little room was home, and she felt too raw and frail to be on the move again.

But she picked up William's basket and carried it down to the car, and turned her face resolutely forward.

The streets around Jamie's mansion block were cleaner and smarter than those of the old, crowded, cosmopolitan neighbourhood she was used to. There were smart little boutiques here, expensive-looking delicatessens, and well-coiffed women parking nippy runabouts on meters. How would she and William fit in here, on their tiny budget?

The cab driver complainingly helped her up to Jamie's door with her bags, and Angharad realized with embarrassment that she hadn't enough money left to tip him properly. He muttered a sour something as he walked away, and she felt irrational tears stinging behind her eyes.

The hallway of the flat and the drawing-room beyond were blurred as she walked through. Was this home, then? Jamie's flat was comfortably, even opulently furnished, but it had a dim air of neglect and unuse. A dirty whisky tumbler stood in a faint film of dust on the glass-and-steel coffee table. Without putting William's basket down, Angharad walked through the silent flat. There was a well-equipped kitchen that looked as if no one had ever used it, a single lemon shrivelling in the fruit bowl. There was a wide bed with a rumpled duvet in Jamie's bedroom. At the end of the corridor, just as he had promised her, Angharad found the two rooms. They had been hastily cleared of the mackintoshes and tennis rackets, but there were dusty patches against the walls where boxes had stood, and the windows were laced with dust. There was a note propped up on the chest of drawers.

'Welcome home. I'm sorry I couldn't be here. Today of all days I have to appear for a client. I'll be back as soon as I can, with provisions. I'll get someone in to clean up. Treat it as your home. J.'

The second room was completely empty. William's basket looked pathetically solitary in it. Angharad leaned against the connecting door and the tears came, burning her cheeks. She had no right to expect anything from Jamie, of course. He was busy, and he had already done more for her than she could possibly have hoped. But there was something about the utter silence of this flat, the emptiness and her solitude, that cut into her. She had blithely expected not to feel lonely with William, but loving and caring for him seemed to drain all her reserves of strength and she had nowhere to turn to replenish them. And then his eyes would open, and she would find herself staring straight down into Harry's face.

It was a bitter shock to realize that she was more alone than ever.

The days that followed were Angharad's worst, worse even than her first weeks in London. At least, then, she had had only herself to fend for. Now her breasts ached, and her stitches shot stabs of pain, and William woke and cried whenever she had fallen into an uneasy sleep.

Jamie was away, immersed in an important and complicated case. In one sense she was thankful for that, but in another way she yearned for ordinary company as she had never done before. On the rare occasions when she did see him she was perversely and determinedly bright, promising to be back at work very soon, although privately she doubted that she could ever do it.

'Give him a chance to get settled first,' Jamie said mildly. 'Don't want him howling in the nether regions and disturbing the diners, do we?'

William fed and slept and fed again. Angharad felt that he was sucking her dry and in her intense love, she was tortured by fears of not giving him enough. A reassuring midwife visited her and told her that he was doing fine, and when Angharad dissolved into helpless tears, she patted her shoulder and said 'Post-baby blues. Quite natural and normal, you know. Haven't you got a friend or a relative who could come and stay with you for a while?'

'I'm quite all right,' Angharad insisted, knowing that she was not. She would look at William, asleep or sucking fiercely at her breast, and feel the terrified conviction that she was incapable of caring for him. How could she sustain this tiny, helpless creature with the strength of her body when she was so hopelessly adrift herself?

If only Harry were here. If only Harry would come, and share with her. She longed desperately and chokingly for him, more and more painfully than she had ever done. But there was no point in letting herself stray further down that avenue. Harry had let her go. It was a blind cul-de-sac.

Then the letter came from her father.

Angharad had written to Gwyn immediately after the birth, and the warm, loving letter that had come back at once had added to the euphoria of the first few days.

'I will tell William,' Gwyn wrote, 'that he has a grandson and a namesake. I don't think, after all this time, that he has any anger left. It might even make him happy, although I doubt that your news will give him as much joy as it has given me. God bless you both. I will try, my darling, to come and see you soon.'

Angharad had sent her address as soon as she was installed at Jamie's. A day or so later she saw an envelope on the doormat and recognized her father's spiky black script. She picked it up with shaking fingers and tore it open.

The words scorched her.

'This is your home as it has always been, although you haven't seen fit to treat it as such . . . you may come back at any time and we will try to forget what's past . . . but I can't shelter a Cotton bastard under my roof, Angharad . . . make whatever arrangements you must for it, and then come home as my daughter again . . .'

A sob tore itself from Angharad's chest. She ran through into William's room and knelt down beside his basket. The baby was wide awake, watching the May sunlight filtering through his window. He turned his head towards her and her tears splashed on his cheek.

'You're not . . .' Angharad sobbed as his fingers closed over hers, '. . . a Cotton bastard. You're mine, and I love you. How could he think that I would ever, ever part with you?'

She screwed up the letter and threw it away. The thought came to her that her father must be slightly mad. Well then, that might be the truth. But if he chose to cut his daughter and grandson off in his mad bitterness, then that was how it would be. She didn't want to hear from him ever again. Moving in a trance, only half conscious of a search for something that would bring normality back into her world, Angharad walked over to the table and picked up a magazine. It was a mother-and-baby publication, left for her by the visiting midwife.

The first picture she looked at showed a radiant young mother rocking her infant in a sunny nursery bright with pictures and mobiles.

Angharad looked through the doorway and saw William lying in the middle of his empty, dusty room. At once her disorientated mind seized feverishly on an idea.

That's it. That's what she would do. She would decorate his room or him. Sunshiny yellow, and she would hang it with mobiles for him to gurgle at, just like in the magazine.

Angharad ran for the kitchen steps and a bucket of water to wash down the grimy walls.

When Jamie came in at ten o'clock, he smelt the fresh paint. Angharad was perched at the top of the step ladder, painting grimly on. She knew that the yellow paint she had hastily chosen was sulphurous and harsh in tone, but she worked on with the image of the golden nursery fixed firmly in her mind.

Jamie stopped in the doorway when he saw her. Her face was grey with exhaustion and her eyes were pitifully swollen. There was a streak of paint across her face, and more in her hair.

'Anne? Anne, for Christ's sake. What are you doing?'

She stared wildly at him and then mumbled, 'I wanted him to have a pretty room like other children. Even if he hasn't got anything else.'

Jamie crossed to her in one stride. He lifted her down from the ladder and wrapped his arms around her.

'Darling, my darling Anne, I didn't realize.' He kissed her hair, smelling the paint and dust. He felt her shaking, and when he looked down he saw the tears spilling from under her eyelashes. 'I should have known it wouldn't do for you. I'm a thoughtless shit. Why didn't you say something? No, I should have damn well known. We'll get a bloody man in tomorrow to paint everywhere, just as you'd like it. Call up Harrods. Look,' he fumbled and then pressed a square of plastic into her hand, 'that's my account. Order whatever you want. Rocking horses. Pale blue furniture with flowers on. Anything. But please, don't look like that. I can't bear it. Do you hear? I can't bear it.'

He rocked her in his arms and Angharad, with the buttons of his waistcoat digging into her face, cried with her helplessness and her hurt, and her relief that he was there.

# CHAPTER SEVEN

At last, Angharad stopped crying.

Jamie lifted her chin so that he could look down at her, and she was too exhausted to try to hide her smeared face.

'Don't,' Jamie said again. There was an odd mixture of tenderness and perplexity in his face. Without letting go of Angharad, he moved to look down at the sleeping baby.

'How long until he wakes up again?'

'I can't tell. Three or four hours, perhaps.'

'Time for you to sleep as well, then.'

Jamie steered her towards the bathroom. He drew the shower curtain and turned the water on for her. Angharad realized that she was aching to her bones. When Jamie had closed the door behind him, she peeled off her filthy clothes and let the scorchingly hot water splash over her. When she came out again she found one of Jamie's thick towelling robes, warmed, hanging behind the door for her. She put it on and wrapped her hair in a towel. Then she crept out, intending to slip back down the corridor to her room, but Jamie called out to her.

'In here, please.'

He was in his bedroom, smoothing a clean sheet over the wide bed. She stared, and then a suspicious shaft penetrated Angharad's numbness. Horrified, she backed away. *Darling*, he had called her, and kissed her hair.

'I can't sleep with you.' The words were out before she could stop them.

Jamie didn't even look at her, but she saw the dull crimson in his face and wished that she could have bitten out her tongue. 'Nor can your baby sleep in the paint fumes you have generated in your own rooms. The general idea was for you to have my bed, and to put William in my dressing-room. But if you're so afraid that I'm going to pounce on you . . .'

'I'm sorry, Jamie. I know you didn't mean anything of the kind.' They looked at each other for a minute, and if Angharad saw the uncertainty in Jamie's face, she didn't try to fathom why it was there.

'Where will you sleep?'

He bent down again to tuck in the corner of the sheet. 'In the sitting-room.' Then he was holding the duvet back for her. 'Get in,' he ordered. Angharad obeyed. She had never slept under a duvet before and it felt exotically light and warm. Jamie left the room again and she looked round at the deep carpet and the drawn curtains, heavy enough to keep out every chink of light and to muffle the pervasive noise of London traffic that had disturbed her sleep for months. There was a pile of new books and glossy magazines on the bedside table.

When Jamie came back again, he was carrying William's basket in one hand and a steaming mug in the other. Casually he deposited the baby in his dressing-room between the ranks of suits and highly polished shoes and gave Angharad her hot drink. It smelled strongly of whisky, and Angharad was so irresistibly reminded of being ministered to by Aunty Gwyn that she half smiled.

'That's better,' Jamie said. The tentativeness had gone, and he was the brisk proprietor of Duff's again. 'Drink that and go to sleep. Tomorrow we'll try to sort things out for you. You haven't made a bad start, but I think you could do with some help, just the same.'

Angharad's independent pride might once have dictated otherwise, but the raw bewilderment of the last few days had changed all that.

'Thank you,' she said simply. She could only hope that Jamie Duff would understand how badly she had needed his help, and how grateful she felt for it.

Jamie was as good as his word.

The very next day a pair of decorators arrived and presented her with colour cards from which to choose paint for her rooms. Another ring at the flat doorbell heralded a delivery from Harrods. When Angharad unpacked the bulky packages, she found a white-painted cot and a chest of

169

drawers, and a nursery table and chair. In another box was a mobile exactly the same as the one in the magazine picture. She realized that Jamie must have seen the picture too, and understood everything.

Angharad ran to the telephone, longing to ring him and thank him for his thoughtfulness. She was holding the receiver when she realized that she had no idea where to find him. Instead, she went to wrap William in his outdoor clothes. They would make their first proper expedition together, shopping. Angharad would cook a wonderful meal for Jamie.

As soon as Jamie came back into the flat that evening, he stood in the hallway and sniffed appreciatively.

'Where are you?'

Angharad was in the kitchen, stirring a saucepan, with a tea-towel wrapped round her waist in the absence of her Duff's apron. She waved the spoon at him and smiled. Jamie stopped short. He had never seen that smile before. It left him groping for something rational to say. He cleared his throat, and tried. 'Mmm. I can't tell you how exciting it is to come home and smell cooking. Don't do it again or I'll start to expect it.'

'I'll do it whenever you like,' Angharad said shyly. 'It's the least I . . .'

'That's enough. What is it?'

'Sole Véronique, but I sort of embroidered a bit.'

'Carry on. Is there time to chill some champagne if I put it in the freezer?'

'Most definitely.'

Jamie lit candles and they sat opposite each other at the kitchen table to eat. Jamie poured the champagne into tall flutes and the atmosphere was instantly festive. He raised his glass and the rising bubbles shot little points of light.

'To Anne and William. Long life and happiness.'

Anne echoed him, 'Especially William.'

They talked about Duff's with the relaxed informality of old friends. 'We need you back, Anne, and soon. Pierre admits it. We'll fix something up for William, don't worry.'

In spite of her doubts, Angharad felt a warm glow at the

idea of being needed. 'I want to come back. You know, I think William smiled at me today?'

'Clearly a prodigy.'

After a dinner they sank into opposite corners of the deep sofa that had been Jamie's bed the night before.

'Whisky?'

Angharad felt warm and comfortable, with drowsiness beginning to blur the corners of the room. It occurred to her that the delicious, unfamiliar sensation was happiness. Was it only yesterday evening that she had been perched on her step ladder in the empty, dusty nursery?

'Why not?' She smiled at Jamie. 'Put lots of soda or something in it, please.'

'My dear Anne, it's a single malt.' Jamie's shocked voice made her giggle, and then they were laughing together.

'You know, you're terribly pretty when you laugh,' Jamie said matter-of-factly. His fingers touched hers when he handed her the whisky glass and she felt no need to jerk her hand abruptly away. She sipped her drink slowly, not thinking, and only half listening to the austere cello suite that Jamie had switched on.

His question startled her with its suddenness.

'Won't you tell me about it? About what happened to you, and him? Whoever he is?'

Angharad's head jerked round and she glimpsed a kind of hunger in Jamie's eyes. Hunger for herself? To know her secrets? Or curiosity? She thought, and the old images came flooding back. There was the lake, and the long ridge of The Mountain, and the two dark heads, opposite faces of the same coin. The same features that she could already see forming in her baby's face, like molten metal taking shape as it cooled.

All that was locked inside her. The narrow bed in the cottage at Heulfryn, and another bed framed by an arch. The two of them there together, and the secrets that would link the three of them for ever.

Those images were reality for Angharad, and this plush flat, and Duff's, and Jamie's face watching her, everything around her now except for William, were grey and

171

insubstantial by comparison. But the greyness was safe, and numb. She didn't want to let the real world leak back into this limbo. Not yet, not even to please Jamie. And she wanted to please him.

'I'll tell you one day,' Angharad lied. 'But not now. I can't, you see.' She reached out and put her glass down on the table. 'Shall I sleep in here so that you can have your own bed back?'

'No,' Jamie said almost brusquely. 'Good night, Anne.'

A day or two later Angharad had a visitor. She opened the door to a woman in her mid-thirties, wearing a navy blazer with a string of pearls showing at the neck. A silk head-scarf was knotted at the chin over her fair, shoulder-length hair.

'Hullo, I'm Caro Gould. Duff, as was. Jamie's sister, y'know.'

Swallowing her surprise, Angharad held the door wide open and Caro strode in, hitching her bag over her shoulder.

'Jamie says you need a spot of female company so I thought I'd drop in. Can I see the babe?'

'Of course.' Angharad's face lit up at the thought of showing William off. She leant over the cot with Caro.

'What a super little chap. But jolly hard work on your own, I should think? God, I've had three and I know. Not that I personally could have done it without help. Not from Charles, of course. He's my husband. Infants are not his strong point. No, I've had a super nanny. It's partly that I've come to see you about.'

Caro beamed at her and Angharad smiled back. Jamie's confident, forthright elder sister seemed as good-natured as he was himself.

'The thing is, my youngest has just started at kindergarten, and so our lovely nanny hasn't a thing to do all day. Here are you with this tiny chap and a job to get back to – quite indispensable, Jamie says – so I thought, why not team up? What d'you say?'

'Well . . .'

'Oh, don't worry. Susie's got a string of qualifications as

long as your arm. Much better with my kids than I am myself.'

'It's not that. It's just that I can't afford to pay for a nanny.'

'Oh,' said Caro airily, 'no need to worry about that. Susie's paid anyway, because we still need her for our three. You'd be doing her a favour by lending her your baby. He's her passport back to all the toddler clubs and sandpit sprees her friends go to. I'm not proposing to provide her with another baby myself, so you'd be doing me a favour too.' Caro smiled, a smile so totally disarming that Angharad smiled back at her in acquiescence.

'We-ell . . .'

'All settled, then. What say we pop round now and introduce them? We only live around the corner.'

There was nothing for it but to follow meekly in Caro Gould's wake.

The Goulds' house was spruce, white-painted and discreetly opulent-looking. In the nursery suite on the top floor, stocked with as many playthings as the toy department of a medium-sized store, they found Susie waiting. Caro's nanny was a plump, freckled Scots girl who pounced on William with cries of delight.

'Oh, the wee thing.'

William, slightly to Angharad's chagrin, gurgled back at her in evident delight. Caro bore Angharad away for coffee and Black Forest gâteau.

'Disastrously fattening. Have a really big piece. A puff of wind would blow you away. I kept on feeding my babies for months because it was such a good excuse for eating like a horse. Not that you need to worry. You know, I'm so glad you've moved in with Jamie. He needs a calming influence.'

'I only share the flat,' Angharad protested. 'Our paths don't cross, except at Duff's.'

'No?' The stream of inconsequential talk stopped as Caro looked at her. Angharad suddenly thought that Jamie's sister was much sharper than she had given her credit for.

Godolphin Mansions, when Angharad and William reached home at last, seemed very quiet indeed.

When Jamie came in, he looked at her with a trace of anxiety.

'Did Caro call?'

'She did.'

'And did she organize you?'

'Organize? I've only just got my breath back.'

They laughed. 'Charles Gould is one of the City's top investment analysts. But at home, the man's a mouse beside Caro. You agreed to her suggestion?'

'I'll start again whenever you like.'

'And your training course?'

'The course too.'

Jamie beamed at her, suddenly very like his sister, as if it was Angharad who was doing him all the favours.

She watched him cross the room to pour himself a drink, loosening his starched shirt collar as he went, and wondered how she was ever going to thank him. William was asleep in his bright nursery. Susie had sent him back with a box of Gould babyclothes, tiny outfits with White House and La Cigogna labels, layered in tissue paper. Angharad herself had a job she enjoyed, and was about to embark on a course under a master chef that could turn her job into a career. She had a home. Even, she thought, remembering Duff's and Caro, friends.

'Jamie?'

'Yep?'

Uncertain of how to say it, Angharad went to him and kissed his cheek. He smelt faintly of cigars and cologne, and he felt firm and solid. With a sharp stab Angharad remembered Harry's leanness, and the way that his bones moved under the skin. *Harry.*

'Thank you,' she said, very softly, turning away to hide the sudden shadow in her face.

'Be careful. Won't you?' Jamie said, just as softly. His hand brushed her hair and then fell again. Angharad nodded. She owed it to him to be careful of them both.

Angharad went back to Duff's.

The first time, she took William in his basket. The staff crowded round, with Mario at the front.

'*Che bello bambino*,' he whispered, and Pierre snorted in derision. But the chef had made a cake, an exotic pagoda of meringue and spun sugar, with '*Bienvenu*' lettered on it. Angharad cut it and handed it round, feeling almost as if she had come home.

Slowly a routine was established. It was very hard work, but she flung herself into it avidly. Work helped her to stop thinking, and it dammed up the memories.

So long as William was well, and happy, as he so obviously was, Angharad could go on from day to day. She let all her love focus on the baby, and he absorbed it and rewarded her with smiles. The rest of her energy and attention went into work.

Most mornings and lunchtimes she worked at the restaurant, and then went to her classes in the afternoon. As soon as it was over she rushed to the Goulds' and William, and took him home for a precious hour before his bathtime. On the evenings when she had to work at Duff's, Susie or one of her friends would come when he was asleep and babysit.

At first Jamie was at home in the evenings only rarely. But slowly, as William grew, Angharad noticed that he appeared more regularly. He would perch beside the bath and play with him, and then feed him his yoghurt with mock-distaste as the baby's fat little hands grabbed for his silk ties. Jamie's first question on coming in changed from 'How many lunches today?' or 'Did the salmon arrive?' to 'Where's Will'm?'

Angharad loved her son fiercely, and it seemed perfectly natural that Jamie should be devoted to him too. William was the thread that linked her back to the real world as his dark hair grew and his eyes took on the same clear stare as Harry's. But he was part of this world too, the featureless rhythm that centred on the Goulds' nursery, class, Duff's and Godolphin Mansions, and in that he belonged to Jamie as well as to Angharad.

The baby's first syllables, as he stood up in the cot rattling the bars, were 'dadadada'.

'No,' Jamie said gently. 'I'm *Jamie*.'

He never asked Angharad again about William's father. She realized, as his attachment to the baby grew, that he didn't want to know any more.

The weeks turned into months, and they were almost a family. Almost.

Angharad was increasingly visited by the eerie sensation that they were all waiting for something – Caro and Charles, Pierre, Jamie himself, even William. Waiting and watching. She began to wonder whether it was worth standing her guard any longer.

At length, Aunty Gwyn was persuaded to pay them a visit. She arrived by train in a nervous flutter of bulging carrier bags, carrying enough food for the journey to supply half an army. Angharad saw from the other end of the platform that she was still wearing her ankle socks, and she ran to her half laughing and half crying.

'*Cariad*, you look so pretty and well. Give me a kiss, there, now.'

'Aunty Gwyn, it's so wonderful to see you. Come on, William's waiting at home for you. You'll love him. He's the most perfect baby in the world.'

It was Gwyn's first visit to London in twenty years, and she exclaimed in amazed excitement all the way back to Chelsea. She exclaimed at the Godolphin Mansions flat, too. Her innocent pleasure made Angharad smile, and made her realize at the same time that she was growing so used to this life that she didn't think about it any more. There was comfort in that, of a sort, but there was a bleak sense of loss too.

'Angharad, where is he?'

It was wonderful to hear her real name again. Anne was changing into somebody else, someone quite different, but Angharad would be the same for ever.

'Through here.'

Susie was playing with him on the nursery rug. William knocked down a tower of bricks with a gurgle of triumph before turning his wide stare on his great-aunt. Gwyn hugged him and kissed him, and told him that he was beautiful, but when Angharad and she were alone together again, she said, 'I don't see anything of you in him at all. It's uncanny.'

'I'm glad he looks like Harry.' Angharad's voice was barely audible.

Inside her head Angharad listened to his name, still hanging in the air between them. If she could talk to anyone about him, she could talk to Gwyn. But she had grown so used to silence that she couldn't find the words now.

Gwyn watched her niece's averted face, and waited. If Angharad had asked, even mentioned him once more, she would have told her, with relief. Harry had come again to the old schoolhouse.

'Where is she?' he asked again.

'I don't know.' This time Gwyn was lying, but she did it because she believed it was what Angharad would have wanted.

Harry left an envelope. 'I'm leaving Wales. If she needs me – ever, for anything at all – a message will reach me from here, wherever I am.' It was an address in New York. Gwyn put the envelope carefully away. But Angharad had never spoken of Harry, and here she was, pretty and happy, building a new life for herself. To Gwyn, the thought of Harry Cotton was a black shadow in this bright, elegant flat. The moment passed.

'Shall we give William his bath?' Angharad asked brightly. 'Jamie comes back at seven, and he likes to play with him before he goes to sleep.'

It wasn't surprising, Gwyn thought. Angharad was happily installed here, with her London friends around her and her job, doing the thing she enjoyed most in the world. And there was this Jamie Duff, too. If she had put it so successfully behind her, why should she want to think back to a dead love affair that had given her so much pain? Harry Cotton's letter could stay where it was, half-forgotten in the recesses of Gwyn's memory.

Gwyn's face brightened, and they went off together to the baby's room.

The visit was a huge success. Jamie and Aunty Gwyn took to each other at once. He treated her with a kind of teasing gravity that made her giggle like a schoolgirl.

'Why didn't you come before?' he asked. 'I've always felt

rather cheated in the aunt department, and you fit the bill perfectly.'

'Now that I know how comfortable it is here,' she retorted, 'and how charming you are, Jamie, I shall probably close up the schoolhouse and move in for good. Then you'll be sorry.'

'On the contrary. It will mean that Anne will have to move out to make room, of course, but that's only a minor consideration. Unless you're proposing a more intimate arrangement?'

They both roared with laughter. Angharad thought that Jamie seemed more at ease with her aunt, these days, than he did with herself. It was as if there was a conspiracy of happiness and normality around her, from which she was excluded only by her own stubbornness.

That's a streak of Dad in me, she told herself grimly.

Gwyn's news of her brother was no different from the few words in her letters. Angharad pressed her, anxious for even a nuance of regret or relentment, but Gwyn shook her head.

'I'm ashamed of him,' she said, 'And so sorry for him, too. He's cut himself off with bitterness, even from me. I know he misses you, love, but he won't give in. It reminds me of how he was after your mother died. Rigid with sorrow and anger and hatred of everything. It took you growing up to break through to him again. That won't happen again, will it? He'll die a lonely, unhappy old man.'

'Die?' Angharad said sharply. 'He isn't ill, is he?'

Gwyn said, gently, 'We're both getting old.'

Angharad rubbed her aunt's knobbly old hands and pressed them against her face, silenced.

When the week's stay was over, Angharad went back with Gwyn to the station to see her off. She stood on the platform and Gwyn, fussed with the anxiety of departure, leaned out of the window to kiss her.

'Give a last hug to the little one from me, won't you? Take care of him.'

'Of course I will. I love him more than anything in the world.'

Gwyn smiled at her, forgetting the train and the clamour around them. 'Yes, my love. You were right to do what you

178

did. I'm proud of you.' The doors were slamming down the length of the train. 'And that nice Jamie, too. You take care of him. You're a very lucky girl, Angharad.'

The guard's whistle blew. In a second the train would be moving, and she would have to shout.

'Jamie and I don't belong to each other, Aunty Gwyn. But I owe him a great deal. And yes, I know how lucky I am. Do you think I should be happy?' Her last words were lost as the train hissed and rolled forward. Gwyn was waving and blowing kisses from her window.

Angharad waved until the train had gone, and then turned to walk towards the Underground. Do you think I should be happy? she repeated to herself. Do you?

Christmas came.

Angharad and William were invited, with Jamie, to spend it at the Goulds'. In return she had offered to cook the Christmas dinner, and had been pleased and amused by Caro's delighted acceptance. The puddings were already made, and were resting in the larder at Godolphin Mansions. In the brief intervals between the pre-Christmas rush at Duff's, Angharad bought her Christmas presents and wrapped them in bright paper. The preparations made her think back to last year, when she had huddled alone in her bedsitter longing to have William for company. She had imagined themselves looking in at the shop windows, watching the lights, alone in their own world.

It hadn't turned out like that at all.

They were caught up in busy, congenial family lives. Angharad found herself going to parties, at Duff's and elsewhere, and meeting dozens of new people. Suddenly she owned pretty clothes, and a diary, and an address book.

Jamie came home bearing a Christmas tree, and they decorated it and turned on the lights before Jamie brought William in to to see it. The baby's mouth and eyes opened in wide, amazed circles and he set off towards the miraculous apparition in his lurching, drunken new crawl.

'Look, Anne! Look at him!'

Watching him, Angharad felt a moment of pure

wistfulness. She longed to be Angharad again, not busy, cheerful Anne. She was sharing her precious baby. And she was losing, slowly, slowly, her hold on the old world. Cefn, and The Mountain, and Harry.

She didn't even know if she loved Harry any more. She had his face, in William, but every day William was more his own self. Not his father. Nor should he be.

'Where's the camera? We must get a picture.'

Angharad went for it, fighting to put the wistfulness behind her, cursing herself for being so stupid. There was no old world to cling to, any more. She didn't have Harry, or her father. It was all memories.

This was what she had now.

Bright lights, warmth, company, interests, a happy and contended child. And a little, cold core of numbness that would never go away.

On Christmas Eve Angharad came home late from Duff's. She turned her key in the lock and breathed in the unmistakeable Christmas scents of spices, tangerines and pine needles. Jamie had stayed at home with William. He was sitting reading, the lamplight shining on his familiar profile. His face lit up when he saw her.

'At last. I thought you were going to stay there all night.'

'Eighty covers. Everyone determined to have the time of their lives.'

'Wish they'd all stayed at home. I'd far rather have had you here.'

Jamie settled her in a corner of the sofa, took off her shoes and rubbed her feet. Angharad smiled at him, and then reached to touch his cheek where a patch of fine, blond hairs caught the lamplight. He looked up at her at once and caught her hand, so tightly that the knuckles grated.

'Jamie,' she said, very softly. She thought, suddenly, how simple it would be. What else was she clinging to?

The gold carriage clock on the mantelpiece struck the hour.

'It's midnight,' Jamie said. 'Happy Christmas.' He leaned to kiss her and from habit she offered her cheek. But with his forefinger at the point of her chin Jamie turned her face and their mouths met. Angharad held her head very still, feeling the hairs prickle at the nape of her neck.

Everything hung in the balance.

Decide for us, Jamie, she begged him silently. Don't make me do it.

He drew back a little and she noticed the length of his blonde eyelashes. Jamie was feeling in the pocket of his jacket.

'I want to give you your Christmas present,' he said. He drew out a little, flat package wrapped in gold paper and a curl of gold ribbon. Angharad held it, then shook it to see if it rattled, her eyes sparkling like a child's.

'What is it?'

'Open it and see.'

Inside the box was a ruff of tissue paper, and under that a little Victorian dress watch. It had a smooth gold case and a round white face with tiny, curly blue enamel numerals, on a narrow black satin ribbon.

'Oh, how beautiful. It's perfect.'

Jamie put the watch on her wrist, tightening the old-fashioned ribbon so that it sat snugly. Then he kissed the inside of her wrist and she felt his tongue against the thin skin where the blue veins showed through.

'Thank you,' she whispered.

Angharad was still wearing her kitchen dress that left her arms bare. Jamie kissed her again, in the warm crook of her arm. His eyes were shut, and she felt that he was shaking. The last of her careful defences fell.

Angharad laid her cheek against his hair. 'It's all right. Jamie, it's all right.'

At once his arms were around her and he was lifting her to her feet. They stood face to face in the glow of the tree lights. Jamie's head bent to hers and he kissed her, reaching for her, with his tongue against hers so her mouth opened and her head fell back. Angharad shut her eyes on the other faces and made herself think only of Jamie, because she knew that he loved her and she wanted to love him back.

His hands were at the neck of her dress, slowly undoing the buttons.

'Come to bed.' His breath felt very warm against her cheek.

181

Angharad thought back to the night when William was tiny, when she had so gauchely rejected an advance that Jamie hadn't even tried to make. Instead he had waited, and he had been right.

Her hand caught his wrist. 'Let's go and look at William first.'

There was a trace of wistfulness in Jamie's teasing smile. 'Mother first and lover second, is that it?'

'Yes.' She answered him seriously, because she wanted to be honest with him from the very beginning.

They went down the corridor to William's room hand in hand.

William was upside down in his cot, one leg thrust through the bars and his arms spread wide in total abandonment to sleep. Angharad picked him up and hugged him, smelling the baby smells of talcum powder and warm skin. He nuzzled against her cheek and made a small, contented sigh.

'I love him, too, you know,' Jamie said as she laid the baby under the covers again.

Angharad nodded, acquiescing.

Then Jamie turned her around and they went away together to his room, where the thick curtains shut out the noise of late-night revellers in the streets and where the door, left ajar for William, showed the coloured glow of the Christmas tree lights that they had left burning across the hall.

Angharad didn't know that love-making could be so gentle. That first time with Jamie was almost dream-like.

In her brief time with Harry she had met his incandescent passion with her own, and they had driven each other on, and further. They had bruised each other, sometimes, but the sweetness had obliterated everything.

But Jamie's touch was as light as if he was afraid of breaking her, and for all his bulk he didn't overpower her. Instead he stroked her skin, gentling her until she felt herself unfold to him. It had been a long time, and her body felt stiff and unfamiliar. Jamie whispered to her, loving secretive things in the dimness of the room, and she smiled against his

182

cheek, feeling its smoothness. He was as gentlemanly and determined in bed as out of it. Yet part of Angharad wanted to be driven, not coaxed like this, and she felt impatience alongside the languor. Harry had been iron and electricity, every muscle and bone apparent under her fingers.

Nothing like this.

But Jamie's way was right, now. The stiffness and impatience vanished together, at last, and the sensations that she thought she had forgotten forever came back to her.

She heard herself cry out, and then Jamie's mouth was hard on hers as he came inside her, urgent for the first time.

'I love you,' he told her, and her fingers dug into the smooth breadth of his back because she was suddenly afraid. But at once pleasure drove away the fear, and she forgot it.

'Anne. Anne, my darling.'

That's right. This was Anne, nobody else, any more.

Afterwards she lay with Jamie's arms wrapped round her, feeling the security of his warmth all through her.

'Jamie?'

'Mmmm?'

'Happy Christmas. To both of us.'

'Oh, I think so. Don't you?'

In the morning when Angharad woke up she was alone again, and she had time to roll over, confused, before Jamie came back. He was carrying a tray with a champagne bottle and glasses, and a big jug of orange juice. There were croissants wrapped in a napkin, and the smell of fresh coffee wafted in with him.

'Champagne in bed? The decadence of it.'

'What else, on this of all mornings? Christmas, I mean, of course.' He handed her a glass of Buck's Fizz with a flourish and they raised their glasses to each other, smiling at the memory of the night before.

'Before you ask, William is fine. Clean, dry, and playing in his cot with a revolting comfort rag and a teddy or two. Now, close your eyes, please. I've got another present for you.'

She did as she was told, and felt a sheet of paper in her hands. She opened her eyes again, laughing and puzzled.

She saw that it was an estate agents' circular. The smudgy picture showed an empty shop-front in a row of prosperous-looking frontages. The caption beneath read 'Ripe for development/conversion'. Angharad scanned the rest of the copy, and whistled at the price.

'Not bad for what it is,' Jamie assured her. 'Just off this end of the King's Road! Well?'

'Well what?'

'It's our new restaurant. Your own kitchen. What do you say? Will you be my partner?'

Angharad caught her breath. It was a dazzlingly generous offer. She was still only an inexperienced chef, and it would give her an unprecedented chance to make her name. It was a daunting thought, but Angharad knew that Jamie's faith in her was justified.

She could do it, if he'd back her.

Partnership, Jamie had said. Angharad took a deep breath and asked, as lightly as she could, 'Is this a business proposition?'

'Yes, darling, that's exactly what it is. The premises will be mine soon. The contracts are almost ready for exchange. You can work for me on the old basis or, if you prefer, you can buy yourself into the business over a set period of time until you own fifty per cent of the shares. I'd have told you about it before this, but . . . well. I wanted to find out a bit more about how our personal partnership stood, first.'

'And does its new standing make any difference? Or if it had stayed just as it was?'

Jamie's blue eyes met hers squarely. 'Not a jot. You are simply the best chef for the job, that's all.'

Angharad smiled her gratitude, and her relief. 'I don't think you'll be sorry,' she said quietly.

'Neither do I.' Jamie took her glass out of her hand and lay down beside her.

'You're asking me to dally here in bed while my son sits alone in his cot?'

Firmly he said, 'That's exactly what I'm asking. Demanding, even.'

It was a very happy Christmas.

When the three of them arrived at the Goulds', Caro took one look and crowed, 'Oh, I say. About time, too.'

'Caro, really,' Charles admonished her. But he was beaming as he produced more champagne.

Angharad groaned. 'How can I possibly organize dinner?'

William sat among the romping Gould children, chewing a piece of purple tissue from the piles of discarded wrapping paper, and smiled his enchanting, reassuring smile at her.

There wasn't any reason, Angharad told herself, her fingers tightening around the stem of her glass, for being alone any longer.

Alone?

Eerily, she heard Harry's voice repeating the word, more clearly than all the voices in the room. The old sensation, half forgotten, that he was somewhere very close at hand came back to her. Close. Closer than any of these people.

'Are you all right?' Jamie's question broke through to her and she shook herself.

'Of course. Of course I am. Can I have some more champagne, please?'

There was a last-minute hitch over the contracts, and it was spring before the shop was finally theirs. Then came the long period of consultation with Jamie's architect and designer, and the attendant devastation in the wake of builders and plumbers. Spring turned into summer, and the first cold breath of autumn was in the air before they were ready to decide on the fine details.

'What are we going to call this place?' Jamie asked. 'We must decide, and do it now. The stationery and china have to be designed, and the sign-painters are waiting to work on the frontage.'

The had debated the question all summer. 'Anne's' was dismissed as too dull, 'Jamie's' as too fey. Other suggestions had seemed pretentious, or cute, or uninteresting.

'I did have one last idea,' Angharad said, hesitatingly.

'Then let's hear it. Time's getting short.'

'What do you think of . . . Le Gallois?'

'Le Gallois? The Welshman?'

185

Angharad waited, a little breathlessly, while he turned the idea over in his mind. The name seemed suddenly important, a talisman.

'For William, you mean? He's still a little Celt, for all the impeccable metropolitan upbringing you're giving him. Oughtn't it to be the Welshwoman?'

'No,' Angharad smiled at him. The name wasn't for William. She wanted it for Harry. It was a sort of tribute, she thought wryly, an acknowledgment of the private fact that he wasn't forgotten. She wasn't hurt, any more. At least, Anne wasn't hurt. Smart London Anne shared everything with Jamie now, even loved him in an unhurried, tranquil way. She wasn't vulnerable, she believed, and she could afford the private memorial of 'Le Gallois'.

'I like it,' Jamie said. He was already doodling the words, tracing out a swooping 'L' and 'G'. 'Yes. I definitely like it. Le Gallois it shall be.'

As if the name was all that was lacking, the last preparations seemed to take no time at all. The new restaurant emerged like a butterfly from the chrysalis of planks and plaster. The walls turned smooth cream, the rough floors disappeared beneath a layer of taupe carpeting. Cream linen cloths and napkins arrived and Angharad smoothed them experimentally over the new tables, smiling to herself as she remembered the riot of hated red and white gingham inside Y Gegin Fach.

She spent less and less time at Duff's, more in the kitchens at Le Gallois working on the new menu. The chic understatement of the restaurant's decor was deliberate. The food was to be paramount. Angharad spent hours, with absorbed fascination, honing her new skills at *la nouvelle cuisine*. The sharp greens of a vegetable terrine gave her more pleasure than a complicated sauce, and the beautiful juxtaposition of the best and freshest ingredients more satisfaction than the most technically demanding traditional dish. Le Gallois was to be a considerable innovation. Angharad was exhilarated by the challenge. In the moments when she had time to think, and was gripped by panic, Jamie was there to reassure her.

A week before the opening party for Le Gallois, when the plane trees were beginning to show brown patches and the tired summer air smelt cold and sharp, reminding her of her early days in London two long years ago, Angharad's defences were tested. She had thought them invulerable, but to her horror they crumbled at once.

She had spent the afternoon at Le Gallois, and on her walk home to the Goulds' to pick up William, she bought an *Evening Standard* from the newsvendor on the corner of Sloane Square. She pushed the folded paper into her basket and hurried on, all her thoughts with William. Their early evenings together were the most treasured part of her day.

William greeted her at the nursery door, shouting 'Mamma! Mamma!' Then he toddled away to where Ned, the youngest Gould, was playing with a line of toy cars. William snatched one up and brandished it.

'See lorry! Lorry!'

Susie and Angharad laughed at him with delighted pride. Every day, it seemed, there was a new word or achievement to enjoy, and to relay to Jamie.

'What did he do today?' Jamie would ask, when he came in.

Tonight William was persuaded reluctantly to climb into his pushchair after the nightly ritual of kisses for all the Goulds. Angharad pushed him back to Godolphin Mansions by the familiar route, stopping as they always did to peer through the basement railings at a fat ginger cat asleep on a windowsill, and at the corner for William to gaze at the colourful blaze of a flower stall.

Once home, the rituals of supper and games in the bath were exactly the same, and as happy, as they always were. At last, William fell asleep in his cot with one fist clenched against his cheek.

For a moment Angharad leaned over him watching the black hair and the dark curve of his eyelashes. Then, sighing with contentment, she walked back into the sitting-room and poured herself a drink.

In an armchair, with her feet drawn up beneath her, she

187

unfolded the newspaper. Immediately, on the Diary page, a picture caught her eye.

It was a stereotyped film publicity shot of a girl in a thin shirt, wet from the sea. Drops of water shone on her skin and the clinging fabric showed off her small breasts. She was looking straight into the camera lens with a practised stare, half smiling, half-pouting. She looked young, and pretty, and taunting. The faintest flicker of a resemblance to someone else, unplaceable, nagged at the back of Angharad's mind. Idly she glanced at the accompanying paragraph.

'Bibi's backing Britain,' she read.

'Bibi Blake, star of the recent talked-about movie *Love All*, is backing Britain in a big way. She's just announced her engagement to the film's assistant director, who's British through and through. The lucky man is Harry Cotton and that, by the way, is a name to watch as carefully as his wife-to-be's.'

Angharad's arms felt like lead, as if there was lead in all her veins, solid to her fingertips so that they stiffened with the newspaper clenched in them and the words dancing smudgy black in front of her eyes.

*His wife-to-be.*

Angharad wanted to drop the paper, but she couldn't. She wanted to stop reading, but she couldn't.

'Cotton cut his directing teeth on New York commercials, but he reached the West Coast as assistant to Dale Preger on *Love All*. Now his name is whispered by those in the know as director of the low-budget, high-profile remake of *Fool's Paradise*. Starring Bibi, of course. For a man only in his early twenties, Cotton already has an enviable reputation as a hell-raiser in the old Hollywood style. But he told me tonight by telephone from the West Coast, 'Of course I shall be settling down. With Bibi. What more could a man ask?' What, indeed? Congratulations to them both. By the way, you can catch Cotton's early British-made short *As the Sun Was Rising* in a programme of similar features this week at the NFT. If you like that kind of thing. Me, I'll be waiting for *Fool's Paradise.*'

The diarist's next piece was about Prince Charles's latest girlfriend.

Slowly, concentrating very hard, Angharad unclenched her fingers and let the newspaper fall. It drifted from her lap on to the carpet and the picture of Bibi Blake pouted up at her.

*Of course I shall be settling down. What more could a man ask?*

Harry had forgotten, then. He had gone away to get all the things he had been so hungry for, and he had forgotten her as completely as if she had never existed.

Harry? Angharad shut her eyes, suddenly swept away by the vivid intensity of her memories. Two years since they had been in Wales together, watching the weather sweep in from the sea to the slopes of The Mountain. Two years since they had sworn, and known, that they loved each other. Two years since she had stumbled on him making love, and hate, and black confusion, with Laura.

Harry had walked away from that, and a world of otherness had swallowed him up. Just as it had done for her, even though she had met it with reluctance, changing Angharad into Anne. It must be happening to Laura too. Laura would be at Cambridge, almost certainly as much of a star in her own world as Harry promised to be in his. At least, Angharad thought, as she looked down into the pert face in the paper, he must be free of Laura now. He must be free, and happy.

Hell-raiser Harry Cotton. Yes. That was how he would be. And then finding what he wanted, settling down. The bitterness rose in Angharad's mouth and she tasted it like bile on her tongue.

What about me? Me, and his son? She stood up stiffly and picked up her drink. Looking down, she was surprised to see that the ice was unmelted. She felt that she had mixed it hours ago. I'll never be free, she realized. Never free of them both. As quickly as it had come, the bitterness vanished. It was replaced by a simple conviction as painful as a stab in

189

the heart. She would never love any man but Harry. No one would ever break through to her again. She would stay as Anne for ever, and Angharad would be lost even to herself.

For the very hopelessness of it she didn't want to cry, but the tears came just the same. She fought against them for a moment, and then let them fall.

She saw how fragile her equilibrium had been, and how misguided. Somehow, without even acknowledging it, she had let herself believe that Harry had gone to cut himself free. To break out of the tangled net that he and Laura had woven for themselves. And she had let herself hope that once he was free Harry would come back for her, and William. He had promised, long ago at the foot of Cefn Hill. A single paragraph in a newspaper had torn holes in that hopeful shroud. Suddenly she understood, with perfect clarity, that Harry had forgotten her. He had made his glib, meaningless promises to disentangle himself from a dull, local girl he had had enough of. Anger was fuelling her tears now. He was nothing to do with herself, or with William, except for the stamp of his features on the child's face. She hated him for his arrogance, and selfishness, and for the way that he had taken what she had to give and then rejected her.

And she loved him.

With the anger came a wild desire to do something, to hit back at Harry in some way that would hurt him in return. She had never tried to find him, and she cursed herself for her passivity. Yet she could try now, surely? Hollywood seemed a million miles away. But a letter to Llyn Fair, or to his film company, might reach him. She could even go to Cambridge, and ask Laura. Laura, where is he? I want him back.

No. She couldn't see Laura.

And even if she found Harry, what could she say?'

*Don't marry your starlet. Marry me instead, remember me? By the way, you've got a son, too. Just like you. Only not like you at all, please God.*

No.

The anger melted away and she stared down at the picture of Bibi Blake, cold with the shock and the utter absence of hope.

Behind her she heard a key turning in the lock and Jamie came in. She didn't look up and he came to her, holding out his hand so that she saw his striped shirt cuff, the gold signet ring on his little finger, the dark stuff of his jacket.

'What is it? Is it Gwyn? Your father? Not the baby?'

Blindly Angharad shook her head, hearing the sudden fear in his voice.

'Tell me then. Please, darling. You look like you used to look, at the beginning. I thought it was all over.'

Angharad could find nothing to say. And by not telling Jamie now, Angharad was shutting him out for good. She wanted to tell him, to let the whole story come spilling out, but the leap from this close-carpeted, elegant flat to Heulfryn, and Cefn, and Llyn Fair, was impossible to make. And her silence now would stay between them like a thick glass wall.

Angharad breathed in, a long, jagged breath. The struggle to hide her shock and grief gave her something to focus on.

'I heard something about someone I used to know. I didn't expect it, and it upset me. But it isn't important. Believe me. Let's not talk about it.' He didn't believe her, and Angharad knew that he didn't. She watched the reckoning in his sharp blue eyes.

At last Jamie said coolly, 'Of course, let's not talk about it, if you think that's the sensible way to deal with whatever it is. I won't look at you, so I won't ask myself what it is that's made you cry. Would you like a drink? No, you've got one. Well, and how was today? Apart from whatever it is, of course.'

She had hurt him, and she wanted to run to him and rub it away. But she didn't, and she felt the silence between them like the glass wall that she had feared.

It was a grey, cold afternoon and the rain came in sudden gusts, sending scudding patterns over the flat face of the river. Angharad crossed by Hungerford Bridge, looking down into the olive green water below her. A train clattered past from Charing Cross and the black iron of the bridge

191

rang dully under her feet. At the steps she walked slowly down, still with her head bent. The concrete heights around her brought welcome shelter from the sharp wind.

At the foot of the steps she looked left and right, taking her bearings. The concrete walls and pillars were stained with grey legs of rain damp, and the fitful eddies of cold air carried drifts of litter into the neglected corners. Her eyes stung with the grit in the air. Angharad blinked and read a sign. The Film Theatre was over to her left, and she turned like an automaton towards it.

She had come to see Harry's film. Unwillingly but inexorably she was drawn even to such a tenuous link with him.

'Young Directors,' the placards read. Angharad paid her membership subscription, bought a ticket, and found her way into the dim warmth of the cinema. It was almost empty. The few faces that she could see in the bluish light were turned intently to the screen. Would-be Young Directors, she realized. Painfully she was reminded of Harry as he had been two years ago. He had come a long way since then. He was on his way up the ladder now.

The first two films were uneven, uninteresting to her. Angharad sat in her seat immobile, mesmerized by the suspense of waiting. Then, without warning, the screen flooded with light. Against the brilliance a long silhouette rose, unbearably familiar. It was The Mountain, from the east, against the rising sun. The glowing rim of the sun edged over the rocky crest and light spilled into the foreground. It revealed the grass close-cropped by sheep, and the few trees licked into humps by the endless wind.

Somewhere behind Harry with his cumbersome camera was Llyn Fair. And ahead, framed for him by the viewfinder, the view of his childhood. Over the top of The Mountain and away.

The simple title credit rolled up the screen.

*As the Sun Was Rising. Harry Cotton.*

Angharad drew her lower lip between her teeth and bit into the flesh so sharply that the blood rose. But she was oblivious of it, and her eyes never left the screen. Above the low music of the soundtrack another sound swelled. It was a lark, singing, a black dot somewhere in the blue overhead. It was the very sound of The Mountain. Angharad had heard it a thousand times, a hundred times with Harry.

The music dropped away altogether and there was only the lark's song, and the wind in the grass. The stuffy darkness of the cinema dissolved around her, and Angharad was at home again.

The camera was moving now, over the grass, gathering speed as if it was flying. (How had he done that? Impressions and sensations flooded at Angharad from all sides). Then it stopped short, at a height somewhere, and looked downwards. A slow skein of sheep fanned out and then began to fold together again, like a pack of cards in a conjuror's hands.

(Beautiful patterns, Harry had said, and Angharad recalled the fierce light in his face. I'm no good if I haven't caught it. But he had caught it. He was good, without question. and his talent had taken him as far away from this film, and from herself, as it was possible to be. To Bibi Blake, and *Love All*.)

Behind the sheep was a busy black shape, the sheepdog. And behind the dog, a tiny figure toiling up the steep slope from the gate in the dry stone wall. The old farmer, Mr Ellis the Bwlch.

Harry's film was utterly simple. It was as if he had simply set up his camera and let it run, capturing the painful rhythm of the old man's days with unobtrusive accuracy. Even Angharad, with her rudimentary knowledge of film techniques, knew how difficult it must have been to achieve that bare simplicity.

The camera's eye saw the littered farmyard, and the few scratching hens. The tattered cockerel fluttered resentfully backwards, displaced by the shiny length of a new car. One of the farmer's sons came visiting, and the shiny shoes crossing the barren yard were left to make their own statement. The slow movements of the farm's life, circumscribed by ancient machinery and the unyielding hill land itself, were echoed exactly by the old man's hobble to

193

the farm gate in his market day corduroys.

The camera saw him in a corner of the Beast Market, hemmed in by other old men with critical eyes on the produce and livestock. Then it moved aside, as if drawn by a shaft of light. With a pain burning in her chest, Angharad saw herself, standing with her market basket balanced on her hip. The sun shone through the bell of hair that Laura had shaped for her, long ago grown out, now, to please Jamie. The girl's eyes were very wide, startled by something as they looked past the camera's unexplaining eye. Angharad felt the gulf between the girl, hardly more than a child, and herself. The old Angharad confronted her for a fleeting second or two. Yet Harry had kept her there, instead of shearing her out. Why? She felt him close again, almost convinced of the warmth of his shoulder next to her, as the rest of the film unrolled in front of her.

It brought a wave of homesickness that was almost suffocating.

Every vista was familiar, even the trees and stones. Harry's touch had given everything a kind of elegiac beauty that she knew didn't truly exist: his film sentimentalized the hill-farmer's life, but it was so exquisite a picture of her home that it stabbed her to the heart. She had had no idea, until this moment, how much she missed it, and how she ached to see it again.

There on the huge screen was the little tin chapel at the crossroads, and the lines of people filing inside. She had left Harry at the gate, and gone in with them. There, inside, was the line of plain glass windows with the morning light strengthening behind them, the severe whitewashed walls, and the rows of stiff Sunday suits. In the middle was the old man, not moving, his hands clenched on his stick.

Angharad's heart was thumping as it all flooded back. She could smell the dust in the chapel, and the faint whiff of boiled sweets and mothballs. Under the forbidding text at the end of the chapel the choir stood up. The hairs at the nape of her neck prickled, just a they had done when she first heard the singing on that August morning.

There was almost no sound recording on the film, but she

realized that somehow Harry had recorded this.

*Ar Hyd Y Nos.* Then, closing on him so that he filled the screen, the old farmer with his handkerchief at his face.

Harry knew how to drive his point home.

At once there came a sharp cut to the contrast of the child's face, the snub-nosed soloist singing *Early One Morning.* Night and morning, old and new. Optimism, and dead ends. Angharad found herself crying with the old farmer. As the solo ended the camera tracked away until it held the whole congregation in such sharp focus that the dancing specks of dust were almost visible in the shafts of light. The last notes died away and they stood up, the long line of dark backs obliterating everything. The screen went black, and there was only the triumphant singing of the anthem.

*Mae hen Wlad fy'Nhadau, yn anwyl i mi . . .*

The old land of my fathers, the words ran in Angharad's head, is beloved to me.

The intrusive lights came up and her hands flew up to shade her eyes. Angharad was protective of her secret, even in this anonymous place. She glanced sideways along the row of seats, and saw that her nearest neighbour was nodding, and scribbling notes.

Yes. Harry could make films. That talent had taken him a thousand miles, a world away.

Angharad made her way out into the bleak daylight, oppressed by a double sense of loss. She stared around at the stained concrete towering over her, the coils of windblown dust and litter, heard the buses grinding overhead along Waterloo Bridge, and hated it all. She couldn't go back home, to The Mountain and the sweet air, however much she longed to. And Harry was even further beyond her reach. The odd feeling of closeness, the sense that he was more real than anything else, was no more than an illusion. Angharad began the trek back across Hungerford Bridge, pulling her jacket around her to shut out the cold wind.

She would go on as she was. For William's sake, and because she could think of no other way to go. She was repaying Jamie's love and generosity with subterfuge, but she could think of no gentle way out of that, either.

'Why this sudden interest in soft porn?' Jamie teased her.

'It's supposed to be a good film,' Angharad answered. 'Lots of people have talked about it. I meant to see it when it first came out.' She hoped that her approximation of carelessness was convincing.

With the feverish secretiveness of an addict she had tracked down *Love All* in the cinema listings. She had to see that, too. Testing the imaginary links, drawn by the painful threads of curiosity.

'It's miles away,' Jamie grumbled.

'I don't mind going on my own. I don't want to drag you . . .' The film was only showing in the evenings, otherwise she would have slipped away alone.

'No, of course I'll come. Might pick up a few ideas. Is that what you think?'

'No.' Angharad was laughing in spite of herself, and with the laughter she was relieved to see the appraising look fade out of Jamie's eyes. He had been looking very closely at her, lately.

The film couldn't have been more different from *As the Sun Was Rising*. It was glossy and pretty in a soft-focus way, with irritating pretensions to seriousness overlying the real reason for its existence, which was to display as much as possible of Bibi Blake.

Harry was clearly being perfectly professional in his climb up the ladder. He was ready to make bad films as well as good ones, if they helped him in any way. Marrying the star couldn't be a hindrance, either.

His name came up, in small letters, in the credit list and Angharad stared at it with the sense that she was pursuing a stranger. She felt disgusted and disorientated. Harry's betrayal was complete. He was betraying himself, as well.

'Oh dear,' Jamie said as they filed out with the seedy-looking crowd, 'I don't think that that warrants anything more than a pizza.' It amused him to grade films on a scale of meals to be eaten afterwards.

'That's fine,' Angharad said dully.

Over the meal Jamie looked across the table at her and said, 'You know, she looks just a little bit like you.'

'Who?'

'Didn't you see enough of her? Booboo or whatever her name is, in the film.' *Click*. The vague familiarity that had nagged at her when she saw the newspaper photograph Under the pout, the heavy eyelids and the direct stare, Bibi Blake's face did indefinably resemble her own.

'She doesn't.' Angharad's knife dropped with a clatter and faces at the nearby tables turned around covertly to stare. 'She looks nothing like me. Don't ever say that again.' The idea was repellent. It was horrible to think of being one in a line of look-alikes.

Another unwelcome thought dawned on her. Perhaps their very attraction, her own and Bibi Blake's with their fair hair and skin, was their physical unlikeness to Laura. Harry's denial of his sister.

'Do you feel ill?' Jamie's voice was gentle, but the sharp eyes missed nothing. Angharad did feel dizzy, and the table seemed a long way down as if she was peering through the wrong end of a telescope. But she steeled herself and picked up her knife again.

'No. I'm fine. Don't tell me I look like that horrible girl, that's all.' They finished their meal, and the thick glass wall of silence had slid between them yet again.

# CHAPTER EIGHT

'Why do we have to come all this way?' one of the girls complained in the taxi. 'Aren't there enough places to eat in Soho? I'm completely ravenous.'

'Harry's idea,' someone answered, as if that was sufficient explanation.

Harry was wedged into his corner, silently watching the London streets slide past the cab window. He might have been miles away from the noisy group of people with whom he had been watching the rough cut of a new film at a Wardour Street preview theatre.

'You a Londoner, Hal?' asked the man from the Coast who had money to invest in a new project.

Harry shook himself out of his reverie. Seeing the tangled ribbons of London streets like this reminded him of the weeks he had spent endlessly looking for Angharad. Millions of faces, jostling and crowding, and never a hope of finding her.

'Me? No, Morty, I'm a Welshman.'

Le Gallois. The Welshman. The name of the new restaurant had sprung out at him from a flyer, and he had decided at once to visit it. It took him back to the days of searching when he had followed up the slenderest connecting threads, like this one, in case they led back to her. How long? Five, six years ago. So much had happened since then, but in another sense nothing had happened at all.

'We're going to Le Gallois,' he had said to the party outside the preview theatre, not caring whether they came or not. They had come, of course, all of them, and now Harry found himself wishing as he did too often nowadays that he was alone.

The taxi pulled up abruptly and the girls fell forward, laughing and exclaiming. Harry put out a steadying hand to one of them and felt the pressure of it returned, too eagerly. He was frowning as he paid the driver and shepherded the little group into the restaurant.

The foyer was cool and wide, and a greeter came hurrying forward, American-style. Morty began to look more cheerful.

'Harry Cotton,' Harry said briefly. 'A table for seven. My office booked it.'

The girl ran her finger down the list in her book, shaking her head. 'I hope there hasn't been a mistake, Mr Cotton. We've been very full since we opened, and this last week...'

Harry leaned over her and pointed. 'That's it. Parallax Productions. I'm sorry, I didn't know my secretary had given the company name.'

Angharad had taken the call, and had written the film company's name in the book herself.

The greeter was smiling, relieved. 'Not at all. This way, sir.'

There was a round table laid for seven in the middle of the room. Harry saw that his guests were seated before looking around him. Cream tablecloths, neutral walls and carpets, a comfortable room full of fashionably dressed people who could equally well have been in New York, or Rome, or Los Angeles. Le Gallois, Harry thought wearily. There was nothing Welsh here at all. It was exactly like a hundred other good restaurants he knew across the world. There was no connection at all with anything that mattered to him. Or rather, anything hat had once mattered before life became a numbing matter of working too hard for oblivion's sake, and playing too hard in an equally vain effort to compensate for that.

The Welshman, indeed. Why should he think there was anything significant about that, any more? He had stopped looking for Angharad Owain long ago. Stopped thinking about her, even, except in odd, anachronistic moments that caught him off his guard like this one. There had been the weeks when, believing that he knew her so well that he knew what she would do, he had come to London, lived on his hunches, and tramped from restaurant to restaurant in an attempt to find where she was working. She loved cooking.

199

That would be her natural choice.

There had been no trace of her, of course.

Harry smiled an involuntary, cynical smile at the futility of his efforts. He must have been hopelessly in love with her. The old lady, her aunt, had never budged an inch. Harry had gone back again and again, begging now to be put in touch with her. But Gwyn Owain's face had remained stony, averted from him.

'If you knew the truth about our two families, boy, you'd understand why I don't want you here. Angharad's never asked for you. Never, ever asked for you. If she had, that would be different. Go away, and forget her because she has forgotten you. She looks prettier and happier than I have ever seen her. She's safe, and secure, and that's the best way for it to be.'

Harry turned away again, trying to blunt the bitterness of having lost her with the knowledge that she was happy.

The last time he had seen Gwyn was years ago, now. She had held firm until the last. 'Angharad has someone to take care of her now. They aren't married yet, but I'm sure they will be. Why don't you leave us alone?'

After that, Harry had stopped searching. Of course Angharad wouldn't need or want him. After what she had seen, knowing what she knew, why had he deluded himself that she still might?

Laura had won. As always, she had been clever enough to see the real threat.

Laura didn't change. Not after her own marriage, not after his own, undertaken in despair and apathy and so soon over. Harry hated himself for that. It was, he reflected at the round table in Le Gallois, one more thing to add to the list that had begun with Laura.

After Angharad, he had denied her, but the responsibility of loving hadn't changed. Laura was wilder now, and sadder. He could do no more than care for her, mitigating her self-destructiveness as gently as he could, but the weight of Laura hung round Harry's neck as heavy as a stone. It was the effort of bearing that weight, not the excesses of his own life, which had drawn the premature lines in Harry's face and feathered the grey streaks in the black hair at his temples.

At the thought of Laura, Harry's fist clenched, the wine glass in his fingers juddered and spread a red stain on the tablecloth. As the waiter swooped behind him Harry heard Morty say, 'You okay? You're kind of quiet.'

In an instant Harry collected himself. He was neglecting his guests at the clinching point of a big deal, the wrong moment to allow his reputation for moodiness to gather weight. If there was no work, there was nothing.

Harry hooked his arm through the back of his chair, trying to relax, and smiled his famous smile.

'I'm sorry,' he said. 'Blame the restaurant. The name of it reminded me, and I was thinking about the first film I ever made, years ago, when I was a kid. I had one creaky camera, and enough ideas to bust a billion dollar budget. The opening scene had to be a tracking shot across a mountain . . .'

Harry launched himself into the story. It was richly amusing, and at his own expense. His audience was laughing, and the atmosphere thawed into appreciative warmth.

It was a convivial meal, and the deal was done.

At the end, Harry excused himself briefly from the table. One of the women, a new actress with hopes of a plum part, turned to the other. 'Tasty guy, wouldn't you say, Dinah?'

The second woman was an agent, enjoying and cultivating her reputation for hard-bittenness. She raised her eyebrows a fraction.

'If you like that sort of thing. A little too perfunctory for my tastes, and chilly behind the spectacular charm. But go ahead and join the queue. There's been no one for longer than a week since Bibi.'

'Why did he marry that birdbrain?'

'Bibi decided to marry him. She just went right ahead and did it. I knew Harry pretty well in those days, and it was just as if he didn't give a damn either way. My theory is that he did it out of boredom, or apathy. Or perhaps to escape something.' Dinah glanced around the table and saw that everyone else was busy talking. She bent her head and whispered, 'I hear that Harry is a man with a past. There is a sister. I met her once. Ve-ery beautiful and glittery. Married to a millionaire. Well, rumour has it that Harry and his sister are as close as this.' Dinah held up her fingers, twined around each other. 'Closer, even. Juicy, no? Hardly surprising it didn't last with Bibi.'

The younger girl's head jerked back. 'I don't beleive that. It's disgusting.' Dinah shrugged and leaned back to light a cigarette.

Harry returned to the table. He stood behind Morty's chair and said easily, 'Okay, people, everyone ready? Two cabs outside. Claridge's for you, Morty. Will you drop the girls in Knightsbridge? And a very reluctant driver to take the rest of the party to fashionable Limehouse. Right, Hugh?'

Out on the pavement in front of the lighted windows emblazoned 'Le Gallois', the pretty actress wound her arms around Harry's neck and kissed him. 'Can't we go dancing? Or at least come back and have a drink.'

Gently, Harry disentangled her arms. 'I'll call you,' he said.

The evening was over at last. He had no intention of prolonging it. The two taxis chugged away.

Harry stood for a moment on the pavement. Then he began to walk slowly away, a lean man huddled into an anonymous raincoat, staring into the bright windows, thinking.

The intercom buzzed on Angharad's desk.

'Anne, will you speak to Gregory Hunt? He wants to book for a private party on the twentieth. I told him it was unlikely, but he wants to talk to you direct.'

Angharad pushed her pile of accounts to one side, sighing, and turned the pages of the restaurant diary.

'The twentieth? Not a chance. But put him through, Louise, will you?' Angharad flicked the intercom switch and leant back in her chair, swivelling it from habit to look out of the window, although the limited view was masked now by the slats of a blind.

'Hello, Gregory. Yes, fine, thanks. Yes, the family too,
Yours? Good. Look, I'm so sorry, but the twentieth is tricky.
We've got two other private parties booked, and the
restaurant nearly full already . . .'

As she talked, Angharad listened mechanically to herself.
Apologetic, placatory, and then tactfully suggesting another
evening. Perhaps the twenty-first? She was efficient,
experienced at her job, coolly pleasant. She knew that she
was good at it, but her heart wasn't in it. Every hour of the
afternoon spent in her office over the Le Gallois dining-room,
instead of in the kitchen, was an hour wasted. But as the time
passed, and the restaurant's reputation grew, it seemed that
she did less and less cooking and more and more
administration. She had a brigade of young chefs to assist her
now, and she felt that they had all the fun while she did all
the dull things up in the office.

Angharad sighed again as she wrote the new booking up
in the diary and then transmitted the instructions through
to Louise.

'Ready for a cup of tea?' the secretary asked. Angharad
glanced at her watch, the Victorian one on the black silk
strap that Jamie had given her for their first Christmas
together. She had another, a tiny wafer of gold, but she
preferred this one.

'No, thanks. I think I'll go home and have tea with
William when he gets back from school. Will you tell them
downstairs that I'll be back about eight?'

Angharad preferred the evenings. There was more
cooking, less business. On her way out of the room she
paused, briefly, at a long mirror to look at herself.
Angharad's fair hair was discreetly blonde-streaked, now,
and fashionably cut. Clever make-up made her wide eyes
wider, and her perfect pale skin was left to speak for itself.
She was wearing a loose, collarless shirt over a calf-length
pleated skirt and expensive black leather boots. A thin gold
chain around her neck was her only jewellery.

She looked, Angharad thought, just what she was. A busy,
successful career woman in her mid-twenties. From her

calm, assured áppearance, no one would have guessed that she was increasingly restless, and increasingly heavy-hearted.

She felt that somewhere, not so very long ago or so that it was even noticeable at the time, she had taken a wrong turning. And now, with every day that passed, it grew harder to remember, let alone to recapture, her old self. That in itself wouldn't be so hard, Angharad reflected, if she didn't feel so disengaged from everything that turning had brought to her. It was pleasant, of course, to be successful and not to worry any more about money. She recognized her luck, and was grateful for it, in having friends, the opportunity to travel, and the close partnership with Jamie. But yet she felt isolated by the thick glass walls, which let her see everything but prevented her from joining in completely.

In the mirror she saw the sadness in her own eyes and wondered if maturity was insidiously deforming her from within. Could it be that she was turning into the emotional amputee that she knew, and pitied, in her remote father? Only her son, William junior, had the power to cut her with fear, or irradiate her with happiness.

Angharad shivered, and turned away from her reflection in the glass. Looking at her watch again, she saw that it wasn't yet four o'clock. If she hurried, she could be home before William and they could spend a few precious hours together.

She snatched her coat from the hanger and ran down the stairs. There would be no one left in the restaurant at this time of day, and it would be quicker to leave by the front door.

As soon as she slipped into the restaurant, she saw that she was mistaken. There was a boisterous group of six or seven men at a table near the door, with brandy glasses ranged in front of them and a blue pall of cigar smoke hanging over their heads. Two bored waiters were hovering at a little distance, and they straightened up when they saw Angharad. She nodded at them, acknowledging their impatience without complicity, and prepared to walk discreetly past the extravagant lunchers. One of the waiters had his hand already on the door to open it for her, when someone touched her sleeve.

'*Angharad? Be ti'wneud?*'

She stopped dead. One of the men at the table had turned round to look at her, and now he was smiling up into her face. The Welsh voice spoke with complete familiarity, as if they had only seen each other yesterday. Still in Welsh, but less confidently now, the man said, 'It *is* Angharad Owan, isn't it?'

The waiters were staring at her in surprise, but she took no notice. The musical content of Welsh, and her own name, had come as such a shock in this distant, citified dining-room.

'Yes,' she answered. The face came back to her: a cheeky little boy with dark eyes and round cheeks. 'You're ... you're one of the Williams twins, aren't you? Dicky, or Gareth?'

'*Da iawn.* Gareth. Well, Angharad, it's a long time, isn't it?'

A very long time. Another life. She remembered the wide, fragrant spaces of Cae Mawr, and the open field and slopes of The Mountain she had explored side by side with the boy that this red-faced, prosperous-looking man had once been. This expense-account Le Gallois luncher had once lived in a little lopsided house down the street at Cefn. He would remember the same cadences of the Sunday church bells, and the ridge of The Mountain against the sky.

She wanted to put her arms around him and beg him, 'Talk to me about it. Anything about it. Won't you, please?' Instead she invited him, 'Won't you join me for a drink, Gareth?'

He waved expansively and began to protest that she must join him, but Angharad raised her eyebrows a fraction at one of the waiters and at once a fresh cloth was smoothed over a table across the room, and the chairs were held out for them. Gareth excused himself to his party, saying that he had met an old friend. A ribald murmur followed him as he walked away. Angharad had placed them already. They were salesmen, celebrating a big contract.

Gareth sat down opposite her and Angharad asked the

waiter, 'Some more coffee and another cognac, please, for Mr Williams, and perhaps you would bring me some tea.'

Gareth's eyebrows had lifted so far that they tangled with his black curly hair. 'You must be quite a regular?'

Angharad smiled. Mischief and pleasure mingled in it. To Gareth Williams, her sophisticated air vanished and she was the skinny nine-year-old tomboy of Cefn again.

'You haven't changed a bit.'

'Oh, yes I have.' For all her vague dissatisfaction, Angharad was proud of her achievement. 'This is my restaurant. What d'you think?'

He whistled admiringly.

'You can't be doing too badly yourself.'

'Computers. It's a Cheshire-based company. I live in Chester now, but I'm in London a good deal. We've just made a sale that'll see us right for a year. Calls for a celebration, you see. Fancy it being your place, Angharad.' They looked at each other appraisingly, and it was Angharad's eyes that dropped first.

'Do you ever go back to Cefn?' she whispered. 'What's it like now?'

'Why didn't you ever come home?' Straight to the point, with native sharpness. No sophisticated verbal fencing at Cefn.

Angharad bluffed quickly. 'Oh, I will. Very soon. I've meant to go back for ages.' Her voice sounded defensive, and she knew it. Gareth was still looking at her. What did they all say about her, back home?

'It's just the same. I was there on Sunday. Trevor the Wagon asleep on the bench outside the Chapel porch, and all of them filing out with their hymnbooks and pretending he was invisible.'

Angharad sat back in her chair and laughed as if she was fifteen again. Old Trevor drove a scrap-metal wagon, and his inability to stay on it, literally or metaphorically, was the basis of a not-very-subtle local joke.

'Remember when we asked him for a ride down the valley?'

'And Dicky sat on the top of an old wash-boiler, and fell

off and broke his nose? Dicky married Jess Rhys, you know. Two kids, now, and a bungalow on the new estate.'

Freckle-faced Jessie Rhys, with her orange-red hair and wide, gappy smile. A wife and mother now, and last time Angharad had seen her she had been a schoolgirl. She knew what had happened, from Gwyn, but she felt the isolation of the exile sharper still.

'The new estate?'

'Don't you know about that? Twenty bungalows on that bit of land beyond the church. There was a lot of fuss when they started going up. Your Dad was the main opponent. Said they ruin the view he's been enjoying for twenty years and had hoped to enjoy for one or two more.' There was a small silence before Gareth said, 'Not too well, now, your Dad, is he?'

Cold fingers of fear touched her. Gwyn had said nothing in her last letter, except that William was tired. Could it be that her aunt was hiding something from her?

'He's been tired lately,' Angharad said quickly. She wasn't sure how much Gareth Williams or anyone else knew about their estrangement, and her instinct was to conceal as much as she could. 'He's not so young, any more.'

To her concern, Gareth looked surprised and unconvinced. 'Ah. Glad it isn't anything more serious.'

To change the subject, she asked for news of other contemporaries from the village. Obligingly Gareth plunged into a stream of stories and gossip. In spite of her sudden anxiety, Angharad listened with fascinated pleasure. The names and the places were so familiar, as were the very cadences of Gareth's voice. Her home came flooding back to her, like a long-closed cupboard door being opened to release a tumble of dusty but precious mementoes. Gareth didn't speak of it, because it wouldn't have occurred to him, but his talk brought back the physical reality of the place too. With sudden clarity, as if she hadn't thought about it for years, Angharad saw the long street with its uneven paving stones, the sun on the grey slate, and the broken line of the old rooftops against the hillside.

'Miss it?' Gareth asked her.

'Yes.' *I hardly know how much. Or even why.*

She had been so absorbed in their talk that she hadn't noticed that Gareth's companions had called for the bill and paid it. Gareth's brandy glass and coffee cup were empty again, and behind him one of the waiters was yawning covertly.

'You ought to come back.'

Angharad collected herself with an effort and gestured at the dining-room, all chic greys and creams, so different from what she knew and what Gareth knew.

'Not easy,' she smiled at him.

'You should, just the same.'

The cold fingers clasped a little tighter. He was warning her of something. They said their goodbyes in the restaurant doorway.

'I'll give your love to Dick and Jessie, shall I?'

'Of course.'

Gareth was on the point of turning away to his impatient colleagues when Jamie arrived. He kissed Angharad and said, 'I hoped I'd catch you. I rang home, and guessed you were still here.'

Angharad had to introduce them. The juxtaposition of the two men struck her as incongruous. 'Jamie Duff. My partner.' Gareth's eyebrows went up once more into his curly black forelock. The two men exchanged pleasantries before Gareth turned away again.

'Goodbye, love,' he said to Angharad in Welsh. It made her feel their bond, and their complicity against the smooth bustle of the King's Road. 'Don't forget your old friends, will you? At least you've got the name to remind you.' And he looked up at the sign of the Gallois, half winked at her, and was gone.

Painfully, she shook her head. Jamie was already steering her away to where his car was sitting on a yellow line.

'Face from the past?' he asked mildly, and they drove away together.

Angharad sat in silence, unseeingly staring out as the car crawled past the brightly-lit windows of Peter Jones, and through the clogged traffic in Sloane Square. It was all invisible to her. She was imagining her father walking down the street in Cefn. He was walking painfully, with a stick, and his skin was waxy-yellow. Aunty Gwyn, Jessie Rhys, Dicky Williams, and the rest were watching him, and shaking their heads. The vividness of the picture shocked her. It was like a premonition.

Angharad was gripped buy a violent, panicky impatience. It grew so fast that it threatened to suffocate her, so that it was torture to go on sitting still in the almost-stationary car. Jamie was whistling and drumming his fingers lightly on the wheel.

If she jumped out now, into the Sloane Square traffic, what could she do? Gwyn had no telephone. Angharad could hardly rush to the station and catch the next train home after an absence of seven years. All she could do was write to Gwyn, ask her for the truth, and wait for the post.

But Angharad knew, with utter conviction, that she must go home. For years she had been closing her mind to the thought, and had expunged it so successfully that, now it had come back to her and she had admitted it, the force of it was doubled. She was afraid for her father, and her fear overcame all the years of silence.

She wanted to see him again. In case he was going to die.

They reached home. Jamie and Angharad were joint owners of their own white-painted terraced house now. The late afternoon spring sunshine shone on daffodils and grape hyacinths in tubs on the steps that led up to the white front door.

Angharad was still silent, preoccupied with her own thoughts, as they went inside together. The latest in the line of successors to Susie greeted them, and William came tumbling down the stairs after her.

In spite of everything, Angharad's face broke into smiles when she saw him.

At six, William was a very normal little boy, dark-haired and with an unusually direct clear blue gaze. Like most mothers, Angharad was fascinated and touched, now, to see her son hovering on the brink between the attachment of babyhood and a trenchant independence that would be all his own. William was growing up with startling speed. Could she take him him, too, before it was too late?

*Not your Cotton bastard*, his grandfather had said.

'Mum! Jamie! Come and see what I've done!'

As he turned to run back upstairs she saw his dark hair over his collar, and the paint stains on his dungarees, and felt the potency of her love for him. All the thwarted love that she had allowed to focus on him. They owed it to Jamie's influence, the two of them, that William was so happy, so unconcerned, and ordinary.

Side by side, they followed the child up to his room. And what about Jamie? What could she say to him, about going home? Not now. She needed to think, first, before too many layers were peeled away.

In William's room they saw that he had rearranged the layout of his model trains. He was a passionate and indiscriminate enthusiast, and models of modern diesels shared the track with replicas of nineteenth-century American wood-burning locomotives. This afternoon he had built an engine-shed, a lopsided gluey edifice of cardboard boxes and tubes.

'That's very handsome,' Jamie said appreciatively. They knelt down together on the carpet and began snaking the engines along the tracks and into the shed.

They couldn't have looked a more perfect picture of a happy family, Angharad thought.

Angharad knelt down too. She wanted to hug William, to reassure herself, but he elbowed her absently aside. The boy was engrossed in demonstrating his construction to Jamie. She smiled, a little lopsidedly, and straightened up.

'You don't need me, you two, do you? I've got some things to do. Sausages for supper, Willum?'

Jamie looked round, but she had already gone. He frowned, hesitating, but William was pulling at his sleeve.

'Isn't it good?' the child crowed. 'Look, a space for every engine.'

Angharad went down to their bedroom. She sank down on the wide bed, looking blankly around at the wicker chairs, the Victorian patchwork quilt that had been her first extravagant present to herself, the pretty, well-polished furniture and her bottles of expensive scent beside Jamie's silver-backed brushes on the tallboy. All the trappings of a comfortable life; a married life.

Not that Jamie and she were married. They had talked briefly about it when they bought the house, and Angharad had said no, as gently and as firmly a she could.

It had been the only possible answer.

Anne, the woman who lived in this sunny house and wore the elegant clothes in the long wardrobe in front of her, might have married Jamie Duff. Just as Anne would matter-of-factly have said that Harry was forgotten, dwindled to barely more than a name from long ago.

But deep inside Anne, Angharad still lived, unacknowledged in this orderly, prosperous life, and Angharad had never forgotten. Nor would she, ever. This afternoon Gareth Williams, who ought to have been no more than a stranger himself, had reached straight out and touched her hidden self. Her old love for Harry, her estrangement from her father, her son's real heritage and the ties that bound her to the village, formed a knot of memories and feelings that she had buried, and then varnished over with Anne's pleasant routines. But to single out one of those buried strands was to expose them all, so that they lay as raw as nervy ganglia under the surgeon's knife.

Gareth had done that. Whether he was obliquely warning her about her father or not, he had brought the fear out. And with the fear came the old bitterness mixed with love, a fierce longing to go home, and knowledge that going back would reawaken too many old memories. How would all those memories affect herself and Jamie, and William, who bore the clear mark of his antecedents in his face?

Angharad shivered and pressed her fingers to her eyes. She had a premonition, and it drew her home so strongly that she knew she shouldn't resist it. But of all the rest, the thousand knotted implications, she was afraid and apprehensive.

She heard a footstep behind her and turned to see William. He was watching her with his head on one side, serious-faced.

211

'Mummy, why are you sad?'

Almost since babyhood, he had had the sensitivity to read her moods. Quickly she smiled, suppressing the urge to snatch him to her and hide herself behind his innocence.

'People do get sad sometimes. You do yourself, don't you?'

'Not today, though.'

Angharad stood up and took his hand. 'I'll try not to be, either. Come on. Let's go and see if we can find you some supper.'

Later, when William was in bed, Jamie and Angharad sat facing each other across the table in the long basement kitchen. The warm light winked on copper pans hung on one wall, and on the plates ranged along the dresser. Jamie drained his glass of wine and said cheerfully, 'Shall we talk about this French trip? We should book soon, to get decent hotels, and to do that we must have an itinerary.'

Jamie loved plans, and maps, and making arrangements. They had been planning an early summer holiday, a slow meander down through Burgundy and the Rhône valley to the Mediterranean. They had always been good at holidays together. Some of their happiest times had been spent in Austria, in Italy and in the remote reaches of provincial France.

Angharad looked up from her glass. 'French holiday?' Her thoughts had been in Cefn, and with the letter she must write to Gwyn.

Jamie's hand closed tightly over hers. She tensed herself to draw back, and then let it lie.

'What is it? You haven't spoken all evening. Don't you want to go on holiday?'

Angharad breathed in deeply. 'I can't go, Jamie. I want to go home, instead.' A pool of silence seeped outwards from the table. Angharad's head was bent so that he couldn't see her face, although he stared sharply at her. He was looking for signs of the old Anne, as he secretly called her. The old Anne was the mysterious, half-tamed girl who had come to his restaurant and begged for a job. And had then borne a child, and wiped their joint histories clean like a slate. She had fascinated him and then unbalanced him into love, but he preferred the woman he had now. 'His' Anne believed in and wanted the same things as he did himself.

Except marriage.

Now he watched with covert anxiety for flickers of the other girl. She had a streak of Celtic wildness in her, and a fierce stubbornness. And she came of a culture that he couldn't begin to understand. It was a measure of her versatility, he thought now, that she had absorbed his own culture so seamlessly. Yet now, alarmingly, it was the other unknowable girl who sat opposite him.

'Home to Wales?'

She nodded. 'A man came to the restaurant this afternoon . . .'

Jamie sat very still. 'A man? The one I met?' He saw again the dark-haired Welshman with the cheeky, confident air. Suddenly an abyss opened at Jamie's feet.

'Just a man I used to know, used to play with, from the village. He said that Dad had been ill. I think . . . he was warning me, telling me I should go back. I've got to, Jamie.'

He flinched from the fire in her eyes, but he felt a wave of relief too. 'Of course. But wouldn't Gwyn have told you if it was anything serious?'

'You know she wouldn't.'

That was no more than the truth. Gwyn's instinct, her judgement blurred by age and isolation, would be to protect one of them against the other. She would hope for William to improve, so that Angharad would not have to be worried at all.

Jamie's hands were chafing comfortingly now. At last she looked directly at him. 'He's an old man. I'm afraid that he's going to die, before we see each other again.'

He said, 'You must go. As soon as you can. And take the boy with you. But write to Gwyn first, won't you? Find out what's really wrong?'

'Yes. Of course that's what I'll do.'

If only it would be as simple as that, she thought. With her heightened perceptions the way they were sitting, facing each other with their hands linked across the table, reminded her of Heulfryn. Past Jamie's shoulder she could see Harry's face, every line of it clear and sharp, and she stared into the eyes.

Was the memory of Harry going to haunt her for ever?

Before bed, Angharad went up to her desk and took out a sheet of writing paper. Quickly she wrote a letter to Gwyn, explaining that she had unexpectedly met Gareth Williams, and he had mentioned her father's illness. *What's really the matter? How serious is it? Please tell me, Aunty Gwyn. I'd much rather know. I can come home at once.*

The letter finished, she folded it and sealed it in an envelope. In rummaging for a stamp her fingers met the edge of a small folder. With a quick backwards glance, Angharad made sure that she was alone. Jamie was still in the kitchen, sitting with the newspaper and a glass of whisky. She took the folder out and opened it. It held a small sheaf of cuttings and photographs.

The first picture, brittle with age now, showed herself, childish, and Laura, sitting together on the school pavilion steps. Angharad had kept the picture pinned on her school bedroom wall for a year because she saw the lines of Harry's face within his sister's. Now, looking down at it, she could only see Laura herself. She was looking into the camera with her challenging, faintly mocking stare.

Underneath the picture lay an announcement roughly torn from *The Times* engagement columns.

The engagement is announced between Laura Veronica, only daughter of Mr and Mrs J. J. Cotton, of Llyn Fair House, Llyn Fair, Clwyd, and Mr Jeremy Argent, of London SW1.

It was dated three years ago, when Laura would have been just out of Cambridge.

The rest of the cuttings were all about Harry.

There were several film reviews, nearly all favourable, although there were one or two that seemed to confuse personal with professional disapproval. The other items, much more numerous, were snippets from gossip columns. One picture showed Harry and his wife arriving in evening dress at a première. The caption archly mentioned wedded bliss. Angharad kept her eyes turned way from it, although she knew the words by heart. Another piece, not much more recent, insinuated that the happy couple weren't quite as happy as all that. Six months later there were reports of a separation, and then a divorce. Bibi Blake was quickly remarried to an older, much-married household name. 'I wish them the best of luck,' Harry was reported as saying. 'Especially him.'

After that Harry's name was coupled with about a dozen others, but hardly more than once. Angharad read the latest one, a few months old now. It was no different from any of the rest.

'Has lovely Helene Oriel set her heart on Harry Cotton, Hollywood's not-such-an-enfant terrible? If she has, our advice would be to think again. My spies tell me that Harry shows no sign yet of wanting to stop playing the field.'

Angharad frowned faintly, puzzled by the vulgarity of it. He sounded so different from the Harry she had known. Had he changed so much? And if he hadn't changed, how could he let them write things like that about him? She gathered up the cuttings and thrust them back into the folder. It was a slender enough history, but it told her as much and more than she needed to know.

She buried the folder again beneath her papers, found a stamp, and stuck it firmly to her letter. Behind her, she could hear Jamie coming up the stairs. He came in, and put his arms round her as she sat still staring down at the envelope.

'Don't worry any more until you know for sure,' he said gently. 'Come on. Let's go to bed.'

Later, with Jamie's arms wound around her, Angharad stared sightlessly up into the dark. They had made love, gently and considerately, as always. It was a pleasant, intimate habit, like so much else in their life together. Jamie had drifted off to sleep. Angharad clenched her teeth, and felt the muscles tighten all along her back and down to her calves, in an effort to lie motionless. Anxiety gnawed at her as she thought back to the meeting with Gareth.

Only this afternoon in her office she had felt remote and

disaffected, cut off from life by the thick glass walls. Just a few words that changed that.

Would they send her home?

Home, perhaps to a dying man. The image of William hobbling along the village street under the concerned eyes was a sickeningly persistent one. It was there, whether she screwed her eyes shut, or went on staring into the dark. Today's had been a chance meeting, she thought, but something like it would have happened sooner or later. She would have had to face the thought of going home, and seeing the old knots come snaking out from their burial place. Involuntarily Angharad rolled her head on the pillow and Jamie stirred in his sleep. He murmured something, and his arms tightened around her.

What was right, for little William, and for Jamie, and herself?

To go on living with the muffled senses that she had come half to accept, or to turn back to Wales and to risk the vivid memories and all their potential for pain?

Angharad didn't know. She felt the years of experience flaking away, to leave her eighteen again.

It was very late when she fell into an uneasy, dream-riddled sleep. Bright light shining into her eyes woke her again, and she lay blinking, trying to grasp the reason for the heaviness and foreboding that made her want to dive back into sleep.

Then she saw that the pretty draped blinds at the window were drawn up, the spring sunshine was striking into her face, and she emembered. The letter to Aunty Gwyn, lying on her desk, ready for the post.

Angharad could hear Jamie whistling in their bathroom.

Then, with the sound of bare scuffling feet, William launched himself from the doorway. He was still in his red pyjamas, and his hair was tousled from sleep. It was his self-appointed job to bring up the post and the newspapers in the morning, and he was carrying them now. He leapt on to the bed, scattering the envelopes, and dived under the covers with her.

'Wake up, it's late. Jamie and I have been up for ages.' He was squirming and kicking, half wanting to be cuddled but

216

too impatient for the day to begin to lie still for more than a second. He wriggled away and began to bounce on the bed. 'Lots of letters. All bills, I bet.' He sounded, for an instant, just like Jamie.

'I bet,' Angharad agreed weakly, and rolled over to pick them up. She saw at once, lying on the pale grey carpet, an envelope with Gwyn's upright handwriting. It had grown much less firm over the last few months.

Angharad snatched it up and her fingers shook at tearing it open. There were two closely-written sheets. She skimmed quickly through them, feeling as if there was ice with the blood in her veins.

William was shouting something and tugging at her arm, and she shook him off with anxious asperity.

'Don't, William. This is an important letter. Go and talk to Jamie, will you?'

The child went away, startled, looking back at her once from the doorway with a wide, puzzled stare.

Angharad smoothed the letter out and read it again, slowly. It was written from Angharad's home, the square house at the end of the village, instead of the old schoolhouse.

Darling Angharad,

I'm afraid that the news isn't so very good this time. You see, William has been poorly lately. At first we thought it was a winter chill, then a stomach bug, and then Dr Hughes thought that he might have an ulcer. He took him in to Queen Mary's for a few tests. I didn't mention it to you, *cariad*, because I didn't want to worry you with you being so busy, and Dr Hughes was sure that it wasn't anything to worry about. Now the tests are done, and the doctor in the hospital wants to keep him there longer for some observation and some treatment. They don't seem sure yet what's the matter, but I know they're doing their best. Your Dad has been in some pain and not in the best of spirits, so I moved myself down the street here to look after him. Now that he's gone in the hospital I'm staying to keep an eye on it in case he's worrying himself. He's much better in the hospital where they can see to him properly, but he's not a good patient, as you can imagine.

I'm sure he will be out and about again soon but, my dear, what would you say to coming home for a few days? I know how hard it will be for you after so long, and with your work down there and everything, but will you try? William hasn't mentioned it, but I know that in his heart he wants to see you, and the boy.

The rest of the letter dealt, with determined cheerfulness, with village news. Don't worry, the last line read. But I think it's time for all these old breaches to be healed, don't you?

Before it's too late, Angharad grimly supplied. I know what's the matter with him. I can hear it in the doctors' very euphemisms, of tests and observation and treatment.

And dear, loving Aunty Gwyn, writing just as she talks, knows it too, but can't bring herself to say it.

Angharad pressed the heels of her hands briefly into her eyes, and then straightened up. She walked briskly through into the bathroom where Jamie was shaving. William was playing with his shaving brush, daubing his own smooth cheeks with blobs of white foam.

Silently, Angharad held out the letter. Jamie took it and read it.

'You must go immediately,' he said. So she wasn't imagining the urgency. Jamie felt it too. 'What are things like at the restaurant for the next couple of weeks?'

'The restaurant?' Angharad frowned, surprised to realize that it hadn't entered her thoughts. 'Oh. Hectic.'

'Louise will have to cope. Pierre and I will help out where we can. We can get a relief manager if . . . if it turns out that you have to stay longer.'

She nodded gratefully, but already London seemed unreal.

*Going home*, she thought.

William's face was turned anxiously up to them.

'Where are you going? Where, Mum?'

The adults' eyes met, and Jamie nodded. He understood, and agreed with her, that it was important for William to go too.

'How would you like,' Angharad asked him, 'to come with me for a holiday to stay with Aunty Gwyn? All the way to Wales?'

'Yes. We're going on holiday, on holiday.' He was already whirling in excitement around the room when a thought struck him. 'Can't Jamie come too?'

Jamie caught him up and swung him round. 'I'll try,' he promised, 'to come for a weekend if you're away for more than a few days.'

He didn't look at Angharad. He was suggesting it so tentatively that he wouldn't say it to her direct, she thought, as she turned away. The years of her life before they met had stayed unspoken of for so long. What would happened now, when all of it was brought back to confront them both?

Angharad was heavy with anxiety and foreboding as she went to send a telegram to Aunty Gwyn.

It took two days to make the necessary arrangements. On the third morning, while Jamie was putting the cases into the car, Angharad stood in their sunny drawing-room. Every book and ornament was familiar, but she felt as if it was somebody else, not herself at all, who had lived here for so long. Down in the street, through the wrought-iron work of the little balcony, she could see William waving impatiently from the car. Quickly Angharad took the first letter to Gwyn from her desk, where it had lain forgotten for three days, and tore it up. Then she locked the drawer on the little secret folder and turned away.

She left the house without looking round again. On the pavement, Jamie reached and put his arms around her. With odd detachment she saw his fair, curling hair, the cleft in his chin, and his concerned blue eyes. He kissed her, and the smooth-shaven cheek felt as familiar as her own.

He wasn't a stranger, was he? He was Jamie, her companion for six years. Jamie, who had given her everything she had now. She was going home strong, and capable, and mistress of her own life. *She must be.* With a quick beat of love that swept aside the self-doubt, and the troubling guilt, Angharad reached and touched his cheek with her fingertips. Then she kissed him, burying her face against the solid warmth of his shoulder. It brought the smile back into Jamie's eyes. He opened the car door for her and settled her gently into her seat.

'Darling,' he said. Then, 'Take care. I love you very much. Both of you.' He stood back, Angharad let in the clutch, and the big car rolled away. He stood and watched until they turned the corner and the quiet little street was empty without them.

Angharad's tense shoulders relaxed. She felt that she had cast off, and was floating on the tide. She turned the wheel sharply and pointed the car towards north London, and the road home.

It was a long, tiring drive. At first William had bounced up and down in his seat, exclaiming and pointing. But as they moved steadily north he grew bored, and then irritable, and finally dozed in his corner.

Angharad wasn't sure that she wanted to be left with only her own thoughts for company.

At the first arrow on the motorway, North Wales Resorts, Angharad felt her throat tighten.

They left the triple stream of northbound traffic and turned westwards across the flat, fertile Cheshire fields. Angharad thought briefly of school, close to here, and with the memory came Laura's oval face and dark, arched brows. And then, Harry. She had no idea where he was, probably thousands of miles away. But every mile that she drove was bringing him alive again for her. Angharad forged on, with their son asleep in the seat behind her. She was as afraid of all the memories almost as much as she was afraid for her father, but still she was drawn back by a thread that had never slackened its hold since she had left Cefn, a lonely girl carrying a suitcase much too heavy for her.

Suddenly, to the west, she saw a long blue line. Immediately it grew, defining itself into receding peaks against the sky. It was the mountains.

'Look, William,' she murmured. 'There's Wales.'

But William slept on without stirring.

The road that she had travelled so often with her father

was different now. A huge bypass had been thrown up around Chester. Angharad lost her bearings in the concrete tangle, and when she found herself again she was home. '*Croeso i Cymru*', the sign at the border flashed at her, with the red Welsh dragon arching its claws and tail. The hills were all around her now, bare-crowned and dark with conifers under the thin sunshine.

It was colder up here. The trees were barely dusted with green, and the high hedges were still winter-brown.

Angharad swallowed to quench the dryness in her throat. Her chest ached, and her fingers were stiff on the wheel.

The road was climbing now, through scattered villages with names as familiar as her own. They came out of a dark tunnel of conifers on to a stetch of bare moorland dotted with limestone outcrops, then they swung to the crest of a hill where the ground dropped sharply away.

Angharad had been expecting it, leaning forward to catch the first glimpses, but still the sight brought a low, involuntary cry. Ahead was the brooding grey-brown profile of The Mountain.

Angharad leaned back, intending to call over her shoulder to William, but he forestalled her. She felt the child's warm breath at the back of her neck as he leant to look over her shoulder. In the mirror she saw his wide eyes, still filmed with sleep, but fixed on the majestic outline as if he recognized it.

'Are we there?' he asked quietly.

'A mile or two more.'

They came down the valley road. At the junction where the road turned up to Cefn was the old stone fountain. Angharad looked at it, and then away again. William was breathing evenly, unusually quiet, his breath still fanning the hair over her collar.

'Nearly home, Willum.'

Under the old trees. The dry stone walls might have been gappier, shrunk farther under the encroaching moss, but nothing else had changed. A tractor chugged past in the opposite direction and Angharad knew without a second glance which of the hill farms it came from. The driver raised his arm in an automatic wave. Everyone knows everyone on this road, Angharad remembered. At the top of the steep hill she saw the oval of sunlight through the trees. The car passed the old oak, still leafless, and she remembered the exact tracery of the bare branches. Ahead of her lay the village street, drowsy, deserted, and just as it had always been. Then they were sliding past the low grey houses. Her eyes sharpened, Angharad saw here and there a splash of fresh paint, a different gate, and the brash new frontage on the village shop. And there at the end was her father's house, so small, almost low enough for her to reach out and touch the sills of the upper windows.

As a child, she had been proud of its square separateness from the tiny terraces.

Beyond it was the stark white geometry of the new estate. No wonder her father had been saddened by it.

The car drew up and Angharad stepped out, cramped and aching from the drive. William tumbled after her. The air was as sweet as milk, and silent except for the high, thin note of the wind off The Mountain. The heavy door of her father's house opened, and the *click* of the old latch was amplified in the quiet afternoon. Am I so used to endless noise, Angharad thought, that this silence seems so wonderful?

Gwyn was standing on the step, wiping her hands on her crossover apron, beaming at them. With William bobbing between them, the two women held out their arms to each other.

'Aunty Gwyn. I'm so glad we've come home.'

Inside the little house the grandfather clock was still ticking under the oak beams, and in the warm kitchen the afternoon sun was shining on the polished range, the old, uneven red tiles, and even the busy lizzies on the windowsill. Only the white cat had gone from the rocking chair.

A sense of peace and strength flowed back into Angharad, as if she had touched solid ground again after too long adrift. It gave her the courage to look into Gwyn's face, and see that it was lined with anxiety. But it was accustomed anxiety, and nothing new. There was no more bad news about her father waiting to greet her, then.

Angharad stooped so that her face was on a level with

William's. The boy was standing quietly, taking in the room with his clear, wide eyes. How like Harry he is, Angharad thought, and then pushed it to one side. Her concern should all be for her father and Gwyn, now, and in drawing little William as gently as possible into this different world.

'This is your home, as much as our house in London is,' she told him. 'I used to live here when I was a girl, and in a way I still belong here. You too, William, if you want to. It's your grandfather's house. He isn't here, because he's ill. In a day or two, we'll go and see him together.'

She touched his cheek with her fingers and he brushed them aside, reassured, and impatient to explore this new place. 'Can I go outside?'

'Of course you can, pet lamb,' Gwyn said. 'Off you go.'

'Mind the road,' Angharad said automatically, and Gwyn smiled.

'He'll be quite safe. Everyone will watch out for him, just like they did with you at that age.'

'But nobody knows him.'

'They do now, love. Haven't they just seen him come here with you?'

Of course. But the scrutiny seemed benevolent now, not irksome as it had done long ago. William would be safe here.

When they were alone, Angharad said, 'How's Dad?'

'About the same. They've put him on some new treatment and they have to wait for him to settle to it.'

'Treatment?'

'Oh, some kind of new drugs.'

Questions brimmed in Angharad, but she would wait to put them to the doctors.

'I told him you were coming, love. He didn't say much. But I know he's pleased, deep down.'

Or does my coming tell him how ill we think he is, she asked herself? No. William's uncomfortably sharp eye wouldn't allow deception, by others or himself. He would know his own condition.

Gwyn was putting the finishing touches to a meal. It was five-thirty, Welsh high tea. The memory of it made Angharad smile, and the sophisticated little dinners in

London seemed to have ended years ago, instead of just yesterday. She moved deftly around the kitchen, taking the worn, initialled silver cutlery out of its drawer, laying three places at the table as she had done a thousand times before.

'When did you leave the schoolhouse?'

'A month or two ago. He needed more help than I could give him from up there.'

Angharad closed her eyes briefly, seeing her father infirm, humiliated by his inability to do simple things for himself. 'If – when he comes out, he'll need me here still. I thought you and the boy might want to take the schoolhouse? Your Jamie will want to come up, and you won't want to be crammed in here.'

She wants me to stay, Angharad realized, and see it all through. Whatever it is. And I want to be here. I couldn't think of being anywhere else. The implications were too far-reaching to be thought about now, that was all.

'That old place is too much for me,' Gwyn said. 'I thought I might make you a present of it. You can turn it into something really grand, your own place up here. And your Dad and I will rub on here into our dotage.' Angharad nodded, as comfortingly as she could.

Gwyn was slicing the ham when the front door banged open again. Two small boys ran through the house and arrived panting at the table. They stood side by side, eyeing the fruit cake.

'Meat first, please,' Gwyn said.

The little boy with William was brandishing a wooden sword and wearing a tin colander on his head, but under it Angharad could see that he had carrot-red hair and a mass of freckles.

'This is Teck,' William told her. 'He said I could play.'

'Tecwyn is Jessie Williams's eldest,' Gwyn said. 'You can stay and have tea with William, love. Hands washed first, please.'

'I can see who he is,' Angharad said softly. The memories of her childhood came flooding back so vividly that she might have been a child herself again. The memories were especially comforting because they were safe. They were of the days before she had known Harry. Jessie and she had played just like this, up and down the street and in and out of the houses all day long. William, coming from his world of well-mannered birthday parties, and children brought to play by appointment and collected again by mothers in their Volvos, knew nothing like it. And suddenly she wanted him to know it. At least, to share it, just for a little while.

Later, in the early evening, Angharad drove to the hospital. William was in the general infirmary in the seaside town a dozen miles away. She followed the road mechanically, every bend familiar although she had never driven herself along it. The Mountain was left behind her, and the road dropped sharply from the high ground where the view of the sea sprang suddenly forward, grey brightening to beaten silver in the west, and on down to the coast road. Inside her head she was busy with her thoughts, working around the bitterness and sense of loss that had crystallized, rock-like, since her estrangement from her father. She wanted to go back, beyond the harshness and the mutual pain of her last months at home. She wanted to find, somewhere, the father she had loved – unquestioningly, even if fearfully – before the Cottons and their history had come between them. To find him again before it was too late was suddenly more important than anything else. She had no idea how he would receive her, but oddly she was no longer afraid.

It had felt so right to come home at last, and it had given her a kind of peaceful strength. She would put it right between her father and herself, somehow. The main street of the seaside resort opened in front of her, lined with souvenir shops and holiday cafés, still boarded up for the winter. The promenade was bare and windswept, with the edge of the deserted roller rink still garlanded with strings of coloured bulbs blown backwards by the gale off the sea. Thudding green and white waves pounded against the little pier.

Angharad left her car in the shelter of the pier theatre and crossed the road, stunned by the cold but breathing in the salt air with grateful gulps. The red-brick Victorian hospital faced the sea, its rows of windows looking out over the grey and white water.

She followed a trickle of visitors in through the main doors. Inside were the immutable hospital smells of disinfectant and ancient radiators. Only at the door of William's ward did she stop short, afraid as much of what she would find as of the memory of their last parting. But it was only a second's hesitation.

Her new determination carried her into the ward, and she saw him at once. At first she thought that he was asleep. He was lying propped up against pillows, very still. His skin was grey, and drawn tight over the prominent bones. Then, as she came closer, she realized that he wasn't asleep at all. He had been watching the door from under heavy eyelids, and now he was watching her.

Angharad stopped at the foot of the bed, and father and daughter looked at each other for a long moment.

Her courage almost failed her before William lifted his hand, very slowly, as if it taxed him to do it, and held it out to her. With a quick movement Angharad took it, and put her arms around him so that her face was against his. His skin was dry and hot, and his bones felt brittle. She understood at once how sick he was.

'Thank you for coming,' William said. Only his voice, light but firm, hadn't changed at all. He was still looking at her, greedily but with a dawning satisfaction. Angharad thought that his illness had stripped away the bitterness, and querulousness, of the last years, to leave the more important realities of the father she had loved. She prayed quickly for the generosity within herself to respond to him.

'I wanted to come. I don't know why it hasn't been before . . . this. I'm sorry, Dad.'

He shook his head with a trace of impatience. 'Don't waste time apologizing.' Was there so little time left, then? 'You look very lovely, Angharad. You've grown up a beauty, like your mother. London must agree with you. I couldn't stand it, myself.' There was a touch of the old asperity there. 'Are you happy?' Through all the uneasy years of her growing up, that would have been an unthinkable question.

'I'm happy to be home.' The evasion troubled her, but William appeared to accept it. There was a queer, half-anxious, half-diffident light in his eyes now, and his fingers tightened briefly on hers.

'Did you bring him? The boy?' With an ache of pity, Angharad saw suddenly how much it mattered to him.

'He's at home with Gwyn,' she said gently. 'Would you like to see him?'

'Yes,' William's voice was very low. 'I'd like to see him. If. If you think that would be appropriate.' They sat without speaking for another moment. Angharad was conscious of the bustle and clatter of visiting time around them, but William seemed to have retreated somewhere within himself.

'William Owain,' he murmured, and then added so softly that she had to bend forward to catch it, 'I'm glad.'

His eyes closed, and he was still for so long that Angharad thought he had fallen asleep. Then he stirred a little and said, 'He's dead, you know.'

The breath froze in her chest. The ward, cream curtains and iron bedsteads and polished floors, swayed giddily before her eyes.

'Who?'

'Joe Cotton.'

It was a moment before the blood began to flow again and the world righted itself. William was still talking. She caught the words without, yet, taking them in. 'Very suddenly. Not all that long ago. Couldn't take any of it with him, could he? I wonder if, in the end, he would have changed places with me? Perhaps not. Neither of us made a very brilliant job of anything, did we?'

He didn't expect an answer. Angharad saw that he really was nearly asleep now. She stood up and took something out of her bag.

'I brought you this edition of Donne.'

Remembering her father's admiration for the old poet's tough, unsentimental verse, and hoping that it might comfort him now, Angharad had found time in the last hectic days to hunt for the volume in an antiquarian bookshop off the Charing Cross Road. William's fingers closed avidly on the smooth leather binding.

'Thank you,' he said. 'That's very clever of you. Jack Donne or Doctor Donne. Which best, for now?' He had lost her, but suddenly his eyes snapped open and he complained. 'Gwyn will keep bringing me detective stories. Has she ever, in seventy-odd years, ever seen me read Agatha Christie?' They were both laughing. She knew that it was the right moment to leave, with this glimpse of the old, impatient William. She kissed him, and saw that he was already sinking back against the pillows, exhausted.

'Don't forget,' he called after her, and she promised, 'I won't forget.' To bring him his grandson, she added for herself, and the tiled corridors swallowed her up again.

It was dark as she drove home again. The car window was rolled half down and as she climbed the air lost its salt sharpness and took on the milky sweetness of the mountains, still startling to her.

Angharad was thinking fiercely.

The weary houseman she had found in the sister's office had told her little more than Gwyn, but it was enough. The disease was advanced when they discovered it, and it was spreading. They were treating him with chemotherapy, a complicated 'cocktail' of drugs. There were the normal side-effects, the doctor told her, weight loss and nausea and so on. But they were hopeful. And it was, of course, an unpredictable malady. There were remissions. Even complete cures.

As she left the hospital Angharad resolved briefly to take her father away with her to London. To the best doctors, specialists, second opinions, the best treatment available. But almost at once she discarded the idea. Why take him away, now, from the place where he had chosen to live all his life, on a tenuous thread of hope?

William was dying, and she was certain that he knew it. If he wanted anything he would ask her. And if he chose to stay where he was, in dignity, that was more than enough. Angharad's fingers gripped the wheel and she stared ahead at the headlights slicing across the twisting road. She would stay here with him.

Penetrating her sadness came anxiety for Jamie, and the realization that she ought to be worrying about Le Gallois. She wasn't, but the thought of Jamie troubled her deeply. Whether she was to stay here, or go back to him, it wasn't simple any more. Coming back had changed it, as she knew that he had feared.

And for herself, to stay here where every line of the horizon, every sound and scent and unfolding vista, breathed Harry to her?

Dizzily, Angharad knew that she wanted it to. Embracing after so long, even the hurt, was bringing her alive again. and the breath of reality, after so much insulation, was poignant, exquisite to her.

It was no use hiding any longer.

As she came up into Cefn and saw the little cluster of lights a wild, enticing plan was beginning to dawn on her.

# CHAPTER NINE

The plane tilted in its last circuit through the dense cloud and swung towards the landing approach.

Harry Cotton stretched wearily and gave up the pretence of sleep. He turned to the tiny window but could see nothing except the wing beneath him and the grey vapour streaming upwards. Manchester, England, he thought. Shrouded in rain. He counted off the obstacles that stood between him and the luxury of bed, and sleep. There was the airport terminal, fetid air and queues, and the baggage carousel. Then the hire car desk, and the drive through the rain, two hours at most, that would take him home.

As the plane came out of the last layer of cloud and swooped towards the ribbon of runway, Harry smiled. Odd that he still, after all, thought of Llyn Fair as home. Out of the jumble of thoughts disconnected by exhaustion, came a moment of pure exultation. Llyn Fair. The secret hollow high up in the hills, the old house, and the black and silver lake with its curtain of trees. For a moment Harry tasted the anticipation, the drive and the first sight of the mountains ahead, and then the road curving and climbing until the peaks soared above him and he was home again.

With a long shrieking roar the plane's wheels touched, bounced, and the brakes bit. The aircraft slowed, swung, and they were taxiing. Harry saw the heavy pall of rain and the loophole of happiness closed. He was aching from the long, cramped flight and he still had the remains of a New York hangover. He felt dirty, unshaven and impatient with himself. This was the last time he would ever come home to Llyn Fair. The house and the lake were to be sold. He was here to sign some papers, to make a sketchy show of filial duty in putting the last of Joe's tangled affairs to rights after his death. But in truth he had come back to say goodbye. And once he had said it, and the house and the lake were gone, then perhaps he could turn away from all of it for good.

Then a vacation, Harry reminded himself. Not in Wales, he didn't want that, but in some quiet, unreminiscent corner where nobody knew him and where the telephone didn't ring. There had been too many films, one after another, too many deals, and so many faces that they had blurred together and left him, after so long, with only two that were still sharp. The plane was stationary now, and the mechanical thanks for coming home with British Airways was crackling over his head. Harry pulled his well-worn leather jacket on over his sweatshirt and jeans and followed the tide of passengers to the exit. In the doorway the hostess saw his dark height coming and brightened her smile, but Harry was for once too tired to see it.

The arrivals queues and delays were exactly as he had known they would be. At length, Harry lifted his single small suitcase from the carousel and turned towards the customs avenue. He was almost through and into the knot of people waiting beyond when he saw Laura.

She was standing a little to one side, completely still, with her hands in the pockets of her loose cream jacket. Her smooth black hair perfectly framed her oval face. She was apparently deep in thought, but she was looking straight at him.

Harry stopped dead, but the press of people behind him pushed him on. Only when Harry was beside her did she take her hands out of her pockets. With the tips of her fingers she touched her mouth, and then his.

'In Christ's name, Laura,' he said, almost roughly. 'What are you doing here?' Looking down, he saw her perfect skin and the dark eyelashes, and smelt his sister's musky, exotic perfume. She looked thinner than when he had last seen her, more fragile, and more beautiful. Her fingers were cool against his wrist now and she was smiling, faintly rueful at the harshness of his greeting.

'Waiting to drive you home. Any objections?'

Harry sighed. 'Want a list? No, forget it. How did you know?'

'Rang the New York office. Not a very taxing process.

They gave me your flight number. And here I am, all excited to see you. Although I can't think why, now I come to look at you. You look a bloody wreck. Is that all?' she asked, nodding at his case. 'Still living like a gipsy?'

'Laura.' Harry took her arm and drew her to him. He moved to kiss her cheek but she turned her head and their lips met. His hand dropped at once, but it was another long second before he raised his head.

'I told you, Laura. Not now. Not ever.'

'I heard you, darling.' Laura's voice was perfectly smooth.

'Good. Well then. I never look my best after a transatlantic flight. You, on the other hand, look exquisite.'

'I have plenty of time to devote to it.' There was no attempt to hide the bitterness in her voice.

'Ah. Where's Jerry?'

'No idea. Tokyo, I think. I've been at Llyn Fair for a couple of weeks. There's a decorator looking at it. I think we should get a much better price if we take out some of Monica's more obvious excesses first.'

Harry shrugged. 'I couldn't care less. Let's just sell it. What does Monica say?'

'Approximately the same as you. She's in Marbella. Widowhood doesn't suit her, she tells me.'

Harry gestured impatiently. 'If you're going to drive me home, shall we set about it? Or would you prefer to stand in the airport all day?' Laura looked at him, past the black frown and the tired creases around his eyes, and straight into his head. With the look the barriers between them melted and they were laughing again, as they had done when they were children.

'Sweet, equable Harry. So lovely to have you back.'

'And to be back, my dear little sister. Lead on, then. I'm clay in your hands, as always.' His voice was light, and he was behind her so her answer was inaudible.

'If only you were. If only. But then, perhaps I wouldn't love you in quite the way I do.'

Laura's car was a silver-grey Mercedes 280SL, with scarlet leather seats. She tossed his case into the boot and held out the ignition keys. 'Want to drive?'

'No, thanks. You show off your pretty toy. Present from Jerry?'

'What else?'

Laura drove recklessly fast, but without Harry's assurance at the wheel. Knowing that she was goading him, he let his eyelids droop and then, quite unexpectedly, real sleep overtook him. Beside him Laura drove on, the ghost of a smile lifting the corners of her mouth.

When he woke up again, with an uncomfortable start, they were almost home. Harry felt a moment of disorientation, thinking that he was still on the plane. Then he saw the ridge of The Mountain, and the hollow in the lee of it that sheltered Heulfryn cottage. A tractor was out on one of old Mr Ellis's fields, inching painfully slowly over the spring ploughing. The Mercedes swept past the old fountain at the foot of Cefn Hill.

Harry winced, as if a stab of cramp had sliced him, and sat upright to light a cigarette that he didn't want.

Laura was humming softly. She broke off to say, 'One for me too, please.' Harry lit one for her and she turned her head a little with her lips parted for him to put it in her mouth. Ignoring that, he held it out and when at last she took it he saw the perfect, varnished ovals of her nails and the assertive glitter of her wedding and engagement rings. 'Jerry's rocks,' she called the square sapphire and its cluster of diamonds. Jeremy Argent appeared to believe that marriage entailed choosing a beautiful wife, loading her with all the right trappings, and then leaving her to her own devices while he pursued his interests elsewhere. Harry had never been able to understand why Laura had married him but, he thought, with a kind of grim humour, he was probably not the best judge of that.

He looked sharply away from Laura and out at the Welsh landscape. The bare hills were still winter-brown and the thorn trees, bent over by the wind so that they looked like old men, showed skeletal fingers against the grey-white sky. The land had a steely grandeur at this time of year that meant more to Harry than the softer, blurred beauty of the brief summer. Only down beside the valley road were the trees misted with pale green, and he knew that in the grass under the shelter of the hawthorn hedges the first violets would be showing. Violets, he thought, savouring the contrast with the steel and concrete wasteland that he had left behind. He played briefly and unguardedly with the idea of asking Laura to stop so that they could search for them together, and then told himself that he could do it alone, tomorrow.

It was ironic that everything he had done in the years since leaving here, all the frenetic escapades, had left him with nothing except a stronger desire to be alone.

A sudden shaft of sunlight swept over the naked ribs of land ahead of him, and Harry was reminded of the sunrise he had filmed with Angharad at the old tin chapel.

Except for Angharad Owain. He would have liked to be with her. He remembered her strange, self-contained sweetness as clearly as he could see the angles of her face in his mind's eye. This landscape brought it back to him. With inexplicable generosity Angharad had shared herself with him, and then she stumbled on him making love to his sister – under the old half-hating and half-intoxicating compulsion that still dragged at him. And Angharad had run away, putting herself beyond his reach with the rigid determination that was as much part of her as her sweetness. She had never asked for him, or mentioned him, her aunt had said. And all this hunting for her had been in vain. Wherever she was now, she was probably happily married, busy at some enviable, even-tenored domestic life. While he was battering about the world and hating it more with every passing day. Over the years he thought he had forgotten her, but coming home again told him that he hadn't.

Home again with Laura sitting beside him, her aquiline profile against the flashing hills. Not even that had changed. Harry sat back again in his red leather seat and Laura couldn't have guessed the tenor of his thoughts from his impassive face.

They came to the crossroads and then began the winding ascent to the high valley. Harry saw that some elms had been felled, and knew that the rooks which had nested there for

234

as long as he could remember would have gone too. The small loss struck him with magnified bitterness.

Yet the approach to Llyn Fair was just the same. The white gate was freshly painted, and the driveway looked spruce and well-swept. Harry had been home for a few hours, in the midst of a tight shooting schedule, for Joe's funeral. There had been no time then to look at anything. But now he looked about him and saw that Laura was seriously pursuing a good sale for the house and estate.

The Mercedes came out of the arch of trees and rolled slowly over the gravel. The silver-grey lake water was shadowed, in this light, with deepest undersea green and there were shivering columns of ripples fanned by the wind over the glassy surface. When he turned to look at it, Harry saw that the house was freshly painted and the wrought-iron curlicues of the verandah looked crisp and white. Scaffolding had been erected against the end gable. It occurred suddenly to Harry that Laura was busy here for the sake of being busy. Keeping herself occupied in the passing of empty, opulent days. None of them needed the money from the sale of Llyn Fair, not Monica or Laura, and certainly not himself.

He felt a quick stirring of sympathy for her and feeling her standing at his shoulder, he put his arm around her. Laura's head rested against him, and he smelt her scent again.

'Welcome home,' she murmured, and although he answered briskly, 'It's time we stopped thinking of it as home,' he knew, and understood, what she meant. He had been looking back at the lake and the trees when he heard the front door slam. Surprised, Harry looked round and saw a man crossing the manicured gravel towards them. He was Laura's age or a little younger, with a tanned face and brown eyes under a mane of sun-bleached hair. He was wearing pale suede trousers and a bright periwinkle-blue shirt.

'Oh, yes,' Laura said smoothly, not moving from the circle of Harry's arm. 'This is Lucian. He's an interior designer.'

Harry looked at him. 'Yes. I see,' he said, smiling agreeably, and Lucian missed the bite in his eyes.

'Hullo, Harry,' he said. 'So exciting to meet you. I'm a great admirer of your movies.' He was holding a sheaf of drawings and waved them at Laura. 'Laura, darling, these are ready now and I wondered if...'

'Not now,' she said sharply. 'I haven't seen my brother for months. It doesn't matter when we talk about what colour the walls should be.' She turned away and walked towards the house, her high heels crunching sharply on the stones.

'Sorry about my sister's manners,' Harry said after a moment.

Lucian laughed. 'That's just Laura,' he said. 'I know her well enough now not to let that worry me.'

Harry followed Laura in under the new white-painted arch and over the stone flags of the hall. The house looked bare, uncomfortable, and undeniably chic. Clearly Laura and her friend had been very busy indeed. Harry's dark frown had returned, and he was feeling the first exhaustion of jet lag.

Drawn by the force of habit he walked through the kitchen, out into the brick-paved yard, and up the flight of wooden steps that led to his old red room over the stables. It was dusty and bare except for a few neglected pieces of furniture. The silence struck him, and he remembered how as a boy he had felt this was his impregnable castle, out of the glare of Joe's domain across the yard.

Harry imagined that Laura had gone up to her own room. Then with a shock that was followed by the recognition of inevitability, he saw that she was sitting, framed by the arch, on his bed. Her chin was cupped in her hands.

She looked sad, and like a little girl again.

Harry walked across to her and knelt down so that their eyes were level. Gently he drew her hands away so that he could look into her face. At once the sadness vanished from her eyes and a smile licked in its place. It was a smile of conspiracy, there was a glimmer of a taunt in it, as well as pleading and clear loneliness. Harry was touched, and at the same time afraid of being so important to her. And afraid, too, of how much she meant to him.

He didn't move.

Laura leant forward. Her breath was warm on his face. Then her lips parted and, as delicately as a butterfly, the tip of her tongue touched his mouth. The room was very still and even the clouds beyond the windows seemed to have stopped in their race. Harry had a sudden, confused memory of smooth skin against his, black hair tangled on the pillow, hunger and fury driving him on, and then the sight of a white, shocked face staring at them from the empty arch that faced him now.

Harry dropped his hands. Slowly, as if some part of him hurt, he stood up. Laura never took her wide eyes from his face, but the sadness flooded back again.

'I don't think I'll sleep up here,' Harry said, as if he was rejecting a hotel room with an unfavourable outlook. 'The old man's gone.'

'Poor Joe,' Laura said, almost to herself, and Harry, thinking about it, said, 'Yes.' It had been impossible, until now, to grieve for his father. Nor could he grieve, exactly, now. Yet Joe was as much a part of the memories that were unravelling today as anyone, and the absence of his commanding bulk struck at his son for the first time.

Harry picked up his case again and walked to the door. 'How long is your gay friend staying?'

Laura chuckled. 'If you think he's gay, why are you jealous of him? He isn't, as it happens. And he's staying until we've finished decorating the house, then we'll sell it for a huge price and have a wonderful spree afterwards.'

'How enticing.' He hadn't come to Llyn Fair for anything of the kind. He realized that he had been hoping for an answer to something, an answer to a question that wasn't even formulated. Instead, now that he was here, he felt that the same old restless tides were threatening to submerge him again. Joe, and Laura, fascination and repugnance. The house and the lake, light and shade. he had escaped once and had stopped the water flooding out of the breach with work, too much of it, and with Bibi and her chain of successors.

Yet he was back again, with nothing to show for the intervening years except material success. Perhaps he had been wrong to come.. Or perhaps he should see the sale through, sever the links finally, and go back to where he didn't belong for good.

'I need some sleep,' he told Laura abruptly.

Laura sat on the bed, unmoving. She listened carefully until his steps had gone away, and then she pressed her hands to her eyes. Her face was haggard.

'You want to do what?'

Jamie's voice crackled out of the receiver. In spite of the difficulty of what she had to say, Angharad smiled. She could see him so clearly, sitting at the desk in their drawing-room, blonde eyebrows drawn together in a frown, running his free hand through his hair so that it stood on end.

Angharad took another deep breath. 'I want to open a restaurant in Gwyn's schoolhouse.'

As she spoke she turned to look through the dusty panes of the public telephone kiosk down the village street. Two or three people were standing with baskets outside the village shop, waiting for the bus. Gwyn was perched on a step ladder, cleaning the windows of William's house. Everyone who passed her stopped for a word. Angharad knew that they were all saying, 'You can come and do mine next,' and it made her smile to think how much it would once have irritated her. Now it merely seemed friendly and natural. She felt that she could follow the conversation outside the shop simply by watching the nods and smiles. Two children were playing a complicated ball game against a house wall, and she knew the half-Welsh, half-nonsense words as well as they did, although she hadn't thought about the game for fifteen years.

*Guto benfelyn, O dyddyn y celyn . . .*

The pips went, and she crammed some more money into the slot.

'And why in God's name can't you use a proper telephone? Haven't they invented them up there yet?'

'There's one in Dad's house,' Angharad said mildly. 'I just feel more . . . private, here.' I really mean anonymous, she told herself. More London-like.

The two halves of me are drifting further and further apart.

'Listen, Anne,' Jamie said. He was clearly trying, with

238

some difficulty, to be patient with her. 'Don't make any more crazy decisions between now and the weekend. I'm up to my eyes in this pharmaceuticals case and Pierre and Maurice are threatening suicide, but I'll try to get up and see you. I'm missing you, Anne. I love you.'

'I know,' she whispered. 'I'm sorry. They don't know how long, at the hospital. It could be days, or months. I must be with him, Jamie. A restaurant would give me a reason . . . and I can see how to make it work . . . it's an idea, but it's not crazy.' And she was already clinging to it tenaciously.

She heard Jamie's distant sigh. 'Let's talk about it when I get there, okay? I must go. Big kiss to William. Goodbye, darling.' Jamie hung up, and after a moment Angharad replaced her receiver.

It had been an inconclusive call, but then she hadn't expected any more than that.

She pushed out of the kiosk and began to walk slowly along the street. There was a stone trough full of daffodils in front of the nearest house, and when she paused to admire them, the owner opened her window to talk. The old lady had taught Angharad at the age of three in Sunday school, helping her to smooth cut-out Old Testament figures on to a felt backdrop.

'Lovely to see you back, Angharad,' she said. 'And your little boy too, I hear. Well done, well done.' Just as if Angharad had successfully added the cut-out group of seven lean kine to the seven fat ones. 'Not missing London, are you?' 'Not a bit,' Angharad smiled at her.

That was how it had been. In two days the village had assimilated her again, taking her long absence and her abrupt reappearance with a six-year-old son in tow completely at face value. Angharad realized with relief that they were only interested in what happened here, in the immediate and understandable vicinity. London was remote and mysterious, and anything could happen there.

She had said as much to Jessie.

Her reunion with her old friend had lasted over several hours and two bottles of wine. She hadn't mentioned Harry, but she had said, warily, 'I'm not married, you know. And Jamie, my . . . partner . . . isn't William's father.'

Jessie had laughed merrily. 'Feeling like the scarlet woman of Cefn? We've moved with the times up here too, you know. You'd be surprised at how free-thinking we all are compared with your day. Nothing like the shame there used to be. Remember poor Eluned Ellis?'

Angharad did. It was the memory of her poor, pregnant walk down the street under the watching eyes that had haunted her in the last horrible days before she had left home. The thought of it brought a quick beat of gratitude and the recollection of how much she owed to Jamie Duff.

Now Angharad said a cheerful goodbye to her old teacher, promising to come again soon for a proper talk. She would go on up to the happy little house on the new estate and see Jessie again.

Jessie saw her coming and waved through the kitchen window. William and his new and inseparable friend Teck were sitting at the formica-topped table busy at some very messy painting. Jessie's little girl was playing under the table, and the baby was asleep in its pram beside the back step.

'I don't want to go yet, Mum,' William said as soon as he spotted her. 'Teck and I are busy.'

'How'd the call go?' Jessie pushed back a bright strand of hair and reached to put the kettle on. Her figure had spread, and her freckles seemed wilder and her hair more unruly than ever, but to Angharad she seemed vibrant with contented happiness, and prettier than her girlhood had ever promised.

'Not exactly a rapturous response.'

Jessie paused with the kettle of water in her hand and looked at her. 'You don't want to go back, do you?'

Angharad was staring out of the kitchen window, watching the wind driving dapples of shadow over The Mountain. 'No.' She heard her answer dropping like a pebble into a clear pool of silence. She thought of London and the shell of life there that she had left behind. Now that she was home, it was inconceivable to think of leaving here again.

'Look, Mum.' William held up his painting, and she smiled at him. What would that mean, for William? And Jamie? Angharad shivered. Talk to Jamie first. Perhaps between them they could make it work.

'Is the restaurant idea an excuse for staying?' Jessie was shrewd.

'No. I can make it work, I'm sure of that. There's nothing like it near here, and it's close enough to holiday places, and business centres, for a wide potential clientele. It'd be very simple, Jess, but very good. Just a few covers, local produce...'

Jessie saw the enthusiasm chasing anxiety out of Angharad's face. She put her teacup down in front of her and said, diffidently, 'Can I help you?'

Angharad knew in a flash that it was just what she needed. To work in tandem with Jessie, practical and cheerful and quick-witted, as she knew of old, was the perfect answer.

'My Mam, or Dicky's, would have the baby so I'd have all the school hours free, and Dicky'd be here in the evenings . . .' There was no mistaking how much Jessie wanted to do it.

They looked at one another with dawning delight.

It would, Angharad realized, be fun. Hard work, because she had already calculated that they would have to open for this summer's season in a matter of weeks. But fun. With a little shock, she realized that that had been missing from her life almost since the beginning of Le Gallois.

Smiling, she raised her cup to Jessie. 'You do realize,' she asked, 'what you're suggesting? We've got a month or so to plan, convert and launch a restaurant? And running it after that? Thirty hours a day?'

Jessie lifted her cup too. A broad grin split the freckles. 'Count me in,' she said.

They drank their toast in lukewarm tea. Glancing away again at the sun and shadow outside, Angharad felt an irrational glow of happiness. For all the obstacles to be surmounted, her wild scheme felt right. Righter than anything had felt for a very long time.

241

An hour later, with the glow still warming her, Angharad was on her way to the hospital once more. This time William was in the seat behind her. The little boy was masking his apprehensiveness at meeting his remote and vaguely threatening grandfather with sulks at being separated from Teck.

'Don't want to go,' he scowled, when Angharad smiled at him in the mirror. 'Don't want a grandpa. I've never had one before. Why should I need one now?'

He had the heartless and unshadowed logic of childhood, Angharad thought, recalling her own. And how she herself had judged her father. She compared that sharpness with the endless, shifting shades of grey that wrapped around her now.

Anxiety began to seep back again. What had seemed for so long to be unthinkable was about to happen. She was taking Harry's son to meet her father. What if the old man turned on him, seeing the stamp of Joe Cotton's features? Worse, what if the boy recoiled in fear from his emaciated, almost other-worldly grandfather?

Angharad winced at the hurt that that could cause.

Could this be the wrong time? Should she wait until later, perhaps another day, another week? If only it could have been sooner.

Then she saw that William's clear blue eyes were watching her face in the driving mirror.

It was now. It must be done now.

'Grandpa has always been here. It's just that I have never brought you to see him. In a way, Willum, it's my fault that you haven't made friends before now. You see, your grandfather and I had a quarrel, years ago, before you were born. I left home and went away to London, and I never felt ... brave, or generous, enough to come back. Now Grandpa is ill, and he wants to see us both, because he loves us. Do you understand?'

William was still mutinous. 'How can he love me if he's never seen me? I don't love him. I've got you, and Jamie. I don't want anybody else.'

Angharad looked back at the road, and at the wide

242

metallic glimmer of the sea ahead. Her fingers tightened on the wheel, and she found herself counting the thumps of her heart.

'He loves you because you're my son.'

She stopped the car again in the shelter of the closed-up theatre, and hand-in-hand they raced across the spray-wet promenade. William was dancing with the exhilaration of the air and shouting over the gusts of salt wind. 'Run, Mum. Look, there's a pier. And miles of sand. Can we go in the arcades?' Angharad remembered how exotic and enticing the slot machines and coloured lights and tinny music had seemed when she was a child. She could almost smell the candyfloss and cockles on the empty April wind. The excitement had communicated itself to William, even though most of the façades were still shuttered against the winter storms.

'The season hasn't begun. They might just open at weekends. Jamie might bring you when he comes.'

'Oh yes.'

They dodged across the road to the red-brick portico. The contrast of close, medicated hospital air with the bright bluster outside was sharp. William was subdued at once. He ducked behind Angharad, holding on to the folds of her skirt.

From the door of the ward she saw the old man. He was propped up against a bank of pillows as before, but this time there were tubes running from his forearm to inverted bottles on a metal stand overshadowing the bed. Angharad braced herself. 'This way.' With her hand on William's shoulder, she steered him towards his grandfather's bed. The boy came reluctantly and stopped a little to one side. The sick man's unnaturally bright eyes, deep in their sockets, saw Angharad at once and then darted to the child.

As she stood with her arm around his shoulder, partly protective and partly offering him to her father's unblinking gaze, she felt their difference. Her own, slight, fair-haired figure beside William, already tall for his age, with his dark hair and distinctive eyes.

Exactly like Harry's.

At last old William held out his free hand. 'Won't you come closer, so that I can look at you?'

243

William stepped out of the circle of his mother's arms and went to him. The veined hand closed over his and there was a long moment of silence.

Then, to Angharad's relief, William chose to display the old-fashioned manners of the Goulds' nursery instead of his own, more natural, unruly self.

'Hello, Grandpa,' he said. 'Are you feeling better?'

'Hello, William.'

Angharad saw the effort it cost him to tighten his hand on the boy's and draw him closer still.

After another moment, with his eyes still greedily on the child's face, he said, 'You're a real little Owain, aren't you?'

'Of course I am,' William said stoutly. 'William Owain, like you. Mum said.'

It took her a moment to understand the words, repeating them foolishly in her head. Then a current of relief flowed through her. Of course.

*A real little Owain.* William was desperately ill. He had no time, now, to see anything but what he wanted to. Somewhere there must be a touch of Angharad, even a reflection of himself, in the boy's face. She had never been able to see it herself.

But then Harry's face had always been more vivid to her than her own. She felt a stab of sorrow for his loss. If he could have been here. Would it have helped the pain of seeing this, too late?

'Sit down here.' Old William's hand was patting the bedclothes. 'Don't let the sister see you.'

Little William's sulks were forgotten. He was already perched on the bed, following his grandfather's directions to locate chocolate in the locker. He broke off a piece and held it out before taking his own.

'Here's yours, Grandpa.'

He shook his head and nodded at the bottles over the bed. 'That's my food in there. Goes straight in. Saves the bother of eating it.' He kept his eyes averted from Angharad's.

William was fascinated but unconvinced. He peered at the tubes disappearing under the white tape binding the emaciated arm.

'It doesn't look very nice. And it isn't a bother to eat chocolate. Not like carrots or something. Hurry up and eat it so that you can come home to Cefn and play with me. Do you know Teck? I haven't got my train-set up here yet, but Mum says we're staying longer than she thought so Jamie can bring it up when he comes. Teck can't play with it, but you can if you want.'

From William, it was an offer of unparalleled generosity. The old man thanked him with serious gratitude and the childish talk ran on as the chocolate disappeared.

Watching, Angharad saw the rapport spring up between them. Old William said almost nothing, but the way he listened and prompted seemed to compel the child. It made her remember, painfully, how fiercely she had loved and admired him as a child herself. More deeply than she had loved Gwyn, even though it was Gwyn who gave all the warmth and sympathy and protection.

At length, William began telling the story of St Winifride's Well, just as he had told it to her on their visit years ago. The little boy listened spellbound, just as she had done. But clearly the effort exhausted him.

'Ask your mother to take you,' he said wearily, when it was over.

'You take me. Please, Grandpa.'

Old William seemed to have shrunk into the bedclothes and his skin was drawn even tighter. 'I'll try,' he said, barely audibly. 'One day.'

'We must go,' Angharad said. 'Grandpa wants to go to sleep now.'

He looked at her, seemingly for the first time since they had arrived. There was a faint, vanishing smile. 'Thank you,' he said.

Thanking her for bringing the boy. Thanking her for her generosity, after so much. Not generous at all, Angharad thought. I've been stupid and blind. Just like you. Poor Dad. She felt the tears stinging her eyes.

Then she looked and saw that her father was crying too. There were tears on his eyelashes. His throat was left bare by his pyjamas, and she could see the thin, clenched muscles

245

working in it. He was too tired to reach out for the handkerchief on the locker.

Angharad put it into his hand and kissed his forehead before turning away. She had never, in all their years, seen him cry before.

So it takes dying, she thought bitterly, to peel the defences of pride away. The boy was waiting for her, tactfully silent.

As they walked down the ward together she felt the weight of her love for him. And with suffocating intensity came the determination never to let barriers like that slide between herself and her own child. It was the knowledge that they surely would, in one way or another, that saddened her more than anything else on that sad day.

They retraced their steps along the gloomy corridors towards the dazzling freshness outside.

'I like my grandfather,' William said.

'I'm glad,' she said, taking her hand in his. 'I'm very glad.'

As she had known he would, Jamie arrived at the weekend. Angharad had driven William and herself up in their unobtrusive estate car, so it was inevitable that Jamie would materialize in the Porsche he used for running about Town, as he put it, only half satirically. Angharad thought that the gleaming, opulent car looked shamefully blatant parked in the narrow road outside the schoolhouse. She said as much to Jessie, wondering what the rest of the village was saying.

'Don't knock it,' Jessie said gleefully. 'It must be the first Porsche ever to do more than blink and miss Cefn. The general opinion is that you must have done ve-ery well for yourself. Everyone also, as I do myself, thinks that the car's owner is impressively distinguished and handsome as well as nice. Everyone except you, that is.'

There was no hiding anything from Jessie's sharp eye.

'I like him very much,' Angharad said, turning away.

'Mm. I like you. And old Jones the butcher. I even like Trevor the Wagon. But it's not quite the way I feel about Dicky.'

'You're married. I'm not married to Jamie.' There was a

note of steel in Angharad's voice that stopped Jessie short.

Angharad saw the flicker of surprised hurt in her friend's face and was contrite at once. 'I'm sorry, Jess. One day, if you have the patience to listen, I'll tell you all of it. But not yet. Not just yet, until . . . I can see it better myself. Is that enough?'

'Of course.'

They sat down together at once to the sheaf of hasty plans for the restaurant that they were to show to Jamie.

From the moment of his arrival, Angharad had felt the incongruity of Jamie's presence in Cefn. It was only partly his country turn-out of corduroys and expensively-cut tweeds, his Porsche, and the obvious fact that he was rich, whereas everyone else, in work-stained farming clothes or unconsidered chain-store outfits, was clearly the opposite. More important, Jamie was citified to the core. He understood metropolitan life perfectly, in all its nuances. As far as country life went, Angharad reflected, he was probably perfectly at home on his cousins' Scottish grouse moor. But in Cefn he was isolated, both socially and culturally. He looked uncomfortable, and Angharad felt reproached both because he was here, and because she was rewarding him for their years together by turning into a different person, apparently overnight.

She had put aside the clever, expensive designer separates that he admired her in, and adopted jeans and sweaters like Jessie's. She tied her hair simply back from her face, and left her skin bare in the clear air rather than applying her careful London make-up. She felt comfortable and happy as she scrambledd about the old schoolhouse with a measuring tape, the local builder admiringly beside her. But when Jamie came, she knew that he saw the London gloss disappearing overnight, and she knew that he was watching, and wondering.

On the first morning of his visit, they walked slowly away from the old schoolhouse and down the village street. Everyone they passed waved at them, or called a greeting.

'You really do know everyone,' Jamie said. 'Don't you find it rather claustrophobic?'

'I used to.'

'It's so small,' he went on, looking around him. It was true. Jamie looked almost as tall as the little houses. 'I'd imagined something bigger, and less . . . grey.'

More like a Cotswold show-village, Angharad thought, with a quiet, bitter defensiveness that surprised her. Jamie seemed only to see the narrowness, and feel the weight of parochial inquisitiveness. He hadn't taken in the grandeur of the humped mountain, and the contrast of the snug village huddled against its protective sweep, or the way that the afternoon light from the west turned the slate and stone from grey to lavender. Nor had he seemed to taste the exotic sweetness of the milky air.

'It's only because you've never talked to me about it,' he said gently, after they had walked the length of the street in silence. He was looking sideways at her, searching for Anne in this thin, simply-dressed girl, younger-looking now than her years. This wasn't Anne, nor was it the strange, untamed girl who had appeared in Duff's so long ago. This woman was anxious, but there was a soft, diffuse glow of calm happiness underlying the anxiety. Jamie thought that he had never seen her look so beautiful, or so desirable in her remoteness from him.

'That's it. You've seen it all,' Angharad said as they stood under the old oak at the end of the street. Jamie put his hand under her elbow and turned her to face him. The street was deserted and so, to him, they were alone. He lifted her chin and kissed her mouth.

Angharad knew that behind the lace and net curtains they were being watched. As Jamie's lips touched hers she knew someone was saying, 'Aaah. Now, isn't that nice?'

Jamie felt that her mouth was stiff, and her skin smooth, but cold. He dropped his hands at once.

'Shall we,' he asked smoothly, 'go up to the pub and have a drink and a sandwich before I take William on this trip to the seaside?'

Angharad was hoping that they might be able to discuss her schemes for the restaurant over lunch. The builder had been encouraging. The old school was sound, and almost

248

ideally laid out. The kitchen would have to be equipped, and the dining-room decorated and furnished. But the obstacles in her immediate path were much less daunting than she had feared.

But when they reached the bar, they found only a handful of people there. Everyone stopped talking when they came in and waited, expectantly. Angharad introduced Jamie. He was a good talker. He asked all the right questions about the village, and within minutes he was the centre of the group while she listened, and watched him. Was she the only one who detected a flicker of cynicism in him? She despised herself for the thought, but it refused to go away.

'They all liked you,' she told him on their way home again.

'I wanted them to, because of you. But I could only understand about half of what they were saying. Rather difficult!' She knew what he meant, and she understood. But it was the wrong answer, setting them both apart from the friendly, beery faces in the bar, and it irked her.

*Jamie*, she thought. I don't want Cefn to come between us. Then, with a chill shiver, she answered herself. Perhaps it always has been there, between us. Perhaps it's always been too late for Jamie and me, right from the beginning. Then they saw William bursting out of the house and racing towards them. Jamie ran too, caught him by the wrists and swung him round until his black hair stood out like a mop and he begged, gasping and laughing, to be put down again.

Angharad was struck by the way that Jamie clung on to him for a second longer, his cheek against the black hair and his arms wrapped around the lithe, wriggling little body. She had seen it in their reunion the day before, a physical expression of how much Jamie had missed the boy, no more than a fleeting shadow, but there just the same. She stood a little apart in the sunshine, watching them romping together.

Jamie had never been possessive of her son. He had never tried to dictate to her about his upbringing. He had simply loved him, and herself, with the same generosity.

Angharad felt confusion, apprehension and fear rising inside her, and the spring sunshine turned suddenly cold.

William was pulling at Jamie's hands. 'Come on, it *must* be time to go to the funfair now. I can't wait any longer.'

'Okay, I'm coming. I'll need my arms in one piece though.'

'Can we go on everything?'

'Oh, of course. The big dipper and the dodgems and the waltzers and the big wheel and the chairplanes . . .'

'And the slot machines and the shooting gallery? Have you got plenty of money?'

'Me? No. I thought we might break open your piggy bank.'

'Oh Jamie, that's not *fair* . . .'

''Bye, both of you. Have a good time. Don't make yourselves sick.'

'Won't you come?' Jamie asked quietly, and she hesitated. They would be like a family again, enjoying the seaside funfair, and they would come home tired and giddy, and sticky with candyfloss. But she had promised to see the builder, and Jessie, and she shook her head regretfully.

'Hurreeee up,' William was clamouring from the Porsche. Jamie touched her cheek. 'We'll have a proper talk about your idea tonight.'

It was a gesture of conciliation, and she smiled, gratefully. Then she kissed him, and for the moment she had forgotten whoever might be watching them.

The afternoon was busy.

The builder came armed with his estimates, laughably modest after London prices. With Jessie beside her, she went through the catalogues of Liverpool catering suppliers, pricing the ovens and sinks and equipment they would need. It would be the bare minimum, but that would be pleasing in itself after the complex machine that was Le Gallois.

Already in her mind's eye Angharad knew how she wanted the little dining-room to look. The main schoolroom had exposed rafters and triangular beams supporting the high roof. When it was decorated it would be a cool, white space arching over the half-dozen tables. The solid slabs of slate that made up the floor would be polished, until they shone, and the tall windows all round the room would be curtained with thick folds to swallow the noise and make the night-time room enclosed and intimate. There would be candlelight, and flowers, and at the end of the room she would have the old stove removed and replaced with an open fireplace. Instead of a bar, she would have low sofas grouped around the fire.

Jessie was as elated by the idea as Angharad herself. The suggestions she made showed that she was inventive, as well as practical. By tea-time, they had arrived at a round figure for the investment that Angharad would have to make before her schoolhouse restaurant could earn a single penny.

To Jessie it seemed enormous. She leant back in her chair, looked around Gwyn's dusty old studio, and whistled. 'It's a fortune.'

Angharad smiled. Compared with the sums of money tied up in Duff's and Le Gallois, it was modest enough. Since becoming Jamie's partner, her share of their profits had accumulated substantially. She had almost enough capital and the rest she was certain she could borrow.

'I think I can manage the money.'

Jessie's ginger eyebrows went up an inch. 'The village is right, then. You have done well for yourself. One more question.'

'What's that?'

'Who's going to eat at this beautiful restaurant?'

'A very good question. It will be Jamie's first one. Look.'

It had helped Angharad, over the last few days, to think about something that wasn't the pain in her father's face, and didn't pull at the chords of memory that drew her back over the hills to Llyn Fair and Harry.

Through a childhood acquaintance she had obtained from the local council a highly unofficial and surprisingly lengthy list of holiday and weekend cottages in the area. After some vigorous telephoning she had compiled her own list too. On it was the new squash club down at the coast, the Rotarians and drama societies, young farmers' clubs and preservation societies, and dozens more.

'We must make sure that all these people know about us. All of them. We'll have a pretty card designed and printed to send out to them. And we'll have an opening day – no, week – with different parties for all the right people. That's where we win out by being local, you see. We know who they are. Once everyone has been once, we can depend on word of mouth . . .'

'It's going to be that good?'

'Yes,' Angharad said quietly. 'I think we can make it that good.' Quickly, because she didn't want to seem cocksure, she went on, 'I think we can hope for local press coverage right away. And it will take longer, but the food guides should visit us too. A country Le Gallois will be interesting enough. I think – no, I'm sure – we can fill the place almost from the start.' And as she looked round the room her face was lit by conviction that made Jessie smile admiringly.

'Yes. Fingers crossed we can convince your partner, then.' Almost as she spoke they heard the throb of the Porsche outside.

There was a second's silence and then William was shouting, relating the afternoon's delights before he was even in the house.

'We went on everything, even the really scary things. You never would've, Mum. There was one thing called the Mad Mouse that went on high rails that stuck out right over the sea. Look!' He was brandishing a helium-filled balloon and a coconut and a lime-green nylon fur snake. 'And look!' In the other hand, a goldfish circling desperately in a bulging polythene bag.

'Oh no.'

'It was that or a tortoise.' Jamie tottered into the room and sank into a chair. 'My stomach. My head.'

'It wasn't. You're fibbing. You didn't score enough points to get a tortoise.'

'Deliberately. Don't you know I'm really a crack shot? Some tea, for God's sake, before I pass out. William won't be needing anything until the day after tomorow. He ate enough fish and chips and horrible sticky things for five people.'

'Cake, please, Mum. I'd like a piece of cake.'

Angharad bent her head over the teacups to hide her face.

The two of them were so happy together, and so important to each other. How could she even let her thoughts run on in the direction they had been taking?

Jessie went away to attend to her own children. In the doorway she touched Angharad's sleeve. 'Good luck.' They smiled at each other. It had suddenly become very important to have Jessie on her side.

Alone together, Angharad and Jamie and William went through the supper and bedtime routines that were accepted rituals at home in their Chelsea house. William fell asleep almost as soon as they had kissed him goodnight, his hair very black against the white pillow.

Jamie said, 'I'm going to have a bath. That funfair was unbelievably grimy. Then we can have a drink and talk.'

She nodded, faintly apprehensive. She wanted his support, and his approval, and knew that she didn't have the right to ask for it.

Jamie went and she watched him go, thinking how well she knew him. He hated baths. What he really wanted was a shower in the spacious, luxurious bathroom adjoining their bedroom at home. He was too big for Gwyn's cramped, turquoise-tiled bathroom and he had to bend uncomfortably to see himself in the tiny square of mirror over the basin. The little room was underheated and glistened with condensation, and there was no room for him to put his things.

Angharad was oblivious of the discomfort on her own behalf, and to William, it was all a huge adventure. But Jamie minded, and she saw it as another manifestation of the way he didn't fit in at Cefn.

She sighed and went back into the kitchen. It was all, all the knot of problems confronting her now, an impossible conundrum.

At least, she reminded herself wryly, there was a fine dinner and a decent bottle of wine waiting for Jamie when he emerged from his bath, and a bottle of Glenmorangie for afterwards. Perhaps that would help him to look on Cefn and the schoolhouse a little more kindly.

At last they were sitting with their chairs drawn up to the

pot-bellied stove. The evening was cold so Angharad had lit it, and now the coke glowed comfortably in the open throat.

'Right,' Jamie said. 'Let's hear it.'

She recognized his businesslike manner, and knew that he would give her proposal his full, formidable attention.

Crisply she took him through her plans and estimates. She outlined the menus she planned to offer, the staff she needed to help her, the cost of decor and furnishings. Forestalling him, she spread out her lists of customer targets and went through them carefully.

She knew that she was right. Even in the time she had been away, the overspill from the big towns over the border had crept closer to Cefn. There were enough prosperous immigrants to fill the restaurant regularly. She wouldn't, and couldn't, rely on special-occasion local trade.

Angharad talked for nearly an hour.

At the end Jamie nodded, but his face didn't clear.

'All right. It makes commercial sense. You can almost certainly make a go of it. It will mean very hard work for you.'

'I don't mind that. You know I don't.'

'Two things, then. One of them is purely business. Are you proposing that Duff & Co. make this investment? Or are you doing it alone?'

His sharp blue eyes met and held hers.

'I want to make the investment myself.'

It might have been imagination. But did she see disappointment in his eyes? 'I see. Well, setting aside the fact that your plan deprives the company – our company – of the best chef it has . . .'

'Jamie, you know that I don't cook any more. I just sign cheques and solve problems.'

But he ignored that, as she had known he would. 'Setting that aside, we come to the second thing. Where does it leave us? You and me, Anne, not Duff & Co.'

She looked away from him, and into the red heart of the stove. It was so bright and hot that it hurt her eyes. Until this moment, she had had no idea how she would answer. Now she found herself talking, talking.

'It's only the summer season. April to October, at most. Perhaps a fortnight over Christmas and the New Year. The rest of the time we can be in London, just like always. And perhaps you can come up here, on and off through the summer, just like now.' Perhaps, she supplied for him. Or perhaps not. Cefn and its environs wouldn't contain Jamie for long, even if he tried it to please her. 'I want to do it, Jamie. It's important. Le Gallois is stifling me. And I want to be here, for Dad's sake. I can't leave him again. Or Aunty Gwyn. She's old and frail too. You saw it yourself.'

Jamie's gaze was cool now. 'Forgive me,' he said. 'But what if your father dies even before you get the place open?'

Angharad's head was bent. 'I've thought of that. Even if . . . that does happen, I'll still want to do it. He would like it. And it would help me to grieve for him. Being here, in the place and with the people he chose. I don't know how I'd do that in London. Anyway,' with a defiant lift of her chin again, 'I don't think he will. He isn't ready yet. If you had seen him with William, I think you would understand.'

Jamie was driven back on to his final defences.

'What about William, then? How can you uproot him from his home and friends and school, and then plonk him down here for half the year?'

And now, she thought, the battle lines are drawn. Jamie, I didn't want it to come to this.

As gently as she could, she said, 'This is his home. Here, where his family belongs. Don't you remember, when you came to see me in the hospital with his teddy and the red roses? "Think about going home," you said. "Back to your own people." Now I have thought about it. And I have come.'

'His schooling, then?'

'He can go with Teck Williams to the local school.'

'Oh Anne, for God's sake . . .' He was angry now, and her own anger flared up to match his.

'Don't be such a snob. I went there for seven years. And won a scholarship at the end of it.'

'You're exceptional, Anne.'

'Isn't William?'

They were staring at each other, with more hostility than she could have believed possible between herself and Jamie. Then, just as suddenly, he was looking away, picking at an invisible thread on his knee.

'Yes. You're both exceptional.'

At once her anger melted and she went to him, putting her arms around him and laying her forefinger against the cleft in his chin. She knew that he loved them both, and she ached at the way she was repaying his love and loyalty. She loved him too, in a certain way, yet in her heart she knew that that certain way wasn't enough.

Later, after their melancholy dinner together and the clearing away in the inconvenient kitchen, they lay together in the hollow of Gwyn's brass bed. Angharad's body was taut as a wire with the day's tension. Beside her, she was vividly aware that Jamie was awake, silently suffering the sagging bed and restricting blankets that would slide away as aoon as he fell asleep. At last, he turned and put his arms around her. His mouth found her ear, her cheek and then her lips.

'Anne,' he whispered. 'Come back.'

Not just to London. Come back much further, from wherever she had retreated. His hands moved over her body and she responded, thinking again, *How familiar. How safe.* And yet, how far away from touching her, or from making her cry silently for him as she did now, 'I love you. Oh, I love you. Where are you? How can I bear to be without you for so long?'

In the grateful darkness tears stung her eyes, and instead of the room she saw the lines of Harry's face, the light and the shadow in it and the command that she couldn't refuse, however much she wanted to deny it and to submerge herself in the simple affection that surrounded her now.

# CHAPTER TEN

Angharad clasped the gold chain around her neck and stood back from the dim mirror, frowning a little. It was odd to see Anne looking out at her again.

For the opening night of The Schoolhouse she had reached back into the rickety wardrobe for the London clothes that had hung there untouched since her return home. Without giving it much thought she had taken out a poppy-red dress with a high neck, which she left unbuttoned, and a demure skirt that only showed the side splits when she spun quickly on her high heels. She turned now, dismissing her reflection with a shrug, and saw Jamie watching her from the doorway. He whistled appreciatively and raised an eyebrow.

'Where've you been, all these weeks?'

As she slipped past him, Angharad reached to straighten his tie. Dark blue silk, white-spotted. A pale blue shirt and a charcoal grey Savile Row suit, tailored to distraction. Jamie was loyally pulling out all the stops for the opening of her eccentric country restaurant.

He caught her elbow. 'Nervous?'

'A little.'

'Well. You've got what you wanted.'

And you never miss an opportunity of reminding me, Angharad thought unfairly. Yet Jamie was here, supporting her as always. He had moved the earth to free himself from business and the restaurants for a few days. And as always, she felt the mixture of tenderness and guilt.

'Ready?'

'Let's just look in at William.'

William was sitting up in bed reading a Superman comic. He frowned at them both. 'You look silly.'

Angharad bit the corners of her mouth to hide the smile. He was right, she thought, seeing their superfluous elegance

257

in the little sloping room with its bare boards and iron bedstead.

'That'll do.' She leant over to kiss him and ruffled his hair. William thought that the party, with all its imagined adult delights, was being unfairly denied to him. He frowned harder and turned back to his comic.

After a brief word with their babysitter, Jessie's youngest sister, Angharad and Jamie ducked out of the dolls'-height front door and stood in the village street. Since the schoolhouse had turned from a home into a restaurant at astonishing speed, Angharad had rented a little house in the middle of the terrace for the summer. She loved its simplicity, the traditional range in the back kitchen and the cotton lace curtains at the windows, but to Jamie it was even pokier and less convenient, if that was possible, than the old schoolhouse had been.

She put her arm through his now and they turned up the street together. The west face of the grey church tower was splashed with late sunshine, and its clockface blazed with reflected light like a mythical shield. As they passed it, Angharad saw and smelt the dense shade under the yews massed by the lychgate, and glimpsed the swallows dipping over the rough meadow not yet enclosed by the sweet green graveyard. The evening air was still, and heavy with the scent of dogroses. A man passed them, his colourless workshirt open at the neck and his throat and chest reddened by the day's work in the sun. He lifted a massive hand and grinned.

'*Iechyd da*. All the best for it, now.'

The tall windows of the schoolhouse were newly white-painted, and the heavy door under the old stone sign *Genethod a Babanod* stood invitingly open. One of Angharad's first tasks had been to plant quick-growing stocks in the bed beside the step, and now they sent up drifts of perfume.

Inside the restaurant, everything glowed with freshness and pale, clear colours reflecting one another. They heard Jessie, singing somewhere, over the rippling piano music from the hidden speakers.

Angharad walked the length of her new domain, quickly, her eyes searching for flaws.

Nothing.

Gwyn had filled little clear glass flutes with fresh cottage-garden flowers. The tall white candles stood ready to be lit, the round tables under their long double skirts of apricot and starched white linen were laid with gleaming cutlery and glass. The sofas were drawn up around the stone hearth. In place of the fire, Gwyn had artfully arranged armfuls of flowers, delphiniums and Canterbury bells and rich purple pansies, so that they looked still moist from the garden.

'You've done well,' Jamie said softly. 'You're a clever girl, Anne.'

Jessie came out of the ktichen. She was wearing an overall over her best dress, and she gave a last flourishing polish to the champagne glass in her hand. Behind her were the waitresses, local girls in dark dresses with barman's plain white aprons over them. Angharad saw past them into the kitchen. Instead of her brigade at Le Gallois she had a boy to help her and Jessie, and the rest of her staff was a washer-up not so very different from Old Lil at Y Gegin Fach, and a genial porter-handyman. But they were all she needed. The food was what she cared about, and she had done it all herself. Now she saw that her knives were laid out ready for her on the long central table. her kitchen whites were hanging up, ready too. After the next nights, the beginning fanfare, she could retreat into her kitchen and do what she loved best.

'Here we go, then.' Angharad looked at her watch and then smiled round at each of them. 'Good luck.'

'There was one thing.' Jessie's eyebrows were drawn together. 'Robina Gwynedd called. She's fratefully sorry, but her party will be four instead of just two. Can we do her a great favah and fit in her deah friends?'

'It's a nuisance, but we must.' Angharad glanced round the tables. They could have filled them three times over from the number of requests. But Lord Gwynedd was the biggest landowner for miles. His daughter Robina made a career out of enjoying herself. She was seldom seen at her father's draughty fourteenth-century castle, but when she was home, and so far as there was a local society, Robina represented

259

the cream of it. It was a coup to have her at the opening.
Local word would make much of it.

'It will mean two cramped tables, but . . . Mary, can you
change the Gwyn-Jones's table to there, and lay this one up
for four? They'll just have to rub elbows a little.'

The little waitress rustled to the job with alacrity.

Angharad heard footsteps, painfully slow, and then an
awkward, humped shadow fell across the polished slate
floor. There was a little silence in the room. Gwyn stood in
the doorway with her brother leaning heavily on her arm.

'Dad. I said I would drive you up.' Angharad was at his
side immediately, but he brushed her away.

'And did I say that I couldn't manage to walk two
hundred yards? Nice job you've made in here. Who'd have
thought, Gwyn, looking at it now, what your mucky old
studio could be turned into? I'm sure it cost enough to do it.'

They helped him to his seat in the corner and Angharad
thought affectionately that that would be all the
congratulation that she could expect from William. She
settled the cushions behind his frail figure and Jamie leaned
solicitously over him.

'Yes, I'll certainly have champagne,' he answered them.
'Why not?'

A brief remission, the doctors had said. It was as if he had
achieved it by determination alone. He wanted to see his
daughter's restaurant open, and he wanted to be with his
grandson. There was no telling how long it would be before
the disease started up its inexorable progress again, but for
now he was allowed to be at home. The old man spent much
of his day sitting contentedly under the grandfather clock,
his back turned firmly on the study door, watching the
comings and goings in the village street. Young William
spent a surprising amount of time playing nearby. The two
of them spoke little, but they seemed to understand each
other.

The room was beginning to fill up now. It was to be a two-
tier party. Angharad had invited a cross-section of village
people, friends of her father's and Gwyn's, Jessie's family
and a handful of others, to christen the restaurant with

champagne. Smiling, she saw Twm Ty Coch come in in his rusty suit and make a bee-line for Gwyn. Later, the paying customers, carefully chosen for their publicity potential, would replace them for the inaugural dinner. As Angharad moved among her guests, laughing and talking and seeing that the glasses were filled, her thoughts were gleefully in the kitchen. Soon after, leaving Jamie as host, she slipped away to the soothing greens of her vegetable purees, the mousse of Dee salmon and the tender Welsh lamb already rolled in its shells of rich pâté and puff pastry, waiting to be roasted just long enough to leave it pink and succulent.

Everything was ready.

Preparing to go out and greet the second wave of arrivals, Angharad glanced at herself in the mirror. The vivid reflection was momentarily startling. Her cheeks were rosy and her eyes bright with excitement.

I'm happy, Angharad realized, with a little shock of gratitude. *I'm happy*. Just for this moment, now and here. If only . . . nothing happens for a little while yet. A little while.

Back in the restaurant the light was changing. Shadows were gathering in the corners and in the cool space above the beams. The waitresses were moving to and fro lighting the candles, and reflected pools of yellow light sprang out, wavered and then shone strongly back again.

Gwyn and William were ready to leave.

'It's lovely,' Gwyn said simply. 'You deserve every success.'

Won't you stay for my dinner? Angharad was going to ask again, and then she saw her father's face. He looked drawn and exhausted and she felt the sharpness of guilt at not seeing him home sooner. She kissed him, gentle with the papery thinness of his skin.

Jamie was waiting. 'I'll drive you,' he said firmly, and she glanced at him in gratitude.

'Not in that infernal machine,' William complained, but let them lead him away. There was a moment of quiet in the empty restaurant. Later Angharad was to remember the scent of flowers, the velevet summer dusk beyond the windows and the purr of a car in the roadway.

The first customers. Angharad smoothed her hair. Behind her Jessie came out of the kitchen and stood beside her as they waited.

The first arrivals were a local solicitor and his wife. Angharad was greeting them when the next party came in. She glimpsed Robina Gwynedd, overdressed but resplendent in a sequinned jacket over billowing silk harem pants, with a pretty blonde boy at her shoulder. Dimly she glimpsed another couple behind them. The solicitor and his wife moved away.

'So pretty,' Robina Gwynedd was saying. 'Who did it for you? Lucian was cross not to be asked, weren't you, darling? But you must know Lucian Lang, the designer? He's done such wonders for Daddy at Castell. And now he's . . .'

But Angharad was looking past Lucian whoever.

Past him, and into Harry's eyes.

The blood sang in her ears and she felt the fine gold chain around her neck as tight as if it would strangle her.

Clear blue eyes, just like her son's, with dark eyebrows drawn close over them. Harry looked back at her without a ghost of greeting, as if they had never been apart, never even stopped looking at each other.

Angharad felt a moment of naked, pure fear.

She stepped back, no more than a single wavering step, and felt Jessie's fingers firm at her wrist.

Nowhere to run to, even if she could have made her limbs work. Why was she afraid?

Robina had sailed away, fluting her approval of the decor to deaf ears. The designer swayed with her.

'Angharad.' Harry's voice was very low, excluding the room, the world beyond it, everything except herself. She remembered his leanness, and the old taut, eagerness flickering behind the weary lines of his face. He looked older and there were clefts beside his mouth that made him look grim. The confident, arrogant boy was all gone now, grown into this authoritative man with his bleak, powerful stare.

'Harry.' As she heard her own voice she knew why she was afraid. She was afraid of the passion within herself, and the power latent between herself and Harry to destroy everything that she, and Jamie, and little William, had so carefully constructed between them.

At a stroke, cold anger replaced the fear.

Why should he appear now, in her place and amongst her friends, to threaten her with her love for him? After so long, when it was so much too late.

Angharad knew that she couldn't stop the love, rising and choking her now so that she wanted to reach out and draw him down to her. But she could try to fight it into submission.

'What a surprise.' The blandness she managed to put into her voice sickened her, and she saw Harry's rejection of it in his eyes before she looked away from him.

Laura was at his side. She was smiling, very faintly, as if the tableau was being staged for her benefit. There was a peardrop diamond at her throat and smaller ones pendant from her ears shot points of candlelight back at Angharad.

'It's been a long time,' Laura said. 'Haven't we all changed?' She took Angharad's hand and held it, proprietorial as she had always been, as she looked around the room. She tilted her head back to look up at the beams and Angharad saw the curve of her lovely neck and remembered that she had seen it reddened with Harry's kisses.

'You know,' Laura was saying, 'I thought it must be you behind this. I made Robina bring us along, to see.'

Angharad had wrenched her eyes from his, and she wasn't going to look at Harry again. She was oblivious of the mixture of surprise, disbelief and cold dislike in the glance that he gave his sister.

'Enjoy your meal,' Angharad said into the air between them. 'I've got a hundred things to do now, if you'll excuse me. Perhaps we'll get a chance to talk later.'

Was that the note she wanted to strike, not hostile, but distant, as if neither of them meant more to her than the grey-suited solicitor with his nose buried in the menu across the room? It sounded intolerably false, and she knew too well the sharpness of their perceptions.

She had half turned away from them, sent a flash of a reassuring smile at Jessie, when Jamie came back.

Jamie, too, saw everything with disconcerting speed. 'Anne. Are you all right?'

'Anne?' Harry's voice crackled.

'Yes, Anne. This is my London partner, Jamie Duff. Laura and Harry Cotton. We were friends years ago, Jamie.'

'And do you think Anne suits you better?' Harry's voice cut through to her from the polite murmurs of introduction. 'Better than Angharad.' He gave it the old, caressing throaty inflection. She quivered again with the sense that he was effortlessly severing them from the rest of the world. Jamie was miles away, diminished, and she fought to get back to him. Jamie's arm settled around her shoulder like a log of wood.

'I've never been able to pronounce it,' Jamie said, and Harry turned his blue appraising stare on him.

'No. Of course you wouldn't.' He was equable, smiling even, but there was no mistaking the truth.

The hair at the nape of Angharad's neck prickled, and all down the length of her spine.

At a glance the two of them hated each other, and she could smell the acrid scent of it between them. She longed to close her eyes and dispel the scene, spiriting herself and Jamie away, but even as she wished it she knew that there was no escape. It would all have to be enacted, step by step, whatever was to come, and the thought of the pain it would cause was like a physical blow.

She lifted her heavy head. 'I should be in the kitchen. Will you look after everyone for me, Jamie?' She crossed the room to the sanctuary of the service doors. Behind her Laura said something and followed it with a low laugh.

Jessie was waiting for her in the kitchen, her bright face tight with concern.

'That was him, wasn't it? Angharad?'

'For God's sake.' She recoiled from what seemed an intolerable intrusion and then, at once, her defences crumbled and broke. Angharad's hand came up to her mouth and then covered her eyes to hide the tears. 'Yes.' If Jessie, an outsider, saw it so clearly and so quickly, then there was no hope. No hope of keeping all the little structures of their life intact. 'It's just the same. Just the same as it always was. I knew it, as soon as I looked into his face.'

Jessie's hands tightened in sympathy on her shoulders. 'And so?' Angharad lifted her head to look at her, showing where the tears had made dark trails through the careful make-up. Her weary, defensive gesture took in the door beyond which Jamie was moving amongst the gathering crowd of diners, and from there to the little house in the terrace where she had left William in bed.

'So nothing.'

'Do you still love him?'

Angharad moved away to the table and picked up one of her familiar knives. The handle fitted snugly into the palm of her hand and she thought longingly of her elated mood of the early evening. Moving amongst the calm order of her kitchen, ready to work at what she loved doing.

'Oh, yes. Yes, God help me. I don't even know why. I'm not even sure he's worth loving. Yes, I still love him. But I can't let that matter, can I?'

'He's William's real father.' Jessie was gentle, but her persistence surprised Angharad. 'That doesn't make it quite a simple choice, does it, to exclude him for the sake of equilibrium?'

Angharad turned sharply. 'His father. Yes. But he hasn't tried to find me in seven years. Jamie's been a thousand times more of a father, and to another man's child. And there's something else.'

The long red room over the stables at Llyn Fair. Tanned bodies locked together, and black hair tangled on the pillow.

'Does he know? Does he know you have his son?'

From beyond the door Angharad thought she heard the cadences of his voice. Impossible that he was here, but true, and they were separated by a wider gulf than they had ever been.

'No,' she said dully. 'No. I never told him. I couldn't have, you see. I never saw him, after . . . that day.' Jessie was staring uncomprehendingly at her. 'I didn't want to see him, with part of myself. I was so shocked, as if everything had turned upside down. I just ran, as far away as I could, and hid, and went on hiding. I wanted to protect myself, and the baby, from them. Him, I mean. But I wanted him to find me too. Somehow to find me, both of us, and to want me more . . . more than . . . But he never came. I used to look for his face in the crowds. I couldn't make the steps to search for him properly, because I was afraid of him hurting us both. I knew that I shouldn't see him again, with the rational part of myself. Stupid, loving like that, isn't it? Doing one thing, and longing for another. You see . . .' Jessie was clearly bewildered, for all the concern in her face, and Angharad shook her head. 'Of course you don't see. He promised once, before I really understood the truth, that he would look for me again when the right time came. He didn't, of course. And I told myself that it didn't matter any more.'

Angharad's voice broke off.

Behind her the door swung open, and the waitresses came in with the first orders. There was work to be done, even though Harry Cotton was there, a few yards away, and had changed everything with a single glance. With jerky, mechanical movements Angharad pulled on her kitchen whites and turned to the long table.

Jessie watched her for a moment, thinking that it was inevitable that Angharad had made a success of her career. Her determination was utterly unwavering. Yet for all her stubbornness she had an extra degree of sensitivity too. And Jessie wondered what that would mean for her and the dark-faced, alarming man outside. She had seen the look that passed between them. And she had seen Jamie Duff's smooth mask drop for a second too.

'Jessie. Would you garnish these for me, please?' Angharad's voice was calm. At once Jessie set to work beside her.

The kitchen ran like clockwork. No one looking in at it would have guessed that Angharad was fighting to keep her hand steady, and her eyes on the succession of dishes in front of her instead of the door and beyond it.

Jamie came in a little later to report the success of the evening. His hand rested for a moment on Angharad's shoulder but their eyes didn't meet.

'Congratulations,' he murmured. 'Everyone has enjoyed every mouthful so far. Atmosphere perfect. Except at your friends' table, perhaps. The women are being very animated, but neither of the men has said more than two words.'

Poor Harry, Angharad thought. An odd complicity flickered within her, beside the anger. Laura had contrived this, somehow, and from the brief glimpse of her, she guessed that she had done it out of malicious curiosity. Laura looked rich, and spoiled, and not very happy.

When the last main dishes had been served, Angharad judged that it was time for her to go out and circulate between the tables. Jessie and the waitresses between them could deal with the puddings.

Angharad went out to the tiled washroom and shook her hair free of the confines of her cap. She stripped off her overall and the gaiety of her red dress mocked her. She didn't want to look into her own face. She made sure that the black smudges had gone, then turned deliberately away from her reflection and went out into the restaurant.

It looked beautiful, she thought with detachment, full of people and muted lights and the ripple of talk and laughter.

She slipped from table to table, accepting the compliments and the well-fed, well-lubricated badinage, conscious all the time of the last table she would reach. At length she had to turn to it, and Harry's stare dragged her eyes to his.

Mystified, she saw the fierceness in his face had melted away. Now there was laughter in it, challenging and as intimate as if he had hugged her to him. It drew her right back across the years to their intoxicated summer together, and she felt her own smile rising to answer his. The confusion fell away and she was left with a beat of happiness. He was here. After she had watched vainly for him for so long.

*I'm deranged*, she thought. *Not in control of myself.*

'. . . so clever,' Robina Gwynedd trilled. 'We'll come every night, Lucian darling, won't we?'

'Not unless Miss Owain lets me design the next five restaurants in her empire to make up for passing me over for this one . . .'

Although Lucian's fingers were ostentatiously linked with

267

Laura's, the brother and sister were ignoring their companions' nonsense.

Harry's low voice cut through it. 'Won't you sit down with us?' he asked.

The laughter was still quivering between them and Laura was watching, cat-like.

The cool amusement in her face had faded to alertness.

'Thank you, but no. There are too many things to do tonight. I'm glad you enjoyed it.' She walked away from the table with her red skirt swirling around her.

Only when she saw Jamie's bulk across the room did the smile die inside her.

The sleek diners sat late over their coffee and the posies of petits fours in their lacy wrappings. The blackness outside the windows was impenetrable, and once or twice a fat grey moth batted against the glass.

Jamie tapped his watch discreetly, and Angharad nodded at him, knowing that it was time for Jessie's little sister to go home. Jamie went, leaving Angharad with her head bent over her sheaf of bills.

Going home to watch over another man's child, she thought, pain swallowing up her happiness again. It was Harry's gaze that followed him to the door. The waitress filled Laura's brandy glass for the third time.

'Time to teeter home, darling?' Lucian said to her. 'Why? When we're having such fun?'

Harry stood up abruptly and drew her chair back for her. His hand was at her elbow when she almost stumbled. Robina and Lucian guided her towards the door. But Laura stopped dead as they passed Angharad. Close to, Angharad could see that there were fine lines beginning to show at the corners of her eyes under the sheen of make-up.

'Must talk soon,' Laura said. 'Friends, like we used to be. Too few in life. Too bloody few.' Her voice was slow and clear. 'Wouldn't you say, Luce?'

'Yes, love.' He was soothing, clearly used to her. The eyes of the other diners were beginning to slide curiously towards them. With her head held high, Laura let Robina and Lucian steer her away.

Angharad knew that Harry was standing beside her, waiting. Robot-like she followed him out into the lobby. Briefly she was cosncious of the cold prickle of stars in the summer sky, and Robina's Gwynedd's tipsy laugh from somewhere in the darkness. Then Harry blotted out everything as he bent to kiss her. Their lips grazed together and she felt the lift of his crooked smile before his hands tightened on her.

'Angharad. At last.'

Her mouth opened beneath his. It was Harry, the reality of muscle and bone under the familiar skin, and she felt the force of her need for him. It took the greatest effort Angharad had ever made to draw away again.

'Why are you laughing?'

'Because I'm happy to have found you again. Just to see you . . .'

Brutally she cut him short. 'You haven't found me again. Do you think that you can just stumble back, Harry, and pick everything up again? I've got . . .'

'I know that. Do you think I can't see what you've got? I'm sorry, darling, I'm sorry.'

There was a new gentleness in Harry, she saw, as if it had taken all his success and self-indulgence to humble him.

'Tomorrow,' he whispered to her.

'No. I can't.' Angharad struggled for conviction. He mustn't come anywhere near here. Nowhere near William, and her father. The old, old restrictions, a thousand times more complex now.

'Yes. You must.'

Outside they were calling him. 'Harreeee, the keys . . . come on . . .' He turned away from her, the arrogant Harry again whom she knew so well. 'Until tomorrow.'

Angharad fled back into the restaurant, only checking her headlong rush when she saw the stares of the last lingering customers. Jessie was writing out their bill, and behind her the waitresses were clearing the last table. There was a smell of hastily snuffed candles in the air, the deflated feeling of the evening's end.

The room was empty, except for Jessie and Angharad

269

sitting exhausted in the sofas in front of the hearth, when the door swung open again. It was Laura.

'Gave them the slip,' she said with a shrug, and a sudden grin that made her look almost a schoolgirl again. 'Came back to have a nightcap with you, Angharad.'

Jessie unfolded her legs from the cushions. She was looking with distrust at Laura, and Angharad smiled inwardly in gratitude for her loyalty.

'I'll be off home then, if there's nothing else that needs doing.'

'Jessie? You were wonderful tonight. Thanks. For everything.' She wanted to stop her going, to keep her here as a shield against Laura, but she resisted the impulse. Laura couldn't hurt her. And Angharad looked unwaveringly back into the eyes that had once seemed so like Harry's.

As soon as they were alone, Laura snapped the two diamond droplets from her ears and dropped them without a glance on the nearest table. Then she ran her fingers through her smooth hair, tousling it until she stood in front of Angharad looking exactly like the girl she had grown up with. For a moment there was no resemblance to Harry at all.

'A long time,' Laura said meditatively. She seemed to have pushed her drunkenness aside, without effort. 'Mayn't I sit down?'

'Of course.'

Laura slid into Jessie's place on the sofa and stretched like a cat.

'And what sort of nightcap would you like?'

'Oh, brandy I think. Thank you.'

Angharad brought the bottle and glasses and set them out between them. When Laura's drink was in her hand she asked, as lightly as if they were old acquaintances who had just bumped into each other at a party, 'What have you being doing, since?'

*Since.* Angharad put the too-vivid image of the red room at Llyn Fair out of her head. She would allow Laura to guess at none of the pain of that. And she knew that she was self-possessed enough now not to let the extremes of tonight's feelings show in her face.

'Working, mostly. Cooking, and learning this business.' The pretty, empty restaurant but with the warmth of a successful evening still lingering in it.

'I envy you that. Work. Your own domain. I married straight out of Cambridge, like a fool. Can't think why. Or yes, I can, but it didn't help anything. I've never done a thing except be a wife, and not a lot of that.'

Wife to Jeremy Argent of London SW1, according to the yellowing *Times* cutting in Angharad's hidden folder.

'Where's your husband?'

'Japan, right now. Making deals, or so the story goes. Oh, it doesn't matter. I used to go with him. You know, successful man with his dedicated wife ever at his side. But have you any idea how bloody boring it is, sitting through dinner after dinner in Japan, or South America, or some godforsaken country whose name you can't even remember, understanding one word in a hundred and smiling, smiling, like a puppet? And during the day, while he's in the meetings, nothing but shopping and salon appointments?'

Laura took a cigarette out of her silk purse and lit it with little, staccato movements. 'No. Well, I don't go any more. Jerry takes one of his pool of PAs or whatever they masquerade as. And I stay here. All mod cons, of course. Flat in Eaton Square, house in the country and another in Switzerland, and so on.' Suddenly she ducked her head and Angharad couldn't see her face. 'Jerry wanted kids. So did I. But I can't have any, as it turns out. So, we keep on keeping busy, in our own ways. Jolly, isn't it?'

Poor Laura. Angharad thought of William, down the village street, asleep in his little room with the Superman comic crumpled beside him. And of her own mixture of joy, pride and anxiety in having him, reinforced by the primeval desire to keep him safe at all costs. Only one emotion that she had ever experienced came close to touching the intensity of that, and Laura, with all her riches, would never know it.

'And what about you?' That was the old, intuitive Laura, probing dangerously close. 'The nice-looking man in the grey suit. He's your husband?'

'My partner. Jamie and I have been together for years, but we aren't married. It's a business relationship as well. We've got two restaurants in London . . .' Keep on talking. About anything so long as it isn't children.

'Duff's and Le Gallois,' Laura interrupted her. 'Pretty name, that. You know, I hadn't connected Anne Owain and you until I saw your picture in *Harper's*.' That was a little giveaway. Perhaps Laura had her secret folder too. 'And this place?'

'My own gamble. Jamie's not sure about it. But my father's very ill. I wanted to come back home for a while.'

Laura flicked the ash from her cigarette and Angharad caught the flash of sapphires and diamonds on her finger. 'Oh, it'll be a huge success. I'm an infallible judge of it in everyone but myself.' She looked around the room and then back at Angharad. Their eyes met, level and appraising. The sudden, vulnerable twist to her mouth surprised Angharad.

'So. Which of us d'you think has come out ahead?'

'It isn't a competition,' Angharad whispered.

'Isn't it? I've been competing. If not with you, then with him. For him.'

Delicately, like the first pawn brought into play, Laura had placed the thought of Harry between them again. But the events of the evening had left Angharad too raw, and the questions they raised were too towering, for her to have been able to respond, even if she had wanted to.

Instead, quickly, she said, 'With me? I was never competition for you, Laura. I just came along behind.'

Laura was laughing. She put her hands out and Angharad almost flinched, then felt relief that she hadn't because there was real warmth and affection in Laura's face. 'Your biggest fault always was underestimating yourself. Then. I don't believe you can possibly still be doing it. When I walked in here tonight and saw you in that red dress, a poppy instead of a windflower, I knew you were winning. I felt quite afraid of you.'

Their hands were still linked. Wondering, feeling the cool

weight of Laura's fingers over hers, Angharad said, 'Don't be. Why should you?'

And was that her own pawn being withdrawn, out of danger?

Smiling a little, Laura disentangled her hands. She picked up her brandy glass and drained it, poured herself another measure, and then began to talk. At first she was the flippant, cynical Laura who had come back from her summer in France. She talked about Cambridge and her effortless success there. She had been one of the innermost coterie of clever, spoilt young people with plenty of money and nothing to do except be more fashionable than one another.

'Amusing for quite a long time,' Laura said with a wry lift to the corner of her mouth, 'But not quite long enough.'

In her last term, Jeremy Argent had appeared like a promise of salvation. Twenty years older than Laura herself or any of her friends, rich, powerful and attractive, he had carved her effortlessly out of a crowded party and, she told herself, she fell in love with him at once.

It was the time of Harry's brief marriage to Bibi Blake.

Laura never sat for her degree. Within weeks she was Mrs Argent. Watching her face as she talked, Angharad saw the flippant mask slide away. Laura described the early disappointments of her marriage, and the humiliating realization that she had made a bad mistake, with a bitter simplicity that touched Angharad's heart. She knew that Laura was telling her what she had told no one else, and she felt the cords of friendship between them vibrate and grow taut again.

Laura was unhappy, and lonely. She had nothing, not the vividness of motherhood or even the steady, unpassionate warmth that Angharad shared with Jamie. Angharad put her arm round Laura's shoulder and kissed her cheek. She was wearing a heavy, musky perfume that was too old for her and Angharad saw that the lobes of her ears were reddened by the dangling weight of the heavy earrings.

'Couldn't you divorce him?' she asked, gently.

Laura looked down at the jewels that she called Jerry's rocks on her fingers. 'What for? I've got all this, and all the freedom I could ask for as well. Jerry likes me to have affairs. It makes him feel better.'

'You might fall in love again. You could marry again.'

Without warning Laura's head jerked upright. Angharad felt the irrelevance of her arm around her shoulders.

'You're not a fool,' Laura whispered. 'You know I couldn't do either of those things. Harry is all I've got. And all I'll ever want. Nothing has changed, and nothing ever will. Because I won't let it. You should know that.'

The words hung between them, tangible with threat, and Angharad knew that they were the stark truth. Slowly, stiffly, she withdrew her arm. The room tilted a little around her and then righted itself. All she could focus on was Laura's stare, her eyes burning brighter than the jewels on her fingers. Wildly she thought, clever, dangerous Laura. To pull the threads tight between us, to disarm me with honesty and draw my sympathy, and then to strike. The same old, immutable warning to stand clear. And so quickly. Before the thought of Harry had quieted enough in me for me to know my own reactions. Laura would have calculated that, too.

And what about Harry himself? He was hardly a pawn to be pushed to and fro between them. Angharad stood up, bright in her red dress, and looked down at Laura. She saw that unhappiness and vulnerability still showed in Laura's face, overlaid with challenge and unwavering determination.

Angharad turned away in confusion. Keeping her voice cool and steady, she said, 'I'm going to lock up now. You'd better leave, if you don't want to spend the night in here with tomorrow's lunches.'

Shrugging, Laura stood up too. She swept the diamond earrings off the table and into her bag without looking at them. Only in the doorway did she pause and, without looking round, she said, 'I suppose we couldn't meet again as friends? I need a friend more than I've ever done in my life.'

Angharad was glad that she couldn't see her face. 'I don't think so. I don't see how we could.'

There. She had admitted it. To Laura and to herself

simultaneously. No stepping down. For all the obstacles that loomed around them she couldn't walk away from Harry now.

'Goodnight, then, Angharad.' Laura rustled away into the darkness. Angharad listened to the throaty roar of her car as it swung away, too fast, in the narrow road.

She moved around the restaurant mechanically, locking the windows and snapping off the lights. Her hands were shaking. At last the door closed behind her and she turned down the dark street. A heavy dew was falling and she shivered in her thin dress, but the air was as sweet as honey. A thin veil of cloud had drawn raggedly across the stars, and the darkness, in the last hour before the summer dawn, was at its deepest. Treading unerringly over the old stones, alert to the tiniest sound of the pebbles under her feet, Angharad made her way home. For all the sharpness of her senses, her head was a racing turmoil. She was sick and afraid, and heavy in her heart for all of them, but yet she was buoyed up with a wild happiness. It was as if a heavy grey blanket had been lifted and left her free to the air again.

Beyond that, tonight, it was impossible to think.

In their cramped bedroom Jamie was asleep. As she undressed in the dim light, Angharad thought that in the creases around his closed eyes there was a shuttered defensiveness that she had never seen before. But when she turned out the light and slipped under the covers he stirred a little. His breath was warm on her cheek, and in the darkness he reached out for her. Angharad turned blindly to him, wishing that he could shut out with his warmth the images that danced in front of her. But that would never be possible. Now or ever. The hot tears squeezed beneath her eyelashes, and in his sleep Jamie kissed them away.

Someone was knocking at the door. Gently at first, and then with growing insistence. From a sleep that felt as deep as if she had been drugged, Angharad struggled towards consciousness. The room was bright, but the coolness of the light told her that it was very early. She groped for her watch on the night table and saw that it was not quite five to six.

The banging grew still louder and then someone was calling her name.

'Angharad. *Cariad*, wake up. Angharad.'

Gwyn. Awake immediately, Angharad flung herself out of bed and across the room. The early morning chill struck through her thin nightdress and the linoleum was icy to her bare feet. Gwyn was standing in the empty street, framed by the early sunlight. She looked frail in her old dressing-gown, and her face over the reassuring plaid was grey.

'It's your Dad, love. He was taken bad in the night. Dr Hughes came, and he rang the ambulance right away.'

'What time?'

'One o'clock.'

*When I was sitting in my restaurant playing Laura's complicated game.*

'Why didn't you come for me then?'

'He wouldn't let me. He said there was no need, on your important night. But the hospital have just rung. They think you should be there.'

The words struck at her like blows, but Angharad felt heself ducking them and already moving single-mindedly. The important thing was to get to him as soon as possible. Behind her Jamie was coming down the stairs, his face still confused with sleep. Past Angharad's shoulder he saw Gwyn still in the street and he read her expression at a glance.

'Shall I come with you?'

From the stairs, Angharad answered. 'No. Stay here with William. I'll go on my own.'

The miles to the hospital had never seemed longer, yet they flashed past her at dreamlike speed. The deserted seafront was beautiful in the pearly light, with the sun shining back off the flat silver sea.

The main doors of the hospital were locked, and it seemed hours before Angharad's fingers pressed to the night bell brought a slow porter to open them. Unthinkingly she brushed past him towards the stairs and the old ward, and she was halfway up the first flight when he called her back, waving a list.

'This way, Miss. Gwynedd Ward.'

She turned and ran back, and saw the discreet blue and white lettering, 'intensive care unit'. Beyond the double doors was a quiet world of silent, purposeful feet and ticking machines. A sister in a plain white overall led her past cubicles where other people were fighting their solitary battles amongst the tubes and dials.

In William's cubicle a nurse was sitting at his shoulder. He looked shrunken with pain but his eyes were undefeated. He looked straight at Angharad, and at once they acknowledged the truth to each other. Not very much longer. The nurse stooped to adjust the machinery and then moved silently away.

'I don't know why they're bothering with all this,' William said at last.

'They have to. It's their job.' Banal words, acknowledging the effort, and the truth that William didn't need it. Angharad bent over the high bed to put her arms around him, turning her face away so that he couldn't see her cry. But then the thought came, why hide it? There has been too much hiding between us. So she took his hands and, sitting in the nurse's chair beside him, she looked into his face through the blur of tears. For a long time neither of them spoke, then William said,

'I'm proud of you, you know. And of the boy. Thank you for bringing him home.'

Behind her father's head Angharad saw the blip, blip of a monitor. It reminded her of the machine's strong, urgent trace when little William was born. But this one was weaker, and slower. So much slower.

'What about his father?'

'I saw him last night,' Angharad told him simply, 'for the first time since . . . I left home.'

William's head turned a little on the pillows. 'I thought from your face that something had happened.'

So obvious, even here?

William seemed to be gathering his meagre reserves of strength. 'I want to tell you that I was wrong. To try to cut you off from those children. Trying to prolong the griefs and hatreds of my own life into yours. Visiting the sins of the

277

fathers, eh? It must have . . . given you a lot of pain that you didn't understand or deserve. It didn't lessen mine, either.'

'I shouldn't have deceived you.'

'No, you shouldn't have done that.' William was quiet again, thinking. 'Would you like me to tell you the story? I think you should know. For the child's sake. It might help you to – decide, if you need to.'

Angharad smiled at him, with all the certainty and reassurance that she could muster. 'Only if you want to. And if it won't tire you.'

'What do I need to rest for, now?' That was so much her father that a true smile broke through and he answered it with his own. Then, looking a little to one side and out past the glass partitions to a distant view that Angharad couldn't see, he began to tell her the old story.

Mary Parry was a fragile, shell-like beauty, the only child of a phthisic farmworker and his tiny wife, when she fell in love and married Will Owain. 'They were pleased with her. They thought I was a catch, God help them, even though I was almost old enough to be her father myself. A scholar, you see, as well as living up in the big house, me and the Owain family for long before that. Your family, Angharad. Yours, and the boy's!' But William checked Angharad's little questioning start with the pressure of his hand, and she sank back again. She was struck with confusion, but she would have to let him tell his story at his own pace.

'They were good people. Within months, they were both dead in the flu epidemic. Mary was never strong, and the shock of that nearly killed her.'

Yet after the first grief was over, Mary and William found that it had knitted them together and they discovered themselves more deeply in love than they had ever been before their marriage. William had been a solitary child and lonely in adulthood, when even Gwyn had been kept at bay, and his delight in Mary doubled. Intense happiness flowered briefly between them. Soon Mary was pregnant. William knew that the child would be a boy and overnight the focus of their happiness changed from the immediate to encompass the future as well.

William's father had not expected to have to work for his living, and had not been trained for it. His only expectation had been to manage the family estate, as his own father had done before him. But years of mishandling had reduced its value almost to nothing. By the time William left home to fight in the war, he had no more than his lieutenant's pay to live on, and when he came home again he had inherited the property and the weight of debts that it had accrued. But now, with an adored wife and a son to be born, he felt galvanized to put his affairs in order. Somehow the debts and mortgages would be paid, and his son's rights restored to him.

Then, in the midst of the happiness, Mary fell ill. It seemed certain that she would lose the baby, but it was as if she hung on to its life with her own.

As he talked, William was still looking past Angharad and back at faces that she couldn't see. She sat with his hand folded in hers, watching him and waiting for him to marshal his strength again.

The sister rustling past the glass wall looked at him and came abruptly to the bedside. Angharad felt her unspoken reprimand for allowing her father to exhaust himself, but William had no attention to spare for anything beyond the goal he had set himself and he said, 'I want to talk to my daughter. Please.'

The sister left them alone again and William's hand tightened briefly on hers. Mary was growing weaker every day. William would have sacrificed himself, the baby, anything to restore her, but it seemed that there was nothing to be done. Then, miraculously, they were offered a straw of hope. A London doctor was specializing in the rare form of anaemia that Mary was suffering from, and was developing a new drug treatment. It was almost untested, and had never been used on a pregnant woman, but William telephoned him and he agreed to see Mary. They left for London at once.

'Money,' William said bitterly. 'We needed money. The treatment was hugely expensive. I told the doctor, and Mary, that I would find it. He had agreed to treat her, and that was all that mattered. I left her there in his clinic

279

and came home to Llyn Fair again.'

Angharad's start jolted William and his eyes closed for a moment against the pain.

'Yes,' he whispered. 'I was born at Llyn Fair. So were your grandfather, and great-grandfather. All that side of the valley belonged to the Owains, once.' Angharad had a sudden crystal-clear vision of the lake, green and silver in its sheltering cup of hills, the fringe of black pines, and the old grey house drowsing in the sunshine.

Home? No. Impossible to think of it like that. It would forever mean Laura and Harry, dark heads bent together and the identical texture of their silky brown skin. Angharad thrust the image out of her head and looked down at the blank white sheet over the bed, struggling to reconcile her father's words with the fact of her own childhood in the little house in Cefn.

'That evening, I saw Joe Cotton. We'd met him half a dozen times before, your mother and I. We liked him. He was very vital, invigorating company. A bright boy, too. He was doing a little building, a little buying and selling land here and there. Determined to get on, and doing quite well at it, I'd half-heard, and not thought very much about it. He lived with his wife and two little children in a house over the hill from Llyn Fair. And I met him that night, when I was walking up and down the lanes, reckoning how to find the money for Mary's doctor. He was standing at the gate to Llyn Fair, looking down towards the lake. There was something fierce in his face that I should have recognized. Covetousness.'

William's voice was fading a little, as if he doubted he would be able to finish the story. Angharad bent her head and willed him to, because he clearly wanted to so much.

'We started talking, there at the gateway. Then he asked me to walk back over the hill with him, to his house. I didn't want to go . . . home, with Mary not there, so I went. And as we walked I found myself telling him about what had happened. I had just a glimmer of an idea. There wasn't much land left by then, but there was one patch up at the head of the valley beyond the lake. It had been grazed for years, no good for anything else, but I suddenly thought that Cotton might be interested in it. There's a fine view from up there. He could put up some jerry-built bungalows. We got back to his house, and there were his wife and the two children. A little black-haired girl, and the boy. Looking . . . like William does now.'

Angharad saw that there was no bitterness or anger in her father's face. Instead there was an infinitely weary amusement that brought cold fingers of fear because it meant that he was slipping away from her.

'Sitting there beside his fire, with his daughter on his knee, Joe Cotton made me a proposal. He didn't want the land himself, he said, but he assured me that I would be able to dispose of it, given time. In the meantime, he would lend me the money I needed. Interest free. He would take the house and lake as security, mortgaged as they were, just as a formality of course. I accepted his offer. I thought he was doing it out of human kindness, because he had his own wife beside him and his pretty children, and I thought he wanted to help me save mine. Within a day he came round to Llyn Fair with the papers, and I signed them out on the verandah while he admired the sunset reflected in the water. By signing those papers I undertook to repay the cost of Mary's medical treatment in full within three months, or to lose our home, worth about forty times as much. Not very clever, was I?'

Angharad couldn't trust herself to speak.

'Desperation makes a poor adviser,' William said softly. 'Mary had her treatment. She was much better. Quite soon I was able to bring her back home. I even learnt how to give her her injections, so that we didn't need to have a nurse. It was a very hot summer, the year you were born, and we would sit together by the lake for hours, not talking, just watching the shadows on the water. It should have been the happiest time, but it was made wretched for me by the struggle to get Joe Cotton's money. I couldn't sell the piece of land. It was unsuitable for building, for some technical reasons, as Cotton understood perfectly well. I couldn't raise the money.

'The deadline came, and I had to go and tell him that I couldn't pay. I thought he might extend the time. Perhaps start charging me punitive interest. But not Joe Cotton. He wanted Llyn Fair. To live there himself, in my house. He was courteous, regretful even, but he said that our agreement was quite clear and he must hold me to it.

'Too late, I got our old solicitor to look at the papers. They were watertight. Joe Cotton was entitled to turn me out of our home. I didn't give him the satisfaction of sending his men to do that. I found a house in Cefn, far enough away, I thought, but not so far that it would mean digging up all our roots. Gwyn helped me, making it as homely as she could. It wasn't much, after Llyn Fair, and neither of us could find it in ourselves even to pretend it was. Then I had to tell Mary. That was the hardest thing of all, Angharad. She loved Llyn Fair more than I did. And I couldn't make her believe that it wasn't her fault, her fault just for being ill.'

The tears were standing out in William's eyes now, and his voice was so low that Angharad had to strain to catch the words.

'The day after, she went into premature labour. You were born a healthy little girl. Mary had a haemorrhage and died in less than an hour.'

At last, after so long, Angharad understood all the pain and grief, and the pent-up bitterness that had shadowed the corners of her childhood, and that had gnawed endlessly at her father until he became the seemingly cold and cruel man who had denied herself and her baby son.

Behind the ache of unshed tears, and the ache of never having known or understood, flickered the flame of gratitude that she and William had not left it too late to come home.

'Why didn't you ever tell me, you and Gwyn?'

'It was past,' William said simply. 'Perhaps we should have done. I don't know. It all seems so long ago, now. So unimportant, when it might have meant you not being here. When it might still mean your being denied your . . . happiness. Don't let my mistakes rob you of that, will you?'

Angharad understood that William was giving her his blessing, whichever path she chose to follow, into whatever future was waiting for her outside this glass-walled room with its unsleeping machines watching them and counting the minutes away.

'I've got William,' she whispered. 'And you, and Gwyn. That's all that matters.'

The ghostly smile, frightening her, still clung around her father's mouth. He knew, and understood, something that she couldn't.

When she looked again through her tears, she saw that William's eyes were shut. She had to lean right over him to hear what he was saying.

'I think I'd like to go to sleep now.'

Angharad kissed the corner of his mouth, and felt the coldness of his skin. William had already drifted away into sleep. For a long time she sat watching him, and then she gently disengaged her fingers from his grasp and laid his hand down on the white sheet. She found the sister writing at her desk. 'My father's gone to sleep.'

The sister ran to him, too quickly, and then turned to her dials and instruments. Another nurse came, and then a doctor, and their rubber soles squeaked as they swooped emotionlessly around his bed.

Angharad sat in her corner, too drained of emotion to move or even to think. The doctor loomed in front of her and said gently, 'Your father is slipping into a coma. He doesn't feel anything, now. He may or may not regain cosnciousness.'

Angharad nodded, knowing already. 'May I stay with him?'

'Of course. There may be no change for quite some time...'

'That doesn't matter. I want to be here.'

Soon they were alone again. She took up his hand and held it, listening to the lullaby of the humming machines.

It was a long, long day and night.

Gwyn came and sat beside her, then Jamie. He took her home to Cefn for an hour, and she played with little William and put him to bed. Then she came back to the hospital, and she and Gwyn sat on into the night in silence. The doctor came back and told them that there was no change. Gwyn let Angharad persuade her to go back home for a few hours' sleep.

Towards dawn the note of the machines changed, then stopped, then faltered on again. The night sister was at the bedside in a second with her silent cohorts and then the doctor, grey-faced with sleep. When the bleep bleep stopped for the second time, it didn't start again. Without seeing him, Angharad knew when the doctor shook his head, just once.

They were surprisingly quick, and gentle with them both. They did whatever they had to do with him, and then they left her alone.

Angharad prayed wordlessly, gratitude inextricably bound up with the sorrow, and then kissed his cheek once more.

Aloud she said, 'I love you.'

The room was quiet, peaceful. Angharad slipped out of the glass cubicle and closed the door silently behind her.

The hospital corridors were deserted, lit with dim globes of light. The floor of the entrance hall was a shining expanse of red and cream tiles with ranks of wooden benches drawn up under the brightly admonishing posters. Someone was sitting on one of the seats, his head sunk against his chest, his face dark and unshaven. But he heard her slow footsteps and looked up at once. Harry was waiting for her.

Angharad stopped, just looking at him.

He came to her and took her hands between his, chafing her stiff fingers. Then he put his arms around her so that her cheek rested in the hollow of his shoulder.

'He's dead,' she said blankly.

Harry's arms tightened, supporting her. Angharad shook her head a little, dazed, but in the bleak dawn suffused with gratitude that he was there.

'I'm sorry.' She had never heard his voice so soft. The roughness of his unshaven jaw grazed hers. He was so close. She saw the soft stuff of his collar, a tiny unravelled thread in his sweater and the pulse at his neck under the angle of his jaw.

'Harry.' The bewilderment was growing. 'How did you know, to be here?'

'I heard. If you would like me to go away, just say.'

She shook her head and felt his arms tighten again.

'Come on.' Gently he led her out of the hospital and into the sea-grey light. The sky to the east was the colour of pearls with a thread of palest pink laid where the sea met the sky. The only sound was the cry of the gulls as they swooped over the pier.

Harry guided her to his car at the kerb. As she sat in the passenger seat and stared out at the red-brick height of the hospital, the first sense of loss dawned on her. She had left her father in there, and he would never come home again. A sob filled her head and broke out of her mouth.

At once Harry's arms were around her again and her face found the angle of his shoulder.

'Cry,' he ordered her. 'Cry, my darling.'

After the first grief had worn itself out, Angharad looked up at the low roof of the car and felt it imprisoning them.

'I want to go outside,' she said.

Harry made her walk across the promenade to a white-painted shelter facing the sea. They sat down side by side on the narrow bench. In front of them the waves spilled over the shingle and the gulls dipped and circled. Angharad drew the cool salty air into her lungs and felt the desperate fingers of the hospital hours loosening their hold. Harry had brought a rug from the car and he wrapped it around her. Now he was fumbling in the bag he had carried with him and she smelt the fragrance of coffee. She realized at once that her mouth was parched, and she was hollow with hunger. Harry broke off squares of chocolate and fed them to her, and before he would let her drink her coffee from the Thermos cup, he uncapped a brandy bottle and tipped the spirit into it.

They ate and drank in silence, listening to the waves and the seagulls.

At last Harry said, 'I wish I'd known your father.'

'He was talking about you, just before he died. About when you were a little boy.'

Harry's stare met hers, and she saw the unchanged blue depths of his eyes.

285

'He told me why. All the reasons why he visited his bitterness on us. He made me understand.'

Angharad was thinking, remembering the effort it had taken him to tell her, and the understanding and sharp love and pity that the story had brought. It was a moment or two before she saw that Harry was waiting, not moving, with his head bent.

'And will you tell me?'

Angharad felt herself the strong one as she picked up his hand and looked down at the shape of it. Clearly remembered, with so much else.

'Yes.'

As she talked, she felt that Harry was listening to her with every particle of himself, but he was looking away from her and out to sea. When she glanced at him she saw the old, impatient lines of his profile that she had loved and clung to in her memories for years overlaid with something new. Perhaps uncertainty. Perhaps the resignation of hoping without expecting. At the end of the long storm, Angharad felt her own exhaustion. Telling it had been William's last effort, and gratitude beat inside her again.

At length Harry's eyes met hers and they looked at each other with a little of the numb fear of children discovering the blackness of adult secrets.

When Harry spoke, she saw that his lips were stiff.

'Your home,' he said. 'All those times and years. Your father and mother. Oh Christ, Joe. He killed your mother. That's what it means, doesn't it?' His voice cracked, and he moved to shade his eyes with one hand, but Angharad caught his wrist and touched her fingers to his mouth.

'Of course it doesn't mean that. Neither of us must think that. She was very ill, and she died. What does matter now is that we should understand why there was so much bitterness. For Dad's sake.'

There was a wildness in Harry's face now as he pulled her to him and kissed her eyelids, the bones of her cheeks and then her mouth, bruising her, laying her open to him as no one had done in all the years they had been apart.

'I love you,' he said. 'I didn't know it properly then, God

286

help me, but I know now. I've known it since that terrible day. I want you, Angharad. It's possible, isn't it? Tell me it's possible?'

Angharad broke away from him. She was too numb, too new to the grief for her father and mother, and too frightened of the insistence that Harry triggered off in her.

'I don't know. Not now. Perhaps not ever.'

William, she was thinking helplessly. Your son, Harry. Then Jamie. And Laura.

'Your grey-flannel lover?' There was a touch of the old arrogance there, and she flared up at it as she would never have done before.

'Yes, Jamie's my lover. And my partner, and my friend. For seven years, through difficult times. Where were you then, Harry?'

He caught her hand, alight with passion.

'I tried to find you. I came to London, not knowing but just believing that's where you would be. I made lists of restaurants, street by street and area by area, and I walked those streets in case I might see you. Have you any idea how many eating-places there are in London?'

Angharad shook her head, numbed. She had been right, then, all those times in London when she had felt him close. How sad, and how wasteful.

'Thousands. It was hopeless, but I couldn't think what else to do. I kept seeing your face, white, like it was . . . that day. I couldn't let you go, and I'd already been a selfish fool and let it happen. I went to your aunt, and begged her to tell me where you were, but she wouldn't. If you asked about me, she said, or ever mentioned me, that would be different. Last time I saw her, she said that you never had. She looked at me as if she hated me. I understand why, now. I gave her an address. Put it into her hands. You could have reached me through that address within hours, any time in the last seven years. I made sure of that.'

Angharad looked sadly away. The sun had come up, a circle of molten colourless light over the burnished rim of the sea.

'I didn't know that,' she said in a small, toneless voice.

'Gwyn never told me.' The heat of anger rose in her, and then she remembered her father and Joe Cotton, and Harry's shocked voice saying *He killed your mother.* Of course Gwyn had hated Harry. Why should she have acted as his messenger? She had been wrong to keep all the secrets, and never to have mentioned Harry, but Angharad understood why she had done it.

And she herself had never spoken of Harry. There had been opportunities and she had let them pass out of a kind of perverse pride. The anger against Gwyn flickered and died, replaced by a knot of frustration. 'I explored every avenue I could think of to find you,' Harry said. 'But you had vanished. Evaporated. I thought I understood, in the end, that you didn't want to be found. And who could blame you, after all.'

Angharad could barely hear the last words, they were spoken so low.

'What about Laura?' she asked, knowing that if all the truths were to be drawn out they should come now.

'Laura, Laura.' With a jerk Harry pulled away from her and stood in the mouth of the shelter, a black silhouette against the sun's glow. 'Do you think I wanted to let you disappear like that? Your last sight of me, screwing my own sister? Not making love, Angharad, do you remember that? Listen. Laura has made sad, bad mistakes and so have I. We pull each other back, and down, and inwards. We can't go on for ever, chewing each other up. If you were mine, Angharad, you could help us both.'

Angharad thought back to the rstaurant, and Laura in her diamonds. I don't believe that, Harry, she repeated to herself. I want to, but I can't.

Harry turned back to her and his face had changed again. There was a new tenderness in it, and it tugged at her.

'If you were mine,' he repeated.

'I don't know.' It was the only answer she could give him. Too much had happened to take in so quickly, and none of the old problems had melted away.

'I understand,' he said at once and brushed the hair back from her face to kiss her forehead. Then he swung her round to look at the sea. 'Look at the sunrise. Do you remember the August Meeting? And the child, singing *Early One Morning*?'

It was as clear in her head as if the notes were soaring around them now. Angharad let her hands fall and walked out of the shelter into the dazzle of light.

'I have to go home,' she said simply. 'To see Gwyn. There are things I have to do, now.'

'I know that,' Harry reassured her. 'When you are ready, I will come back again.'

He took her hand and led her back to his car, and she felt in that moment as clear and certain as she had done seven years ago.

# CHAPTER ELEVEN

The meadow over the grey stone churchyard wall was
fringed with the foaming lace of cow parsley. Beyond it the
ground sloped down to Cae Mawr, where the Cefn children
always built their Guy Fawkes bonfire, and then rose once
more to the bracken folds of The Mountain. The humped
back of it stood dark against the brilliant blue sky.

Angharad looked back again, to the sweet dark earth at
the gravemouth and the vicar who was reading her father's
burial service in his slow Welsh cadences. He had christened
her in the same tiny church. Around her was the silent crowd
of her father's neighbours and friends, dark compact people,
their heads respectfully bent and forgetful for a moment of
whether they were Church or Chapel. Jamie Duff in his sleek
dark suit towered above their ranks like a being from another
world.

The slow, momentous words were balm to her spirit.
Angharad felt the sun hot on her head, and the peace
spreading from the churchayrd to encompass the village and
the hills beyond. She could even believe that a little of it
settled on Harry and Laura, side by side yet not together, at
the far edge of the group. Laura had stopped twisting the
rings on her fingers, and Harry stood very still, his face
intent, looking into the dense shade under the yew trees.

Angharad understood why they had come. They had done
no more than murmur a word to her at the church door. It
was for her father's sake, and after all the years, for Joe.

The service was over. The moist earth fell back again as
the sexton bent to his work. Angharad knew him as the
cowhand from Tyn-y-Caeau farm. The mourners were
beginning to turn aside from the grave in twos and threes.
Without looking, Angharad was aware that Harry and
Laura had already slipped away. She turned to Gwyn. Her
seamed faced was wet with tears but she was scrubbing them

290

away with her folded handkerchief. Firmly she told Angharad, 'We'd best get back. Everyone will be wanting something to eat and drink.' The expectations were distinct. As soon as the cards on each of the wreaths had been read and their appropriateness commented upon, there would be an eddy of people back to the house. There should be sandwiches, *bara brith* and cake, tea and whisky, and the atmosphere would lighten perceptibly until it became almost jolly again. Only then would people consider it appropriate to leave.

Angharad knew that her father would have attended dozens of such gatherings, and she knew too that for all his cynicism, it was what he would have wanted for himself. She had done all the preparing with due care.

Now she walked back down the street to her old home, flanked by Gwyn and the vicar. In the window she glimpsed little William's pale, serious face. He had been left in the care of Jessie's mother who was cutting the obligatory triangular sandwiches. Angharad went quickly in to him, but he met her at the door.

'Will Grandpa come home now?'

'No, William. He won't come back. But he's safe. We shouldn't be unhappy any more.' She watched the transparency of emotions in the little boy's face. At last the one she had been waiting for broke through. It was impatience, with the muffled quiet of the house and the sombre days just past. William looked out of the window and saw the blue sky.

'C'n I go and find Teck?'

'Of course you can.'

He was gone at once, ducking between the groups of his grandfather's friends at the front door, and away up the village street. Watching him, his head tucked down and his bare legs flying, Angharad thought she might have been seeing herself twenty years ago.

She turned back to the little room, lined with her father's books and possessions, and crowded with the cluster of friends who would remember those days too. They came to shake hands or put their arms around her shoulder, restrained in their sympathy, perfectly at home with emotions that the day demanded. They were comfortable with her too, because they could place her exactly. How could it be like this in London, Angharad thought? I belong here. Amongst these dark, dignified people.

Her old Sunday school teacher had just come in.

'A sad day,' she murmured to Angharad. 'But beautifully done. A lovely service.'

'Thank you, Mrs Parry. Will you have some tea? Or something stronger, perhaps?'

'Well, I don't know that I should. But William always was a whisky man, wasn't he? Perhaps just a very small one, in respect, mind.'

Angharad looked round at the little community, drawn tight around Aunty Gwyn, and herself if she should need it. Her own generation were here too, Jessie and her husband, and Gareth Williams whom she had last seen in Le Gallois. He looked much more natural here. The faces were brighter now. Over by the window, where the late sunlight was strongest, she heard the first low laugh muffled by a discreet cough. Jamie was plying the whisky bottle. Angharad smiled to herself. The gathering was proceeding exactly as it should.

Her father would have enjoyed it.

How can I leave? she thought with a sudden pang. I don't want to go away again. *This is my home*.

It was well on into the evening when Angharad and Jamie at last made their way back to the rented cottage with its whitened step and discreet lace curtains at the window. They had left Gwyn sitting in the darkening room with a trio of friends, the grandfather clock ticking securely behind them. William had begged to spend the night at Teck's house, and had been dispatched to Jessie's cheerfully elastic household. Angharad and Jamie were alone for almost the first time since she had come home from the hospital four days ago.

Angharad knew that Jamie was watching her and, aware of her own cowardice, she busied herself with the preparations for a meal rather than face him at once. In spite of the hot weather, a low fire was kept burning in the old range to heat the water. Angharad checked and found that the old bread oven was hot. She would make a soufflé, and they could have a simple salad. While she whisked up the egg whites, Jamie stood half-turned away from her, his head almost touching the black oak beams, looking through the curtains down the deserted street. She could sense his taut impatience. He had already given her more time than he could easily afford.

They ate the meal in almost unbroken silence. At last Jamie put his plate to one side.

'Anne?'

It sounded very strong now, that London name.

'I know. Jamie, I . . .'

'Wait. I want to ask you, first. I miss you, Anne. I understand, of course, that you wanted to be with your father, and that it was natural and good that you and William found a way of staying here with him until he didn't need you any longer. I could see how happy it made you, and I even recognized it in him. You were right, and it was astonishingly generous of you.'

*Selfish, as much as generous, Jamie. You are the generous one.*

'But now, will you come back with me? To our life? I love you, Anne, and I love William too. I want to take you both home again.'

*Home? Oh, Jamie, I know how much you love us. If only, if only.*

'Will you come?'

Angharad thought of their pretty Chelsea house with its careful antiques, blue-and-white china, and the flowers blooming in the tubs on the steps. Her office over the Le Gallois dining-room, with her appointment book beside the telephone and the brigade of people downstairs doing all the things she had enjoyed herself. None of it, not a single thing, seemed as real or important as this little rented house and the street beyond it.

Prevaricating, and hating herself for it, she said, 'There's The Schoolhouse. It's been closed for four days. I want to open it and start it working properly again. I can't just leave it now, Jamie.'

'There's also Le Gallois.'

'I don't cook there any more. Any efficient manager could

293

do what I do. I'll come back and appoint one.' She was looking down at the tablecloth, not wanting to see his face. 'It isn't just The Schoolhouse. There's Aunty Gwyn . . .'

'Gwyn can come and live with us, of course.'

Generous Jamie, city-rooted. He couldn't understand what it would be like to be torn away from this gentle, powerful place.

The silence gaped between them.

'Tell me the truth, Anne,' Jamie said.

*And what was that?* Layers of truth, corroded and fused and tangled together.

The truth that now she had come home she couldn't sever herself from it again? Or the other, where Harry's dark height fell between them and Jamie, and which she couldn't look into herself, yet, because of the ache it set off in her heart?

'I want to stay here in Cefn. Will you let us do that, Jamie?'

Perhaps she should have cut the ties between them then, but she couldn't find the strength to do it altogether. Part of herself still clung to him, the vulnerable self that had been so painfully exposed when she first came to London. And now habit and familiarity clung to their years together, and to the times that they could go on spending in just the same way. Jamie was kind, and good. She could never be in love with him. But was love what she needed? If it was the agonizing wrench that she felt for Harry, her spirit was beginning to tell her that she did not. The steel core of independence strengthening within told her that what she needed now was peace, and solitude, and her son alone.

'Tell me the truth,' Jamie said again, very quietly. 'The man at the opening night. Harry. He was Harry Cotton the director?'

'Yes.'

'And he is William's father.' Not a question. A long breathed-out sigh of despair.

'Yes.'

'Does he know you have his son?'

'No.'

'You can't keep that a secret, Anne. Not up here. He'll find out, and he'll want him as well as you, and he won't let go easily. What man could?' The first bitterness she had seen in Jamie, and she had bred it. The pain stabbed at her. 'I saw him looking at you in the restaurant. I know the Harry Cottons of this world. They're single-minded, and they're hard, and they are never quitters. Don't let him devour you, Anne. Don't you let him smash you back to the girl you were when you walked into Duff's and asked for a job. And don't let him do anything of the kind to William. Even if he is his real father.'

Jamie swung back to the window and stared out at the mild little view as if he hated it. Angharad went to him and put her hands on his sleeves. Soft flannel, hand-tailored for him, the very familiarity biting at her now.

'I won't let him,' she whispered. 'If I never do anything else, I will keep William safe and happy. I loved Harry Cotton when I was a girl of eighteen. I didn't know anything or understand anything. His father had cheated mine, a long time ago, and I was forbidden even to know him and his sister. But I loved them both and they loved me, in their own way. Harry was very young and wild, then. I was pregnant, and I ran away. The rest you know. I didn't see him again until the night of the opening.'

Angharad lifted her head to look into his eyes. 'I'm grown up, now, Jamie. I'm a mother, and I'm myself. I'm not afraid of Harry Cotton. You asked for the truth. The truth is that I don't know what I feel for Harry. Whether I hate him. Or love him. Or whether he doesn't matter any more. It's so tied up with many other things. With my father. With this place, and another called Llyn Fair. Where . . . Harry used to live.

'But I do know what I want, and need. I want to stay here in Cefn, living with William and seeing him grow up with the people and the way of life that I knew. We're not going anywhere, Jamie. We're still here, if you want us. I'm sorry about London.'

The paucity of the words struck her, but she could find no others.

He smiled at her, reaching out to touch her cheek and then kissing the corner of her mouth with his old gentleness.

'I know you are,' he said. But Jamie couldn't disguise the sadness in his eyes, and he turned away to the dim little room because there was nothing else for them to say.

In the dark night Angharad sensed that Jamie was as wide awake as she was herself, watching the black square of the window soften at last with grey light. But he didn't whisper *Are you awake?* as he had done so often in the past, nor did they turn inwards to try to find again the warmth that was fading away between them. Angharad tasted regret in her mouth, and impotence, and when Harry's dark face slid in front of her eyes, she closed them against him as if he was an intruder.

Jamie was to leave very early the next morning for London, and she sensed the relief when it was time for them to get up. They moved awkwardly to and fro, bumping into each other in the confined spaces of the cottage. Jamie carried his suitcases out to the Porsche while she made coffee and toast, and then they sat facing each other in the back kitchen in what seemed to Angharad a cruelly painful parody of all their other mornings together.

'I'll got up to Jessie's and say goodbye to William,' Jamie said tonelessly. Almost as he spoke they heard flying feet along the pavement and William erupted into the house.

'I was afraid you'd be gone,' he said, clambering up into Jamie's lap and leaning back so that his black hair fanned out over Jamie's smooth shirtfront.

Jamie stroked it lightly and said, 'Of course I wouldn't go without seeing you. What are you doing today?'

'It's the best day. Football after school. When will you be coming back?'

A pause, fractional, hovering between them all. Angharad turned to the dishes with her throat tight.

'I'm not sure. William, your mother and I have been talking about things. Trying to decide how best to arrange everything because I have to work in London and now we have The Schoolhouse here, and Aunty Gwyn as well. Which would you like better, to live here or in London?'

Angharad rounded on him. Don't ever use William

between us, her eyes flashed at him, but then she checked herself. Jamie loved William too. He was simply asking him, as it was fair to do.

William was thinking, serious-faced. She saw, and knew that it was the beginning for him, the first sight of adult paths with their divergences and mysterious turnings. Questions would begin to loom for him as they had done in her own childhood. How would she avoid his grandfather's mistakes when already she was hiding so much?

Looking from one to the other of them, William said with a puzzled face that roused her fierce protectiveness, 'I'd like to stay here. But only if you can too, Jamie.'

With the utmost gentleness he answered, 'I can't do that.'

'Teck's Dad works here. Why can't you?'

'I couldn't do my kind of work in Cefn. William, I'm not your Dad. I thought you understood that.'

'I want you to be.'

Angharad was shaking, her hands clattering the lid of the butter dish. Was this what she really wanted, this wanton destructiveness of her child's secure world? Yet they had never, ever tried to pretend. From the very first, when William's stumbling syllables had formed 'dada' they had corrected him, with gentleness. Not Dada. Jamie. How long would it be, now, before the question came, 'Where is my Dad? Where has he been?' And how would she answer that?

Jamie had smoothed William's hair once more and now he set him down squarely on his feet. 'I know,' he said softly. 'But I'm Jamie. Same as always. And I'll be back next weekend. As often as I can.'

'Promise?'

'Of course I promise.'

There was gratitude in Angharad's eyes as she looked over his head, and William was years too young to interpret the hollow effort at conviction in the two faces important to his world.

They followed Jamie out to the car, and waved until he had swept around the corner under the oak tree and vanished from their sight.

You did it to him, and yourself, Angharad told herself

savagely as she steered solemn William to the school bus. You did it, as she walked up the little road to the restaurant, tore the apologetic notice from the door and once inside took the explanatory tape from the answering machine.

You, yourself. And Harry. Harry, will your fingers dig into my flesh for the rest of my life?

Jessie came in in her apron, took one look at her face and brewed coffee so strong and black that it puckered Angharad's mouth, but stopped her hands shaking at last.

'Talk?' she asked, but Angharad smiled crookedly and shook her head.

'You know everything,' she said. 'Let's work. Just work.' But the brief pressure of her old friend's arm around her shoulder comforted her, and helped her to cling to the flickering conviction that she was right. She had to be right.

They worked.

The restaurant was open again for lunch that day, although there were only five customers. There were nine for dinner, more the next day, and on the third they were booked up again. Angharad flung herself into it as she hadn't done since the early days at Duff's with Pierre's eyes on her and the mysterious unfolding force of the baby inside her. The difference was that all she carried now was the weight of her thoughts and memories, and the reverberating, endless questions.

Should she, after all, hack through the little totem of her independence and take William back to London, marry Jamie and be his Anne for the rest of her life? Or stay here in Cefn with her son, living as simply and with the happiness they found in spite of so much, as they were doing now? Or go to find Harry? Seek him out as she hadn't done years ago, and say, This is your son? And me, can I explore the way that you still hold me, taut and braced against the pain of it, whatever comes?

No.

She wouldn't do that. The answer came back clearly every time.

Angharad rigidly ordered her days so that the precious hours between the return of the school bus and William's bedtime were spent uninterruptedly with him. She found a pleasure in his company much stronger than the busy, distracted love that had reigned in London. They read books together, and then played long, involved imaginative games based on the stories that then had to be repeated exactly the next day. On Sundays and Mondays the restaurant was closed, and on their first Sunday alone together Angharad drove them west to the great stone castle at Caernarfon. They ran up and down the battlements with the wind in their faces and the jackdaws tumbling in the air below them, and huddled awestruck at the foot of the great cliffs of towers.

William avidly soaked up all the meagre information about the place that she had absorbed from her own father, and begged for more.

'We'll look in Grandpa's books. and then there's Harlech, and Conwy as well . . .'

'Can we go now? Today?'

His eagerness surprised and delighted her. 'Too far today. Next Sunday we'll come, with all the books and a picnic, and the camera, and we'll make a castle scrapbook, if you like.'

William fell asleep in the car on the way home, exhausted with the air and exercise. Looking back at him, Angharad felt pride at the success of the day healing a little of the rawness of anxiety.

On other afternoons they went walking. Walks in London had meant the Embankment, or Kensington Gardens to look at the ducks and sailing boats on the Round Pond. But in Cefn they could strike past the church and over Cae Mawr, and up on to the springy turf of The Mountain. Once they were dawdling up the rutted track over the lower slopes, looking at the wildflowers sheltered in the mossy ditch.

'Herb robert,' Angharad recited to him, 'crosswort, vetch, celandine and campion.' Delightedly she spotted the curved green spires of wild arum in the coolest hollow. 'Look, lords and ladies. See, inside their green cloaks, the lords in purple and the ladies in cream.'

William bent to examine them, and the ferns sprouting from the bankside brushed their intent faces. Then he straightened up again as something else caught his attention, and he was scrambling over the gate and running exuberantly away from her in a wide diagonal across the bracken-crisp slope.

Angharad heard the crackle of a footstep in the dry undergrowth. She felt his closeness even before she looked up, and then his eyes drew hers and she stared into Harry's face.

Atavistic terror gripped her.

'What do you want?' Her instinct, surprising her even in that split second, was to turn aggressor. She wanted to drive him back, away from here and her playing child, as if he were a predator. She moved like a cat to block the gate, and his view over it to the mountain slope.

Harry stepped back, unbalanced by the fury in her face.

'To see you. To ask how you are. Is that so very terrible? What's wrong, Angharad?'

'You've been following me. Spying on me.'

Gently, as if to soothe a child, he said, 'Of course I haven't. I was walking up there.' He gestured to the ridge. 'And I saw you coming up. Remember how we used to walk together? Miles and miles, talking.'

'I don't want to talk now.'

His face was concerned, eyes measuring her. Angharad fought the impulse to turn and run. 'Of course not, if you don't want to.'

*You can't keep it a secret, Anne, not up here,* she heard Jamie warning her. Harry was much taller than her, and he could look over the gate.

'Who's that? A local kid?'

The blood roared in Angharad's ears and the innocent blue sky turned threatening and dark. She reached out for the gate's support and held it, and heard her own voice come through cracking lips.

'That's right. A local kid.'

Then, as high as the cry of a curlew on the wind, she heard William calling as he flew back down the slope. 'Mummy. Mummy, look at me.'

The mountainside went very still. There was only the little boy with his black hair blown back as he ran, and then his laughter, and his panting breath as he reached the gate and

300

scrambled over. She put her arms around him and felt the sharpness of his shoulder blades and the firm straight line of his backbone. Healthy and strong, happy and well-loved, an ordinary little boy. What now?

'William,' she turned him round, 'this is Harry. An old friend of mine.' Only with the child's shy smile did she look from his clear face to Harry's, and at once the likeness struck her like a thunderclap. She had always known it, but not until she saw them face to face did she recognize how close it was. And in Harry's eyes she saw something that frightened her, yet made her want to hold him just as she held William now.

William sensed the atmosphere between them and wriggled awkwardly.

'Can I go down the hill? There's a stream at the bottom.'

'If you stay where I can see you,' she said automatically, and he was off again. Angharad could not look to see, but Harry's eyes were fixed on the dark, bobbing head.

The silence welled between them, as unbroken as if the rustle of wind in the grass, the skylarks and the throaty complaint of the distant sheep belonged in another world, light-years remote from theirs.

Angharad had braced herself, expecting the iron grip of his hand at her wrist, or the pressure of his fingers on her shoulder. But Harry hadn't moved. She could see his right hand hanging at his side, loose, almost helpless.

At last he said, 'He's mine, isn't he?'

Bewilderment, sadness and loss in his voice, with none of the anger or aggression she had steeled herself for. 'Yes. You are his father.'

'Angharad.' There was a break in his voice. 'Why?' Harry moved to lean on the gate, his head bent, the loose hand up to shade his eyes. 'Why didn't you tell me that you were having a child? I have had a son, your son, for all these years and never known him. Years of Hollywood. Years of nothing. While you . . . and he . . . have been alone . . .'

She wanted to reach out and touch him now, but knew that she couldn't dissipate the shock reverberating through him. Not yet. And if ever they were to draw close again, this

301

moment must stand clear and undistorted by half-truths.

'I came to tell you, that day, and to ask for your help. The day that I found you and Laura together.' Too clearly, she saw the flicker of pain lick upwards in him. 'After that I ran away. I hid in London. I didn't want you to find us, and yet I did. So badly. I thought that you could find us if you wanted to. I didn't know that Gwyn was trying to protect me.'

'I tried. God help me, if I'd known I would have moved the earth to find you.'

As it had always done, Laura's name quivered between them. Angharad waited for him to say it, admitting it, but cruelly he would not. Instead he turned to her and took her in his arms, lifting her face up to his and examining it minutely as if he had never seen her properly before. She knew that he was searching for words, discarding them. She had never seen bewilderment in Harry until this moment. The arrogance and impatience that had marked him were cracking, dissolving before her eyes, and she looked back at him as if it were for the first time too. She saw the clefts that his bitter-edged smile had dug at the corners of his mouth, and the weary lines around his eyes. He looked older than his years, and yet at this moment younger and more at a loss than she had ever known him.

'I feel,' he said uncertainly, 'as if a slice of time has been taken away, and handed back translated into a dimension I don't recognize.' He drew her closer still so that she felt his heart beating. 'Tell me what he's like.'

Angharad half-smiled at the impossibility. 'He likes trains, and football. He wakes up too early and disturbs the whole house. He's very rational, in the most irrational ways. Harry, he's a little boy . . .'

'. . . And he thinks that your grey-flannel lover is his father?'

'Jamie. His name is Jamie.'

'He thinks that Jamie is his father?'

'No. He hasn't asked, yet, why his friends have fathers and he has Jamie.'

'And when he does?'

As gently as she could, she said, 'I don't know, Harry.

That's a decision that Jamie and I have to make.

He'll find you out, Jamie had said, and he'll want William as well as you, and he won't let go easily. Angharad waited tensely, but Harry did no more than drop his arms and turn silently away. They looked across the slope and saw William climbing towards them.

'Look what I've found!'

He came rolling over the gate and held out his treasure for them to examine. It was a sheep's jawbone with all the teeth and fragments of gum clinging to it, smelling ripely. Nothing could have been more fascinating for William. Angharad took a deep breath and gamely bent over it. She was aware of Harry hesitating for an instant and then kneeling down too. His hand reached out, wanting to touch the child's shoulder, and then withdrew again. William was rattling his jawbone, absorbed, and it was Harry who was struck with shyness. Angharad watched the hunger grow in his face, checked by diffidence, and felt the tremor of old judgements and old values sliding aside to make room for new ones. Perhaps she didn't know Harry Cotton at all.

'I'm not very well up on sheep,' she mumbled in reply to an urgent question of William's. It was Harry's hand that reached out for the gruesome object and turned it for the child's inspection.

Dark heads, close together.

'Sheep eat grass, don't they?' Harry said. 'See, all the teeth are flat for chewing it, with all the ridges running that way.'

Even their hands are the same shape.

'Our teeth, and all meat-eating animals', are pointed for tearing at our food.'

'So if I ate grass,' William said, 'my teeth would be like this?'

'Oh, definitely.'

'Huh. I don't think I'll bother, actually.'

And then they were both looking up at her, the same intense blue eyes, and William's face a softer, rounded version of his father's. Father and son. Angharad felt the heat of the sunlight rippling over the cropped turf, and the wind scented with cut hay, and she smiled. At once the flash of

303

Harry's old smile answered hers, and all the weariness and bewilderment was gone from his face.

'Can I keep it, Mum? Please, Mum.'

'In the back garden. As far from the back door as possible.'

'That's no good.' But they were both laughing now, over William's head. For an instant all the fear lifted from Angharad and she felt as happy as she had done so many summers ago when she and Harry had ranged in freedom over the empty mountainside.

'William, d'you want to see something really interesting?'

He looked up at Harry at once, inquisitive. 'What is it?'

'Come with me. I saw it on the way down. Follow me along this path, and tread as softly as you can.'

They filed obediently along the path, the arches of bracken brushing at their legs, until Harry turned back to them with his finger at his lips.

'Shh. Come here, William.' He reached out for the child and swung him to safety on his shoulders, and then stretched a restraining hand towards Angharad. Looking past him she saw why. Basking in the warmth of the sunlight on the narrow path was an intricate coil of mottled bodies, flat heads and tapering tails.

'Oh, Harry. Snakes,' breathed William, as if he had been handed the gold from the end of the rainbow. 'I want to get down.'

'Stay where you are,' Harry advised him. 'See the V markings at the backs of their heads? They're adders, and their bite is poisonous.'

Angharad stepped back with her knuckles rammed against her teeth. The vibration disturbed the snakes and slowly they stirred, raising their malevolent heads before they slid one by one into the shelter of the bracken. William watched, transfixed, until the last one had vanished and the green fronds were only stirred by the wind.

'That was fantastic,' he breathed. 'Wait 'til I get home and tell Teck.'

'William,' Angharad said, hearing the sharp note of panic in her voice, 'you are never, do you hear me, to come up here without boots on? I didn't know there were snakes.'

304

Harry was grinning at her, delighted, with the mockery and mischief that she remembered so vividly. 'Afraid of snakes? And you a country girl? They're very unlikely to hurt you unless you step right on them. Just remember to look where you're treading in the bracken, that's all.'

At once the mild green sea around her became a threatening mass of rustles. She took one step and faltered, peering between the sappy stalks.

'Want me to carry you back to the track?'

'Just carry William,' she snapped at him. 'I'll take care of myself.'

'It's a very rare sight,' Harry called at her retreating back. 'We're very lucky.'

'Very lucky,' William echoed, and Harry came cantering down the path with the little boy clinging on and whooping with reckless delight. Once she had regained the safety of the track and saw how pleased with themselves they were, Angharad had to laugh again in spite of herself.

'I shall never be able to walk here again without waders,' she groaned. 'Harry, you've ruined it for me.'

'I would be very sad if I thought that was the truth,' he said with sudden seriousness, and they were quiet again, remembering.

It was a moment before she realized that William was looking speculatively between them. She glanced down at her watch and forced a lightness into her voice.

'Supper time, and we've got a long way to walk home. Come on, Willum.'

He was about to demur, clutching at his new friend, but Harry said, 'And I'm going back over that way. Goodbye, William.' Angharad thanked him silently for his tact. William began to run away down towards Cefn and Harry said in a low voice, 'I think we should talk, Angharad. We owe each other that, wouldn't you say? I won't ask you for anything else, not you or him, if you're afraid of that. Will you just give me an hour or two, to tell me about you and the child? I have to go away very soon.' He gestured, hopelessly again. 'Another bloody film. It would make it easier for me to leave. Not that there's any reason why you should, of course.' The bitterness had flooded back too.

Angharad fought the impulse to say, *Don't go. Not so soon.* Instead she nodded, quickly. 'Tomorrow night. You know where I am.'

Then, abruptly because it was hard to leave him, she began to walk away to where William was calling for her. Without looking around, she knew that Harry watched them until the deep hedge around Cae Mawr had swallowed them up.

As she hoisted him down from the last stile before the village, William said suddenly, 'Did you love Harry when he was your old friend?'

She stopped, seeing the grey wedge of the church tower against the fading blue and the weight of the summer trees shading the lane. A cloud of midges danced in the green chasm ahead of them.

The truth was important. She had learned that from her father.

'Yes. I did. A long time ago, William. You know that people can love each other in different ways? I loved Harry in a way that wasn't right for that time. A different way from the way I love you, or Grandpa, or Jamie.'

*A different way, and perhaps the only way that will ever truly matter to me. Too early, and too late now.*

William saw the flicker in her face and, uncomprehending, wound his arms around her neck until her head came down to his. He kissed her awkwardly and said,

'I love you.'

It was the first time from his heart, with none of the litany of babyhood.

'That's all I want,' she told him gravely.

Then she swung him down from the stile and they walked home to the little house hand in hand.

Gwyn came with her knitting bag the next evening, to babysit for William. She knew that the restaurant was closed, yet didn't ask where Angharad was going. Through all the days since the opening of the restaurant they hadn't spoken of Harry, and Angharad felt the constraint deepening between them. She was afraid to broach the subject in case, however she might struggle to hide it, her bitter regret that Gwyn had kept Harry from her would show and hurt her aunt.

Nor had Angharad told Gwyn that she knew her parents' story. She had needed time to understand it herself, and to reason out that the bitterness and tragedy of the past should not be allowed to visit itself on the future.

Now Gwyn was watching her as she passed in and out of the tiny living-room. Angharad had changed her clothes three times, like an adolescent before a date, and the sound of a car slowing outside made her drop her handbag from shaking hands. The car rumbled past, and as Angharad fumbled for the contents of her bag at Gwyn's feet she felt her aunt's eyes on her, waiting fearfully for something.

Angharad took a deep breath and put her hands over her aunt's.

'I'm going to see Harry Cotton,' she said gently.

Gwyn flinched, and then her mouth set in a steely, straight line.

'Why?' she asked. 'Why, after so long? You don't need him, or anything to do with that family. You've got your good, kind Jamie, and the boy is happy. I thought you'd forgotten the other one, the way you never spoke of him. And when he came here, looking for you . . .'

Angharad's hands tightened, silencing her. That damage was done, and there was nothing to be gained from raking over it.

'I know why you feel as you do. Dad told me before he died. I should have been allowed to know earlier, and it would have been better to let me decide about the Cottons for myself.'

Gwyn's face was suddenly ugly, distorted with hatred.

'That man. That monster. He killed your poor mother, you know. As good as murdered her. She was ill, and carrying you, and he forced her out of the place she loved. It broke her heart, and her body. She lived one day after she left Llyn Fair. One day. Angharad.' Tears glittered in her eyes, softening the ugliness of hatred.

'I know. It was a terrible thing to do. But no amount of

307

bitterness now will bring any of them back. Father and son aren't one and the same, Aunty Gwyn. Harry shouldn't suffer any more for what his father did. He and his sister have suffered enough already.'

Their unity against Joe had driven them closer together, Angharad thought. Too dangerously close, and they lived under the weight of that still.

'Listen, Aunty Gwyn. I love Harry, and I've loved him from the day I first knew him. He didn't always do the right thing when he was younger, but that doesn't matter to me. I haven't always done the right things either. None of us has, not you, or Dad, or anyone. Harry and I have learned by our mistakes now. I believe we have a chance of happiness now and I can't – I won't – let it go by again. You see, Harry's got a greater depth of love in him than anyone I've ever known. He doesn't give it easily, but once it's there, it's for ever. I believe that love is mine. Please, Aunty Gwyn. Please see that William and I need him.'

Angharad's voice dropped. 'I don't think I can go on without him any longer. It's been a long, long time.'

She was looking away from her aunt to the curtain over the street door. Another car approached, and this time stopped outside. Harry, with native awareness of the village eyes, would wait for her there.

Gwyn's hands dropped, and she sighed. 'Go on, then,' she said heavily. 'I can't understand, but I believe you. Anyone would, seeing that look in your face. Go to your Harry, then. Should you have gone seven years ago?'

Angharad whirled round at the door and ran back to her. She wrapped her arms around the old woman and kissed the top of her bent head. 'That doesn't matter, now. Don't let any of the past matter today. I love you, Gwyn.'

Only the present. Only now, and Harry waiting for her outside.

'Go on, then,' Gwyn repeated. She watched the door close, heard the car start up and purr away, and went on sitting, staring into the lamplight. It was a long, long time before she picked up her knitting again.

*

The car door swung open and Angharad slid into the low seat. The knot of memories unravelled instantly to set her bewilderingly free from all her anxieties. She was fifteen again, joyriding with Harry in Joe Cotton's white Jaguar; seventeen again, drunk with love and Harry in his grey van bound for their kingdom within the thick walls of Heulfryn Cottage. And she was grown-up too, mistress of herself, with Harry beside her and his remembered hands with the brown fingers loosely curled close to her own.

It wasn't too late. It wasn't ever, ever too late. The happiness sang in her head.

She felt Harry pick up the vibrancy at once. Angharad laughed, and he laughed back at her, losing his success-ingrained weariness and impatience, his cynicism and bitterness, and he was Harry again, as she had always loved him.

'Where to, my love?'

'I don't know. I don't care.'

'Dinner?'

'I couldn't eat a mouthful.'

'Neither could I.'

He drove to the remote pub on the mountain road where they had gone in their first days together. Nothing had changed. Even the fairylights festooned over the bar were the same, and the boisterous rock-climbers retelling their feats. Angharad felt that she loved them all. They sat in a shadowy corner, and she was so stunned that Harry had to wind her fingers around her glass for her before she could muster the concentratation needed to lift it.

'Why?' she asked him. 'Why do we feel so happy?'

'Don't ask,' he said fiercely. 'Take it. I want you to talk to me. Tell me about all the years I've missed, not being with you, and William.' His insistence made her almost afraid again, and she shook her head.

'Not yet. I need another drink. You tell me, first. Tell me about getting famous.' She smiled at him. 'I cut out all your film reviews. and all the gossip column stories. I even saw *As the Sun was Rising*.'

'With you in the Beast Market with your basket. I could

never watch it myself, after it was finished. It reproached me.'

'Go on.' She felt as if she was starving, confronted with a banquet and not knowing where to begin.

Harry gripped her fingers and with their linked hands gestured it all behind him as if it meant nothing at all.

'I'm not proud of it. Of the films I've made, perhaps two have been honest. The rest have been deals. There's no glamour in it, my darling, for all the stuff in the gossip columns. It's dirty, and hard, and it affects people in the same way. I've got one, two more deals to honour. That's why I have to leave tomorrow.'

The thought clouded their faces, and they pushed it away again at once.

'Listen, after that I'm free. No more of that world. Oh, don't worry. There's more than enough money to take care of you both.' ·

Angharad dropped his hands as if they burned her. 'No. I look after William. We don't need anything.'

Gently he lifted her hand again and brushed the back of it with his mouth. She was burning once more, a different kind of fire. The friendly pub with its winking lights and brasses was an intrusion.

'If you should need it. Only if, Angharad. Come on,' his voice went rough as he saw her face. 'I don't think we can stay here any longer.'

They were out in the soft air, and then driving again. Angharad watched the dark towers of the trees sweeping past and the prickle of stars in the night sky between them. The time for decisions, the capability for doing or not doing, was past for both of them. They were borne along together, powerless against the torrent.

When they stopped again Angharad sensed that they were miles from anywhere. The silence that enveloped them was complete, the more impenetrable for the mysterious rustles and the sighs of the wind, and because of the distance from the noise of humanity.

Harry laced her fingers in his and they crossed some rough grass to the dense wall of trees rearing in front of them, then as they came into the blackness Angharad caught the sharp scent and knew that they were in one of the pine forests that blanketed the hills. For an instant it brought back Llyn Fair with its sentinel trees. The ground under their feet was thickly carpeted with fallen needles, as dry and soft as a vast blanket.

They walked in silence until the trees had swallowed them up. The branches overhead were so dense that not a star was visible. The remoteness was eerie, and comforting because it gave them a world that was theirs alone.

'Tell me about you and William,' Harry commanded. 'What happened when he was born? Who was with you?'

'Nobody. A medical student with a tired smile, and the nurses. I didn't want anything, only the baby. I felt that for a long time afterwards. He looked so like you, Harry, from the moment he was born.'

'Was it very hard for you, being alone?'

'Not after the beginning. We were lucky.'

'Jamie took care of you?'

'Yes.'

They couldn't talk about Jamie now.

'I wish I could thank him for that. Tell me some more. About his first birthday. The first time he saw the sea. The elephants at the Zoo.'

He was no more than a darker shape at her side, but the raw hunger in his voice and the clutch of his hand unlocked her tongue. They walked on and on over the soft carpet and she talked, the trivial, affectionate details of their lives tumbling out.

At last, dry-throated and exhausted, she stopped and leaned back against the rough bark of a tree.

'Thank you,' Harry said simply. 'Tell me, do you think it's possible to love a son you have only seen once, and known for only a few hours? Even though those hours feel more important than all the rest of your life?'

Angharad loved the diffidence in his voice, and the soft side of himself that he was laying bare for her. 'Yes.'

'And will you let me love him?'

There was a longer silence and Angharad could just make out his profile turned away from her, a harder-minted version of William's, painfully waiting. 'Yes, if you want to.'

'Of course I do.' The words were like a whip and in an instant he had turned, drawn her again to him as if he would never let her go. 'And you, Angharad?'

It was important to be honest now, without pride or pretence. Awkwardly, she said, 'I think you know that I have always loved you. I couldn't, can't, see how that love was going to be replaced. I tried, and it made me sad.' She heard the low groan in Harry's throat. He bent so that his forehead rested against hers.

'It's so cheap to say I'm sorry that I'm ashamed. But I am sorry. For the way that I was when I was nineteen, and for what Joe did before that, and for what has happened since.'

Angharad put her fingers up to his mouth, silencing him. And as she touched his face she shivered, not with cold. She felt the answer within him at once, but Harry was waiting. His hands raked the hair back from her face as they clung together in the darkness and she sensed, rather than saw, the question.

Harry wouldn't take from her, any more.

She must meet him fully, and the flicker within her that she though she had forgotten rose up at once to do it. She drew his face down to meet hers, her hands quite steady now, and he felt the curve of her smile against his mouth.

'Angharad.' A note of not daring to believe, and warning, in his voice. She kissed him in answer, feeling the hardness of his jaw, the softness behind it and the taste of him that she had never forgotten. Her old, old fears and doubt vanished like mist in the sunlight. There was nothing but happiness, and needing him.

'Angharad.'

A different voice this time, low in his throat, shutting out even their kingdom of silence under the pines.

They had sunk to their knees in soft fallen needles, clinging to one another like lost explorers. Now Harry wrenched off his jacket and spread it for them on the ground. His shirt glimmered palely as he drew her down to him again and they measured themselves against each other in the sweet, resiny bed. For a moment they lay still as the languor of happiness

312

possessed them, and then they were swept by impatience and each scrap of clothing, each secret step of rediscovery, was an intolerable obstacle until at last they had freed themselves. For an instant he was poised above her and even in the darkness she saw the love and tenderness in his face. And then he repossessed her and she moaned, for he was just the same, and yet he was different with all the difference of their years apart. He was the old, insistent Harry who had driven her into delight within the stone walls of Heulfryn, yet he was gentler and more certain, slower, yet more alive to her response. And whilst he drove her on until she cried aloud again, his mouth was soft against her bare shoulders and over the curve of her breasts.

'I love you,' he whispered as the tide within her receded at last to leave her body washed as smooth and pale as the mother-of-pearl lining to a shell, and 'I love you' was torn from him as his own climax possessed him and threw him against her like a great wave smashing and breaking over the sea wall.

The timbre of his voice in that brief instant of surrender, or perhaps the angle of his head and throat as he arched away from her, brought back the long red room and the image of Laura beneath him, dark next to dark. But then the image was gone again, as incredible in this moment as it was hateful to her. She turned from the malign shadow of it to the light of Harry with his arms locked round her and the calmness of extinguished passion in his eyes.

She wanted to laugh for pure happiness, and at finding herself here, naked under the branches and with the prickle of dead needles in her hair. The laugh bubbled up and he rolled over with her in his arms, mock-indignant.

'Be careful. I may not be the tireless satyr I was at nineteen, but if you laugh too uncontrollably you could just undermine my fragile confidence.'

'Your what? Hell-raiser Harry Cotton?'

'Oh, darling, darling. The cuttings. I'd forgotten.' His hair brushed her face and his mouth found hers again. 'All a myth. Practically a myth. Listen.' The laughter ebbed and he said seriously. 'In all the years, through all the cockeyed things I've done, there hasn't ever been a day like today. Because of William, but,' he drew her closer against him, 'much more because of you. Seeing you out on The Mountain, with that wild, angry look of protectiveness for him, and here now, like this, under these trees.'

His voice sank to a whisper, within her head, within her being. 'Loving you in this place felt better and sweeter than anything I've ever known. Like coming home, Angharad. I don't ever want to leave again. Stay here with me. You, and William. Stay here with me.'

Beyond the safe haven of their warmth, the pine forest spread over the hillside, and beyond that lay the calm green turf and grey rock country that Angharad loved as much as she loved Harry because the two belonged together, inseparable. She felt the closeness of him, familiar yet so erotically different that she ached for him all over again, and beneath them the solid earth, unchanging. The wild hope that they might be together after all, the three of them at home in the shadow of The Mountain, surged up in her and spilled over into dazzling certainty.

It was all she could see now, and the other faces faded away in the brilliance.

'I will be here. If you leave tomorow, to go and do whatever it is you have to do,' their hands tightened on each other at the thought of it, 'and then come back again, I'll still be here.'

'As soon as I can. The first minute. I love you.'

A wind had sprung up, and it sighed in the high branches above them.

'And I love you.'

More gently and more truly than either of them had ever spoken it, yet it was as if the wind brought a chill, warning finger and laid it on her warm skin, and Angharad shivered. Harry had reached imperiously for her again, but he felt it and lifted her up at once.

'You're cold. Here, put this on.' With a deftness that surprised her he found her scattered clothes and buttoned them up for her, wrapping her at last in the warmth of his jacket. He helped her to her feet and kissed her forehead, and his gentleness dispelled the chill again.

'Home,' he said, and with laced fingers they began to retrace their steps over the springy needles, and then suddenly they were running, faster and faster, weaving between the trees in a downhill plunge that brought them out from under the canopy of trees and into the moonlight gasping, and laughing, like breathless children. They almost stumbled on the slippery grass and the laughter turned to shouts as they swooped down to the car. Then they saw that the moonlight had turned the rocks and the road to beaten silver, and the beauty of it caught the laughter in their throats. Silenced, they turned back to one another and their mouths brushed just once more.

'As soon as I can,' Harry repeated.

In the lights of the car he picked the pine needles out of her hair, and then they turned and drove the long road back to Cefn with the happiness so solid between them that Angharad felt she could have stretched out the tips of her fingers and touched it.

The village street was in darkness except for the single square of yellow light in Angharad's cottage. Harry stopped at the door and she saw the questioning rake of his black eyebrows.

'Don't vanish yet,' she commanded him. With Harry at her shoulder, she lifted the latch of the old door and stepped into the little house. Gwyn had been dozing in her chair with her spectacles askew and her knitting in her lap, but her head jerked up at once.

She saw the brilliance in Angharad's eyes, and Harry's commanding height squarely beside her. She saw that their fingertips were still touching, as if they couldn't bear to let go of one another altogether. A sigh escaped her, almost inaudible, and her hand lifted to settle her spectacles again. Angharad was beside her at once, kneeling and smiling up into her face.

'I'm very happy, Aunty Gwyn,' she whispered.

'I see that,' Gwyn said, and lifted herself heavily out of her armchair. From her niece's bright face she looked to Harry, searching for the impatient, demanding boy who had come

315

to the schoolhouse long ago. But the boy had vanished.

'You've changed,' she said, and Harry smiled crookedly at the grudging edge of her voice. Gwyn was as protective of Angharad as she had been when he had come in search of her.

'I think so,' he answered. 'I hope so.'

Gwyn gathered up her things and marched to the door. 'I'll say goodnight, then.'

'Won't you let me see you home?' Harry asked gravely.

'One hundred yards down Cefn street?' she asked him. 'I think I can manage that, thank you, young man.'

The door closed behind her stiff back and they looked at one another, and irreverent laughter leapt up again. Shaking with it, Angharad reached out her hands to him.

'It will be all right,' she promised him. 'Everything, all of it, will be all right.'

The little room reflected heir warmth back at them. Light glowed off the copper kettle on the mantelpiece, and the silver-framed photographs of William that flanked it. It shone on the white tablecloth smoothed over the red velvet one with the bobble fringe beneath it, and made oval pools on the old walnut upright piano against one wall. Harry lifted the lid and played a single mellow bass note that hung in the air.

'May I go up and look at William?' he asked her. She had raised her hand, intending to point at the door. The steep, narrow stairs wound up behind it.

But another sound distracted her. Tap, tap. It sounded like a claw, tapping on the glass.

Angharad turned around, icy premonition congealing the warm race in her veins. At the window she saw a white hand, hooked so that it looked like a claw too, lifted to tap again. Behind the hand, disembodied in the blackness, dead white and with the wide eyes staring in at them, she saw a face.

Laura.

A scream rose in her throat but she crammed her knuckles into her mouth to stifle it. The piano lid dropped with a clatter. Harry had made for the door, but Laura was quicker. It swung open silently and she slid into the room with them, her hand still raised.

'Oh no,' she whispered. 'You can't, you know. Hide from me. Hide from Laura. Did you think that you could, poor things?' Her voice was throaty, almost caressing, but it raised fear in Angharad that prickled with the hair at the nape of her neck. This was a Laura she had never seen before. Her hair was a tangled black cloud, and her clothes were stained with dark, damp patches. In the paper-whiteness of her face the pupils of her eyes had shrunk to tiny, glittering points of light.

But Harry knew her. Anger, and pity, and the shadow of revulsion tautened his face. The creases that the evening had rubbed away sharpened again. He snatched at the wrist of her raised arm, drawing it down, his knuckles showing white with the force that it took. ·

'Stop it, Laura,' he said in a low voice. 'Don't do this now.'

She whirled around to face him. 'Not now? Not now, of all times. You've been with her, haven't you? Out on the hills somewhere, in some little hollow? Our hills, Harry. Well? Is she as good as I used to be, Harry, do you remember? She wasn't, once upon a time, was she? You still came limping back to me, because I was what you really wanted. Like a drug, wasn't I? You had to have more and more. Over and over again, for all you said that you hated me, and it, and what I did to you.'

Harry's hand passed over his face in a vain attempt to rub out the weariness and despair.

'Stop,' he said again. 'Haven't we wrecked enough of each other's lives already? Let go, Laura, for God's sake, while you still can.'

Angharad read the hopelessness, and the ice set hard and ugly in her veins. This scene was no more than a repeat of others, stretching away behind them into the remote cradle of Llyn Fair valley itself. She was struck by the thought that this was the heritage that Joe Cotton had bestowed on his children along with his house and the lovely lake, and she had to struggle against the wild urge to laugh.

'The only wreck in my life,' Laura was saying, in the same caressing, infinitely threatening voice, 'is not having you. But I do really, don't I, my darling?' And Laura did laugh,

317

with a crazy triumphant ring to it that made Angharad want
to turn and run away from her, away from Laura's malign
influence that had snatched away the little, gilded happiness
she had shared with Harry tonight. Harry had taken Laura's
other wrist, and he had lifted her up with the force of
thrusting her away from him.

Disgust stamped out the quiver of everything else in his
face.

'Get out,' he said. 'Go. Now, Laura. Everything is finished
between you and me. I don't want to see you again. I hate
you, and I pity you, but I don't even feel those things as
strongly for you as I do for myself. Go,' he repeated. 'Leave
us alone.'

Through her own fear and horror Angharad saw how stiff,
and numb he was. The pain would come later for him. Love
surged more strongly through her than it had ever done
before, and she understood fully, for the very first time, the
black conundrum of Harry and Laura that had puzzled, and
thwarted, and excluded her for so long.

She ran to him.

'No,' she heard him warn her. 'Keep out of it.' But her
desire to break the dark chain at last was stronger. She
pushed relentlessly between them until Laura's glittering
eyes fixed on her. Her old friend's fingers curled around her
forearm and she felt their chill, and the manicured nails dug
painfully into her flesh.

'Yes, Laura,' she answered her. 'Harry and I were
together tonight. I love him. I always have, and nothing will
change that.'

They stared at each other. Angharad knew that she was
fighting for everything, and that the real battle had always,
always been with Laura herself. The cold premonition came
that she could not win now, because the real Laura had gone
away somewhere and this mad-eyed stranger was fighting
for her life, with weapons that Angharad didn't even
understand. But she pushed the fear behind her again and
faced up to the shell of her friend.

'I love him,' Laura said. 'You can't even guess how, my
china shepherdess.'

'The difference is, Laura, that I'm not his sister. You cannot marry him, but I can.' *Or bear his children, Laura, poor Laura.* 'I can and will, Laura, and we'll be happy together.'

Harry moved like lightning to protect her, but he was far too slow. Laura's white hand with its long, curved nails flashed out and Angharad felt the gouge of it like fire and acid in her face. She stood stricken, with the trickle of blood starting on her cheek. She lifted her fingers to touch the place, and stared uncomprehendingly at the smear on them.

Laura's glittering eyes followed the movement too, and the slashes on Angharad's cheek a they reddened and spread. For a moment her face was blank, as if she was wondering who could have caused them. Harry's movement beside her, as he reached for Angharad, aroused her again. Her mouth went slack, ugly lines deepening beside it, and even the unhealthy glitter in her eyes went out. And then she moaned, a low, terrifying sound that rose in pitch until it was a scream. Harry turned on her and shook her so that her head flopped like a rag doll's, and then he slapped her face with he flat of his hand. The scream was bitten off at once and Laura crumpled against him. Her eyes closed and tears spurted from under the lids. Her mouth opened again and Angharad flinched before the sound, but all that came was a shuddering, hopeless sob. Laura clung to her brother, her firsts beating at him as the storm of weeping possessed her.

Angharad turned away, but not before she had seen Harry's dark head bend unwillingly over his sister's and the revulsion in him give way once more to despairing pity.

Laura cried for a long time. Her tearing sobs were the only sound in the silent cottage. At last the storm died away again. Laura pushed the wet coils of hair back from her ravaged face and drew herself up straight. The vengeful glitter sparked up again. Angharad saw that she was still driven by whatever mixture of despair and jealousy, drink and more, that had fuelled her attack.

'I will not let him go,' Laura said.

'Laura. You don't possess me.' Harry's voice was iron, but Laura was oblivious. She was deadly calm now, all her attention focussed on Angharad.

'Never. Never, never. Listen to me. I'll do anything to stop you taking him. I'll kill you, even.'

Angharad stared at her, transfixed.

It was impossible that Laura was saying these words. Her friend, Harry's sister. Here in the cosy, old-fashioned cottage parlour. The same light on the shiny kettle, polished wood and figured velvet.

'I want you to believe me,' Laura said. 'If I have to, you know, I'll go for whatever you care about most. If you destroy, so will I. I'll do whatever will cause you the greatest grief, the same pain that you have caused me.' The soft silence fell around them. In the heart of it Angharad heard a tiny sound. It was no more than a sigh, and a creak, as William stirred in his sleep upstairs.

*Whatever you care about most, I will destroy.*

Laura was watching her like a cat, ready to spring. Angharad believed what she had said, believed it so implicitly that her skin crawled with terror. Laura was mad, and Laura was dangerous.

And upstairs Harry's child lay asleep, the dearest thing to Angharad in all the world.

Laura didn't know about him, and she must never find out. One glance at Harry's ash-grey face confirmed her fear, and her resolution.

The wild, protective impulse galvanized Angharad. She had half-sprung to bar the stairway door but she checked and made herself freeze into stillness again.

Her one thought was to get Laura out, far away and for ever. She made herself nod her head, submissively, although the little movement of surrender shot pain all through the core of her.

Laura was smiling now, and the glitter was intensified. 'Sensible,' she said. 'Expedient. Thank you. I think we should say goodnight, Harry, don't you?' Her voice was conversational. If it were not for her livid face she might have been taking her leave after a dinner party. 'Goodbye, Angharad,' she said softly from the doorway and stepped out into the darkness.

'She would do it,' Harry whispered, and the words fell like cinders on the burned-out pyre of their happiness. Angharad understood him as she had never done, and bled for him, and for the hideous burden that had kept him running, and hiding, all the years.

There was nothing to say.

'Take her with you tomorrow. Away. For him, Harry.' Her voice was high and child-like, thin against the wastes stretching ahead of them.

Harry's hands grasped hers, burning them, and she caught the closeness of him for the last time. 'What should I do?' he asked her, without hope. 'The police? Certify her? She's my sister, Angharad. And what we did we did together, at the beginning.'

*I know. You love her still. I understand that. There's nothing to be done.*

Angharad said nothing, and her eyes were on the door in the fear that Laura might come back again.

Slowly, slowly, Harry turned away. 'Kiss my son goodnight for me,' and he was gone.

With trembling hands Angharad slid the bolts at the top and bottom of the door. She went into the kitchen and searched for the key to the back door, which she had never locked. She found it at last hanging from one of the hooks on the dresser, and the lock grated as she secured it.

Only when she had made sure that all the curtains were drawn so tightly as not to permit a chink of light to escape, did she allow herself to go upstairs. William was fast asleep, his knees drawn up to his chest and one fist clenched against his cheek.

She bent over him to listen to his even breathing, and brushed the tangle of sleep-damp black hair away from his face. Deliberately she made herself see only the sleeping child, her son alone. She closed her eyes to his innocent likeness to the other two faces which had vanished now for ever.

Angharad crossed the little landing to her own room and sat down in the low chair beside the window. She was numb, and cold, and unable to think or even to move. She was still sitting, motionless, when the incongruous sun came up and the little street below her came to life again.

It was her stubborn sense of independence that saved her in the end. In the first terrible days after the numbness wore off, when wild, aching longing for Harry alternated with the fear that Laura would somehow discover William and come slipping into the cottage for him in the dark, she had clung weakly to the thought of Jamie.

Jamie meant safety, and she could turn tail and run away back to London with him. Back to the burglar-proofed walls of his Chelsea house, and the ranks of protective minions at Le Gallois.

*Change the name, first.*

Then Jamie came, as he had promised, sliding up outside the cottage in his Porsche and stepping out in his grey suit with a silk tie she had once given him as a present. She wanted to run to him like a child, asking for shelter, but she could not. She felt too cold and still, and too aware, like an unhealed gash in her flesh, of the heat Harry had reawakened in her. With the memory of that carried within her, turned bitter by Laura's poison, everything that followed was dim and remote. Talking to Jamie, she heard her voice coming from somewhere outside her head, muffled by distance. She saw him watching her strangely, and saw the good-humoured stranger's face stiffen and turn away from her. She wanted, but it was no use. and yet she didn't want. To be alone was her truest need, to learn to live with the emptiness and to answer the demand for survival for herself and William. When the numbness ebbed away and the pain that followed would allow it, that was her paramount thought. To cling to anything else was wrong. Hopeless, and wrong.

The inevitable time came when Jamie made her sit down to face him. He talked with all his old gentleness, and it warmed her face into a sad smile.

'You haven't smiled, Anne, for do you know how many weeks? Do you know how much that hurts me, and William?'

'I'm sorry.'

322

It cut her like a knife, and she knew that it was true. But William and she would survive together. The little boy had edged a little closer to the reality of his mother, and to a dim understanding.

Jamie was rubbing his broad face wearily. 'I don't understand why, Anne. But I think we both know that it's the end. It hurts me too much that we should go on pretending.'

He picked up her hand and looked at the fingers. 'I won't come back to Cefn again.'

Then the bright blue eyes met hers, and acknowledgement stole between them. Acceptance, and the relief of honesty, lifted the veil that had blurred their sight of each other. The stranger became Jamie again, and Jamie and she were friends. Or would be friends, when Anne was forgotten and replaced and Angharad had learned to live whole again. They smiled at each other, and Jamie laid her hand gently back in her lap.

'Will you let William come and stay with me in London?'

'Whenever you want. Whenever he wants. Much too often for you, I should think.'

'Don't cry, Anne.'

'Jamie. Thank you.'

The time came for her to stand with William in the little street, when Jamie had kissed them both and strapped himself into his sleek car. They lifted their hands to wave, and Angharad couldn't see his last look at her because her eyes were full of tears. Then he was gone, and they were left alone.

William had watched the car until it was out of sight. Then blindly he turned to Angharad and buried his face in the soft stuff of her skirt. She smoothed his head, and blinked back the burning tears for him, and knelt down to enclose him in the circle of her arms.

'William?' she said softly.

He jerked his head up, and she saw the tear-marks on his face. 'I can look after us,' he told her, and she smiled at him.

'You could, I know. But there isn't any need. Jamie is our best friend, and we have Aunty Gwyn, and all our other friends here, where we belong, and Cefn. We'll be quite safe together, you and me. Shall we go inside, William?'

They went in, and Angharad made sure that the door was quite secure, as she always did.

Angharad had cut herself free, with surgical precision, and as the days began to slip past, her ability to survive reassured her. While she worked she could forget, and when she was not working, tiredness helped to foreclose the memories and keep the fears at bay. The demands of the restaurant became her bleak comforter, and she met them and rose to confront fresh ones.

The Old Schoolhouse was an outstanding success, and the slow weeks passing piled up security and even a kind of resignation. She began to laugh again with Jessie, and Gwyn stopped watching her covertly and waiting for the break in her composure that never came.

She was working in the kitchen one afternoon, utterly absorbed, when the young waitress came in and leant across the table to her.

'Gentleman in the restaurant would like to see you for a moment, if that's convenient.'

'What's his name?'

'Mr Lang.'

Angharad frowned, unable to place him, but she dried her hands and went out into the restaurant. At a table by the window Lucian Lang was sitting in a buttercup-yellow shirt. At once Angharad remembered who she had seen him with, and stepped back so quickly that she almost stumbled.

Lucian smiled crookedly, acknowledging it. He held out a chair for her and she sat down, her hands cold.

'I saw our friends,' he told her pleasantly. 'Just a few days ago. Harry is filming in Hong Kong, and Laura is with him.'

Half a world away. No need to lock the doors tonight, then. Harry, true to his protective promise. Angharad's hand went colder at the thought of what it must cost him.

'How are they?'

Lucian's face tightened a little. 'Laura is not very well. But she is quite safe. You know, Harry has never struck me as the most generous or unselfish of men. But he is generous to

324

Laura.' Delicately Lucian added, 'Who hardly deserves it, as I think you know.' And in a low voice that she could barely hear, 'Whether she is responsible for her own actions or not.'

Angharad bent her head. 'Thank you for telling me. Did . . . did he ask you to?'

'Not in so many words. But I told him that I was coming home, and I think that was his oblique intention.'

'Thank you,' she said again. 'I'd . . . better go back to work.'

Lucian nodded at her, and turned gracefully to stare out of the window.

In the kitchen she bent over her work again.

*Generous*, she heard Lucian's light voice.

Harry was so far away, and he could never come back. The certainty of their love for one another had never left her.

Angharad pushed away the pretty whorls of vegetable that she had been preparing, the sharp knife and the plates that were waiting for her, and laid her head down on the table.

Painfully, unpractised, she began to cry, for herself and for what Harry was bearing, and for the bitter, immoveable wedge of Laura driven between them.

# CHAPTER TWELVE

'It's been a year,' Jessie said.

Angharad sighed, and slid her glasses down to the end of her nose so that she could peer at Jessie over the top of them. It was one of the best times of the day, when the last diners had left the restaurant and she and Jessie sat down at opposite ends of one of the sofas to make plans for tomorrow before going home.

The glasses were new. They were glamorous ones with grey smoked lenses, but Angharad felt that the glasses more than anything else marked the change in her. She was quiescent now, with her path marked neatly out for her. Its boundaries were William, and Cefn, and the restaurant. And she suddenly needed spectacles for reading. She played up to them, taking them out of their case with a flourish and peering exaggeratedly over the rims, but she still needed them.

'A year,' Jessie repeated firmly. 'More or less.'

Easter was later that year, and although it was a month past, it was still cold enough to keep the log fire burning in the hearth, and the sofas drawn up close to it.

'Eleven months,' Angharad corrected her automatically, 'since we opened.' And since her father's death, and almost eleven months since Harry had gone. Not long ago they had held William's eighth birthday party here in the restaurant.

'You should take a holiday,' Jessie persisted. 'Why not? I can manage perfectly well. I might not have been able to at the beginning, but I can now.'

Angharad smiled at her. Then she pushed the glasses back into place before looking down at her notepad. 'I know you can, Jess. It's just that I don't want a holiday, that's all. William is going to Jamie in London tomorrow for half-term. I'll do a bit less this week.' She began scribbling at the marketing list for the next day. It still gave her pleasure to buy vegetables at the Beast Market, although it was no longer strictly necessary.

A holiday? Where could she go, and for what?

'Angharad.' Jessie was persistent. 'Do you think it's altogether . . . balanced for you, living here alone . . .'

'I'm not alone.'

'You know what I mean. Unvaryingly. Working all the time, and living just for William. If you went on holiday you might meet new people. Feel different.'

Angharad smiled again. It was a new, crooked smile that didn't quite reach her eyes behind the smoked lenses. 'Meet a man, d'you mean? Do you think that's what I need?'

'It might just help.'

The smile deepened the lines at the side of Angharad's mouth. 'I don't want a lover. I don't want anyone else for company except William, and Gwyn, and you and Dickie, and all the people here.'

Jessie looked at her for a long moment, trying to see her friend's eyes behind the pale grey shields. 'For ever? Won't he come back?' she dared to ask.

Angharad stood up abruptly and turned away to the windows. She shook out the folds of the curtains, and stood back to look at them as if the effect was important. 'It isn't that he won't,' she said at last, almost to herself. 'He can't. That's all.' The tone of her voice made clear that the subject was closed.

Then she was circling the restaurant, searching for anything out of place that she could put right, anything to focus her attention upon. At the little bar she stopped and picked up a bottle. 'Shall we have a nightcap?'

Jessie looked at her watch. 'I ought to go, really. Dickie . . .'

She could have kicked herself for her thoughtlessness. Jessie saw the cloak of loneliness around Angharad, although Angharad was assuring her at once that there was nothing more to do and she could close up alone. There was no possibility of staying to keep her company for just a little while longer. Their goodnights were muted and soon done.

When she was alone Angharad looked down at the bottle on the bar, and then slammed it into the cupboard and locked the door. She moved quickly round the restaurant, checking the locks and the lights, and then closed the front door and double-locked it.

The air outside was cold, and clean, and still, and she breathed it in gratefully. Sometimes, just sometimes, she felt that her flourishing business was no more than a yoke and harness that kept her treading round and round the same flat, well-worn and familiar path.

A holiday, Angharad thought again, and once more, Where, and for what? Heavily she turned for home, and the air seemed to have lost a little of its sweetness.

The three of them, Gwyn and William and Angharad, had moved back into her father's old, square house that had once marked the end of the village. Now Cefn straggled on beyond it into the cluster of new estate houses that old William had hated so much.

Angharad let herself into the silent house. Gwyn and William were asleep, William with his bag, ready-packed for the enchantment of a week in London, beside his bed.

In the dimness Angharad saw the white moon-face of the grandfather clock, and listened for a moment to a steady ticking. Eleven months. No time, and it felt like forever. Time to try to sleep again, and it was market day tomorrow. Angharad climbed the steep stairs, stepping over the one that creaked as she had done ever since she was a little girl. She felt too sad tonight even to go into William's room and whisper goodnight to him. Instead she went and sat down on her own bed, and shook the sleeping tablet from the phial into the palm of her hand. Just one, never even a quarter more, even if sleep didn't come at all.

Before she lay down she turned the hands of her alarm clock. Market day tomorrow. The uninterrupted, even, unbreakable and yet vulnerable edifice of her life.

What for? she asked herself just once, before the set replies came trotting back at her and she closed her eyes wearily on all of them and turned to the pursuit of sleep. She dreamt of the Beast Market, and of Harry waiting for her in the angle between light and shade, reaching out to take her heavy basket.

When the shrill alarm fractured her dream and Angharad got up to grope around the silent house, pulling on her boots and a thick sweater against the morning chill, and then sat down with a mug of tea in the cold kitchen, she was still possessed by the sense that he was close to her. She tilted her head, listening to the silence, trying to imagine his nearness.

And Laura.

She put her mug down. Quickly she went upstairs and saw that William was still asleep. Only a dream, she told herself, the kind of just-before-waking dream whose fingers reach out and try to cling on to the stronger day. She put the mixture of wild hope and fear that it aroused in her as far behind her as she could. Before she left the house she glanced at the secure lock on the back door. The front door lock clicked solidly behind her.

The Beast Market was alive with people. In the soft grey light the vegetable stalls were beacons of colour behind the dun-coloured crowds. Angharad slipped among them, nodding to her acquaintances. Her network of contacts was fully established and she bought most of her supplies direct from source, choosing the pick of the produce before it came anywhere near the stalls. But the Beast Market was her earpiece now, and she used it to the full. It was here in the cobbled square, casually talking, that she heard which farmer's wife had started making her own creamy butter again in the old-fashioned dairy, and which reclusive old man was growing exquisite apricots against the south wall of his overgrown kitchen garden, and might well be willing to part with a couple of baskets. It was here too, rather than in the confines of The Schoolhouse, that inconspicuous men approached her with news of fine salmon, or fat pheasants and the occasional deer, into whose antecedents she didn't want to enquire too closely.

Today she walked slowly, but she didn't fall into conversation with anyone. When she had crossed the square she made herself look round, slowly but deliberately, into the corner where she had stood with her market basket. It was empty. In the place where she had seen Harry behind the black eye of his camera, and where she had dreamt him this morning, old Mr Ellis the Bwlch was standing with his black and white sheepdog at his feet.

Harry's film, with the skeins of sheep making beautiful patterns over the hillside, and the man and his dog tiny specks behind them. Angharad had never seen the old man at the Beast Market, in all the months since she had opened The Schoolhouse.

Coincidence, she told herself, and went through the physical motions of turning away, even finding a taut smile. But she was shaking. Harry felt as close to her as if the dark hairs on his arms brushed against her bare skin. She was hot, and at the same time there was another cold breath, chilling her with fear and sadness, and she thought of Laura. Suddenly she was possessed with a violent need to get back to William. She swung round in the crowded place and almost stumbled.

A hand touched her arm, then steadied her. 'Up too early, is it? Or too late last night?'

It was another farmer, a young man who worked the opposite side of the hill from Mr Ellis. Angharad bought eggs from his wife's hens, little speckled eggs with thick shells and orange-yellow yolks.

'A bit of both, I think.' She was still shivering, and the farmer's arm had the reassuring solidity of a rock.

'You don't look too good. Come on in the pub now and we'll get something to put you right.'

The pub was busy, with condensation running down the old engraved glass and spilled rings on the bar. Angharad's rescuer found her a seat and put a glass in her hand. The whisky warmed her and she sipped gratefully at it, wedged into her place between the corduroy legs and ancient tweed shoulders. Angharad listened to the blurred cadences of Welsh all around her, and breathed in the thick, warm atmosphere compounded of beer and cattle cake, damp wool and tobacco. She blinked, and the dream's fingers released their hold. The eerie sensation was gone, and the sight of Mr Ellis was no more than what it really had been, a coincidental glimpse of an old farmer in a place where she might have expected to see him any day. Relief surged through her, and she smiled around the little bar.

Market day, market people, homely and safe.

'Feeling better?'

'Much. Thank you for the drink.'

'Thought you were going to pass out, back there. Have another?'

'Not if I'm going to drive home.' Angharad's smile was for him too, and under the effect of it, he rose gallantly and escorted her to her car.

'Nancy's got four dozen eggs for you. Drop them in, shall I?'

'Any time. I owe you a drink.'

Angharad drove slowly back to Cefn through the dappled light, relishing the calm, puzzled by the intense certainty of something unexplained that had made her skin crawl.

William was sitting at the kitchen table, meekly eating Rice Krispies under Gwyn's watchful eye.

'He can't go to London without a proper breakfast inside him.'

'Most certainly not,' Angharad agreed.

William grinned at her, his round face crinkly with excitement. 'Why're you so late, Mum? We'll miss my train.'

'I've been to market. It's hours till your train.' She sat down beside him, and began devouring toast as quickly as Gwyn coud make it. The kitchen was warm now, with sun on the red tiles and on Gwyn's knitting folded up in the rocking chair. Angharad licked a blob of marmalade from her fingers. Secure contentment had utterly replaced her anxiety, and she smiled at her own susceptibility.

'Mum, it's time.'

On his visits to Jamie in the past, Angharad had taken William down to London herself. Now, with his eighth birthday behind him, he insisted that he could do it on his own. It was a through train, Jamie woud be waiting at the other end, and she was reluctant to head off his independence. By making discreet inquiries, Angharad had discovered a neighbour who would be taking the same train.

He could be watched over, from a tactful distance.

They reached the station far too early, so that there was time to walk to the far end of the platform and examine minutely the signalling system and the marshalling yard beyond. William's excitement had mounted steadily until he could barely keep still. He was full of speculation about the week of treats that Jamie would have in store for him.

The train came in and he ran to find a seat, forgetting Angharad in his headlong rush. She was smiling when she caught up, but she was touched by another, plangent sadness now. The little boy was growing up, out of their close circle of two, just as he should be doing. Soon, and she clenched her fists in her pockets, counting the curled fingers, in ten years at the most, he would be gone altogether. Hungrily she reached for him and pulled his warm dark head against her. He suffered the kiss and then wriggled away.

'Can I sit in this carriage?'

Angharad checked, and saw the reassuring nod of her ally. She helped William in with his suitcase, and kissed his cheek, brown skin, just like his father's.'

Doors slammed, and she stepped back to the platform. William was waving, sliding past her, out of her reach, and then he was gone. Angharad watched the end of the train as it rolled away around the curve, tears sharp in her eyes.

In ten years, when he was really gone, what then?

She lifted her chin and stared defiantly back at the blank tracks. She would occupy herself with her work and with her friends, just as she was doing now. Jessie was all kindness, nudging her gently into looking for more than that, but Angharad knew with cold certainty, lonely certainty, that she would never love anyone in the way that she had loved Harry.

To occupy herself.

Was that the object, then, after so much pain, and such happiness, never to be hoped for again?

Defiantly blinking back the tears, Angharad walked out on to the concourse and found a telephone booth. Jamie answered at once.

'I've just put him on the train, Jamie.'

'Fine. I'll be there. Is he excited?'

'Yes.'

'I'm going to take him for a weekend's sailing.'

'Yes.'

'Are you all right? Is anything the matter?'

Kind Jamie, no longer a refuge, just a friend a long way off now. Her own doing, because she could never love anyone in the way that she had loved Harry.

Angharad smiled her lopsided smile. 'Yes, I'm all right. It's a strange day, that's all.'

'Take care of yourself, Anne.'

Who? So far away, now.

'Of course. Enjoy yourselves.'

The booth was stuffy. The big clock over the concourse told her that it was almost midday. The restaurant was waiting for her, of course. Work, to occupy herself. When Angharad came into The Schoolhouse she saw that the tables were all laid up ready for lunch, and a great armful of white-lipped scarlet tulips was arranged on the hearth in place of the winter fire. She nodded her approval and turned to the list of bookings clipped to the table by the door.

*1 p.m., Lucian Lang. Table for 3.*

Coming again, bringing them with him?

Fear swooped back, prickling along her back and congealing in her throat, tight in her chest. William was almost halfway to Jamie and London now. Safe enough, surely safe enough? Angharad saw Laura's lifted white hand, and the sharp red nails tipping it.

And with the fear came hope, never disunited, fluttering up through the slough of it. If only Harry were here. If her instincts were right and he was really close. Just to see him for an hour. That would dispel the long, the endlessly long, eleven months, and more.

Angharad walked through the kitchen as if she was hypnotized. Jessie pushed a strand of orange-red hair back under her cap, watching her.

In the washroom mirror Angharad stared at herself. Would he see that she was thin, and that there were lines in her face? Her hands shook as she brushed colour over her cheeks. She put her glasses on, shielding her eyes, and then

333

tore them off again. There was more brightness in her eyes now than there had been for months.

She went to her station in the kitchen and began work, barely hearing what Jessie and the waitresses were saying to her. The red minute-hand of the kitchen clock crept around with painful slowness and then suddenly swept forward with hallucinatory speed.

At one-twenty Angharad told herself that they must have arrived by now. She crossed to the restaurant door and inched it open no more than a crack. Across the room Lucian Lang was sitting at table in a pale cream suit. He was leaning forward deferentially, listening hard. His companions were a middle-aged couple, prosperous-looking, strangers to her. It was only Lucian and some prospective clients, out for a flattering lunch before they engaged him to do a lucrative job.

Angharad let the door close silently. She could have laughed, in bitterness, at her own pathetic hope and her neurotic fear. They were still thousands of miles away, both of them. Real miles or not, it made no difference.

She went back to her place, where they were waiting for her to carve and garnish again.

Once more, Angharad was the last to leave when lunch was over. William wasn't there, and Gwyn would be having her afternoon sleep. There was no one to hurry home for. The sense of emptiness oppressed her again as she scoured the already spotless kitchen and prowled through the dining-room, moving a vase of flowers, refolding a starched napkin. At length, when she could no longer even pretend to be busy, she saw that it was four o'clock. In an hour or so, she could legitimately come back and start the evening's work. Reassured by a sense of purpose, Angharad took her jacket down from its peg and went out into the schoolyard. There were tubs of flowers now, and a newly-planted hanging basket suspended over the doorway. It was a clear afternoon, with the hard-edged, chill brightness of the late spring.

Lucian Lang was sitting on the low wall, smoking, waiting for her. He stood up as she crossed to him, and Angharad thought that he had lost his habitual air of modish weariness.

'Do you have a minute of time to spare?' he asked her.

'All the time in the world.'

'Perhaps we could walk?' He pointed to the path that led down to the slope of Cae Mawr, and beyond to the track up the side of The Mountain. The idea struck Angharad as incongruous and she laughed.

'If you don't mind getting grass-stains and worse on your client-lunch suit.' Then she saw that Lucian was looking at her, speculative, without a trace of a smile, and the laugh died in her throat. 'I'm coming,' she whispered.

They turned in silence down the lane, the only sound the grasses brushing their legs. Lucian was walking fast, stiff-armed, as if he wanted to escape all possibility of being overheard or overlooked. At the stile where little William had told Angharad 'I love you,' they stopped. Lucian's face was stiff too, and Angharad looked at him with fear reawakening within her. A blackbird began to sing, mockingly golden notes.

'You haven't heard?' he asked her, shaking his head, and then answering himself while she still stared at him in frozen bewilderment. 'You can't have done. I thought, perhaps the local papers . . .'

Angharad's hand reached out. She was aware of her fingers crumpling the pale cloth, digging into his arm. 'Heard what?'

Don't tell me, don't tell me, I'm afraid to hear, the words bubbled in her head.

The blackbird finished its song, and the silence that followed it was absolute.

'Laura's dead.'

Angharad swayed a little, temporarily dodging the words like a boxer deflecting a blow. 'Harry?'

Lucian's arm came round her, pressing her face awkwardly against him. Too vividly she saw the tiny threads in the cloth, the stitching around the lapels. 'Not Harry. Laura, I said Laura.'

'Harry's safe?'

'Of course he is.'

She let go of Lucian's arm and stood back, numbly

shaking her head. 'How?' Following the shock, the floodgates opening, letting out the first of the questions swirling up within her.

Painfully, he said, 'They . . . we . . . think . . . it was an accident. I was with her. It happened in Hong Kong. Laura liked it there. At least, she didn't dislike it. She had begun to dislike everything, you know. Harry was away, just for ten days, in LA. Laura wouldn't go. She hated LA, and tried to stop him going. There was another terrible row, and he left. We had agreed, towards the end, Harry and I, that one of us should always be with her. So I stayed, although I should have been back in London. On the night . . . it happened, we had been out together. I ate a meal, Laura played with hers, and drank. That was all she did, towards the end. Usually we'd have a nightcap, but that night she went straight to her room. She said she was tired. She . . . never got up much before midday. The next morning I waited for her at lunch, and she didn't come. I sat there on the terrace, looking at the view, and suddenly I knew what had happened. I ran to her room. The door was locked, and the houseboy helped me to break it down. She was dead.'

Laura, her childhood defender, unbowed by the stupidity of school. Laura, laughing by the lake. Laura in Harry's red room, the flare of triumph in her face. Laura, with her white hand raised to tap on the cottage window. Laura, with her challenging, tormented eyes closed for ever. The images danced in front of her, a hundred and then multiplying into thousands, mocking her because the real Laura had gone out of their reach and would never come back again.

Angharad felt the cold wind blowing.

'It was a mistake,' Lucian was saying. 'Do you see? She must have been desperate for sleep. She was drunk, and careless with her pills. Accidental death, that was the official verdict.'

He was asking her for reassurance, and she gave it. 'Of course. It must have been shocking for you. When did it happen?'

'A month ago. There were formalities. A post mortem. It took a long time, out there . . .'

A month, and she hadn't heard. More questions, surging up, threatening to choke her. She made herself voice just one, clearly, so that there should be no mistake.

'Where's Harry now?'

'I came to tell you.' Lucian, the messenger between them again? 'He's at Llyn Fair.'

So near. Looking at Lucian, anger at his intrusion melted in Angharad. She saw that he loved them both, Harry and Laura, just as she did herself. That was enough. 'I think . . .' he said, 'I think he needs you.'

She had already turned away from him, measuring the lane in front of her. 'I've got to go now,' she told him. Then she had to call back over her shoulder, because she was already running, 'Thank you, Lucian.'

She ran, and ran. Past the Schoolhouse without a glance, and down to the village street with the breath beginning to sob in her chest. Past her home, and between the new estate houses, blind to the trim painted fences and the neat gardens. When she reached Jessie's she was stumbling, her fist gouged deep into the pain in her side. Jessie's back door opened before she could hammer on it, and Jessie stood in front of her with her hair wound up in a towel and her cheeks stiff with a face-pack. Her eyes and mouth were round pink circles of concern.

'What . . . ?'

'No time.' The words burned in Angharad's chest. 'You said . . . you'd cover for me. Tonight?'

'You know I will.'

'And for as long as it takes?'

Jessie nodded and Angharad was running again. 'Tell Gwyn for me. Tell her I've gone to Harry.'

'Yes,' Jessie shouted after her, the smile of delight cracking her white cheeks. 'And yes.'

Angharad didn't hear. She reached her car, parked outside the house, and the engine roared at once in answer to her prayer. A glance at the dial told her that there was enough petrol. The little terrace houses slid away behind her, the old oak on the corner, and she was plunging down the tunnel of trees to the valley and the Llyn Fair road.

To get to Harry was her only thought now. There would be time for all the questions, bitter as well as gentle ones, but not yet. Grimly she focussed her attention on the road, willing the car to eat up the miles until she reached him. At the crossroads she remembered the other, terrible headlong rush to Llyn Fair, when she had bicycled there against the slashing rain with the sick weight in her stomach. And had found them, locked together, triumph and torment.

*No more.*

She swung the car at the crossroads and began the climb up to the remote little valley. Harry had driven her up here, that first sunlit day. A laughing boy in a white shirt, showing off his pretty car to his sister's friend. What would she find now, behind the white gates?

The gates glimmered ahead of her in the shadow of the trees. They were closed and she had to stop the car and climb out, running to them with her legs heavy and trembling. They swung open smoothly and she was back in the car, revving the car engine so that it shot forward up the gravelled drive. The shade under the trees was lighter, the sharp green leaves overhead not yet fully unfurled. But it slid back in just the same way, like a sun-blind, leaving her blinking against the splinter of light on the windshield. The lake was smooth green glass, sheltered by the slope of the hills and the pine trees.

Angharad stopped the car by the crescent of clipped grass, and saw that the roses were pruned. Someone was caring for the house and the gardens. A dusty saloon car, unremarkable, was parked beneath the windows.

The wild urgency had left Angharad now that she was here. She walked slowly to the house and stood under the verandah, listening to the endless splash of water. As she stood there a breeze shivered the glassy water, and it carried the scent of the pines across to her. Sharply, back came the dark forest and the silver rocks of her last night under the moon with Harry.

The memory gave her the courage to start walking again. She skirted the end of the house and came into the little brick-paved rear yard. The herb bed where Harry had picked herbs for their first lunch was gone, but everytning else was the same. The steps still led up to the long room over the stable block. Angharad climbed them, her feet ringing hollow on the wooden treads and the baluster splintery and warm under her fingers.

She reached out to the latch, waiting for the door to swing inwards under her touch, but the latch clicked uselessly up and down. The door was locked.

Angharad moved sideways to look in through the window. The sun behind her head was bright on the pane, and she had to peer through the dazzle into darkness. Her heart thumped painfully.

For an instant, in the reddish glow, she thought that something moved. She thought she saw black hair, arms and fingers wound together. Chilled to the bone, she leant her face against the glass, shading her eyes with her hand. But the red paint was gone, and so was the low bed and the clutter of possessions. There was a sitting-room now, with neat modern furniture and square cushions. Through the arch Angharad glimpsed a new kitchen. A polished kettle stood on the worktop with a flowered melamine tray behind it.

A housekeeper's flat. The red room was gone.

Angharad shook her head numbly, but the memory of it in that instant lost its sharpness too. The colour drained from the image that had been printed behind her eyes for so long, leaving it like a sepia photograph of people she no longer recognized.

Of course Harry wouldn't be there, not in that room any more.

She turned her back on the locked door and walked slowly down the steps and across the yard. The kitchen door opened when she pushed it. The house was quiet, smelling of polish and fresh paint. She walked through the kitchen and into the hallway. The signs of Laura's and Lucian's improvements were everywhere. The walls were stippled in pale, clear colours and most of Monica Cotton's ornate furniture was gone. It was a spare, elegant, showpiece house now, not made for living in.

Angharad walked from room to room, looking. It was as if the Cottons had never been there. She tried to think of her father and mother in these light, bare rooms, and shivered. This was no one's home now.

Who was left? Harry, and herself.

'Harry?' Her voice sounded frightened, high and thin with a quiver in it. 'Harry, are you here?'

She heard the creak of old boards, then footsteps. She ran back into the hallway. Harry was standing at the head of the stairs, staring downwards.

'Who is it? Who is it?'

She saw the shadows in the unshaven hollows of his cheeks. The sheet of paper that he had been holding slipped from his fingers and drifted down towards her. Then she was running to him.

Harry sat down on the top step and she knelt beside him. Their arms came round each other, their foreheads touched, and it was like a circle closing, seamlessly, so that the join would be invisible for ever. In that moment Angharad felt her own strength, and knew that Harry needed her, and knew too it was that need which had been missing all the years. Harry's eyes closed, and the weight of his head lay against hers.

She saw that he was crying, the tears deepening the pain lines in his cheeks.

'Why didn't you come to me?' she asked him.

'To say that my sister's dead, I'm free?'

She understood, and rocked the weight of him against her.

'I would have come, in the end,' he said. 'But thank God you're here now. I need you so much.'

Angharad let his head rest against her until the tears of grief, exhaustion and bitterness had spent themselves. It was as if he hadn't cried for his sister until this moment and Angharad waited for him, patiently, with her cheek against his bowed head.

At last there was silence, and Harry folded her hands between his. They stood up together at the top of the stairs. Angharad's eyes were dry. She would grieve for her friend later, when she was alone, and in the days to come. There

340

was no room for it now, because Harry was her only thought. He lifted her face so that he could look into it.

'I love you,' he said. 'Do you have any idea how much?'

There was dappled light on the floor and stairs, and tiny specks of dust dancing in it. With her head close to his chest Angharad could hear his heart beating.

'Let's go outside,' Harry said gently. 'I don't want to be in this house.'

The late afternoon was warm with the first hint of summer. With their hands clasped Harry and Angharad turned to the path that led around the lake, under the lee of the hills and into the trees. At the far point of the little cup of valley a long stone lay half-buried in the grass. Harry stopped beside it, stooping to touch the pockmarked surface where the yellow lichens grew.

'It was here,' he said softly, 'that we first kissed.' He looked up at her, and his eyes were washed an intensely clear blue. 'Angharad, I want to tell you this because it is important, and then I don't want to talk about it ever again. It's finished. Thank God, it's finished. It was September, hot, with thunder in the air. We must have been twelve and ten. We had been picking blackberries. Laura had a long bramble scratch on the cheek, and her mouth was purple. She was sitting on the stone, looking up at me and laughing, and her tongue was like a red flower. I kissed her, and she tasted of fruit and grass.'

A mayfly skimmed past them, low over the water. There was a plop, and spreading ripples, as a trout rose to it inches away from them.

'It was the most delicious fruit, for both of us, and we understood that it was poisoned but we couldn't stop eating it. It took a long time, years, but the end was inevitable. It's important that you should understand it was my fault. I led her into it. The cruellest part is that by the end, when you found us out, it was Laura who was trapped. I knew it, and there was nothing I could do. Somehow I was free, and she couldn't be.' Harry spread his fingers and looked hopelessly down through them. 'It's my fault she's dead. I might as well have killed her myself. I couldn't love her in the way she

341

wanted, and she wanted nothing else.'

Angharad snatched at his hand, wrenching her own fingers in her urgency. 'It was an accident. Don't blame yourself, ever, do you hear me?'

Harry's face was stiff, and when he spoke again it was as if the words cut at his mouth.

'It wasn't an accident. She wrote me a letter. I was in LA, did Lucian tell you that? I guess it was Lucian?'

Angharad nodded dumbly, shock rippling within her all over again.

'The bitterest letter. There was no threatening, any more. The end was a simple statement. She said that if she couldn't have me, she didn't want anything. I was ready to leave for Hong Kong again within an hour, and it was as I was leaving that I got Lucian's call. She was . . . already dead.'

There was a long, long silence while the water lapped into the soft edge of the bank. So Laura had taken herself away.

Angharad wondered what had happened, in the end, to the sharp sight and vivid intelligence that she had loved as a girl and had learned to fear in the last months.

As she lifted her head to look out over the water again, Angharad breathed in, very slowly, as if trying to detect the scent of corruption and decay. But there was nothing. It had drifted away, to leave only scoured emptiness. By contrast she became acutely aware of Harry and herself, warm skin over the breathing network of veins and nerves, unfairly living in the sunlight. She saw Harry more clearly than she had ever done. The cuffs off his faded blue shirt were rolled back, and she saw the knobs of his wrists, the sinews on the backs of his hands. She saw his bent head, and it was as if she looked right through it into the suffering. She knew in that instant by the lake what it had been like to Harry to live with Laura, and what it had cost him. He had paid, if it was necessary to pay, for the blackberry afternoons of long ago.

Angharad reached for his hand and felt its warmth, the ridge of the knuckles in her palm and the tiny movements beneath it, the pulse of blood and the twitch of muscle.

They were alone, now.

The sadness that had possessed her ebbed away for a

moment, and although she knew that it would come back, that there would always be times when the loss of Laura would reclaim them, she was filled now with a sense of completeness. She loved Harry herself, and she was certain that he loved her in return, and it was right that they should love each other.

She turned to face him, putting her arms around him and drawing his head down so that it rested against her. The strength was hers now, and it would bring them both through.

'Tell me,' she whispered, 'about the rest of it.'

With his face still hidden against her, Harry talked of the last, hunted months. Laura had come on location with him, and while he worked she sat in his trailer behind the drawn shades. At night she would come into his room with a glass in her hand, her eyes burning hard and bright or softened by the glaze of tears. And he would sit with her, talking and holding her, until she fell asleep. When Harry was not working they drifted between hotels and luxurious borrowed houses, sometimes with Lucian and sometimes alone, waiting for they didn't know what.

'I thought of you and William all the time,' Harry said. 'I could see you quite clearly, here in the mountains. It was like staring into the background of a Renaissance picture. Very beautiful, exquisitely detailed, but a long way off. And untouchable. I didn't write, or telephone. What could I have said?'

Angharad laced her arms around him. 'I love you.'

'After all the horrible things that had to be done . . . afterwards, were over,' Harry went on, as if he had a last, important thing to say, 'Lucian and I took a boat one evening, out of Hong Kong harbour. It was teeming with life, a great ant-heap that had spilled out over the water, under one of those dull, beaten-copper evening suns that they have out there. We slid between the boats, through the cooking smells and the music and shouting, and a little way out to sea. The sun was vast, almost touching the horizon, and the mainland was a scribbled line behind us. They gave us a little box, at the ugly British chapel. We dropped it into the sea. There were tiny ripples, and after that nothing.'

Harry turned his head away from her, looking out over the lake water, and at the ripples there of fish rising to the mayfly.

'I asked myself if I could come back, walking into the beautiful picture background, and expect you to face up to that with me.'

He was asking her, and not looking at her because it was so important that he couldn't bear to.

Angharad thought. There must be no mistake now, for there would be no going back over it.

The completeness was still with her, a seamless circle enclosing ecstasy as well as pain. They were grown up now, whole people for better or worse. Harry and she would have to learn to live together, and part of that lesson would be the shadows of the waste, and loss of Laura, in the corners of their sunny house.

Their eyes met now. Angharad saw her son's gaze looking back at her, and more. There was a certainty that she had never dared to hope for, a counterweight to her own, love and need and knowing all together.

'Who else?' she asked him softly. 'Yes. I'll face it with you. Laura, and those ripples on the sea, and whatever else comes. So long as we're together. It's been so long, Harry. It's been so long.'

Harry moved, a flash of blue and black, and his arms swallowed her up and thee was no need to say any more, or to tell any more, because they had found one another and they had come home.

He kissed her eyelids, and the angles of her cheeks, and they took possession of each other as they had never done before.

'I hadn't even hoped,' he told her, and she remembered the arrogant boy in his Morgan, and the thoughtless young man she had first loved. The knowledge of how the change must have been brought about hurt her for his sake.

As the sun dropped behind the pine trees and the jagged edge of shadow moved over the water's surface, they walked on around the lake, into the shade and out again to the splash over the dam where the green weed tangled like hair in the silvery spray.

It was cool when they reached the house again, but they turned away from the open front door, reluctant to go into the silence. Instead they sat on the verandah where the new leaves were beginning to cast the familiar waving patterns over the white table-top.

'Your home,' Harry said. It was a mark of the peace between them that there was no compulsion for him to add, with bitterness, 'Until Joe took it.' Instead the memories spooled backwards, silently. Angharad tried to see her father here, and her mother pregnant with herself, down at the lake-edge perhaps where the old bench sat beside the jetty. But the picture refused to form itself. Too many fresher images overlay it. And Llyn Fair was too neutrally elegant now, with its pale walls and cool Italian furniture, for her to imagine old William here amongst his books. Even the sense of belonging here in the quiet valley that she had felt on her first visit was gone. It was no more than a beautiful, faintly sad house beside a secretive lake.

Beside her Harry stood up. His basket chair creaked and she looked at its emptiness as he went quickly into the house. She didn't want to lose him for even a moment. He came back almost at once with a thick wad of cracked, yellowing paper in his hand. The papers were tied with a dark ribbon. He put the bundle down on the table-top in front of her.

'What is it?' she asked. To stop looking at him and focus on anything else was an irrelevance.

'The deeds,' he said simply. 'I was sorting through the papers when you came.' Seeing the uncomprehending stare he said again, 'The deeds, to the house and the lake. All the property. A fair acreage of useless land. It's yours, of course.'

Angharad heard the crackle of the old papers on the table, and she smiled at him. The smile made Harry draw in his breath, and see afresh the colour of her skin and the fine down of hair on her forearms.

'Do you love Llyn Fair?' Angharad asked him.

Harry shook his head violently. 'No. Too much has happened here. But you know that isn't why I want you to have it. It belongs rightfully to you.'

345

*Too much has happened here.*

Angharad thought of the unhappiness that the old house had visited on their two families. It was like a dark knot, coiled in the valley in defiance of the hills' ancient shelter. If there was to be another family, regenerated in herself and Harry and little William, it would never be here.

'Thank you,' she whispered. 'I don't want to keep it. I don't want to be anywhere except with you, and how can we be here?'

His hands found hers and folded them together. They sat and listened to the water and the sighing wind in the trees.

'Sell it, then,' he answered her.

'We could give the money to a good cause. Perhaps that would lay it to rest.'

'Which one do you have in mind?' he asked her, only half-attending.

'Unmarried mothers?' she answered him innocently. She was rewarded by the first glimmer of laughter in his eyes.

We shall be happy, you and I. Not yet, how could we be, but one day we'll be happier than ever we could have hoped or dreamed.

'I think that would be a very appropriate way to dispose of your house. I admire you, Angharad. I don't deserve you, and I love you and I want you. You, and the boy.'

He kissed the angle of her neck under the warmth of her hair. 'Where is he?'

'He's gone to stay in London, with Jamie, for a week. They're still very close.'

The clarity that was important, now, in everything between them.

'I'm glad. Can I see him, when he comes back?'

She loved him again for his tentativeness, and for letting her see his vulnerability.

'He's your son, Harry.'

The silence wrapped round them again as they looked at each other.

At last Harry said, 'Does that mean that you don't have to go away anywhere, now, this minute?'

Jessie was at the restaurant. She would have told Gwyn.

'I don't have to go anywhere.'

Harry stood up and walked to the old front door. He swung it closed and then as an afterthought he posted the folded deeds in through the letterbox. Then he held out his hands to lift Angharad from her chair. She followed him unquestioning across the gravel sweep to his anonymous car. He opened the door for her and she climbed in, watching the realness of him as he settled into his seat beside her. As he turned she saw the challenge in him, the challenge that he had always offered to her and which she had wanted nothing more than to meet, and answer.

'Come with me, Angharad. Away from here. Anywhere, I don't care where it is. We need to be together. No, that isn't the truth. I can't bear to be alone any more, and I am alone, without you.' His voice grew softer and he reached out to touch the curve of her mouth with the tip of his finger. 'Haven't we lived for long enough without each other?'

He was tired, and his face was hollow with exhaustion, but the old crackle was still alive in him. Angharad smiled, and the crookedness had gone.

'I'll come. I want to go somewhere in Wales, a long way from everything, like the last time we saw each other.'

The shadow fell at once, as it would do often and many times yet. Gently she said, 'Before that. Under the pine trees, do you remember, where there was no one else at all?'

'I remember.'

The car was moving, rolling across the gravel. Without a backward glance they slid under the tunnel of trees and then away through the white gates for the last time.

They were alone where once they had been three, joy-riding in the white Jaguar with Laura's hand on the radio dial. The sadness came again, dropping its folds over them like a cloak. And they would learn to live with that, as they had already learned to live with so much else.

They turned down the steep road to the valley and Angharad thought that they might almost collide with themselves ten years ago, racing upwards with Harry laughing at the wheel and his black hair blown back from his suntanned face.

*If we could go back*, she thought, and then she checked herself. There could be no going back. We shall be happy, you and I. There would be time for that, and time, when they were ready.

Angharad looked at him once again, to make sure that it was really Harry and that he was truly there, and then turned resolutely to face the empty valley road.

They reached the crossroads. The car turned west, away from Llyn Fair and the lake basking in its remote cup of valley.

*Also by Rosie Thomas*

# WHITE

Rosie Thomas

'Terrific stuff ... a real weepy' *Sunday Times*

For Sam McGrath a brief encounter with a young woman, on a turbulent flight, changes his life. On impulse, crazily attracted to her, he vows to follow her – all the way to Nepal.

Finch Buchanan is flying out as a doctor to an expedition. But when she reaches the Himalayas she will be reunited with a man she has never been able to forget.

Al Hood has made a promise to his daughter. Once he has conquered this last peak, he will leave the mountains behind forever.

Everest towers over the group, silent and beautiful. And the passionate relationship between Finch, Al and Sam – two men driven by their own demons, and a woman with a dream of her own – begins to play itself out, with tragic consequences ...

'A story full of passion ... will keep you reading long after bedtime' *New Woman*

'Outstanding' *The Good Book Guide*

'A superb storyteller ... *White* is an epic mix of passion and drama' *Hampstead and Highgate Express*

*Also Available in Arrow*

# CHARMED LIVES

## Susannah Bates

*'Penny Vincenzi fans will devour this – unputdownable'*
Louise Bagshawe

Kate Leonard is a high-flying young lawyer. Smart, sexy and successful, she seems to have it all except a life outside the office … until she meets Tom Faulkener.

Tom comes from a different world: the privileged, idle world of private incomes, breathtaking bills and the pursuit of pleasure. The last thing he wants is a relationship … until he meets Kate.

But as Kate tries to juggle her hectic existence with the temptations of Tom's exclusive circle – irresponsible society photographer Charlie, shy but kind-hearted Douglas, and Tom's lovely but neurotic ex-wife Arabella – she begins to see through the careless glamour of their charmed lives …

# LILY-JOSEPHINE

## Kate Saunders

*'I loved Lily Josephine. Kate Saunders is such a wonderful writer ...'* Jilly Cooper

Lily-Josephine had a talent for love. Wilful, enchanting and passionate, she was the centre of a charmed universe – until her foolish, indulgent father maried again.

Like Snow-Drop in Grimm's fairy tale, Lily ran from her jealous stepmother one idyllic summer evening in 1941. She escaped to find sanctuary but, at Randalls, she discovered a love far greater than any she had ever known ...

A generation later the events set in train that night begin to unravel when Sophie Gently falls in love with Octavius Randall and the bizarre and tragic history linking their families is uncovered. Not until ancient passions and betrayals have been confronted can Lily-Josephine – long gone but never forgotten – truly be laid to rest.

Praise for Kate Saunders
'Hugely enjoyable, glossy, sexy and wittily turned'
*The Times*
'Gripping and entertaining' *Sunday Telegraph*
'A marvellous read' Jilly Cooper
'Fabulous stuff' *Evening Standard*
'Vivid, sexy, funny, clever and BIG' Amanda Craig,
*Literary Review*

## AVAILABLE IN ARROW

| | | |
|---|---|---|
| ☐ White | Rosie Thomas | £ 5.99 |
| ☐ Bad Girls, Good Woman | Rosie Thomas | £ 6.99 |
| ☐ Other People's Marriages | Rosie Thomas | £ 6.99 |
| ☐ Charmed Lives | Susannah Bates | £ 5.99 |
| ☐ Lily-Josephine | Kate Saunders | £ 5.99 |
| ☐ Night Shall Overtake Us | Kate Saunders | £ 6.99 |
| ☐ Wild Young Bohemians | Kate Saunders | £ 5.99 |
| ☐ Old Sins | Penny Vincenzi | £ 6.99 |

ALL ARROW BOOKS ARE AVAILABLE THROUGH MAIL ORDER OR FROM YOUR LOCAL BOOKSHOP.

PAYMENT MAY BE MADE USING ACCESS, VISA, MASTER-CARD, DINERS CLUB, SWITCH AND AMEX, OR CHEQUE, EUROCHEQUE, POSTAL ORDER (STERLING ONLY).

EXPIRY DATE ..................... SWITCH ISSUE NO. 

SIGNATURE ................................................................................

PLEASE ALLOW £2.50 FOR POST AND PACKING FOR THE FIRST BOOK AND £1.00 PER BOOK THEREAFTER.

ORDER TOTAL: £.............................(INCLUDING P&P)

ALL ORDERS TO:
ARROW BOOKS, BOOKS BY POST, TBS LIMITED, THE BOOK SERVICE, COLCHESTER ROAD, FRATING GREEN, COLCHESTER, ESSEX, CO7 7DW, UK.

TELEPHONE:  (01206) 256 000
FAX:    (01206) 255 914

NAME ................................................................................
ADDRESS ................................................................................
................................................................................

Please allow 28 days for delivery. Please tick box if you do not wish to receive any additional information ☐
Prices and availability subject to change without notice.